She dared to rob him of his clothes.
He swore to get revenge . . .

The Scarlet Temptress turned to Jason next, holding out the bag. "If you please, Lord . . . ?"

"Windhall, the Viscount of Westland, at your service. And I am sorry to disappoint you, madam, but I am without a farthing."

Searing anger burned through her veins. He was the only reason she'd stopped this blasted coach! "But sir, you are poorly mistaken." She cast him a wicked little smile. "For I see much of value in your fine . . . apparel."

Jason went rigid. *"What?"*

"Please, your lordship, if you would be so kind as to remove your clothing. *At once."*

"You won't get away with this." He forced a shrill note into his voice to keep it from lowering in rage.

She watched him strip down until he had removed his shirt. "The breeches now, if you please."

Jason clenched his teeth and undid the buttons to his pants before sliding them down, then with both feet firmly on the ground, slightly spread, he straightened to his full towering height and placed his hands on his bare hips.

Samantha nearly strangled on her own gasp. Her eyes widened in disbelief. My God! Why wasn't the man wearing undergarments? . . .

The Scarlet Temptress

Sue Rich

POCKET BOOKS

New York   London   Toronto   Sydney   Tokyo   Singapore

An *Original* Publication of POCKET BOOKS

POCKET BOOKS, a division of Simon & Schuster Inc.
1230 Avenue of the Americas, New York, NY 10020

ISBN: 0-671-73625-6

First Pocket Books printing September 1991

10 9 8 7 6 5 4 3 2 1

THIS BOOK IS DEDICATED TO

JIM RICH. My husband. My inspiration. For the
warmth and laughter you so generously share.
I love you.

MY CHILDREN. For their unwavering loyalty—even
when Mom didn't deserve it.

DEBBIE BAILEY, DIANNA CRAWFORD,
SALLY LAITY, JEANNIE LEVIG, and MARY LOU
RICH. My critics. My friends. I thank you.

I would like to add a very special note of appreciation
to my agent, ROB COHEN, and my editor,
CAROLINE TOLLEY. For making it happen.

The Scarlet Temptress

CHAPTER 1

Lynch's Ferry, Virginia
January 1774

At the sound of approaching hoofbeats David Brown quickened his pace. The frozen ground crunched beneath his worn boots as he hurried toward a lean-to at the side of the shed. "God preserve us," he whispered, reaching for the team's harness. "We're caught sure as it rains in England."

Icy wind whipped around his coattail and tugged at the edge of his tricorn. A shiver raced up his spine. Why had he ever gotten involved in this mess in the first place? Just because he knew how to run a printing press didn't mean he *had* to help. A body could get hanged for what he was doing.

Another tremor rippled along his back, but whether from fear or cold he couldn't be certain. Pulling at the harness with one hand, he tucked the other into the warmth of his pocket and hunched forward. He was getting too damn old for all this excitement.

The thundering hooves rumbled to a stop in front of the shed. A spiral of dread curled through David's chest. He jerked the team to a halt and released the harness; then, edging toward the rear of the building, he peered between the half-open double doors, afraid of what he might see.

Shadows from a single candle danced over the bare gray walls inside the abandoned tobacco shed. David watched his companion, Carl Malderon, step quickly away from a wood table near the front window. He ducked his lanky frame behind a wagon in the middle of the floor and raised a musket, his body rigid, his alert brown eyes fastened on the entrance.

The door burst wide, crashing against an empty barrel. Like an apparition of Satan a towering black-clad figure filled the opening. A silk domino concealed his upper features beneath the shadow of a lowered tricorn. Broad shoulders and powerful arms strained against an ebony shirt of fine linen. Snow whipped wildly around dark breeches that fit snugly over lean hips and long legs before disappearing into shiny black riding boots.

A mournful wind howled. The candle flickered. Then all went still.

"Soldiers are coming." The masked man's smooth, deep voice cut into the silence. "I'll try to distract them while you move the press."

Carl's shoulders slumped, and he lowered the musket. He drew in a deep breath, then jerked his silver head in a nod of agreement. "Be careful, Jas—"

David gasped in belated recognition. "The *Devilrider.*"

The man in black swung his head in David's direction, pinning him with cold eyes visible behind the slits in the domino.

Swallowing against the terror clogging his throat, David tried to think, but his thoughts whirled in panic. Wasn't the outlaw supposed to be a friend of the colonists? Hadn't he saved McDaniels from the hangman just last week? Didn't he risk his own life distributing those pamphlets? David nervously eyed the masked figure again. Still, one never knew when a man like that might turn on you.

Suddenly, like the demon he was named for, the Devilrider flashed his startling white teeth, and he chuckled wickedly, almost as if he'd read David's thoughts. Then, with a swirl of his billowing black cape, he vanished from the doorway.

David's breath whooshed from his lungs, and he looked quickly at Carl.

Carl offered a small understanding smile. "You heard the man. Let's go." Tossing the musket on the wagon, Carl hurried to gather the remaining evidence of the operation. Lifting a bundle of Samuel Adams's newly printed pamphlets, he heaved them on the bed of the wagon and shoved them beneath the press, then paused and turned. "David? I suggest you forget what you saw just now."

David couldn't have agreed more. If there was anything he *didn't* want, it was to make an enemy of the Devil-rider.

Jason Kincaid smiled as he brushed the black cape back from his shoulders and swung atop his horse, Adversary. Poor David. The man was a mass of nerves. He really should get out of this business. And Carl, standing there with that musket raised as if he would use it. God's teeth. If a soldier had entered the doorway, Carl would probably have thrown the weapon and run. He just didn't have it in him to harm another human being.

Jason's grin deepened as he jerked the reins and spun Adversary toward the advancing soldiers. He didn't doubt that Carl and David would escape. They kept the press mounted on the bed of the wagon for just that purpose. But they needed a little time, and Jason would see that they got it. "Come on, Addy. Let's give those British bastards something to tell their grandchildren."

The glistening stallion reared its powerful ebony head and snorted as if in agreement.

Jason laughed and nudged the horse into a gallop, his body taut with exhilaration. Pitting himself against the British was a trial Jason couldn't resist. Of course, Nick would think him deranged. But then his twin brother had never understood, had never needed the excitement and sense of challenge that Jason craved.

At the sight of the approaching riders Jason wheeled Adversary around, ready for the chase. A volley of gunshots echoed across the frozen valley, and one nearly found its mark as a ball whizzed close to Jason's ear. His pulse quickened, and he spurred the stallion forward. "Bungling buffoons. They couldn't hit the side of a tree if the ends of their barrels were against it."

Steam spewed from Adversary's nostrils. Muddy soil sprayed across the snow-covered field as his long strides increased the distance between Jason and the soldiers.

Jason's blood ignited at the feel of power straining beneath him. He tightened his thighs and focused on the area just ahead. Through the darkness he could see the dim outline of the forest. He darted a glance back over his shoulder. Four red-coated soldiers whipped wildly at their mounts as they rumbled across the rolling terrain of a winter-barren tobacco field.

A tingling sense of danger fired his pulse. He had to lose them soon, or forfeit his life. "Bloody hounds," he grumbled, kicking Adversary.

The powerful steed lurched, charging into the trees with reckless speed.

As the foliage closed around him, Jason turned sharply up a steep incline. He jerked the reins back and forth, forcing Adversary to zigzag through the trees.

Heavy undergrowth slapped at Jason's legs, but he barely noticed the annoying sting. Tree limbs became live fingers, clawing at his face and hood as snow fell from upper branches, plummeting onto his head. He shivered against the cold and ducked lower.

The pounding hooves of the detachment thundered in his ears, then gradually grew distant. At last he heard the soldiers' horses receding in a different direction. He felt the coil of tension loosen, and a satisfied smile slid into place. Then, turning the stallion toward the river, he straightened in the saddle and let out a slow breath. Now all he had to do was make it to the plantation on time.

Iron Sword's urgent warning that the soldiers had learned the location of Carl's hidden press had come at the most inopportune moment. Jason had been about to dress for the Wainwrights' soiree. At any other time, being late wouldn't have mattered. He would simply have gone to warn Carl and been tardy to the affair. But tonight, of all nights, he had agreed to accompany Peter Hawksley in the younger man's carriage. Knowing his timing was going to be close, he'd thrown on the Devilrider costume. It certainly wouldn't have done for the king's men to recognize his all-too-familiar face—the face of Lord Montague Windhall, or so

4

they believed. But now he was hopelessly late. Peter would arrive at Crystal Terrace any moment.

When the James River came into view Jason slowed the horse and scanned the area. Should he take the safer route, north, and risk being even later, or south toward the narrowest part of the river—and pray it was frozen enough to cross? A thrill of challenge raced through his veins. He never had been one to take the easy route. With a wry smile he reined to the south.

Guiding Adversary along the rocky, thickly wooded bank, Jason scoured the river's surface. A thick sheet of ice—at least he hoped it was thick—covered the deadly waters from bank to bank. He leaned forward and stroked Adversary's neck. "Well, old boy, what do you think?"

The stallion shook its head.

Jason grinned. "Makes you nervous, does it?" He studied the frozen ribbon again. "You're not alone, Addy. But we're out of time."

Knowing the horse's footing was going to be tedious at best, Jason slipped out of the saddle and gingerly led Adversary forward. An eerie silence surrounded them, almost as if nature was holding her breath, afraid that the slightest sound might split the frozen covering. Only the hollow thump of Adversary's hooves striking ice disturbed the unnatural quiet.

The ice creaked beneath the pressure of their weight. With Jason's own footing unsure, he gripped the bit tighter for balance as well as control. Cold seeped through his clothing, and his pace quickened.

Just as the stallion's front hooves again touched solid ground the ice gave a chilling crack.

Jason wrenched forward on the bit. The ice broke.

Adversary's hindquarters sank back. The animal rolled its eyes wildly and reared its head.

Jason felt his arm jerk, then his feet left the ground. A high whinny shrilled an instant before arctic water surged over his head. Cold, so painful it stunned, engulfed him. His limbs instantly lost their strength. He felt a momentary

5

wave of panic but held it at bay. If he lost control now, he was a dead man.

Forcing himself to remain calm, he pushed upward until he broke the surface. He ripped off the sodden mask and tricorn, then flung them toward the shore. He drew in great gulps of air. But the breath tried to freeze in his lungs.

Commanding his lifeless limbs to respond, he groped for the rocky shore. Shards of ice tore into his gloved palms. Needles of pain stabbed into his hands. Adversary's body slammed against his side, and Jason lost his footing, plunging again into the frigid water. Resurfacing, he sputtered and frantically searched the area.

A tree root protruded from the bank, just out of his reach. He focused on it, willing it closer. Raising a leaden arm, he stretched and strained, pushing forward. Numbness retarded his movements. His arms felt weighted, his legs like iron anvils.

In desperation he lunged for the root, touched it. A spear of pain cut into his fingers as they curled stiffly around the fragile lifeline. Muscles straining, nearly paralyzed from cold, he dragged himself out of the water, groaning as he collapsed on the ground.

Adversary gave another frantic screech.

Jason's head jerked upward, and he clenched his teeth. Fear for the horse's life replaced thoughts of his own suffering. Forcing himself to stand, he stumbled across the bank and reached for Addy's reins.

The frightened animal tossed its head. Deadly front hooves rose up from the water, pawing the air.

Jason ducked and slipped on the slick bank. His back struck the hard ground, slamming the air from his body. A groan hissed from between his teeth.

Struggling to his feet again, he sprang for the horse and caught the bit. Then, using every ounce of strength he possessed, he gave a hard yank.

Adversary shot up out of the water and bolted forward. Jason leapt to the side to avoid being trampled.

The horse stopped, then shuddered and stomped, swinging its powerful head.

"Easy, boy," Jason rasped softly, stroking the animal's quivering jaw. "It's all right now, Addy. You're just fine." Untying the cape from his shoulders, Jason wrung out the excess water and dried the horse as best he could, then spread the cloak over its rump. "I know it isn't much, boy. But it's the best I can do for now." Retrieving his hat and the mask, Jason shoved a boot in the stirrup and mounted.

Though it had been only minutes, it seemed like hours before the familiar cave, nestled in the pines near the base of the mountains, finally came into view. Keeping his teeth clamped together to stop their chattering, he leapt down and led Adversary into the hidden stable.

After pulling the frosty saddle and cape from the animal's back he found a woolen blanket draped over the end stall and thoroughly dried the stallion. "Looks like you fared better than I did."

Adversary whickered as Jason stepped swiftly out of the cave opening. Half running, half limping on numb legs, he raced through the underground tunnel that led to the house. Once inside his bedchamber he bellowed for the housekeeper. "Dahlia! Get up here!"

Crossing the spacious bedroom he'd called his own for the last two months, he stripped the sodden clothes from his body and tossed them onto a cedar trunk at the foot of the brass bed, knowing he'd have to return them to the cave later. Then, turning toward the richly carved armoire, he searched through the rows of elaborate ensembles. His hand stilled. A blotch of bright crimson stained one of the garments. "God's teeth!"

"Jason?" Dahlia called from the other side of the door.

"One moment!" He snatched a sheet from the bed and wrapped it around his waist. "All right, Dahlia, enter."

The door opened, and the portly housekeeper waddled into the bedroom. "What's all the fuss about?" Her eyes widened when she saw the blood staining the front of the sheet he held. She inhaled sharply. "Good heavens! What happened?"

He waved a hand. "It's nothing. Just some cuts. But I need your help. Find me something to wipe my hands, then go downstairs and wait for Peter Hawksley's arrival. Stall him while I dress."

Dahlia's gray head bobbed in agreement beneath her dustcap as she raced to the washstand and withdrew a clean cloth. "Here, use this." She tossed it to him. "I'll get the salve." Bustling across the room to the chest-on-chest, she stretched her squat frame upward to retrieve a jar from its top. "This should do it."

Cleaning the blood from his palms, Jason accepted the salve and smeared it over the cuts on his hands. Only a few beads of crimson managed to seep through the pasty ointment. "That's fine, Dahlia. Thank you. Now off with you. I've got to get dressed."

"You young fool," Dahlia mumbled as she hurried from the room. But he didn't miss the concern in her voice.

Releasing a slow, soft sigh, he turned away from the door and dropped the sheet before returning to the armoire. Naked and shivering, he rummaged through the wardrobe until he decided on a pair of yellow brocade breeches. His nose wrinkled in distaste. Lord, those garments were disgusting. He turned to probe the drawers for dry undergarments, but at that moment Peter Hawksley's carriage pulled up out front. "Bloody hell!" Jason swore again, shoving a foot into a pant leg. He had no time to spare. Dragging the breeches up over his naked hips, he reached for a frilly white shirt.

After tucking in the long ends of the blouse he tied a lacy cravat beneath his chin, then moved to the bureau. He bit back a foul word as he picked up a tin of white powder and applied it to his face with quick pats. Hesitating a moment, he scowled at his reflection in a gold-framed mirror. He looked like a bloody ghoul! Damn Carl and his brilliant ideas. "Just pretend to be a lord of the realm," he mocked.

"That way you will be able to carry on with your activities without fear of discovery."

Jason glared at the powder. "But you forgot to mention, old friend, that I'd be forced to act and *dress* the part of a mewling fop!"

He gritted his teeth against the injustice of it all. Why did the mere name Jason Deverall Kincaid inspire such suspicion with the king's men, just because, *a couple of times,* he'd shown adversity to a raise in taxes?

Locating two star-shaped beauty patches next to the powder, he slapped them on his square jaw and reached for a short white wig. It sported two sausage curls on either side and a tiny queue at the back, tied with a large black bow. Snarling at the hairpiece as if it were alive, he slammed it down atop his head.

Moments later Jason descended the staircase to join Peter Hawksley, the powdered wig concealing his thick black hair completely. His toes were pinched inside the white stockings and buckle shoes with high red heels. Too, he could barely move beneath the tight yellow waistcoat and matching redingote. His stepmother's brother, the *real* Lord Windhall, was a slightly smaller man.

As Jason reached the bottom step he tucked a canary-yellow tricorn beneath his arm and finished pulling on his leather gloves, deftly hiding the cuts on his palms. He drew his lips into a prim line and took a deep breath. "Peter, my good fellow." He waved his lace-trimmed handkerchief as the painfully thin man peered up from the entry. "How good of you to be so prompt."

Peter sniffed regally, creasing the customary layer of powder covering his parrotlike features. "'Tis my pleasure, your lordship."

Behind Peter's shoulder Dahlia rolled her eyes.

Jason cast her a warning glare, then brought the handkerchief up to dab at his nose before again regarding the baronet. "Shall we be off, then?"

At Peter's nod Jason crossed the spacious tiled entry and

took a cape from Dahlia's outstretched hand. His stern look promised the servant retaliation as he set the tricorn on a small Edwardian table, then flung the satin-lined mantle around his shoulders. Retrieving the plume-edged hat, he turned to Peter and gestured toward the door. "After you."

Cold wind whipped the cape as he and Peter descended the steps of the front veranda, and Jason felt the chill all the way to his bones. Damnation. Would he ever be warm again? Suddenly a sound from the waiting carriage drew his attention, and he looked up.

Minerva Carstairs hung out the window of Hawksley's shiny black coach, her large bosom heaving, nearly spilling over the bodice of her chartreuse gown. "Yoo-hoo. Montague." She swung her arm briskly from side to side. Her towering hair swayed, the springy locks near her heavily rouged cheeks bouncing wildly. "I wager you didn't expect to see me here, did you?"

Jason stifled an agonizing groan. God's teeth! Hadn't his day been bad enough already? He glanced at Peter. The younger man's lips were set in a narrow line of disgust. Obviously the blonde had weaseled an invitation out of him.

As if they realized at the same time that the last man in the carriage would be forced to sit next to Minerva, both he and Peter dived for the coach door. Their shoulders collided, and Peter's slight frame bounced sideways.

Minerva giggled behind a gloved hand.

Peter's face reddened with embarrassment beneath the powder. "G-Good heavens, your l-lordship. Excuse my manners."

Jason felt a twinge of sympathy for the man, but not enough to let him enter the coach first. Dipping his head, Jason sniffed. "That's quite all right." Brushing at the side of the cape as if Peter's touch had damaged it, he climbed in the coach and sat opposite Minerva. He tossed the tricorn on the seat beside him; then, resigning himself to an evening in the cloying ninnyhammer's company, he pulled the wool rug across his lap.

Peter frowned as he entered the carriage and took the seat

next to the blonde. He edged his skinny body as far away from her as possible while still sharing the same seat.

Minerva didn't seem to notice as she leaned forward and tapped the back of Jason's hand with her finger. "Good evening, your lordship. It's nice to see you again."

Her unctuous voice oozed from between her lips, giving Jason the shivers. Or was it just the cold? The carriage lurched forward, and he leaned back. "It's good to see you too, Mrs. Carstairs. I trust you are faring well in this ghastly weather?" That seemed like a safe enough subject.

Minerva tittered. "In weather like this a widow such as myself often wishes for the warmth of another." Her eyes explored his torso slowly, suggestively.

Peter shifted in his seat.

Jason lifted his chin to hide a grimace. "Yes, quite." Then, clamping his mouth shut lest he say something he might later regret, he parted the curtains with his finger and stared out at the night-darkened scenery, hoping to pass the majority of the hour-long trip in silence, knowing that his companions wouldn't be surprised by his cold dismissal. It was expected of the Viscount of Westland.

Towering, snow-covered pines, occasionally separated by small meadows, lined both sides of the road as silver fingers of moonlight speared through the branches to pool on frozen beds of pine needles.

Peter and Minerva's presence receded as the steady thud of horses' hooves and periodic squeak of carriage springs lulled Jason into reverent memories of the past.

He was twelve again, racing bareback across the summer fields near Halcyon, his father's plantation. Hawk and Nick were behind him. Hawk, the young Shawnee half-breed, even at the tender age of five, managed to outdistance the overly cautious Nick. His shoulder-length black hair flapped wildly around his face. Thin brown arms swung determinedly as he flailed his pony in an effort to catch Jason.

Nick and Jason laughed at the little brave's attempts. Nemesis, Adversary's sire, had never been beaten. But Hawk remained undaunted. He ignored their gentle teasing and pushed the sorrel pony he'd been given for his birthday to the limit. So adamant was he in his quest for victory that he refused to name the pony until it had beaten Nemesis.

Week after week the race took place on the day before the Sabbath. The sorrel grew to adulthood but never won. Once or twice Jason even considered slowing Nemesis to end the boy's torment, but Jason knew it wouldn't have been fair to the brave. Hawk's intent was more than just to be the victor. He needed to prove himself their equal. If he was to succeed in honor, it had to be a genuine coup.

Then it finally happened. The great sorrel accomplished the impossible. It overtook Nemesis in the last yards of the race. And on that day Hawk gave the sorrel its name, Ataraxia. For at last Hawk's heart had found peace.

But Jason's hadn't. Only days later his mother died of fever. Forcing back the painful memory, he tried again to concentrate on the happy times. The summers had been long then, the tobacco crop prosperous. Filled with excitement, the trio had found a new adventure at every turn.

It was the time before Hawk's mother had deserted him; before Jason and Nick were sent away; before Father's murder—no! Jason fought back a wave of aching anger. He couldn't think about that, *wouldn't* think about it, not until he found the man responsible—the scarred soldier.

Drawing in a long, settling breath, he dropped the curtain back into place and turned his attention to the occupants of the carriage.

Minerva had propped her elbow on the ledge of the window and cupped her chin with a gloved hand, her attention fixed on Jason's chest.

Peter sat staring out the opposite window, his expression one of boredom.

Jason pulled out the lacy handkerchief he'd shoved in his cuff and gave it a flick. "Peter, my good fellow, I understand that Joshua Minter will arrive soon."

Peter jerked his head around, then brightened as he straightened his ivory satin waistcoat and raised his chin importantly. "Yes, 'tis so. On the morrow. My uncle's business with Governor Dunmore is concluded, and he must return to his portentous duties here as customs official." His narrow nose wrinkled in the semblance of a silent sniff. "'Tis most tedious to have one of the king's emissaries milling about Hawksley Manor. The constant stream of influential visitors tends to become quite bothersome at times." A stricken look suddenly contorted his features. "Oh! I meant no reflection on *you,* your lordship."

Jason coughed to hide a chuckle. He couldn't help but like Peter. He just wished the younger man wouldn't strive so hard for social importance. Waving his hand airily, Jason dipped his head. "That's quite all right. I knew exactly what you meant."

Peter opened his mouth but was saved from making a comment when the coach pulled up in front of the Wainwrights' plantation.

A richly garbed servant placed a stepping box in front of the carriage door before opening it, then offered a hand to help Minerva down.

Minerva cast Jason a coquettish smile and descended from the carriage with a regal air.

Somehow Jason managed to keep from showing his distaste.

When the servant reached inside again, extending his palm, Jason fought the urge to brush it aside and daintily placed two gloved fingers on the footman's hand.

As Jason's high-heeled shoes sank into the snow he turned to see the Wainwrights silhouetted in the brightly lit doorway of their elegant three-story mansion and released a silent sigh. It was going to be another long, boring evening.

CHAPTER 2

Samantha Fleming's slender fingers shook as she tugged on a pair of red kidskin gloves. Though the small fireplace barely kept the bedchamber warm, she knew her trembling wasn't just from the cold.

Raising her arms, she straightened a velvet hood of deep crimson over a billowing white wig that concealed her thick raven hair from view. Shoulder-length, the hairpiece fluffed out at the sides and curled riotously about her cheeks.

Turning to a gilt-edged mirror mounted above a plain oak dresser, she considered her likeness. The reflection that stared back at her was that of a seductive enchantress in a revealing gown of scarlet velvet and black lace. It had taken an eternity, but finally, sometime during the past seven months, she'd become accustomed to the image that was so contrary to her true nature. She was the daughter of an earl, for goodness sake! Not the sultry strumpet the soldiers believed her to be. Still . . .

With a resigned sigh she lifted a red satin ball mask from atop the bureau and placed it over her eyes, shading their vibrant green color behind shadowed slits. The crimson material reflected off her smooth, ivory skin, giving it a pinkish tint, as if she'd pinched her cheeks repeatedly. The satin came down low, concealing her uptilted nose behind a small rise in the stiff fabric, but did nothing to hide her full lips. To compensate she had used a lip rouge of deep red to mask their natural pink blush.

Satisfied with her appearance, she tied the crimson cape beneath her chin, then turned toward the bed to retrieve a blunderbuss lying on a thick flannel quilt of apple green.

The weapon belonged to Carl, though she was quite sure

14

he'd never used it to hold up a carriage. More than likely he took it on his many hunting ventures with Jedediah Blackburn.

"So—"

Samantha swung toward the door.

Her twin sister stood in the now-open portal, hands on hips. "You still have not given up this foolishness."

"Blast it, Christine." Samantha clutched her chest to still the wild pounding of her heart. "Don't sneak up on me like that. There are enough perils in my life without adding apoplexy to the list."

Christine's delicate, fine-boned features softened. "Do not do this, Samantha. Do not risk your life. Surely there are other means to appropriate the money."

Samantha sighed and lowered her hands. She had hoped to avoid this conflict. "Twin, we've been over this more times than I care to recall. It's something I *must* do. You know the amount required to buy Father's escape. Lord Windhall's reputed to have considerable funds, and I intend to relieve him of a small portion. Besides, you were the one who told me the viscount would be riding in Hawksley's coach."

Her boots made no sound on the worn carpet as she crossed the small bedroom to stand before her sister. "I understand your fears, but please stop worrying so. There isn't as much danger as you might think," Samantha lied convincingly. "I'll be perfectly fine."

Christine didn't appear in the least mollified. If anything, she looked angry. "Do not worry?" Christine's clear emerald eyes, identical to Samantha's own, darkened to a stormy sea green. Her rose-petal mouth tightened, and her full breasts rose and fell rapidly beneath her peach gown.

Samantha cringed inwardly. Her sister's temper was rising like steam from a teapot.

"What am I supposed to do, pray tell?" Christine hissed through small clenched teeth. "Wait calmly for word of your demise? That is, if I do not *feel* it first?"

Samantha shook her head. "Of course not." She had

heard that others who had shared their mother's womb experienced each other's pain, much like she and her twin. And she and Christine were definitely twins—outwardly, at least. But inside they were as different as satin and wool. Samantha being wool, of course, the coarser of the two; the one who shunned propriety by riding astride a horse; the one who preferred fencing to stitchery; the one the London School for Young Ladies prayed they never saw again; the one who gave Father most of his gray hairs.

Visions of her father's silver curls and softly lined face tore at her heart. Swallowing against the pain, she turned toward the small fireplace and stared down into the dancing yellow flames. "Christine, please try to understand. Father—"

"Father is in the London Tower"—Christine's voice quivered with emotion—"not *Newgate*. He is not suffering, Samantha. Why can you not see that? He most likely has a servant in attendance and is quite comfortable. You must know that your fears are groundless."

Samantha spun back to face her sister, her pulse pounding. *"Groundless?* Father is in prison on a charge of treason! And you think my fears are groundless? Blast it, Christine. If he goes to trial, they'll hang him. He can't prove he didn't know about that damnable cargo."

The injustice of her father's imprisonment fired her blood. Just because that Williamsburg customs official had found gun powder on one of her father's ships the magistrate automatically assumed her father had been smuggling contraband to Patrick Henry and his rebels. Her father—the king's most loyal subject—a rebel. Her hands tightened into fists. That wretched Captain Cordell! Her father probably hadn't even known about the blasted cargo. "I have to get Father out of there." Samantha glared at her twin. "And I'll get the money to rescue him if I have to rob the governor himself!"

Whirling back to the bed, she grabbed the blunderbuss and stalked from the room, her fingers in a stranglehold around the blameless weapon. Christine's unquestioning faith in the sovereign would never allow her to understand.

But as always, by the time Samantha reached the foot of the stairs her temper had cooled, and she sorely regretted her outburst. Christine's concern for their father matched her own ... only Christine didn't believe him to be in immediate danger, so she wasn't of a mind to do anything about his quandary.

Making a mental promise to apologize later, Samantha stepped onto the dull slate tiles of the entry hall. She walked slowly, quietly, not wanting to alert Effie, the maid, to her presence. The servant, like her twin, heartily disapproved of Samantha's escapades.

Hearing the sound of clinking dishes, and knowing that Effie was occupied elsewhere, Samantha skirted around the dining room and tiptoed into the servants' quarters. With barely a sound she lifted the latch of the side door and crept out into the night.

The wintry white grounds gleamed blue under the glow of the full moon. Everything looked clean and new. Even the peeling sides of the low gray barn appeared presentable, its crudeness disguised by shadows and snowflakes.

She turned her attention to the window where a tiny yellow light flickered from inside. Blast. Carl's groom, Hadley, was obviously still at work. Steeling herself for the next skirmish, she reached for the handle.

The door creaked when she pushed it open, and the slave turned his shiny balding head toward her, the broom stopping mid-sweep. His ebony face beamed behind silver whiskers as he set the broom aside and moved his portly frame in her direction. "Evenin', Missy." Kind velvet-brown eyes made a quick inspection of her costume, and his round features sagged. "Lord Malderon ain't gonna like dis. Da massa done tole ya, gal, dat he don' want no mo' shenanigans."

"Oh, Hadley, not you, too."

His expression gentled. "Missy, I know ya wants ta he'p

yo' papa, an' I don' blame ya. I'd be hawd put not ta maself. But thin's like dis is best left ta da menfolk. A li'l gal like you's bound ta come ta hawm."

"I'll be careful, Hadley. I swear by all that's holy, I will. Now no more arguments, no matter how well intended. Please, just saddle Starburst for me. I've got to go before it's too late."

Hadley shook his head, and light glinted off nappy gray curls above his ears. "I don' like dis, Missy. I sho'ly don'. But I ain't gonna say no mo'. Mostly 'cause ya is jest too stubb'n ta listen anyways." Moving to the end stall, he opened the gate and stepped inside.

Starburst's speckled head reared up, and he whinnied nervously when Hadley threw a saddle blanket over his back.

The stallion's anxiousness around other people never ceased to amaze Samantha. Even Hadley, who'd been tending Starburst since birth, caused the horse to skitter uneasily.

When she had first arrived Carl had ordered her to stay away from the spirited beast. But as usual, she hadn't listened. And from the first moment she'd stroked its smooth pink muzzle the horse had taken to her. And he learned quickly. In just a few short lessons she'd taught him the commands she'd learned from the grooms at Willowglen, to come when she whistled and to kneel. Her cheek dimpled. Then she'd added a command of her own—play dead.

Carl had been livid the first time he saw her ride the hunter, probably because she'd blatantly disobeyed him. But he soon resigned himself to her determination, although not silently. "That damnable Fleming bullheadedness," he had moaned often. But that was Carl.

After her father's arrest, when he had insisted that she and Christine go to his friend in the colonies, they had been skeptical of this man called Carl Malderon. But after one week in his home both she and her twin realized that he was just like their father, all grumble and noise, yet soft as a downy pillow. And he cared about them. Deeply. She could hear it in the gentleness of his voice, see it in the lines that worried his handsome brow when one of them didn't return when expected.

Her smile softened fondly. Tonight she would try to ease his trepidation. She would make an effort to be home before he returned from his mysterious jaunt.

When Hadley finished saddling Starburst and moved out of the stall Samantha entered and slid her hand over the animal's bulging gray chest. "How you doing, boy?" She leaned forward and rubbed her cheek against his sleek neck. "Ready for a little exercise?"

Almost as if he understood her words, the stallion nickered softly. Raising her foot, she touched the toe of her boot to his hoof. "All right, fella. Kneel."

Starburst instantly curled one front leg and lowered his massive body. He bowed his head, enabling Samantha to mount without assistance.

Reining her mount around the servant, she guided him outside. The frosty breath of winter caused her to shudder and snuggle down into her cape as she rode across the yard. Again she thanked Effie's foresight in having made the scarlet gown. She had padded the velvet cape with cotton batting before stitching in the red satin lining. She had done the same with the skirt, all the while grumbling because Samantha had insisted it be split so she could ride a horse astride. Effie, like her husband Hadley, had shaken her head yet done as instructed. But her disgust had shown in the downward pull of her fleshy umber cheeks.

When Samantha had first come to Riversedge Carl had told her that Hadley and Effie were completely trustworthy. Although she doubted he realized then just what Samantha would entrust them with. Carl had said that the slaves had been with him since he, her father, and Cousin Beau Kincaid had first come to America back in '41. The servants had known her father and respected him deeply, which had been to her advantage when Samantha approached them with her somewhat outrageous plan.

At first they had been scandalized. But later, after realizing she would persist with or without them, they agreed to help, albeit with much-voiced disapproval.

She smiled at the memory and leaned forward in the saddle, nudging Starburst into a gallop. He raced across an open field toward a stand of trees, his hooves thudding heavily, his stride long and sure.

At the edge of the meadow she slowed the stallion to a trot and guided him into the forest; then, reining to the left, she turned Starburst toward the main road that led into Lynch's Ferry. A few miles this side of the settlement she remembered a fork leading to the Windhall plantation. Half a mile before that the forest-lined road narrowed to the width of a single carriage. She'd learned from experience that if an obstacle lay in the path, nothing could pass.

She grinned beneath the satin mask and tapped her heels against Starburst's sides, directing him toward the lane.

"The perfect place for a robbery."

CHAPTER 3

Jason still shook with chills as he climbed back into Peter's carriage. That dip in the James must have frozen his blood. He felt terrible. And the nauseating scent of Minerva's perfume caused his stomach to churn. Propriety had demanded that he dance with the annoying blonde. But did she have to rub against him every time the music brought their bodies close? Not that he was averse to the feel of a woman's body next to his own. Quite the opposite. But he truly preferred to make the advances himself.

The carriage bounded forward, springs creaking under the swaying weight of the coach, and Jason shifted in an attempt to stretch his long legs. He had been fortunate tonight in one respect, he thought. With the soldiers out looking for the Devilrider there had been none of the stiff-necked bastards in attendance at the Wainwrights'. Thank Providence. Attending these ghastly affairs was bad enough without having to endure *their* presence, too.

He still didn't see how Nick managed to live and work among them without slitting a few of their throats. Even if working in the governor's office did afford Nick the information he needed for the Williamsburg smuggling operation, Jason still didn't know how his brother kept himself in control. Jason knew he himself couldn't have done it. But then Nick always had been the more sensible of the two.

Again Jason squirmed, trying to relieve the constriction of the tight brocade. He couldn't wait to get home and take off the god-awful clothes.

Glancing across at Peter, he noticed the younger man still babbled to Minerva about the goodly wager he'd lost to George Wainwright. Jason knew Peter was upset merely because he hadn't won. The sum was of little importance. As the son of a deceased baronet who'd made his fortune raising indigo, Peter had little worry over funds.

Evidently feeling the weight of Jason's perusal, Peter turned to him, then leaned forward in the seat. "Did you have occasion to speak with Lydia Millworth this evening?"

"Alas, no, I did not." He'd managed to avoid the wretched gossip all evening—thank heavens. "Her husband, Davidson, barely left my side during the entire affair."

"Then you haven't heard the news?" Peter's face brightened. "Bartholomew Dungworth was set upon last evening." He straightened his hedgehog wig, which had slipped to one side. Then, raising an arm, he swung a skeletal hand, indicating the outside surroundings. "In this very area. 'Twas that female bandit, they say. The Scarlet Temptress."

Peter looked at Minerva, who was seated beside Jason. "'Tis said she took his purse, his rings, his snuffbox, and his wife's jewels." He leaned closer for emphasis. "And if that wasn't enough, why, the wench took the wig from his very head. Said it was just in case she needed a spare. Can you imagine?"

Hardly. Jason had heard several tales of the bandit's exploits since his arrival in Lynch's Ferry. Not that he believed them. A woman who rode astride a horse? In a dress? Not bloody likely. It was probably a scrawny lad disguised as a female.

"My word!" Minerva Carstairs sidled closer to Jason, and he cursed himself for taking pity on Hawksley and switching places with him for the ride home. Her towering curls bobbed as she clutched the lap robe, drawing it close to her barely concealed bosom. "How positively horrid. Bartholomew's poor wife. Why, she was surely frightened to tears." Cutting a look at Jason, she gave a delicate shudder. "I know I would have been." She edged closer yet, then lowered her short blond lashes. "Unless, of course, I had a courageous protector at my side."

Jason fought the urge to roll his eyes heavenward. He didn't know which struck him as funnier—Minerva ogling him as a protector when he'd spent the past two months emulating a simpering dandy, or the thought of Bartholomew's hulking frame groveling at the feet of a gun-toting strumpet.

Minerva slid her hand through the crook in Jason's elbow, and her breasts rubbed against his arm. Her sickly sweet perfume attacked his nostrils, and her voice dropped to a low, nauseating mewl. "Nothing would frighten me with you at my side."

Jason drew in a slow breath. "I'm honored that you think so highly of my capabilities, Mrs. Carstairs. But I sincerely hope my valor is never put to the test. One never knows what one will do under such frightening circumstances."

"Well I, for one, wouldn't cower 'neath that harlot's assault," Peter inserted, his narrow nose elevated haughtily. "A Hawksley bows to no one."

"Quite so," he replied dryly. Peter reminded him of an underfed bantam rooster. Jason might loathe playing the

part of a fop, but he had to admit some of the people he'd encountered were very entertaining.

Suddenly the carriage jerked. It slowed rapidly as it bucked and swayed to a wrenching halt. Peter stumbled to his feet and leaned out the window. "What is it, Isaac?" he called to the driver. "Why are we stopping?"

A thread of nervousness laced the driver's response. "It be a horse, suh, layin' in da middle of da road. Looks like it be dead."

"Well, move the wretched thing out of the way, and be quick about it." Peter slid back into his seat. "Bloody nuisance, that's what 'tis. What's a horse doing in the middle of the road, anyway? In the middle of the night?" He pulled the rug back over his bony knees, snorting in distaste. "Incompetent colonials."

Jason frowned. Incompetent colonials? He doubted that. The horse could very well be serving as a ruse to stop the carriage so it could be robbed. Making his hand tremble in an attempt to appear nervous, Jason brought his handkerchief up to his temple. "Didn't you say this is the area the bandit haunts?"

"Yes, 'tis." Peter nodded, then he cast him a reassuring smile. "But fear not, your lordship. The outlaw has never been known to strike in the same vicinity two nights in succession. 'Twould be too great a risk with a detachment of soldiers patrolling the area."

And it never snows in Virginia, Jason thought. His hand automatically slid to the waist of his breeches, but he checked the urge to withdraw the pistol tucked safely beneath the folds of his shirt. Slowly, so as not to draw attention to himself, he slid his hand down again and picked up the tricorn lying across his knees. He drew it to his breast like a shield, in a gesture that he hoped emulated fear, while secretly removing his purse of gold. A highwayman couldn't steal what he couldn't find.

"Oh, my," he said, drawing the tricorn closer to his chin, distracting the others while he slid the purse behind a gap in the velvet lining just below the coach window. He'd have to

retrieve it another day, he thought. "I do hope you're right. I'd hate to think some fearsome rogue might be nearby."

Peter chuckled. "Lord Windhall, the rogue is a woman. A very beautiful woman, from what I hear. If she can elude the king's men for over six months, she's not fool enough to change her strategy at this late date." He straightened the lace on his cuffs. "I quite admire her cunning—even if she is a hoydenish outlaw."

Minerva clutched Jason's arm fearfully. "Do you think we're going to be robbed?" There was genuine terror in the woman's high-pitched voice.

Jason wished he'd kept his mouth shut. Dropping the tricorn, he turned in the seat to face her fully. He patted her hand while easing out of her grasp. "There, there, my dear. How thoughtless of me. I should never have said such a thing. Of course Peter is right. The outlaw would never attempt another robbery so soon—"

"Care to wager your life on that?" a woman's low, sultry voice asked from behind Jason.

Minerva and Peter cried out in unison as they stared over his shoulder.

Jason's anger surged. God's blood! Would this wretched day never end? He felt the twitch of a muscle in his jaw and turned slowly to face the window. The wide barrel of a blunderbuss was visible through a part in the curtains, pointed directly at his head.

"If you would be so kind as to step out," the throaty voice commanded.

Suppressing the desire to jerk the bandit through the window, he resigned himself to his role. "Oh, my! Oh, my!" Oh, hell.

A horrified screech escaped Minerva's throat, and her fingers clamped around his wrist. "Oh, please, don't let her kill me. I don't want to die."

Jason gnashed his teeth. He wanted to shake some sense into her. God save him from whining women. He glanced at Peter. Hawksley didn't look as though he fared much better. The man looked as if he were made of wood. So much for

24

bravado. What was the matter with these people? Didn't they realize that showing fear would only give the outlaw more confidence? Lord, what he would give if Peter and Minerva weren't here. He would have no trouble dealing with the bothersome bandit.

For a fleeting instant Jason considered overpowering the miscreant. But to do so would destroy his image. And above all else, his identity must not be questioned.

"Your lordships," the bandit said from the shadows beyond the curtain, "I'm waiting."

Jason refrained from telling her she could wait until hell cooled for all he cared. Instead he climbed slowly from the carriage. Raising his hand, he gently assisted Minerva down and watched as Peter nervously joined them.

Jason turned to face the outlaw for the first time—and inhaled sharply. She looked like an ethereal goddess bathed in silver. She was so small, so fragile.

An unwanted emotion slithered through him when he explored the creamy swell of flesh rising above the bodice of a dark crimson gown. His loins tightened. This was definitely no lad. At least none that he'd ever seen. Slowly he examined every well-formed inch of her small frame. Come to think of it, he hadn't encountered many *women* who looked like that, either. She was magnificent.

He traced the full rise of her breasts straining against the tight velvet. Very nice. Entranced, his attention moved down her narrow rib cage to a tiny waist that, no doubt, his hands could span with ease.

With some surprise he noticed that she wore no panniers. The material of the skirt clung enticingly to the curves of her nicely rounded hips.

Jason inspected her childlike gloved hand holding the gun, then looked up a slender, velvet-encased arm to the edge of a short cape. It hid her shoulders from his view. But the strings tied at her neck drew him to the throbbing pulse at the base of her smooth throat. He felt the ungodly urge to touch his lips to the exposed flesh.

Shocked, he forced himself to resume his inspection. He

saw the stubborn tilt of her chin and, farther up, her delicately curved jawline. An array of curls shimmered in the moonlight like spun silver as they peeked from beneath the hood of her cape. He tried to detect the true color of her hair at the edge of the white wig but couldn't.

Remembering his own disguise, he wondered momentarily how she would react to the Devilrider. His mouth tilted, and he returned his attention to the red satin ball mask, trying to see her eyes behind the narrow slits. He couldn't tell, yet somehow he knew they would be as breathtaking as the rest of her.

A chilly breeze stirred, and he caught the faint scent of roses the same instant he saw her mouth. He felt another spiral of tautness coil through his lower abdomen. He wanted to pull his stare away from her lips. And he tried. But they held him mesmerized. They were full and moist, the kind that would tempt a man to crush them beneath his own. The kind a man would plunder again and again as he lowered her to the bed and eased between her—God's teeth! What was the matter with him? She's nothing but a bloody outlaw! No wonder they called her the Scarlet *Temptress*.

Samantha felt a quiver run along her spine as the man's stare burned a slow, scorching path over her body. Her flesh tingled as if he'd actually touched her. No one had ever looked at her in such a manner. It was indecent!

Was this Lord Windhall? She caught sight of the lace handkerchief protruding from his cuff. Yes, he must be the prissy fop she'd heard so much about. Her gaze rose to meet the startling impact of his. Those blue, blue eyes seemed to say something completely different than his manner. Even in those outrageous clothes there was a danger about him. He had an assurance and confidence that was in direct contrast to his vain appearance.

He was ruggedly handsome, excitingly so, even though his chiseled features were covered by that disgusting white powder. Eyes the color of a summer sky, surrounded by thick black lashes, studied her with frightening intensity.

Along the firmness of his jaw a shadow revealed that he needed to spend more time than most with a razor. Above the square chin his beautifully carved mouth was accentuated by a determined lower lip that hinted at a sensuality she instinctively knew this man would take pains to hide. Something stirred in her breast.

Disturbed by her own musings, she quickly pulled her attention from his face and directed it toward Peter Hawksley. Holding tightly to the gun, she raised her other hand and revealed a black cloth bag. "Place your valuables inside and make haste." She smiled sweetly. "And gentlemen, don't forget your fat purses."

Jason felt a rush of smug satisfaction. With his purse of gold hidden in the carriage, he had nothing of value on him. He wore no jewelry. And not even for the guise of Lord Windhall would he suffer beringed hands and a stickpin that shoved his cravat up under his nose. How would she accept the loss?

Peter, the first to respond, quickly removed his ruby ring, a gold snuffbox, and the timepiece from his fob pocket, dropping each into the bag. An embarrassingly light purse followed.

The outlaw frowned.

Next Minerva shakily unclasped her emerald necklace, her melonlike breasts jiggling with nerves. She cast Jason a fearful look, then removed her earbobs and plunged all into the bag.

The Scarlet Temptress turned to him next, holding out the bag. "If you please, Lord . . . ?"

"Windhall, the Viscount of Westland, at your service." He bowed stiffly, then shrugged. "And I am sorry to disappoint you, madam, but I am without a farthing."

Samantha started in surprise at the sound of his whining voice. It certainly didn't match his powerful appearance, and she suppressed an odd feeling of disappointment. Then his words penetrated her brain, and she saw his lips quirk. Minor explosions erupted in her temples. She clutched the

SUE RICH

bag until she felt her knuckles grow numb beneath the gloves. Her temper rose to a slow boil. The lying popinjay! How dare he play her for a fool? Did he think her a simpleton?

She made a quick inventory of his pockets. There didn't appear to be a bulging purse, nor even the outline of a snuffbox. Blast. He was the only reason she'd stopped this coach! What had he done with his money? Hidden it away? Left it home? Her eyes narrowed. Bloody peacock!

The blunderbuss wavered, and she forced herself to relax, then tilted her head, in what she hoped was a casual manner. "Oh? Is that a fact, milord?"

Jason nodded and flashed a patronizing smile while removing the handkerchief to dab at his nose. "It most certainly is, madam."

Samantha felt her back muscles stiffen. Why, you preening milksop, she wanted to shout. You vain cur. You . . . you . . . Unable to come up with another scathing imprecation, she drew in a slow breath and tried to think.

So the prissy fool wants to play games, does he? Then so be it. "But sir, you are poorly mistaken." She cast him a wicked little smile. "For I see much of value in your fine . . . apparel."

Jason went rigid. She wouldn't. She damn well better not! A muscle drummed along his jaw as he fought his own rapidly rising ire. *"What?"*

"Please, your lordship, if you would be so kind as to remove your clothing. *At once.*"

She would! Damn her! "You won't get away with this." He forced a shrill note into his voice to keep it from lowering in rage. "You bloody wretch!" Silently he raged, I'd give my right ear to spend five minutes alone with you, vixen. Just five minutes. Clamping his teeth together, he mentally dismembered every limb from her lovely little body.

Glaring down at the gun she held, he weighed his chances. No doubt he could disarm her. But what if someone got hurt in the process? Possibly even the bandit herself. Although he couldn't discern why *that* should bother him. And what

28

about his charade? The whole guise could well depend on this moment.

Smoldering with a fury so great it nearly singed him, he ripped off his gloves and tore the yellow redingote from his shoulders, tossing them on the frozen ground. He resisted the urge to grind them beneath his heel. The snow-white cravat and waistcoat followed the same path. Uncaring of the damage he did to the shirt, he snapped off several buttons in his anger and haste. But he managed to contain his anger long enough to conceal his pistol in its white folds.

Samantha blinked with surprise when he first removed the gloves. His hands were golden bronze, slim, well shaped —and cut. How? What had a man of his obvious breeding done to acquire such injuries?

Her attention shifted to the width of his sinewy torso when he stripped off the shirt. Soft dark hairs curled gently over his solid, muscular chest, widening to encircle male nipples, then arrowing down the hard, flat stomach to disappear into the waistband of his breeches. Dragging her stare from the intimate sight, she swallowed against a sudden constriction in her throat.

Jason's muscles tightened as the frigid January air slid its icy fingers over his bare flesh. Using more care now, he dropped the shirt on the stack of clothing, hoping to cloak his weapon, but the bloody pistol plopped out. It bounced and landed at the woman's feet.

Biting back a string of curses, he risked a quick glance at Peter and Minerva, praying they hadn't seen the pistol. Minerva was whispering something in Peter's ear, causing the younger man's face to redden. Thank Providence they hadn't seen the weapon.

But the outlaw had. She scooped it up and dropped it into the bag, the corners of her lips tipping upward.

Jason tensed, and his hands balled into fists. He wanted to throttle her! That pistol had been the last birthday present his father had ever given him.

Samantha noticed that the viscount had stopped undressing. Did the man think she had all night? Was he stalling for time, hoping the soldiers would come? She was anxious to be gone. And more, impatient to see the arrogant lord redden with embarrassment. She knew he would have to travel home in his undergarments. Smiling, she jerked the blunderbuss toward him. "The breeches now, if you please."

Until this night Jason had never in his life thought of hurting a woman. But he could almost feel his hands tightening around her slender throat.

"Your lordship," Samantha repeated. "Do make haste."

Shivering from cold—and anger—he stepped out of his shoes, his toes curling against the frozen ground. Bending, he reached for the bands of his stockings.

"Leave them," Samantha said, not bothering to hide her grin. "I wouldn't want your modesty threatened more than necessary."

Jason straightened. "How thoughtful of you."

Samantha nodded, a dimple creasing her right cheek. "Yes, isn't it." Her smile faded. "The breeches."

Jason clenched his teeth and undid the buttons of his pants before sliding them down over his lean flanks. He kicked the garment aside. Then, planting both feet firmly on the ground, slightly spread, he straightened to his full towering height and placed his hands on his bare hips.

Minerva, as if awakened from the dead, shrieked at the sight of his nakedness and collapsed in Peter's arms.

Peter nearly dropped her as he, too, sucked in a sharp breath at the blatant display of undeniable maleness.

The coachman made a choking sound.

Samantha nearly strangled on her own gasp. Her eyes widened in disbelief. My God! Why wasn't the man wearing undergarments? Her face flamed beneath the mask. Why hadn't he warned her? He was no gentleman. A gentleman would never stand there like some jackanapes—with a smirk plastered across his arrogant face!

She looked quickly away. But the picture of that hard body was stamped on her brain. Did all men look like that without their clothes? So powerful? So dangerous?

Feeling the heat in her cheeks rise even higher, she wrenched her thoughts from his manliness and met his laughing blue eyes. Laughing. Her anger blazed. For one awful moment she nearly pulled the trigger. And oh, how she wanted to. But her fingers loosened. She couldn't kill a man—especially not *this* man.

Startled, she blinked and watched his mouth widen into a knowing smile—almost as if he'd read her mind. Her teeth ground together. So he thought to make sport of her, did he? The bounder. She'd show him a thing or two!

Slowly she bent to pick up his discarded clothing, her eyes on his, while keeping the gun leveled at an angle that would definitely threaten his future heirs should he make a sudden move. Scooping up the shoes and costume, she crushed the bundle to her breast and instantly noticed the clean aroma of pine soap, leather, and his own manly scent. Her senses tingled, but she quickly brushed the feeling aside to motion the widow and Peter into the carriage. When the viscount moved to follow she stopped him abruptly. "Remain where you are." Without taking her eyes from the man she whistled for her horse.

Starburst, lying motionless in the path, jerked to his feet and trotted to her.

With her eyes locked on Lord Windhall's Samantha spoke to the driver, who still sat rigidly atop the carriage. "Be gone with you. And don't stop until you've reached your destination."

The driver, obviously unmindful of the naked viscount, snapped his whip, startling the team into a gallop, and the carriage raced away.

Jason faced the woman, his bare skin protesting the cold, his teeth chattering. What was she going to do with him? The thought intrigued him. Since he'd taken on the guise of Lord Windhall he'd been without a woman, and he sorely felt the neglect. Folding his arms across his chest, he studied her bodice.

Samantha chose that moment to glance up—and her fury

soared. Even as his breath formed little clouds of steam he
stared at her roguishly . . . lecherously. Her lips drew into a
tight line. Snatching up the hunter's reins, she raised the gun
and stepped back, then tapped Starburst's hoof with her
boot. "Kneel," she commanded, and the gray stallion instantly dropped into a low bow.

It was all Jason could do to keep from sputtering in
surprise. Then he received another jolt when the woman
lifted a booted foot and swung her leg over the saddle,
revealing a skirt that resembled loose breeches.

As the stallion rose to its feet and sidestepped anxiously
Jason frowned and looked up at the Scarlet Temptress. What
of him? He rubbed his hands together for warmth.
"Madam?"

Samantha nudged the horse away from his reach. "You,
sir," she ground out slowly, "will walk."

"*What?* Are you daft, woman? It's freezing out here!"
Already his toes were numb. "You can't be serious."

Samantha ignored his outburst and urged the horse
farther away. Windhall looked angry enough to hurt someone.

The viscount stepped forward threateningly, all pretense
of meekness having disappeared. "The game has gone on
long enough." His tone lowered dangerously. "Now give me
my clothes."

Samantha felt a coil of fear. The hunter nickered nervously. With blinding clarity she realized the viscount's vain
facade had been a ruse. This man could, and probably
would, harm her.

"Damn it, woman, if you leave me out here like this, I'll
hunt you to the ends of the earth. And when I catch
you—and I *will* catch you"—his voiced deepened to a
chilling rasp—"I'll destroy you."

She knew he meant it, but she'd be damned before she'd
let *him* know it. Drawing on the Fleming courage, she cast
him an impish smile. "I tremble at the thought, milord."
Then, raising her fingers to her lips, she blew him a kiss
before reining the horse toward the forest.

Jason watched her slim form disappear, and his hands drew into fists. His temples throbbed. "You won't escape me, vixen," he vowed softly to the shadows. "As God is my witness, you won't escape my wrath."

CHAPTER 4

Samantha jerked the stallion to a halt. A freezing wind whipped her cape and stung her cheeks. The viscount's shuddering form wavered in her vision. Dear God, what had she done? "I can't leave him out there to die!"

Starburst pricked up his ears.

She pulled the reins, turning back in the direction of the narrow lane. "Blast my unruly temper."

Her great-grandfather had been renowned for his volatile temper. It was his Irish heritage, they said. And now Samantha was blessed, or was it cursed, with Falkner Fleming's wretched disposition. Just once, she'd like to be able to control herself long enough to think rationally *before* she acted. Well, there was no help for it now. She must go back. She might be a thief, but she most certainly wasn't a murderer. Shivering from cold, and knowing the viscount must be faring far worse, she kicked Starburst into a canter.

She didn't know how she planned to get the viscount home, but first she must return his clothing. Perhaps then she could alert someone to his dilemma.

Advancing through the last stand of trees, she reined in. The road was deserted. She trembled against the cold and frowned in confusion. Where was he? "Your lordship?" she called softly. She scanned each shadow, her ears honed to the slightest sound. A small furry animal skittered across the path, but all remained silent.

"Lord Windhall!" she called louder, then she tilted her

head to listen. Again nothing. Real concern rose. Blast it! Where could he have gone? The bloody fool didn't have a shred of sense. He'd undoubtedly left the safety of the road to wander through the forests. "Jackanapes! He'll cause his own death, and it'll be on *my* conscience."

After a fruitless search Samantha entered the stables at Riversedge, her limbs numb from cold, frustration swirling through her breast. She'd probed the entire area between the fork and the Carstairs plantation but hadn't found a single trace of the viscount. Had the carriage returned for him? Perhaps one of the king's soldiers had happened by. That must be it. Please, God, let that be it.

Sighing, Samantha tried to shake off the hollow feeling in her stomach. She unsaddled the hunter and rubbed his coat until it was dry, then led him into his stall. Feeling an almost desperate need for a hot bath and steaming cup of tea, she left the stable and strode quickly toward the house.

As she neared the manor she caught a glimpse of the small, white two-level house that sat amid a circle of spruce less than a hundred yards from the edge of the James River. It wasn't pretty, or even passably attractive. Yet, though small by many standards, it had managed to weather more than two score years.

Her father had told her about this place many times, about his trip to the colonies with his cousin, Beau Kincaid, and Carl when they were mere lads of nineteen. The trio had been so eager to see America, he had said, so set for adventure. But Father's part in the exploit had lasted less than two years. He had had to return to England to take up his duties as the Earl of Willowglen when his father died unexpectedly. Beau and Carl had remained, determined to make their fortunes.

Samantha smiled. How she wished she'd known the adventurous threesome in their younger days. For hours she had listened in rapt silence to her father's tales of their wild escapades; tales of how they'd saved the life of a trapper named Jedediah Blackburn, who later taught them the trade; of how they'd been captured by a band of Indians and became friends with the chief, Flaming Wing; and of how they all fell in love with the same woman, Lucinda Buford —with Beau as the victor.

A sadness touched her heart for her father's loss. Though they were cousins by birth, her father had looked upon Beau Kincaid with all the affection of a brother.

Releasing a slow breath, she entered the house and picked up a lone lighted candle from a small table in the entry hall. The flame from the taper wavered as she moved toward the door leading to a cupboard beneath the curving staircase. She stepped inside the small cubicle and inched toward the back, pushing hard on the rear wall. A low screech reverberated from the hinges of a concealed door as it swung open to reveal a cold, dark storage area.

Setting the candle on a barrel she knew contained tea, she removed her mask and tossed it down beside the taper. Eerie shadows danced over the dusty jars of ink, type, and stacks of parchment that lined the gray shelves. Carl's secret engagements, she'd concluded long ago, must have something to do with printing.

Placing the viscount's bundle of clothing and shoes in a cedar chest on the floor, she peeled off her cape and gloves, adding them to the trunk. Cold seeped up through the spaces in the floorboards. She shivered in earnest and decided the rest could wait until she reached the warmth of her bedroom. Leaving the concealed area quickly, she started to mount the stairs.

Murmured voices penetrated the silent hall.

Stopping with one foot on the steps, she listened. The voices seemed to be coming from the parlor. Who in the world could that be at this hour? Moving stealthily lest it be a member of the king's army calling, she crept up to the partially open parlor door and peeked around the edge.

Carl and Christine sat with their backs to her, facing a white marble fireplace. Light from several candles flickered over the blue and silver high-backed chairs. Sparks from the burning logs popped out onto the low hearth, glowing for a moment before fading to tiny black specks. Samantha let out a soft moan. They were waiting for her. Blast.

Christine's head was bent over her needlework, her dark hair fanned out around her shoulders like a shimmering black cape.

Samantha's attention moved to Carl, who sat rigidly in the opposite chair, gnawing on an unlit pipe. She looked fleetingly back at the stairway leading to her room, but she knew a decent night's rest wouldn't be possible until she'd faced the inevitable confrontation with Carl. Quietly she pulled the door open and stepped inside the parlor.

"Shouldn't she be back by now?" Carl asked suddenly, lowering his pipe.

"She will be here," her sister returned confidently. "Just give her time."

Staring into the flames, Carl shook his head. "How much time does it take to rob a carriage, for bloody sakes?"

Samantha could see the lines of worry creasing his face and bit her lower lip, trying to ward off a surge of guilt.

"Surely she's had enough time," Carl continued. "Damn it, Christine. If anything happens to her, I'll never forgive myself. I should have put my foot down. Prevented her from risking her life on such foolishness." He shook his silver head. "Your father will never forgive me."

"There are very few people who can prevent Samantha from doing something she wants to do," Christine consoled.

"The fault will nonetheless lie at my door. Derrick trusted me to take care of you girls. If she gets injured or, God forbid, killed . . ."

Samantha felt the ponderous weight of blame settle on her shoulders. Unable to bear yet another burden this night, she stepped forward. "I'd forgive you, Carl."

His head snapped around, and he leapt to his feet.

"If anything happens to me, it will be because of my own carelessness," she added gently.

"Where have you been? You should have been home hours ago. Do you think all we have to do around here is wait while you meander about the countryside?"

Samantha's and Christine's eyes met in mutual humor.

Carl was behaving just like their father. Turning back to Carl, she tried to look contrite. "I'm sorry. A small problem came up."

"Problem?" He instantly scanned her person. "What problem?"

"One of the passengers." She reassured him quickly. "He claimed to have no valuables."

Carl frowned. "So? What happened? What detained you?"

Samantha stole a peek at Christine. Her sister, too, had her brows raised in silent query. Samantha stifled a sigh. Her oh-so-proper twin was probably going to swoon at this. "A gentleman, Lord Windhall—the one supposedly without funds. Well, I felt he should be taught a lesson lest his peers decide to try something similar."

Carl flinched. "Wind—what *kind* of lesson?"

Samantha avoided looking at Christine and crossed to the fireplace to warm her hands. "Nothing too drastic. I just took his clothing and sent the carriage on without him."

Christine sucked in a sharp breath.

Samantha cringed.

"You *what?*" Carl bellowed. "It's freezing out there!" He placed a hand to his forehead and kneaded his temples as if trying to calm himself. "Where did you leave him?"

Was Carl coming down with the ague? He sounded hoarse. "Near the fork. Why? He's not there anymore. I went back, but he'd already gone." She edged her back to the fire. "The carriage must have returned. Or perhaps a rider came along." At least she *hoped* that's what had happened.

"What if neither did? What if he's out there freezing?" Carl voiced her fears. "What if he wandered off in another direction? He could die out there." Something almost savage flared in his expression before he abruptly reeled away. "I'm going to look for him," he rasped harshly. "And you'd better pray I find him."

"I'll go with you."

"No!" he fairly shouted. "You've done enough damage for one night." He grabbed his coat from a hook by the door. "I warned you in the beginning that someone might get hurt." He jerked on his redingote, then flung a wool cape around his shoulders. When he turned back to her his expression was fierce. "There will be no more of this!" Yanking at the ties of his cape in a futile effort to secure them, he glared menacingly. "Don't bother to wait up for me. We'll talk again in the morning." With something between a snarl and a growl he spun on his heels and stomped from the room.

"What was that about?" Christine asked when the door closed behind him.

"I have no idea," Samantha answered tiredly. Pulling the wig from her head, she tossed it to Christine and shook out her hair. Lord, it felt good to take that thing off.

Christine absently stroked the hairpiece. "I have never seen Carl so angry before—or so worried. Except when fretting over you, that is. Mayhap the man is a friend of his."

Remembering the foppish dress and manner of the viscount, Samantha shook her head. "I doubt that. Lord Windhall appeared to be a dandy of the first water." Samantha's forehead creased. Or was he?

"Well, I just hope for your sake that the gentleman makes it home safely."

"Believe me, twin, so do I," Samantha replied. Her fingers moved to undo the buttons down the front of the scarlet gown as she turned toward the entry hall. "I don't think I could live with the man's death on my hands." Her fingers stalled on the buttons. Just the thought of that handsome face, stilled forever in death . . .

"I know," Christine agreed gently. "And like Carl, I feared something like this would happen." She reached for the staircase banister and paused. "Mayhap now you will give up this foolishness."

Samantha stopped but didn't turn to face her sister. A maelstrom of emotions ran rampant: guilt, worry, anger, but above all, concern for her father. "I can't," she whispered raggedly.

As they entered the bedroom Samantha crossed to the fire while Christine retrieved a towel from below the washstand.

When Samantha turned she saw Christine studying the dull, marred finish of the old stand.

"Why do you think Father sent us here?" her twin asked suddenly. "I mean here to America?"

Samantha stepped out of the velvet dress and tossed it across the back of an upholstered chair. "He didn't have much of a choice." She peeled off her chemise and laid it beside the dress, her bare flesh tingling from the warmth of the fire. "When the magistrate seized Willowglen we had nowhere else to go. The *ton* now considers Father a traitor. And you know yourself how our social invitations halted the moment his imprisonment was announced. Heavens, Christine, even pending engagements were canceled."

"Oh, I understand all that. But he could have sent us somewhere else—someplace more suitable, like France."

Samantha arched a brow at her sister. "Without a chaperon? Or have you forgotten that not one single person applied for the position when we were in such need?"

"No," Christine conceded. "And I thought it terribly ingenious of you to disguise yourself as an elderly woman and pose as *my* chaperon for the voyage over here. But that still does not answer my question. Why here?"

Samantha shrugged. "Because he trusts Carl. And, too, should we find ourselves pressed, we have relatives here."

Christine gave an unladylike snort. "We do not even know our estranged cousins, the Kincaids. Their father died when we were mere babes, and they have lived in these wretched colonies the whole time. Why, they never once even bothered to communicate." She tossed the towel down. "I sorely resent being sent to this horrid place. What chance do you or I have of finding a suitable match when all the eligible gentlemen are an ocean away?"

"I'm not looking for a match, suitable or otherwise," Samantha pointed out as she stepped into the warm water Christine intuitively had prepared. The occurrence was so common that she barely gave it thought anymore.

Christine sighed. "You know, we may be identical in appearance, but believe me, Samantha, that is where our similarity ends. Not that I blame you. I do not. It was all Father's fault. If he had not allowed you such freedom—''

Samantha opened her mouth to defend her father, but Christine raised a slim hand to stay the words.

"Oh, I know how much you adore him—so do I, for that matter. But still, he should have listened to Aunt Katherine instead of encouraging you to tag along with him and dally around those smelly stables. You learned nothing of what a proper lady should know—especially concerning matrimony.'' She moved closer. "How many times have I heard you claim that marriage was for weak, spineless women who need a man to tell them what to do? A hundred?"

Samantha grinned. "That's a fair estimate."

Christine looked as if she wanted to stomp her foot. "This is not humorous.'' She dropped the soap in the water directly in front of Samantha. It splashed fatly, sending a shower of droplets into Samantha's face. "If only our mother had lived, you might have turned out properly.''

Samantha brushed the water off her face and blinked at her twin. "And how would you know that? Our mother died the night we were born. We never even knew her.''

"Well,'' Christine hedged, "I am certain she would not have tolerated it, anyway.''

Samantha couldn't stop her smile. It was an old argument. "Well, it's no use discussing what might have been. It won't change the way I am. Just let it be, twin, and help me wash my hair, hmm?"

With her bath complete, a cup of hot tea inside her, and a long flannel gown around her, Samantha paced before the fireplace. Visions of the viscount rose up to haunt her when she thought of how he had trembled with cold. How was he faring? Had he found his way home? Or was he lying on the frozen earth somewhere, drawing his last breath? Surely the carriage had returned for him. But what if it hadn't? a damning little voice asked. What if he were to die?

"You did not really make Lord Windhall disrobe, did you?" Christine asked, uncannily picking up on Samantha's direction of thought as she folded the red velvet gown.

"Yes."

Christine frowned. "Is he not that elderly, overweight gentleman whose lips are always dribbling?"

"No, you're thinking of Lord Wainwright. Lord Windhall is younger—a score and ten, or thereabouts. It's a shame, too. He wouldn't be half bad if he wasn't such a peacock."

"I wager he really looked quite humorous in his unmentionables," Christine said, glancing up from the bureau, then blushed at her own boldness.

"He wasn't wearing any."

"What?" Christine inhaled sharply. "You mean . . ."

"Exactly."

"My goodness! Were you not embarrassed? Was he not? Oh, Samantha, how *could* you have done such a thing?"

"It was really quite simple. I merely held him at gunpoint and told him to remove his clothing, and he did."

After placing the crimson gown inside the bureau and locking the drawer securely Christine rose to her feet. "Was it frightening?"

"A little."

"Was he beastly?"

"No." Samantha again envisioned his handsome countenance. "Not beastly. Overwhelming, or intimidating perhaps, and very . . . *manly.*"

"Oh," Christine said in a small voice. "I think I would have swooned."

"That's exactly what Minerva Carstairs did." Samantha chuckled. "Right into Peter Hawksley's arms."

"Oh, the poor dear."

Samantha sought patience from the ceiling. "Christine, there isn't one thing remotely dear about Minerva. Quite the contrary. She is, in my opinion, about as dear as a strumpet is to a preacher's wife."

"Samantha! What a terrible thing to say."

"But true. You may be blinded by her oh-so-sophisticated manner, twin, but I'm not. I've seen the way she mentally devours every eligible bachelor."

"How mean. Besides, if Minerva had not taken me under

her wing when we first arrived from England seven months ago, why, it could have been ages before I was introduced to what little society there is here, so far from London and the court." She flipped a raven curl back over her shoulder. "And if the relevance of that statement does not permeate, if it were not for all the invitations I receive, you would not know when and where all the rich and influential people will gather. So you see, without Minerva's help in launching me, the money you so urgently seek would not be forthcoming."

Samantha held up her hand to halt her sister's tirade. "All right, twin. I yield. Forgive my insolence. And the next time I say something against your precious Minerva, just cut my tongue out and be done with it."

"Oh, Samantha, do be serious."

Serious? Robbing carriages wasn't serious enough? Risking her life wasn't serious? Lord have mercy, she'd never been more *serious* in her life. "I'll try," Samantha conceded rather than arguing further. Bringing a hand to the back of her neck, she paced again, and in doing so missed half of her sister's words.

". . . at Lydia Millworth's tomorrow afternoon."

"What?" Samantha's attention snapped to her twin.

"I said do not forget that you are to attend a tea at Lydia Millworth's tomorrow afternoon."

"As your elderly chaperon," Samantha moaned. "I'd forgotten all about that." She cast a pleading look at her twin. "Couldn't you go in my place just this once? You enjoy those sickly sweet tea parties so much more than I do."

Christine shook her head, her mouth pressed into a stubborn line. "Oh, I just could not. That awful Aunt Madeline disguise is too stifling for my delicate constitution. Surely you know that. Besides, I have an engagement to go shopping with Pamela."

Shopping? Again? Good Lord, was that all Christine thought about? Samantha shuddered at the thought of wearing that awful Aunt Madeline disguise again. The elderly woman's guise was now used to keep the authorities from discovering she and Christine were twins, thus protecting Samantha's ruse as the Scarlet Temptress. "Christine, I—"

"And you have not had to wear that costume for almost a fortnight now, just because I keep telling everyone how ill and senile Aunt Madeline has become."

"Couldn't she claim illness tomorrow?" Samantha crossed her fingers behind her back.

"No. Carl informed me this evening *while we were waiting for you* that Peter's sister Virginia plans to attend. She is to return with her uncle Joshua from Williamsburg tomorrow morning and will no doubt be most eager to impart the latest news. There is a good chance you might learn something of importance from her." Christine walked to the door and opened it. "Something pertaining to the rumored tax shipment, mayhap?" she baited softly before closing the door behind her.

Samantha unlocked her fingers and drew her hands into fists. She hated it when Christine was right. And she was—this time. It was imperative that Samantha attend the function—she needed to know about that shipment. Releasing a defeated sigh, she glared at the pale green carpet. Like it or not, she was going to have to dress as Madeline Traynor. *Again*.

CHAPTER 5

Carl Malderon urged his horse into a faster gait, cringing against the biting cold that reddened his cheeks. He had to find Jason. In weather like this a man could die from exposure in no time.

He had nearly swallowed his own tongue when Samantha told him what she'd done. One of these days he was going to thrash that girl! Of all the idiotic, featherbrained things for her to do. And to his best agent! It was hard enough trying to protect his people from the soldiers without having to protect them from each other, too!

And God have mercy on his soul if anything should happen to Jason. He'd hate to have to face Nick with such news. There was nothing worse than Nick Kincaid's anger—unless it was Jason's. If Jason lived through this, Carl just hoped the man never got his hands on Samantha. There was no telling what he might do.

The shadowed road leading to the Carstairs' tobacco plantation was completely deserted. Carl sighed. What else was to be expected at two o'clock in the morning? He just hoped that Jason had enough sense to stay near the road; otherwise, he might never find him.

He didn't doubt that his godson was still out there somewhere. Jason wouldn't have remained motionless while Samantha made up her mind to return. Certainly he would have found something with which to cover himself, then surely he would have started for the closest shelter.

Carl drew his horse to a halt. Or would he? Would he head for Carstairs? Or Crystal Terrace? Carl sucked in a deep breath. Jason would most definitely head for home. Jerking his horse around, Carl nudged the roan toward the shortcut he was certain Jason would have taken.

Less than a mile from the private bridge that led to Crystal Terrace a movement off to the right caught his attention. Relief spilled over him. Jason leaned heavily against the base of an oak.

Spurring the horse, Carl raced toward him. By the light of the moon he could see that Jason had done just as he'd predicted—tried to cover himself by hugging branches to his waist. The limbs concealed his nakedness but did little to ward off the cold. At any other time the sight might have struck Carl as quite funny—but not now. Not with the way Jason was shivering.

Barely giving the horse time to stop, Carl leapt out of the saddle and rushed to his godson's side. He tore the cape from his own shoulders and flung it around the trembling man. "Jason, are you all right? Can you speak to me?"

Jason lifted his head slowly, as if it took great effort. "I'll—get her—for this." He rasped the death knell from between chattering teeth. His strength seemed to diminish, and he lowered his lashes.

Fear shot through Carl. "Jason? Damn it, Jason, wake up! I've got to get you home. Can you hear me? Come on, son, help me."

Slowly, stiffly, as if by sheer force of will, Jason raised his head and pushed away from the tree. Dropping the branches, he attempted to stand, but his knees buckled.

Carl swore as he caught him. Then, bracing Jason's tall frame against his shoulder, he led the younger man in slow, laborious steps to the horse. He urged him to mount. Another oath escaped when Jason didn't move to comply. Leaning his godson against the animal, Carl moved behind Jason, then grasped him around the thighs and heaved him up across the saddle, pushing his leg over the horse.

Swinging up behind him, Carl pulled the shaking form against his chest in an attempt to share his body heat, then kicked the horse into a gallop. Why on earth had he involved Jason in this? It was one thing to recruit an acquaintance to a dangerous cause, and entirely another when it was someone you'd watched grow up from infancy. Hell, Jason was like his own son.

When Jason's mother died of the fever in '56 his father had lost touch with the world. After his beloved Lucinda's death nothing mattered to Beau anymore. Not his life; not his plantation, Halcyon; not their friendship. He became wild and reckless, taking too many chances.

Then Beau met his second wife, Sybil Windhall, and for a while Carl thought he might straighten out his life. It wasn't hard to understand why Beau married Sybil. She was very beautiful. But her loveliness didn't go beyond the first layer of skin. Carl knew Beau wanted a mother for his sons. Sybil, on the other hand, wanted nothing to do with the children and immediately convinced Beau to send them to boarding school in Italy.

And that wasn't the only thing Sybil didn't like. She hated the seclusion, the isolation, of Halcyon. She begged Beau to sell it. But at least in that he remained firm. Although he did attempt to pacify her by purchasing Crystal Terrace from her brother, Montague Windhall.

But Beau Kincaid had changed. Being parted from his sons had driven him into a deeper depression. He began spending more and more time away from Crystal Terrace, in Williamsburg and Richmond. Three years after his sons' departure Beau was killed on the wharf in Williamsburg. Pain cut into Carl's heart like a fine-edged razor. Would the grief never end? Would he ever stop hurting for the man he'd loved like a brother? Somehow he didn't think so.

Shortly after Beau's death Carl heard rumors that the murder had not been committed by miscreants, as they'd first thought, and he began investigating. The more he pried, the more convinced he became that Beau had been murdered by a soldier.

Jason and Nick, two hotheaded adolescents at the time, returned from Italy in a fury. Jason, after listening to Carl's tale, had to be physically restrained from going after the entire British army. Nick, on the other hand, had remained unusually silent.

Carl would have taken the boys home with him, but as unpredictable and angry as Jason was over his father's death, and with Nick so strangely remote, Carl thought it best to send them back to Italy to finish their education and give them time to come to terms with what had happened.

Four years later, when Nick and Jason returned, they had changed. They had grown into men, and they immediately began probing into Beau's death again. The good folks of Williamsburg were happy to relate the tales of the lord of the realm's demise. They pointed the twins to the owner of a small lumberyard near the docks, a man named Charlie August. Charlie's brother, Luke August, was one of three men who had witnessed Beau's murder. But when the bodies of Luke's two friends washed up on the shore Luke had fled, fearing the same fate. All Charlie could tell Jason and Nick was that his brother had rushed home in a panic, saying only that he'd seen the murder and that one of the killers was a soldier with a scarred face. They found Luke's body a week later.

After learning of Luke August's death Jason and Nick went their separate ways. Nick chose to remain in Williamsburg and join other patriots in forming the First Continental Congress. With his status as a loyal nobleman Nick was able to win Governor Dunmore's trust, and he used the association to further the patriots' cause.

Jason went in search of the nameless soldier. During his travels through the colonies he met Patrick Henry and Samuel Adams. Samuel asked Jason to deliver pamphlets during his wanderings, and Jason agreed. So by day he became a lord of the realm looking for his father's murderer, and by night he was the outlaw Devilrider, who churned up the colonists with blasphemous pamphlets.

Finally, three years before, Jason had given up the search and returned home to Halcyon. But even there he couldn't stay out of trouble. He openly defied England's taxes and leadership and soon became known to the British as a nonconformist. And, too, he continued his secret activities as the Devilrider.

Then, two months ago, Carl had asked Jason for help with Samuel Adams's new printing operation. Because suspicion followed Jason Kincaid everywhere he went, he chose to come to Lynch's Ferry disguised as his stepmother's brother, Lord Montague Windhall. It was a good thing that Sybil had gone to England following her own father's death and had no plans to return, although Carl couldn't help silently thanking her for the opportunity she afforded the rebels.

Jason's sharp wit and keen intelligence had been a god-send to the operation. The only drawback was that some-times Jason took too many chances and risked his life unnecessarily. But he was damn good at what he did, and he had never let Carl down.

Carl's arms tightened around his godson and by all that was holy, Carl wasn't going to let Jason down now.

When Crystal Terrace finally came into view Carl nearly sobbed with relief. Quickly reining his horse around back, he bellowed for the servant. "Bromley!" When no response came immediately, he swore loudly. "Damn it, Bromley. Get out here and help me!"

A moment later the door to the servants' quarters swung open, and a thin, sleepy-eyed Negro youth of twenty appeared. Wearing only a baggy pair of breeches, he scratched a thick crop of rumpled black curls and squinted in Carl's direction. "Who dere?" He suddenly shot forward. "Mistah Mald-ron, suh? What is it? Is de massa hurt? Oh, Lawdy me. He ain't dead, he is?"

"No, he isn't dead. Not yet, anyway. Help me get him into the house, then go fetch the physician."

Lowering Jason from the saddle, they carried him into the drawing room.

"Dahlia!" Carl shouted for the housekeeper.

"What's all the ruckus?" Dahlia grumbled from the top of the stairs as she tucked a strand of gray hair beneath her nightcap.

Carl waited until he heard the door slam behind Bromley before answering. "Get down here, woman. And bring some blankets—Jason's in trouble."

Easing the younger man down on the blue velvet settee before the glowing fireplace, Carl rubbed his godson's hands and arms, trying to increase circulation.

Shortly Dahlia rushed into the room carrying an armload of quilts. "What happened?" she demanded, inspecting Jason worriedly.

"I'll tell you about it later." Carl waved a dismissing hand. "Right now, just help me get these blankets around him, then heat some water for a bath."

After Jason was firmly encased in mounds of flannel and

wool Dahlia hurried out to heat the water, and Carl went to fetch a bottle of Jason's strongest whiskey from the study. He didn't know who needed it most, him or Jason. He looked at the younger man, then back at the bottle, and poured himself a drink.

By the time the tub was filled Jason's shivering had increased to racking shudders. His skin felt ice-cold and leathery to the touch. Helping him to his feet, Carl led him into the parlor, where the tub sat before a blazing fire.

"Bring the whiskey," Carl called to Dahlia, who had disappeared into the hall while Jason disrobed.

"Bloody hell!" Jason swore as he sank his long body into the tub of warm water.

Carl stepped behind him to massage his shoulders. "Too hot?"

Jason snarled something unintelligible and sneezed.

Carl's mouth twitched. "That's a good sign, son. At least one part of your body is starting to work."

Jason sneezed again and cast a murderous glare in Carl's direction.

Dahlia knocked at the door, and Carl moved to take the bottle of whiskey from her gnarled hands.

"How is he?" she asked, peeking worriedly over Carl's shoulder, trying to see Jason.

"He'll live another day or two," Carl quipped, feeling relaxed now that the crisis was over.

Dahlia, obviously not in the mood for teasing, shot him a disapproving frown. Turning from the door, she stomped off toward the stairs, mumbling to herself, "Got no respect for the ill. None a-tall."

Smiling, Carl filled two glasses and handed one to Jason. "Come on, son, take a big swig of this. It'll help thaw out your insides."

Jason took the crystal in his trembling hands and tossed back the fiery brew. He fought for breath and coughed, then leaned his head against the rim of the tub. "Did you get the press moved?"

"Yes, thanks to you."

"Thank Iron Sword. He sent the warning through your man Hadley."

"But you risked your life to deliver it."

Jason shrugged, then studied his empty goblet. "Tell me what you know about the Scarlet Temptress."

Carl stared at him thoughtfully. "I imagine I've heard pretty much the same things you have. She robs only those who can afford the loss. She has never killed anyone. And she's reported to be very beautiful."

"I hear she's a patriot champion." Jason drew in a ragged breath. "Is that true?"

"If that were true, then I'd be the first one to know about it, wouldn't I?"

"Yes," Jason said, closing his eyes as another tremor shook him. "I suppose so."

Carl rose and took the empty glass from Jason's hands. "Come on, let's get you out of that tub and into bed. Your body has taken all the abuse it can handle for one day."

"You don't know the half of it," Jason grated as he gripped the sides of the tub in order to rise.

Carl frowned. What the hell did that mean? Shrugging, he guided Jason toward the upstairs bedroom. Since his godson had never outgrown his abhorrence of nightclothes, Carl helped him into bed and pulled the brown flannel quilts up to his chin before he'd allow Dahlia in the room to check her charge.

Dahlia had been in the Kincaids' service since the twins were twelve, shortly before Lucinda's death. She was completely devoted to them and had lovingly taken over as their substitute mother. When Jason took up the guise of Lord Windhall Dahlia had insisted on accompanying him to Crystal Terrace. And since she had long ago discovered his ruse as the Devilrider, Jason saw no reason to deny her request. Though it was often difficult to fool Dahlia with their antics, the twins could still confuse her about their identities when necessary.

After Dahlia had seen to Jason's welfare and retired to her room Carl took a seat next to the bed. "How did you get into this mess?" he asked unnecessarily. "It was the Scarlet Temptress, I presume."

"Yes."

Carl tried to look thoughtful, but inside he trembled with laughter. He had known the Flemings and Kincaids would meet one day, but he never dreamed it would be like this. Carl felt tears of mirth threaten. What would Jason say if he knew his nemesis was a relative of his? That their grandparents had been fraternal twins? That the elder Flemings had passed down not only their tendency for dual births, but their fiery tempers as well? "Did she rob you?"

"Of my clothing . . . and my pride," Jason spat, then he lapsed into a fit of hoarse, congested coughing.

Carl felt the constriction in his own chest.

When the attack subsided Jason drew in a deep breath. "What were you doing out at this time of night?"

"I was on my way to meet a contact. At the fork." Carl added credibility to the lie. "I just barely saw you leaning against that tree. Hell, I nearly missed you."

"What contact?"

"Now, Jason, you know I can't divulge that information. If I could, I'd have satisfied your curiosity long ago about Iron Sword—and his about you. But the identity of the others involved is my knowledge alone. It's for everyone's protection. If any of you were captured, it would be impossible to reveal what you don't know." He paused, then added quickly, "Not that you would." He knew that was true. Jason would die himself before he'd reveal a comrade's identity. But it was a practice Carl firmly believed in, for everyone's protection. And he made no exceptions— especially now that Samantha had entered the fray.

"Well, thank you for that much, anyway." Jason sighed tiredly.

Carl sat quietly until the young man drifted off to sleep. Listening to the raspy rattle in Jason's breathing, he didn't need to await the physician's confirmation to know that his godson was going to be too ill to meet with Samuel Adams's emissary in Richmond next week.

Carl rubbed the back of his neck. With Jason down, that only left one person to attend to the vital meeting—Nick Kincaid. And Nick was not going to like it.

Rising, Carl stood for a moment looking down at the sleeping man. God, how he hated to have to tell Nick about this. Nick was worse than a protective mother bear with a cub where Jason was concerned. And he knew without a doubt that the moment the meeting in Richmond was over Nick would come to check on Jason.

Carl shook his head and sighed. "Lord have mercy on us all."

CHAPTER 6

When the first rays of sunlight filtered through a part in the drapes Samantha rose from the chair she'd been sitting in. Sleep had been impossible. Every time she'd attempted it the viscount's shivering visage rose to spur her guilt. Had he arrived safely home? Or would she hear of his death this morning?

A hollow shaking began in the pit of her stomach and spread to encompass her entire body. Hugging her arms over her waist, she crossed to the fireplace and tossed another log on the glowing embers. The magnitude of what she'd done gouged into her composure like a hoe into soft earth. That she, Samantha Fleming, the daughter of an earl, could be responsible for taking a life was unimaginable.

Her stomach gave a warning lurch. Taking a deep restoring breath, she walked to the armoire and retrieved her riding habit. This attack of conscience had to cease before she became bedridden. She had to think. And the best way to do that was on Starburst.

Moments later the stallion's great hooves churned the earth as she raced him along the river's edge toward the mountains. Freezing wind stung her cheeks, her unbound hair whipped wildly around her head and shoulders, and her lungs filled with frigid, healing air. On and on she rode through the forest, over hills, and across vast fields until at last, feeling the flush in her cheeks and the rapid laboring in her chest, she drew the hunter to a halt in a small clearing. Snow blanketed the tiny meadow, and towering pines, like protective sentinels, guarded it on all sides.

Samantha sighed and slid from the saddle, her boots sinking into the soft snow. Dropping the stallion's reins, she allowed him to roam freely while she trudged toward a dry patch of earth beneath a canopy of snow-covered branches. There, leaning back against the trunk of a tree, she snuggled deeper into her cape and stared out at the majestic scenery. Everything looked clean and new, untouched by humans.

Something moved beside her.

She spun sharply. A man clad in buckskins stood motionless not six feet away. Her heart jumped to her throat. "Who are you?"

The man's gray eyes made a slow, lazy exploration of her body, then returned to her face, but he didn't speak.

She felt a knot of fear tighten in her belly. "What do you want? Am I trespassing?" She tried to think, which was extremely difficult with him staring at her. Had she ridden farther than she thought? Was she on someone's private property? She searched his face for some sign of anger. There didn't seem to be any. His firm lips appeared relaxed. There was no flaring of nostrils in the straight, aristocratic nose. The muscles in his smooth, square jaw were taut but not tense, and the pulse at the base of his strong brown throat beat slow and steady. He held his arms loosely at his sides, but she wasn't fooled by the easy stance. Every nuance of his manner said he could and would move with the speed of a striking rattler if the need arose. But he didn't seem threatening.

Samantha felt the tension leave her body. "Who are you?" she repeated forcefully.

The man's smooth bronze features remained stoic. "I am called Hawk," he said softly, his deep voice stroking her senses like a velvet hand.

Samantha swallowed and stepped back a pace. There was something decidedly different about this man. Hawk? What kind of name was that? She examined him closely. His hair was gleaming black and pulled into a queue at the back of his neck. The buckskin shirt he wore had long pieces of fringe down the outside of the arms and across his wide chest from shoulder to shoulder, then repeated again down the outside edges of his breeches. He looked like a trapper, yet he didn't.

"If I'm trespassing, I certainly didn't mean to be, and I'll leave immediately."

His attention fastened on her mouth as she spoke, and Samantha shifted uneasily. He had a most disconcerting way of looking at her.

"You are not trespassing," he rasped in a liquid voice.

A tingling excitement raced along her spine. "Then why are you here?"

He lazily explored the contours of her face. "Why does any man approach a beautiful woman?"

Samantha's tongue stuck to the roof of her mouth. She had never met a man like him before, and she didn't quite know what to say. Looking away, she tried to think of a suitable retort. Deciding to reprimand him for his boldness, an act that was not only proper but expected, she turned back to him.

But he was gone.

Closing her mouth, she quickly searched the glen. He was nowhere in sight—as if he'd never been there at all. She shook off a feeling of eeriness and with hurried strides crossed to the huner. "Kneel," she whispered, tapping his hoof with the toe of her boot.

Starburst bowed, and Samantha mounted instantly, anxious to be away from this strange meadow—and its even stranger occupants.

When she reached the house she found Effie setting a plate of warm biscuits on the table.

"Dere ya are, chile. De massa were lookin' fer ya. He done left now, though. I figured ya was out on dat demon horse a yours, an' I tole him dat. He were smokin' round de colla, I can tell ya dat. He said fo' ya t' stay put till he come back." Her voice softened. "What'd ya do t' nettle de massa dis time?"

"I robbed another carriage." Samantha slipped out of her cape and handed it to Effie.

"Oh, chile. Don't ya know he be afraid ya's gwine t' get hurt? De massa cares 'bout ya, li'l one, an' he don' want t' see ya come t' no harm."

"I know, Effie. But I have to do something. Father won't be free until I do." She cast a pleading look at the warm brown face. "And please, before you start, no more lectures. I'm not up to it right now." Crossing to the hall door, she turned back. "Is Christine up yet?"

Effie's full lips pressed together, but her black eyes said all the things Samantha didn't want to hear. Then, shaking her head, the servant answered, "No, Missy. She ain't been down yet dis mornin'."

Samantha sighed. "Would you have some water brought up for my bath? I have to attend a tea this afternoon."

"Are ya gwine t' go as yo'self or dat ol' woman again?"

Samantha felt the weight of Effie's disapproval. The servant had often voiced her opinion about Samantha's elderly disguise, although not quite as boisterously as she did the Scarlet Temptress ruse. Drawing in a deep breath, Samantha turned back to the door. "I'm going as Madeline Traynor."

Christine didn't make an appearance until Pamela

Millworth's carriage arrived; then it was just a brief stop to advise Samantha of her departure. And though her sister didn't say anything, her look clearly suggested that Christine would not want to be in Samantha's shoes when Carl returned.

Samantha didn't particularly want to be in them either. Carl could be quite formidable when really angered. And last night he had been angrier than she'd ever seen him.

When the clock in the hall struck three o'clock Samantha felt a wave of relief. It was time to get dressed for her engagement. And Carl still hadn't returned.

Moving quickly to the fireplace, she found a small piece of charred wood near the edge of the hearth, then crossed to the dresser, where she stood before the mirror. She drew thin lines near her temples, then repeated the pattern on her cheeks, at the corners of her mouth, and across her brow. The effect was startling. In the space of a few moments her face transformed from one of eighteen years into that of an old woman.

Lifting a tin of white powder from the chest, she liberally coated the "wrinkled" areas as if to conceal the lines, which deftly hid the fact that there was no depth to them. Heavens, she looked atrocious.

She moved to the bed and picked up a heavy silver hairpiece. It resembled a frizzy hedgehog wig with a small topknot. Yanking it down on her head, she tucked all of her ebony strands out of sight. Then, moving back to the mirror, she tugged at the curls around the hairline until they concealed the smoothness of the skin not covered by "wrinkles".

The gray wool gown lying atop the bedcovers had once belonged to Lady Sara Heatherton, Nichole Heatherton's mother. Her friend Nichole had thought her deranged when Samantha asked to borrow a few of the overlarge gowns, until Samantha explained that she needed to provide Christine with a chaperon for their voyage.

Slipping out of her dressing gown, Samantha pulled on the chemise Christine had enlarged and smoothed it over the generous expanse of her breast. She grinned. No need for padding here—unless she wanted to appear deformed. She stuffed towels into the side pockets Christine had stitched on, and into the large one across her rear. It made her hips look full and wide.

After adding several layers of petticoats she wriggled into the gray gown and buttoned it up the front all the way to her chin. The loose, puffy sleeves hid her slender arms down to her wrists, and as a final touch she pulled on short gray velvet gloves to hide her smooth hands. To complete the disguise she picked up a fat black reticule that contained a spare tin of powder, just in case she found a need for repairs.

As Hadley brought the carriage around Samantha waddled down the stairs and slipped into a heavy wool cape of mule gray.

The ride to the Millworths' took little time, and for that Samantha was grateful. Even though the sun shone brightly, the late January cold penetrated the woolen gown and cape.

As Hadley turned the coach into the drive Samantha raised a hand to straighten the wig and sat forward in the seat to peer out the carriage window.

Davidson Millworth's tobacco plantation was one of the wealthiest in the area, superseded only by Windhall's Crystal Terrace and the Wainwright plantation. The Millworths had spared no expense creating the English grandeur of their home and surrounding gardens. Suddenly, nostalgic memories of home cut into her chest.

However, she didn't have time to dwell on her thoughts as a thin, elderly maid met her at the door and took the heavy cape.

"Madeline, my dear," Lydia Millworth gushed as she emerged from a room on the left. She swung her extensive girth in Samantha's direction. "How good to see you."

Enduring a brief hug, Samantha forced a smile. Then, using what she called her "Madeline voice," she returned scruffily, "Well, Lydia, I see you still haven't managed to rid yourself of that oppressive surplus yet."

Lydia at first looked confused, then clamped her teeth

tightly together and took a deep breath. With a strained smile she patted a bulging hip that made Samantha's padding appear slim by comparison. "I know, dear, but I really do try—well, most of the time, anyway. Now come along and join the others, won't you? Peter Hawksley's sister Virginia is here. You do remember Peter, don't you? And," she said, waving her hand airily, "you'll never guess who else is here."

"That blond tart Minerva, no doubt," Samantha rasped, finding at least one thing she liked about the disguise—the liberty to say whatever she pleased. Actually, she made the outlandish remarks hoping to offend enough people so as not to receive further social invitations. No invitations—no Madeline.

Lydia stifled a chuckle. "Now Madeline, you mustn't say such terrible things. What will people think? But of course, you are right. Minerva is here. Now come along, dear, let's not keep the others waiting. There are so many tidbits of news, one hardly knows where to begin."

Sighing, Samantha followed Lydia into the drawing room.

Between two plush gold settees sat a low, round wood table laden with china cups, saucers, and a gleaming silver tea service. Sally Blankenship, a young woman about Samantha's age, shared one of the seats with Minerva. Rather shy and unassuming, Sally had a sweet, gentle nature, and under normal circumstances Samantha would have enjoyed a friendly companionship with the beautiful redhead.

A thin, plain-looking girl with stringy brown hair and features that closely resembled Peter Hawksley's sat on the other settee.

Samantha suffered through an introduction to Virginia, then greeted the others as Lydia led her to a comfortable brocade chair near the fireplace—next to Minerva. For a while Samantha was content to sip the raspberry tea Lydia had offered and sit back, listening to the foolish falderal about the recent Paris fashions, Bertha Dungworth's latest dinner party, and the new seamstress who'd recently moved to Lynch's Ferry. Samantha knew it wouldn't take long for the conversation to turn to last night's events—and it didn't.

"Oh, Lady Traynor," Minerva purred, tapping the back of Samantha's gloved hand with her finger. "Have you heard the news?" She glanced around the room as if to make certain she had everyone's attention. Apparently satisfied, she turned back to Samantha. "Peter and I, and Lord Windhall—I don't believe you've met him yet—were accosted by that awful bandit last evening—on the way back from the Wainwrights' party. The one they call the Scarlet Temptress." She gave a disgusted snort. "Although why they call her that I cannot fathom, when the Scarlet *Trollop* would be so much more appropriate."

Samantha's expression remained blank, but her hand tightened on the straps of her reticule. Trollop? She fumed. Why, you mule-faced cow. Clenching her teeth to stay the words, she gave an indignant sniff. "Humph. You don't look as if you suffered. She must not have done too much accosting."

Minerva tittered. "Well, that is true. But it was so terrifying. Why, just imagine how you would feel if someone held a gun on you and threatened to end your life if you so much as breathed."

Unable to point out that she hadn't threatened anyone, Samantha leaned back and smoldered in silence.

"It was terrible, I tell you," Minerva wailed. "Positively terrible!" She squeezed out a small tear and sniffed. "But I wouldn't let the outlaw know how frightened I was. Oh, no, she wasn't going to have me pawing the ground and quivering like some mewling simpleton. And I guess my strength must have impressed her, for she did let me go unscathed."

This time, Samantha barely kept herself from saying.

A round of sighs followed Minerva's announcement, and the other ladies murmured among themselves about her bravery.

It was more than Samantha could stand. Especially when she clearly remembered how the whimpering blonde had clutched at Lord Windhall's arm, begging him not to let the bandit kill her. "Minerva Carstairs, I find it quite amazing that you profess such bravery. That's quite a feat for one who usually exerts about as much backbone as a bowl of pudding."

"Well, I never!" Minerva spat, raising her nose in the air. Tossing her pale curls, she turned to Sally Blankenship. "Some people are so rude."

Sally's huge violet eyes twinkled as she glanced over Minerva's shoulder and smiled at Samantha. "I'm sure she didn't mean to be, Mrs. Carstairs. You must try to remember that she is getting on in years and is not always responsible for an occasional lapse in decorum."

Samantha felt the powder crease at the corners of her mouth and leaned back into the cushions. Dear Sally. She was always trying to smooth over Madeline's contemptuous remarks.

"I know Peter was still quaking in his wig when I arrived home this morning," Virginia spouted. The statement drew all eyes in her direction, causing her to blush profusely.

"Why isn't something being done about that wretched bandit?" Lydia grated.

"Oh, there is." Virginia's face brightened. "Posters have been placed all over Williamsburg, Richmond, and Lynch's Ferry, offering an outrageously large reward for the outlaw's capture." She leaned forward. "And that's not all. It's only rumor, mind you, but I hear tell that Bartholomew Dungworth is going to summon his cousin, Captain Harvey Langford of the king's army, to handle the matter personally."

"Harvey Langford?" Lydia frowned. "I don't believe I know him."

Virginia lifted her thin shoulders. "Nor I, but I understand he's quite ruthless."

Samantha twisted the straps on her reticule. She didn't know this Langford person, but she well remembered Lord Bartholomew Dungworth, the blubbering infant. He had nearly burst into tears when she took his wig. Of course, after she'd seen the tiny spikes of gray hair sticking out all over his head she'd almost felt sorry enough to return it.

"Well, I for one am certainly glad to hear that," Lydia said. "Especially after what that vile female did to that nice young man Montague Windhall."

Samantha's attention shot to Lydia.

"Oh? What was that?" Sally asked before Samantha could open her mouth. "Did something happen to him?"

"Oh, yes!" Lydia nodded vigorously. "That outlaw stole the clothes from his very back and left him out in the cold. The physician's wife, Dorothea Falwick, said her husband didn't think the viscount was going to live."

Liquid cold poured over Samantha, and the room receded in a dark, whirling mist. What have I done? Oh, God, please don't make this man pay the price for my stupid prank.

"Well"—Virginia raised a bony hand—"I certainly hope they capture her before that shipment of tax money passes through here on the way to Concord. My uncle Joshua—the customs official, you know—said a detachment of soldiers was going to be sent here to ensure its safe passage." She turned to Lydia. "As a matter of fact, Lady Millworth, the governor was most eager to receive an invitation from you to house some of his men."

Lydia's face brightened. "The governor? Oh, my. Why, yes. Yes, of course. I'd be delighted." She beamed at the other ladies. "I have so much room here, it would be a shame not to put it to good use." She turned back to Virginia. "Did the governor say when he expects to send them?"

Virginia shook her head. "No. But I'm sure he'll be in contact with you for the arrangements."

"Certainly. Why, I'll post a letter to him at once and extend an invitation." She smiled at the others. "After all, it's quite important that we all do our duty."

"Speaking of duty," Minerva spoke up, "don't you think it's our Christian duty to see how Lord Windhall fares?"

"I'll pay him a call when I leave here," Samantha said in a voice tight with emotion. It's the least I can do.

"I'll come with you," Minerva offered.

That was the last thing Samantha wanted. "Mrs. Carstairs, we *would* like to see the gentleman recover."

Several titters echoed around the room.

Minerva gasped in outrage, "How dare you?"

Samantha wasn't in the mood for Minerva's tantrum. "I dare anything I like, Mrs. Carstairs. Now if you'll excuse me, I'll be on my way." She rose and turned to Lydia. "Would you have my cape brought in?"

Lydia, speechless for once, nodded as she scurried out of the room. But Samantha didn't miss the suppressed laughter causing the woman's shoulders to bob up and down.

Normally it was less than an hour's ride from the Millworth's plantation to Crystal Terrace, but the afternoon sun had melted the ice-covered road and turned it into mud.

Samantha tucked the rug around her legs and pulled the gray cloak closer to ward off the growing evening chill.

She had never seen this plantation, but somehow she'd always envisioned it as a rather mystical place.

Suddenly the carriage emerged from the wall of trees onto the drive of a stately plantation.

Architecturally a masterpiece, the gray stone house commanded a view of rolling hills, now barren of tobacco. A dome-shaped second story centered the building. White pillars lined the wide front veranda, supporting the roof and matching the sparkling alabaster curve of the dome. Little round windows trimmed in white encircled the entire cupola, creating the appearance of a crystal crown. Samantha stared. So this was Crystal Terrace. How fascinating.

A lean young Negro assisted her down from the carriage and ushered her into the parlor. His dark eyes were warm and bright, his smile engaging. Bowing respectfully, he excused himself to summon the housekeeper.

Samantha explored the elaborately furnished room that

bespoke lordly wealth. Wall coverings of apricot silk matched windows lavishly draped in the same hue, contrasting greatly with the gray marble fireplace inlaid with swirls of gold. Plush settees of rose flanked the fireplace, and against the opposite wall a harpsichord of polished pine dominated a quarter of the room beneath a gold-framed portrait of a mysteriously beautiful woman.

"How may I help you?"

Startled, Samantha whirled around. A pleasant-looking woman dressed in an aproned homespun that declared her station stood in the archway separating the parlor from the entry. Her gray hair, pulled back into a neat bun beneath a dustcap, emphasized her plump features. Then Samantha noticed dark smudges under the woman's eyes and the lines of worry creasing the aged forehead, giving evidence of a sleepless night.

Samantha's stomach knotted. Was she responsible for this? "I'm Madeline Traynor, a houseguest of Lord Malderon's."

The woman's features brightened. "How do you do?" She looked relieved. "Has Lord Malderon sent you?"

Samantha tried to hide her surprise. Carl did know Lord Windhall, after all. Why had he never mentioned him? "Yes, he did," Samantha lied. "How is he? Is his condition as serious as we've been led to believe?"

The woman looked down at the floor, her expression troubled. "I don't know what you've heard, but I can tell you this: Jason's in a bad way." She shook her head. "A very bad way."

Samantha's heart plummeted. Taking a moment to gather her suddenly shattered composure, she surveyed the room. "Jason? Who is he?"

The maid looked confused, then stricken. "L-Lord Windhall. Forgive me. I forgot myself. I-It's his—um—middle name. I call him that sometimes."

"I see." Samantha nodded. "Are you taking care of him by yourself?"

"Yes," the housekeeper said stiffly, looking as if Samantha might question her ability to care for her patient.

"Now, now, Mrs. . . . ?"

"Murphy."

"Murphy. Don't take offense where none was intended. I can see that your concern for the viscount is great. Carl just thought you might have need of my help. And I know you must have other pressing duties."

The woman hesitated. "Well, I don't think—"

"Of course," Samantha interrupted. "I'm sure your master won't mind a cluttered house and soiled garments when he recovers, since all of your time *is* being spent on his care."

Mrs. Murphy looked perplexed. "Well, I—"

"And, too," Samantha pressed on, "you do appear quite capable of handling a twenty-four-hour vigil, day after day. Preparing meals, carrying heavy trays and linens up and down those stairs"—she nodded toward the curving staircase—"and sitting at his bedside throughout the night. Yes, indeed, you must be commended. I wonder if the viscount realizes what a gem he has running his household."

The housekeeper looked deflated. Her shoulders slumped. "I'm not nearly as strong as I look. But I am trying, for Ja—Montague's sake. I already have a backache, and my legs feel like knotted tree trunks." She lifted her head scornfully. "Not that I can't manage, mind you. But I worry what might happen if I get down in my back. Who would look after him then?"

Worried hazel eyes met Samantha's, and affection for the woman surged. She reached out and patted Mrs. Murphy's hand. "I'm sure you do, my dear. And, as I've said, you've done admirably. But we all have our limitations." She smiled warmly. "Please accept my small measure of help."

Obviously undecided, the woman merely stared.

Samantha didn't wait for an answer. She shook the cape from her shoulders and handed it to the housekeeper. "There now, it's all settled. Now, if you would be so kind as to tell me which room is Lord Windhall's, I'll go up and check on him while you tell my driver to deliver a message to Riversedge to let them know I'll be staying."

Mrs. Murphy studied her quietly for a moment, then, obviously coming to a decision, nodded. "Of course, your ladyship. The master's room is upstairs on the right."

As soon as the housekeeper stepped out the front door Samantha lifted the dowdy, matronly skirt above her knees and sprinted up the stairs, anxious to find Lord Windhall's room and see for herself how he fared.

Locating the room after two attempts, she slipped inside and closed the door behind her. It was a wicked feeling, being inside a gentleman's bedroom, and she couldn't help glancing around curiously.

Heavy drapes of gold velvet enclosed the cavernous room against the last of the evening light. Next to a stone fireplace stood a chest and armoire of richly carved cherrywood. Directly opposite them sat a massive oak desk.

Bookshelves filled with tomes in varying sizes and bindings lined the north wall, and a russet silk dressing screen stood just beyond the bed. Behind that a tapestry portraying the hunt hung from ceiling to floor. She frowned. What an odd place for a wall covering.

Shrugging, she shifted her attention to the commode on the opposite side of the fireplace. Its linen-covered surface supported a white pitcher and bowl. But what drew her attention was the biggest four-poster bed she'd ever seen. It looked to be at least ten feet square.

Beneath a rich brown flannel quilt the viscount's masculine form was visible, and she moved in for a closer peek. For a moment she thought she might have entered the wrong room. The man lying in the bed looked nothing like the pompous aristocrat she'd robbed.

This man had silky black hair that was so clean it caught blue shadows from the flickering candlelight. His face, deeply tanned and lean, only vaguely resembled the man she remembered from last evening. Gone were the concealing rice powder and beauty patches. Although pale, his skin had a healthy golden glow, a ruggedness, as if he'd spent a lot of time outdoors. The proud, straight nose was the same, but his lips looked somehow fuller; though still firm, they held a marked trace of sensuality.

A quiver rippled across her senses, and she stared at his broad bare shoulders. Before last night, other than the slaves in the field, she had never seen a man without his shirt—not even her father.

Intrigued despite her moral upbringing, she allowed her gaze to wander freely over his naked chest. She marveled at the soft dark hairs that curled against flawless sculptured bronze skin. With each rasping breath he took his smooth, flat stomach rose and fell, the tight muscles rippling.

She watched the pulse throbbing at the base of his throat. He looked so vulnerable. . . . Dear God, what had possessed her? Removing her glove, she reached out a trembling hand to stroke his cheek—something she knew she wouldn't dare do if he were awake. A day's growth of beard shadowed his jawline and scraped at her fingers. Heat from his cheek seeped into her fingertips. He was hot. Too hot.

Jerking her hand back, she closed her eyes and desperately tried to remember Aunt Katherine's teachings concerning illness. Water. A feverish person needs water.

Raising her lashes, Samantha saw a ewer and glass gracing the bedside table. She poured some water and, returning to the viscount's side, gently slipped her arm beneath his neck and raised his head. His hair felt silky against her arm, and his familiar scent rose up to tease her. He smelled clean and earthy, as he had the previous night.

She touched the glass to his lips, and he turned his face, burying his nose against her bosom, mumbling something incoherent. The warmth of his breath penetrated the woolen gown. Her nipple grew taut. Shocked by her body's reaction, she quickly eased his head back onto the pillow and moved away from the bed, but the heat of his breath still lingered on her breast like a warm hand.

Swallowing against the unexplained tightness in her throat, she set the glass back on the table and looked around for another means to relieve his fever.

On the washstand lay a damp rag. Removing her other glove, she retrieved the cloth and rinsed it out, then returned and tenderly placed it against his hot brow.

Suddenly he cried out, "No! You can't do this to me. Damn you, woman!"

Samantha's hand flew to her throat, and she flinched at the venom in his voice. She watched helplessly as his head twisted from side to side.

"Trollop! Hellish vixen! Damn you!" he bellowed, swinging his arm as if to strike out at someone. His hand hit the glass. It crashed to the floor and shattered.

Samantha jumped back. Tiny slivers of glass peppered her shoes and skirt.

The door burst open, and Mrs. Murphy hurried into the room, her expression anxious. "What happened?"

Samantha felt the blood drain from her cheeks. Lord Windhall's hateful words had been meant for her. Snapping her attention to the housekeeper, and remembering her hands were bare, she quickly slid them into the folds of her skirt before answering. "He's delirious."

The woman looked at her strangely for a moment, and Samantha realized she'd forgotten to disguise her voice. Evidently the housekeeper thought it just the strain of the moment, because she merely shrugged. "He's been that way all night. He must have suffered a horrible ordeal with that outlaw."

"I'm sure he did." Samantha nodded numbly, hoping her wince had gone unnoticed. "He was saying things like 'damn her, trollop,' and such."

The older woman smiled. "That's not near as bad as some of the things he's been saying. I know I sure wouldn't want to be in that woman's boots when he gets hold of her."

"Nor I," Samantha returned honestly, recalling the display of temper he'd made shortly before she left him. Giving herself a mental shake, she turned to the older woman. "I'll take over now, Mrs. Murphy. You must get some rest."

"Your ladyship? I know it's proper for you to call me Mrs. Murphy, but truly, I prefer my given name, Dahlia."

"Dahlia," Samantha repeated softly. "That's a lovely name. And, I would be pleased if you would call me Sam—Madeline."

Dahlia lifted her chin regally. "No. It isn't right." Her voice softened. "I am a servant, even though I don't act like it sometimes."

If Samantha hadn't been so upset over her own near slip, she probably wouldn't have given in so easily. "Very well, Dahlia, as you wish. Now off you go. And I don't want to see your face again before morning. Is that understood?"

Dahlia chuckled. "Yes, Lady Traynor. But first I'll clean up the broken glass and fix a tray for you."

The instant the maid left Samantha slipped on her gloves and moved away from the bed.

Dahlia returned shortly with a tray for Samantha and a cup of chicken broth for Montague.

When the maid finally retired for the night Samantha set aside her untouched supper tray and tried to coax the viscount in to drinking some of the broth, being very careful to keep his head some distance from her breast. He took a few swallows and afterward seemed to rest a bit easier.

With little else to do, she roamed the shelves of books and selected a collection of stories, then pulled a blanket from the foot of the bed and curled up in a scratchy gray horsehair covered chair. Resting her head against the back, she tried to concentrate on the story, but after her own sleepless night she soon felt her eyelids grow heavy.

A low moaning sound aroused Samantha from her slumped position in the chair. Her eyes shot open. She looked around wildly for a moment. Then her senses cleared, and she realized she was in Lord Windhall's bedroom.

It took a moment, but her brain finally connected the sound she'd heard with the viscount, and she glanced toward the bed.

Montague moved restlessly against the sheets, his body gleaming with perspiration. He had kicked the coverlets down to his feet—and was completely naked.

Samantha's breath caught. Was she forever destined to see this man without his clothes? She lurched to her feet and reached for the blankets. But her traitorous stare absorbed every beautiful inch of his powerful body.

The sheen of moisture glistened against his golden skin, inviting her with its rich, tantalizing appearance. His dark hair curled and clung damply to the nape of his strong neck. The hollow at the base of his throat throbbed, nearly hypnotizing her with its quick, rhythmic beat. Silky black hairs veiled his chest as it rose and fell with his uneven breathing. She mentally followed the tempting trail of curls until they arrowed down beyond the hard, flat plain of his stomach to widen out again.

Embarrassed, she skipped to the long legs moving against the sheet. She marveled at the strong calves and the slender shape of his feet. Of their own volition her eyes moved back up the long muscular expanse of his legs, stopping a moment to inspect a jagged scar on his inner thigh before continuing upward. Her breath stopped. Spellbound, she stared boldly at the generous evidence of his masculinity, wondering what it would feel like to touch him.

Appalled by her thoughts, she jerked the covers up, and her hands flew to her face in a futile gesture to cool her hot cheeks. Her gloved hands came in contact with the thick makeup that had grown sticky from her own glowing face.

Anxious to concentrate on something—*anything*—other than Montague Windhall's body, she turned her thoughts to the sensitive skin complaining beneath its layer of powder. If she didn't remove the mess soon, she would resemble someone with the pox.

Certain that Dahlia would sleep through the night, and equally certain that the viscount wouldn't remember even if he did awaken, she moved to the wash basin to remove her disguise. She knew she wouldn't have any trouble replacing it since bits of charred wood were available in every household.

Standing before the cherrywood chest, her face once again clean, she removed the wig and ran her fingers through her hair. Lord, that felt good. If only she didn't have to wear that awful hairpiece. Knowing there was no choice in the matter, she shrugged and picked up the book that had fallen to the floor, then resumed her seat.

She settled in the blanket and returned her attention to the pages, trying to read the printed words. But her decadent musings on Montague's virile body continued.

"Nick!"

Startled, Samantha's head whipped up from the book.

"Damn it Nick, help me . . ." Montague arched his back and slammed his arm against the bedsheet. "You can feel the pain. . . ."

Frightened by his thrashing, she rose and hastily approached the bed. She touched his brow and bit back a curse. His fever had risen.

"Luke August . . . scarred soldier . . ."

She turned quickly to the washstand and withdrew a clean cloth from the lower shelf. After dampening it in cold water and returning to his side she sat on the edge of the bed, her lower lip held between her teeth, and gently pressed the cloth to his forehead.

The coolness seemed to settle him.

Trailing the cloth over his fevered brow, she brushed back a heavy lock of hair, then stroked his thick eyebrows, his temples, and his leanly carved cheeks. Sliding the cloth lower, she traced it across his chest and swirled it through soft hairs, not noticing for some moments that the motion had become a caress. She swallowed and tried not to be affected by the way his muscles bunched and tightened beneath her touch.

Again and again she slid the moist cloth over his exposed body. But try as she might, she couldn't stop her hands from trembling when they came in contact with his smooth, hot flesh.

"No!" he shouted suddenly.

Samantha's breath caught as his steellike fingers gripped her upper arms and jerked her forward, trapping her hands between their bodies. She instantly became aware of the hardness of his naked stomach against her palms, of the way her breasts pressed against the firmness of his chest, of the musky scent of his heated skin and the way her pulse leapt and quickened in response. Startled, her gaze flew to his face.

Glittering blue eyes bore into hers.

The breath left her body. Her heart slammed wildly against her chest.

"Did you come back to finish the job, Temptress?" he ground out slowly, his fingers tightening, if that were possible. "Or did you come to witness the results of your folly?" A shuddering tremor shook him.

Samantha froze, fear holding her immobile. How had he recognized her? The only time he'd ever seen her she'd been masked. She took in the sculptured lines of his face. Long, thick black lashes rested against fever-brightened cheeks. He hadn't recognized her. He was delirious.

Slowly, lazily, his silky lashes raised. "Black hair," he rasped softly. "I wondered." He pulled her closer, so close the heat of his breath caressed her lips. His fingers eased the pressure on her arms, and his thumbs began a slow, sensuous stroking motion. "And beautiful emerald eyes . . . so very beautiful . . ." His voice thickened huskily, and his gaze darkened as it lowered to her lips. "So tempting . . ."

Her chest tightened, and she quivered.

As if he'd felt her response he groaned and jerked her forward, capturing her mouth with his.

Nothing in her life had prepared her for the raw passion in this man's fevered kiss. Fiercely his lips plundered and ravaged her softness before his tongue boldly penetrated her trembling lips. Heat curled up through her belly, and she felt herself falling into a swirling ocean of sensation. Every instinct warned her to pull away, but the hunger in his kiss sliced into her restraint, neatly severing her resistance.

His hands rose and burrowed into her hair, holding her trapped while his mouth seized hers again and again with an exquisite half-tender, half-brutal invasion.

The room tilted crazily, and she pressed closer, her body

straining against his strength, no longer able nor wanting to resist. Timidly her tongue touched his, and he groaned low in his throat. Passion blazed, and their mouths melded in savage communion.

Suddenly his grip in her hair tightened, and he thrust her from him. "No!" he roared. "I won't be taken in by your beauty. Vixen! I'll destroy you . . . destroy you."

CHAPTER 7

Stunned by the searing kiss and the way Montague had thrust her from him, Samantha pressed her fingers against swollen lips that still throbbed from his ruthless assault. Her arms and legs quivered weakly, threatening to splinter into fragments as she shakily rose from the bed.

He was asleep again, his chest rising and falling with labored breathing. The white cloth she'd used to soothe him lay on his tight, flat stomach. The hard planes of his face were tinted with the crimson flush of fever. He hadn't really seen her. Please, God. He couldn't have.

On unsteady legs she stepped back to the bed and gingerly removed the cloth, placing it on the washstand. Returning to the chair, she buried herself in the blanket. But of their own volition her eyes clung to the sleeping man, and she again raised a hand to touch her tender lips. She could still feel the incredible warmth of his mouth . . . the heady taste of him.

Confused by her mind's ramblings, she jerked her hand down. What was happening to her? Why hadn't she tried to stop him? Had something happened to her in the last seven months? Had the unvirtuous Scarlet Temptress overtaken her senses, turning her into a wanton?

She grimaced at the thought and reached for the book lying on the floor. Picking it up, she opened the weathered pages, needing something to occupy her thoughts. She didn't want to think about anything, especially not the viscount—or her reaction to him. But try as she might, she couldn't prevent the printed words from wavering and sliding together. Capricious daydreams clouded her intent, and soon she again felt her lashes grow heavy.

When she next opened her eyes her limbs ached from their cramped position in the scratchy chair. Moving slowly, she shoved away a heavy lock of hair and looked around blankly for a moment. Then it came back to her—the night just past, the viscount's illness, his fever . . . his kiss. Shaking her head, Samantha touched a palm to her cheek. Her thoughts froze. Her other hand flew up to cup the opposite jaw. Oh, no. She had forgotten her disguise!

Frantically she raced to the fireplace and grabbed a small piece of charred wood near the edge of the blazing flames. She paused for a second, trying to remember when she'd added more logs. Unable to come up with the answer immediately, she shrugged and rose. There was no time to ponder the thought—not now. She hurried to where her reticule lay on the bureau and withdrew the tin of powder.

With her makeup complete and the wig in place she moved her head from side to side until satisfied with her appearance in the mirror. Able to relax now, she cleared away the evidence of her ruse and returned to the bed.

Placing a hand against Montague's brow, she found him still feverish and reached for a half-filled water glass on the bedside table. As she brought the glass to his lips in an attempt to give him a drink her puzzled gaze settled on the crystal goblet. She couldn't remember replacing the broken glass from last evening.

The door opened suddenly, and Dahlia entered with a tray of tea and biscuits. "I thought you might be up," she said brightly. Setting the tray down next to Samantha's untouched one from the night before, she scowled. "Madam Traynor? Are you well? I see you didn't eat anything."

Samantha straightened and set the goblet on the small table. "Of course I'm well." She inflicted gruffness in her voice. "Just because I don't eat like a starving sow is no reason to assume illness."

The housekeeper's eyes twinkled. "I see. Of course, I meant no offense."

Samantha waved her hand apologetically. "Forgive my loose tongue. I'm not always at my best in the morning." She inspected the tray Dahlia had brought in. "Perhaps some of that tea would improve my disposition."

Chuckling, Dahlia poured a steaming cup and handed it to Samantha. "How did his lordship fare last night? Did you have any problems with him?"

Yes, she thought. He kissed me. She took a sip of tea to swallow the words. "No. His fever rose, and he was quite delirious at times, but he seems to be resting better this morning."

Dahlia nodded and looked at the sleeping man. "The physician will be here soon. I just pray his report is favorable."

"I'm sure it will be." Samantha hoped she appeared much more confident than she felt. After another drink she set the cup aside and crossed to where she'd dropped her reticule moments ago. "As for myself, I must return to Riversedge for a change of attire. Would you see that a carriage is brought around? And don't press yourself while I'm gone. Anything to do with the house can wait until my return, which shouldn't be more than a couple of hours."

"Of course, madam." Dahlia nodded as she left the room.

Samantha moved to Montague's side and smoothed his brow. He looked so handsome he took her breath away. Grazing his dark cheek with her gloved fingers, she smiled, then quietly left him.

At Riversedge Samantha found that Christine's intuitive feelings had again come into play, and a hot bath awaited her.

Stripping the coarse woolen gown from her body with a speed that surely revealed her ambivalent state, she sank deeply into the warm, sweet rose-scented water.

"How is he?" Christine asked, handing Samantha the soap.

"I'm not sure. He's still very ill. He had a bad night, and a bevy of nightmares and fever kept him from resting." She met her twin's inquiring look. "Do you know how dreadful that makes me feel?"

"Mm." Christine nodded. "I imagine I do."

"To think that I am responsible for his condition. That *my* actions put him in what could very well be his deathbed makes me consider the hangman a fitting end."

"What did the physician say?"

"I haven't spoken to him yet. He's probably with him now."

Christine smiled gently. "In that case, why do you not wait until you hear *his* conclusions before volunteering your neck?" She turned for the door. "All will be well, Samantha. Of that I am certain." A dimple creased her left cheek. "But just for good measure, I will see if I might assist."

Samantha frowned as her sister breezed out the door. What was she up to now?

Once again disguised as Madeline Traynor, Samantha found her sister in Carl's study. Christine sat at his desk with several bottles lined up before her.

"Christine, those aren't what I think they are, are they?" Her twin smiled impishly. "Yes."

"Oh no," Samantha moaned. "You don't really expect me to inflict *that* on Lord Windhall, do you? Hasn't the poor man suffered enough already?"

"Samantha." Christine rose, her hands planted on her slim hips. "Aunt Katherine would scratch her coffin lid if she heard you talk that way about her unrivaled healing potion. The castor-oil plant is renowned for its rejuvenating qualities. It certainly could not hurt the man, and it just may cure him."

Samantha rolled her eyes. "Twin, have you forgotten how that stuff tastes? The castor oil alone is bad enough, but with the ground tobacco leaves in it, along with all those other

SUE RICH

herbs, it tastes like spoiled grease—once your mouth stops burning."

"Nevertheless, it is an excellent healing agent," her sister said primly, shoving the bottles into a satchel. "And after all, I am only attempting to keep the man alive for *your* sake."

Shaking her head, Samantha gingerly took the satchel and set it on the chair next to her reticule. "Where's Carl this morning?" She wanted to avoid him if possible.

Christine shrugged stiffly. "I do not know. Shortly after we received your note yesterday he raced out of here mumbling something about a message. I believe I heard him mention the name Nick, though I cannot be certain. I merely overheard him muttering to himself as he passed on his way out. That was the last I saw of him."

"Nick? I think I've heard that name somewhere before." Samantha shrugged, her thoughts on more pressing concerns. "Has Carl's anger subsided any?"

"Not that I have noticed."

Samantha sighed and turned for the door. "Tell him I'll be spending a few days at Crystal Terrace." She met her twin's knowing look. "Until the viscount has recovered."

A thin brow arched up Christine's forehead. "And to give our guardian time to compose himself, mayhap?"

"I hope so," Samantha whispered as she closed the door.

Arriving back at Crystal Terrace, she was met in the entry by a teary-eyed Dahlia. Samantha's heart sank. Had the physician's verdict been grave? Her palms grew moist inside the gloves, and her voice felt constricted when she spoke. "What did Mr. Falwick say?"

Dahlia sniffed. "That his lordship is greatly improved."

Samantha felt a surge of relief so great that the room actually swayed.

Dahlia sniffed again. "Not that the master is out of danger yet, and things could always get worse, but the physician seemed very hopeful."

"Then why are you crying?"

76

"Because I'm so happy." Dahlia dabbed at her cheeks with a handkerchief.

Samantha relaxed. "I see." She gestured toward the satchel she'd dropped in a nearby chair. "In that case, I have something to make you even happier. An elderly aunt of mine, now deceased, was something of a miracle worker. She passed a healing potion down to me." Slipping the cape off of her shoulders, she crossed to the chair. "If you would brew a cup of tea, I'll mix some for his lordship."

Samantha carried one of the bottles upstairs to the bedroom, where she found Montague still asleep, and waited for Dahlia to bring the tray.

After pouring the tea Samantha dumped an overly generous portion of the vile concoction into the viscount's cup. Hiding her distaste as she stirred the brew, she then instructed the housekeeper to raise Montague's head. While Dahlia held his mouth open Samantha trickled the medicine between his parted lips.

Montague's eyes shot open, and he buckled into a sitting position. He choked, and shuddered, and coughed, and cursed—all at the same time.

Samantha smiled. His reaction had been the same as hers had been the first time she tasted the drink.

"Who are you?" he snarled when he could breathe normally again. "And what in the hell was that stuff? Poison? Have you been sent by the Scarlet Temptress to finish the job?"

Dahlia's mouth quirked. "Have a care now, your lordship. This lady is a guest of Lord Malderon's—"

"It figures."

"—Madeline Traynor," she continued firmly. "She's been helping me look after you. And that *stuff,* as you call it, is a healing potion that's bound to hurry your recovery."

"Or demise," he grumbled, falling back against the pillows.

Dahlia snorted and swung her ample figure toward the door. "Young people nowadays," she muttered. "Got no respect for their elders. None a-tall. Young buck needs a good strapping, that's what I say."

Samantha felt tears of laughter sting her eyes as they met Montague's.

"A good strapping?"

Assuming Madeline's disdainful air, she lifted her chin. "A good horsewhipping is more my preference." She lifted powdered brows. "Its impact is much more forceful."

Montague's lips clamped together in a scowl.

Samantha walked over to the bookshelves and withdrew the book Dahlia had evidently replaced. When she collected herself and turned around she found him watching her. "Would you like for me to read to you, young man?" She purposefully swayed her hips in a waddling motion as she moved back to the chair.

Settling back against the pillows, he shrugged. "Do whatever pleases you, madam." He drew in a ragged breath, then lapsed into a fit of congested coughing.

Her own chest tightened with empathy. Fearing he might notice her distress, she quickly lowered her padded hips into the chair and opened the book. When the attack subsided she didn't dare look up, wary of what her expression might reveal. Instead she began to read the story she'd started the previous evening.

A few minutes later, pulling her attention from the pages, she peeked up at the viscount.

He studied her curiously.

Didn't he like the way she read? Her father had always loved to hear her read. He said she brought the characters to life. Perhaps he didn't care for the story. "Do you disapprove of mysteries, milord?"

Montague shook his head. "Quiet the contrary, Lady Traynor. Solving mysteries is one of my favorite pastimes."

What was that supposed to mean? "Then perhaps you disapprove of the way I read."

"No. I find you a very entertaining storyteller."

She shifted uncomfortably. Something about his manner

made her decidedly wary. "Then why are you looking at me so strangely?"

He smiled, showing strong, even white teeth.

Samantha's heart tripped over a beat.

"Was I?" he asked a trifle too innocently. "I didn't realize."

And bees don't build hives. Was he toying with her? "Well, do tell me, young man, if I start to bore you."

Unsettled by that strange light in his eyes, she bent over the pages of the book again. But in her peripheral vision she saw him smile. And she could have sworn she heard him whisper, "You could never bore me. . . ."

At the sound of Montague's deep breathing a moment later Samantha lowered the book. As usual, Aunt Katherine's potion had done its work well. Sleep was the real healing agent, her aunt had often said. And Samantha agreed. Montague needed all the rest he could get to help his body heal itself.

Closing the book, she rose and crossed the room to replace the volume on its shelf. Her fingers traced the leather bindings on the splendid array of tomes. Did all these belong to him? Had he read them? If so, he certainly had varied interests. The books ranged from humorous light plays to deep philosophy, to animal husbandry, agriculture, and law.

She lowered a hand to her padded hip and tilted her head thoughtfully. Quite an assortment for a dandy. Where were his books on etiquette, fencing, and fashion?

Surveying the room, she frowned. Everything, with the exception of the wig and rice powder, bespoke bold masculinity. Hardly the type of room she'd associate with a milksop. And what about the way he slept? What gentleman would sleep in the . . . without his night attire? She ignored the leap in her breast at the thought. What was this aversion he seemed to have to nightclothes? Could it be an allergy? Perhaps sensitive skin? Was that, too, why he wore no undergarments beneath his clothing?

She looked back to the bed and studied the strong, clean lines of his face, shoulders, and chest. His skin, smooth, flawless, and deeply tanned, hardly seemed the type to break out in a rash. But if it wasn't an allergy, what other reason could a gentleman have for shunning such propriety? Her gaze returned to his attractive face. Unless he wasn't a dandy at all.

Remembering his fury the other evening, she gnawed her lower lip in concentration. He had certainly dropped his dandified airs after Peter and Minerva had departed.

She moved closer to the bed and lifted one of his hands. His fingers were long and slim, with neatly trimmed nails. But they weren't soft-looking. They were the hands of a man who wasn't afraid of hard work, a man who had, perhaps, spent many laborious hours in the sun. His muscular arms, so firm and solid, were definitely not those of a fop, nor were the hard muscles in his stomach. What was his game? Why would he pretend to be something he was not?

"Lady Traynor?"

Samantha jumped and dropped Montague's hand. Her heart pounded as she spun toward the door. How embarrassing to be caught holding the hand of a sleeping man. What must Dahlia think? Swallowing tightly, Samantha cleared her throat. "Yes, Dahlia? What is it?"

Dahlia's expression revealed no indication that she'd witnessed anything inappropriate. "I'll be leaving in a few minutes to have Bromley take me into town, seeing as I need some supplies. Anything you want me to bring you?"

Samantha shook her head, then stopped suddenly. "As a matter of fact, there is something. . . ."

After their departure Samantha straightened the bedroom, then took last night's tray and the damp cloths downstairs. Depositing the tray in the kitchen, she went in search of the laundry. Behind one of the doors in the long hall beneath the stairs she came across the Windhall gallery and stopped for a moment to admire the portraits. But upon reaching the last one she cocked her head to one side and frowned. Why wasn't Montague's likeness among them? Still puzzled, she left the room to continue her search for the laundry. Locating it at last, she placed the bundle of soiled cloths in a basket, then returned to the bedroom, where she found Montague awake.

"Who are you? Where's Dahlia?" He looked stunned.

"Don't you remember? We were introduced. I'm Madeline Traynor." Samantha shut the door and waddled over to the chair. "And Dahlia went into town with your manservant."

A confused expression crimped his brow. "When?"

"Not long ago."

"Do you know who I—" He looked uncomfortable. "I mean, I'm hungry."

Samantha smiled, feeling her skin stretch beneath the heavy powder on her cheeks. "Would you like some broth?"

He seemed to relax but still looked unsure of himself. "Do I have a choice?"

"No."

He sighed heavily. "Then broth it is."

Drawing the chair up closer to the bed, Samantha picked up the bowl and a spoon.

Montague reached for them.

"No. You're not yet strong enough to feed yourself. Just open your mouth, and I'll do the rest."

Like a petulant child he clamped his lips together. "Madam," he hissed softly between clenched teeth, "I am quite capable of feeding myself."

"It matters not," Samantha said haughtily. "You see, at the moment I am in charge. And either you do as I say"—she leaned forward—"or you do without."

His crystal-blue gaze challenged hers for a moment, then drifted to the bowl. Releasing a slow, disgruntled breath, he opened his mouth.

Samantha ducked her head as she scooped up some liquid and slid the spoon between his lips.

"Why are you here?" he asked after swallowing.

"I think that should be obvious. Dahlia's a lovely and very capable woman, but hardly able to carry on a twenty-four-hour vigil at your side along with the rest of her responsibilities."

"How long have I been ill?"

"Two days."

His clear blue eyes flashed beneath thick black lashes. "Two days? Hell's breath. I thought it was the morning after the robbery. Why hasn't Carl sent someone to help Dahlia? He knows she's in no condition to take on extra duties."

"He has," she pointed out. "Me."

Again he drew his brows together in a confused frown. "When did you arrive?"

"Yesterday. Don't you remember anything?" Did he remember the kiss?

"No. I don't."

Why was her relief mixed with offense that he didn't remember kissing her? Heavens, she didn't *want* him to remember. "I'm Madeline Traynor, a guest of Carl Malderon's. We were introduced yesterday."

"Sorry. I don't recall," he rasped, and he began to cough, deep and jarring, leaving him gasping for breath.

Samantha rose from the chair and poured a cup of tea. She added another dose of Aunt Katherine's healing potion and returned to the bed. "Here, drink this."

He stared at the mug. "What is it?"

Amusement clogged her throat as she realized he really didn't remember. "Tea."

Slipping her hand behind his head, she raised him to a sitting position and placed the rim of the cup against his lips. "Down it all at once."

When he opened his mouth she quickly dumped the contents of the cup, forcing him to swallow rapidly.

His eyes opened wide. He sputtered. "Bloody hell!" His chest rose and fell heavily as he fought to breathe. "What *was* that?"

She smiled sympathetically. "A medicinal tea that my deceased aunt concocted."

"What did she die of? Drinking it?"

Samantha burst out laughing.

Montague blinked and stared at her in bewilderment.

Seeing his confused expression, she grimaced inwardly. She had forgotten her charade. Her laugh was definitely not that of an old woman. Blast. Well, there was no help for it now. Maybe if she just ignored his observation.

She drew her features into a haughty frown and sat rigidly in the chair. "No, she did not, young man. And I suggest you cease this foolishness and go to sleep. Your condition will remain unsettled until you've had the proper rest to restore it."

Montague watched her curiously for a moment. Then his gaze wavered, and he lowered his lashes.

For what seemed like forever Samantha sat stiffly in the chair until she heard the sound of his even breathing. Her shoulders slumped. Thank goodness Aunt Katherine's tea had taken effect.

After Samantha watched Montague sleep for a long while she rose, wishing she could rid herself of her wretched disguise for a while.

The screen on the other side of the bed caught her attention. She could if she stayed behind the partition, couldn't she? If he awakened, she would hear him and be able to dress before she let him know of her presence in the room.

A few minutes later, having retrieved a washing bowl full of heated water, she removed her clothing down to her own underchemise and dropped to her knees, then bent over the kettle to scrub the powder from her skin.

The white wig lay beside her heap of clothing on a chair, and her hair tumbled down her back in a wild disarray of black curls. Arching her neck, she raised the washcloth and slid its coolness down her chest.

Not wanting to dally, she dried, then straightened, reveling for a moment in the pleasure of smooth, clean skin. Lord, but it seemed she'd worn that disguise forever.

"Nick?"

Montague's voice startled her, and she sucked in a sharp breath.

"Nick, where are you? I need you."

Samantha peeked around the corner of the screen. He was still asleep, but he moved restlessly. She relaxed. He was just having another dream. And who *was* this Nick? Was it the same one Carl had mentioned?

Montague moaned low and lashed out with his hand, his body twisting in a wild thrashing motion against the bed. Without giving thought to her state of undress Samantha grabbed her damp cloth and raced to his side.

The cool rag did nothing to calm him. His skin burned with fever. Deep, agonizing moans wrenched from his throat. His dark head swung from side to side. "Scarred . . ."

Self-loathing burned through her. It was her fault, and she had never felt so helpless in her life. Why had she let her temper get the better of her? Why had she left him? She closed her eyes, unconcerned with the tears sliding down her cheeks.

She was so wrapped up in her own misery that it took a moment for her to realize the room had grown still. Slowly, half afraid of what she might see, she opened her eyes to meet the narrowed blue impact of his.

"Who are you?" he rasped.

Samantha felt the blood leave her face. Oh, God. Please don't let him be coherent. Not now. Not when she sat before him without her disguise and clothed only in a thin chemise. And how could she answer him? What could she say?

She said nothing.

"You're so beautiful," he murmured in a soft, lazy voice. "Like a mystical siren."

His hands rose to slide up her naked arms. "So soft, so real." He smiled sleepily. "But for how long? Will your image fade when I close my eyes again?" His fingers pressed gently around her arms, and he slowly pulled her toward him. "You're only a dream," he whispered, his breath caressing her lips. "But I want you. I want to feel your lips against mine. I want to touch you . . . taste you." His gaze slid into hers. "Make love to you."

Paralyzed, as if in a dream, Samantha watched his unhurried movements as he closed the distance between them.

The softness of his lips upon hers generated an immediate and uncontrollable response. She couldn't think or breathe. And worse, she didn't care if she ever did so again. All that mattered was the wonderful sensations this man caused deep within her. A small whimper escaped her throat, and she helplessly softened beneath his kiss.

A thrill of pleasure spiraled through her body when his warm, exploring tongue melted between her parted lips to conquer the recess of her mouth. With slow, lazy strokes he retreated to trace her lips with the tip of his tongue before penetrating again with sensual mastery. Unable to control the chaotic emotions that toppled her senses, she moaned powerlessly and pressed closer.

Finally, languidly, he pulled his lips from hers. He smiled drowsily. "Lord, how I wish you were real." Then, releasing a heavy sigh, he closed his eyes.

She didn't know how long she sat there before she realized that his hands had fallen away, and he was asleep.

Trembling from the contact, she rose to her feet and moved stiffly to dress in her disguise and dispose of the water, her thoughts in uneasy turmoil. Why did this man stir such unfamiliar feelings within her? No other man had ever affected her so. Never touched her so. And why had she allowed it? Oh, certainly he was handsome. But so were a hundred other men. She didn't even know this man, for goodness sake—didn't *want* to know him.

Forcing thoughts of Montague Windhall aside, she restored the room to order and pulled the chair over to the window. She sat down and gazed out, her face half turned toward the sleeping viscount. As they had done so many times before, her thoughts drifted to home and family.

Everything had been so simple in England: the serene, endless days riding along the beach, the horse races and fox hunts. She missed the old stone castle at Willowglen. She missed her room, her friends . . . her gentle father.

Tears clouded her vision. An ache of intense longing grew in her chest until the pain was unbearable. Oh, Papa, I miss you. I need you so much. A sob rose, and she cleared her throat, then channeled her thoughts to another direction. If only there was another way to obtain the money needed to free Father, to obtain the coin for the guard's bribe, the money the contacts demanded before they'd attempt the rescue.

Her father had always teasingly called her a vixen, but she'd never truly felt like one until now. She was a criminal—a *real* criminal. This wasn't a game of make-believe. And one small mistake could place her neck in the hangman's noose. Her hand rose to her throat, and she swallowed against the imagined tightness forming beneath her palm.

For the first time in her life she was scared—really scared. But she had no choice. Her father's life was at risk. And to have her father back and safe was worth any price.

Staring out the window, she sat motionless for over an hour, carefully keeping her thoughts from home. But they returned again and again, weighing down her heart.

"What brings about such sadness, Lady Traynor?" Montague asked gently from the bed.

Samantha jumped in surprise. Quickly schooling her features, she turned to face him fully. "Sadness?" she rasped gruffly, forcing a smile. "What could I possibly have to be sad about? I was merely enjoying the view."

"My mistake," he said softly, then he looked around the room. "What do you do here all day? How do you keep yourself entertained?"

She shrugged. "I read, mostly."

"Ah, yes, the story of the fisherman, I remember." His gaze slid back to hers. "Do you play games?"

"What kind of games?"

"Whist?"

"No. But I have been known to play an occasional game of chess."

"Truly?" A slow smile spread across his handsome face. "Chess is my favorite." He eased up into a sitting position, wincing as he maneuvered back against the pillows. "Would you care for a match?"

She eyed him skeptically. "Are you sure you're feeling up to it?"

He chuckled warmly, a deep rumbling sound that caused her heart to beat an odd tune. "Madam Traynor, chess takes very little physical effort." He gestured toward the door with a nod of his head. An unruly curl fell onto his forehead, and he impatiently brushed it aside. "I believe you'll find the board in the parlor near the harpsichord."

"Very well," Samantha said, rising. "But I want it understood that if you find it tiring, you'll tell me at once."

Montague dipped his raven head. "Agreed."

After closing the bedroom door Samantha raised the hem of her skirt and raced down the stairs. She couldn't hold back her smile any longer. She hadn't been beaten at a game of chess since she was twelve years old—much to her father's chagrin. How many times had he jokingly claimed that he'd created an insatiable, bloodthirsty opponent who impudently showed no mercy, even to her poor sire?

Retrieving the board and chessmen, she bolted back up the stairs. When she reached the door she stopped to smooth down her skirt and compose herself. Hoping her triumphant expression didn't give her away, she opened the door.

Samantha won the first two games in three moves and the next two in six moves.

Montague said something beneath his breath, then glared at her. "Woman, I believe you've played me false."

She blinked innocently. "Oh?"

"For someone who plays *occasionally,* you show remarkable expertise."

"Oh, that." She grinned, hoping her dimple didn't show beneath the powder. "I had a good teacher."

"Obviously," he grumbled.

They played three more games, and Samantha won unabashedly.

Montague began to chuckle. "Lord have mercy. Lady Traynor, have you ever considered the fortune you could make simply by challenging the men of Lynch's Ferry to a game of chess? You could become independently wealthy."

Samantha frowned. "Do you mean play for money?" Why hadn't she thought of that before? A *legal* way to appropriate funds. Her hopes rose, then immediately plummeted. How would it look for an elderly woman to engage in such activity? Society might overlook such behavior in a younger person, but not in a woman supposedly in her fifties. Suddenly a thought struck her. What if Christine . . . She held back a smile. "I doubt if I'm good enough for that," she said humbly.

Montague raised his chin. "Madam, I am considered one of the better players in the area, and as you can see, you've tromped me mercilessly." He bent his head to one side. "Have you ever been beaten?"

This was her chance. "Yes. Quite frequently." She smiled. "By Christine." Sorry, twin.

"Christine?"

She nodded. "My niece, Christine Fleming."

"Good Lord, you mean it runs in the family?"

At his look of utter astonishment Samantha couldn't stop the burst of laughter. Besides, Christine had never played chess in her life. Tears threatened, and her shoulders shook. "No," she said finally, managing to compose herself. "It's only the two of us."

"How old is your niece?"

"Eighteen."

"And she can beat you at chess? Unbelievable." Then

something in his manner changed suddenly. "Is she by chance related to Cous—Derrick Fleming?"

"Yes." Samantha bit her lower lip. What did that have to do with anything? "Do you know him?"

"No. I've heard of him, though." He studied her closely. "Does your niece look like you?"

Startled, Samantha nodded. "Perhaps when I was younger." Was he remembering her from his delirium?

A soft smile touched his lips. "In that case, I can't wait to meet her."

Samantha sobered instantly, despairing at the thought of Christine meeting Lord Windhall, though why it should bother her she didn't know. "I'm afraid you'll have to wait until after you've recovered. I certainly don't intend to bring her to a gentleman's bedroom for an introduction."

Montague shook his head. "Nor would I expect you to. Of course I meant at a later time." He straightened the sheet over his naked chest and smiled. "Now, madam, I demand another chance to repair my shattered ego."

Samantha's happy mood returned, and she arranged the chess pieces. She won another game before she finally felt sorry for him and let him win.

"If I wasn't so happy about the victory, I'd cry foul," Montague chided.

Samantha clutched her chest in feigned insult. "Lord Windhall, how could you think that I would deliberately lose? It was simply misjudgment on my part."

His brow peaked. "Of course."

Suddenly the bedroom door opened, and Dahlia entered. "Well, your lordship, I see you're feeling a mite better."

"I am."

"Good." She strolled over to the bed and tossed a package down beside him. "Then you'll be able to use this."

He looked confused as he picked up the package. "What do you mean? What's this?"

Dahlia grinned, and she winked at Samantha. "A present from Lady Traynor."

Samantha grinned. "Go ahead. Open it."

"Why would you buy me a present?" He frowned, then he sighed and reached for the string.

How Samantha wished she could have captured his expression when he opened the package.

Carefully untying the twine, he peeled back the paper. His mouth dropped open. After a frozen moment his burst of laughter filled the room. "A red nightshirt."

CHAPTER 8

Samantha awakened late the next morning. Aware that Dahlia must truly be exhausted from sitting with Montague and in dire need of relief, she dressed quickly in another of her Madeline gowns, this one of dull blue, and rushed out the door. Hurrying down the hall in quick strides, quite unlike the elderly lady she was trying to portray, she rounded the corner and nearly collided with the housekeeper.

"Oh!" Dahlia sputtered, attempting to steady the wobbling tray she held. "You startled me."

Samantha clutched a hand to her own pounding chest. "You retaliated quite nicely. My nerves will never be the same."

Dahlia chuckled softly.

"Now, my dear." Samantha placed her hands on her padded hips. "I recall telling you last eve that I wished to be roused early." She tilted her head to one side. "Well? Why were my instructions so blatantly ignored?"

Dahlia smiled cheekily, appearing not at all offended by the rebuke. "It was his lordship's idea. He said you'd been pushing yourself too hard, and you needed the rest."

Samantha pursed her lips, trying to hide the leap in her

breast at his concern. "I see. And of course, *his* wishes far outweigh mine."

The older woman's eyes crinkled at the corners. "He *is* my master, Lady Traynor. Besides, I think it has something to do with a surprise he has for you."

"Surprise? What surprise?" Samantha's spine rippled uneasily at the maid's manner. "Dahlia?"

The housekeeper's face broke into a wide grin, and she turned hurriedly, then peeked back over her shoulder. "His lordship is waiting for you."

Samantha stared at the woman's retreating back. What was going on? With a frown creasing her brow she continued down the hall until she stood before Montague's bedroom door. From the other side she heard his voice raised in a lilting cadence but couldn't catch the words. Who was he talking to?

She gave the handle a yank and swung the door open. An all-encompassing glance told her that the viscount was alone in the room. Her frown deepened as she looked at Montague. At the sight that met her eyes her jaw dropped. Braced in a sitting position by mounds of feather pillows, Montague preened at his reflection before a small looking glass. He wore the red flannel nightshirt she'd given him, but he'd embellished its design. At his throat he'd added a silky black cravat that billowed under his nose, adorned by a gaudy gold stickpin. Beneath a wig his heavily powdered face had *three* beauty patches speckling his jaw. A purple tricorn with bright yellow plumes sat next to him on the bed.

His haughty gaze rose to meet hers, his lips pursed tightly, as if he'd been sampling alum. His wig sat cockeyed, one curl dangling over his left brow.

Samantha erupted into peals of laughter. Her shoulders shook, and her stomach clenched in an uncontrollable siege.

He stared at her with a confused expression. But catching her attention, he reverted to his pompous facade. "Madam, your humor sorely offends." He motioned to the flannel costume. "I merely tried to please you by donning the garment you so graciously supplied." He arched a brow. "Does this attire not meet with your approval?"

Somewhat sobered now, Samantha dabbed at the tears of laughter that threatened to overflow and ruin her disguise. She managed a nod, but she couldn't have spoken at that moment to save herself from the hangman's noose.

Montague brought a frilly lace kerchief to his nose and sniffed disdainfully. "Good." He nodded with a regal air. "Then see well to your inspection, madam, for I will not have my lack of propriety challenged again."

Taking a deep breath to still the quivering in her stomach, Samantha cleared her throat. "I am quite impressed, your lordship. I had no idea that you valued my opinion so highly."

He flicked the kerchief. "Well, be that as it may . . ." His features rounded innocently, resembling those of a small boy seeking admiration. "Do you approve?"

Samantha stared at him as if his teeth had fallen out. Was he serious? He couldn't be. Could he? "Well, I—" Heavens, what could she say? "Uh—of course, Montague. You look . . . quite grand."

He folded his hands primly across his chest. "Yes, I do, don't I?" He tilted his head to look admiringly down into the looking glass braced on his lap. "That's what I was just telling myself."

Samantha blinked in astonishment. He *was* serious. But what had she expected? She'd seen this side of him before. Only during his illness had he let down his dandified airs. She opened her mouth to make an uncharitable remark, but Dahlia's entrance halted the words.

"Here's your brandy, your lordship."

With his attention now directed at the older woman as she carried a tray over to the desk, Samantha regained her composure and moved to the foot of the bed, watching him nod in response to something Dahlia said. She noticed that beneath the heavy layer of powder shadows darkened the area below his eyes. Lines of strain and fatigue grooved the sides of his mouth. His chest labored beneath the folds of the nightshirt. Montague was putting up a front. He was still very, very ill.

Samantha quickly ushered Dahlia out of the room. She took the glass of brandy from his unsteady hand and set it aside. "I think that you have quite overdone yourself, young man," she scolded, using her no-nonsense voice. Pouring a cup of Aunt Katherine's tea, she handed it to him. "Drink."

Montague curled his lip. "I'd rather be ill."

"Either you drink it on your own, or *I* will help." She arched a brow. "Well? Which is it to be?"

Mumbling something beneath his breath that she was probably fortunate not to have heard, he tossed back the liquid. He choked and pressed his lips tightly together. His eyes watered as he handed her the empty cup.

After setting the mug on the bedside table Samantha pulled several of the pillows from behind him and flung them carelessly across the room. Slipping off his wig, she tossed it in the direction of the armoire. His gleaming black hair tumbled over his brow. Ignoring the beguiling sight, she pointed to the remaining pillows. "Lie back."

He did so, albeit with obvious reluctance at having to obey her brusque command.

She removed the black patches from his jaw and, with a damp cloth from the bedside table, washed the powder from his face. Absently she brushed the strands of hair from his forehead before her fingers trailed along his firm jaw.

As she worked to remove the cravat and stickpin his sapphire gaze rose leisurely to lock with hers. Her hands stilled. He peered into her very soul, drawing her, beckoning her. Time seemed suspended as she struggled to surface from the depths of his eyes.

Finally, after a lifetime—or was it only moments?—his thick lashes slowly lowered and released her from their hold.

"Get some sleep, Montague," she whispered. "You'll have plenty of time to admire your finery later."

He sighed deeply, his lips softening into a slow, satisfied smile. "Beautiful green eyes," he murmured before surrendering to the pull of healing slumber.

Samantha stared down at him for a long moment. She didn't understand why this man's mere presence touched her in hidden places—places she hadn't known existed. What was it about him that set him above all other men? He was a combination of bold masculinity and irritating foppishness; an enigma that defied propriety, then embellished it; a dandy with a pulsating sensuality that demanded recognition.

Giving herself a mental shake, she retreated to the chair. She didn't have the time or inclination for affairs of the heart. Her father's freedom—his very life—depended on her ability to get the money needed for his escape. At this moment her only objectives were to see that Montague recovered from the illness her brash actions had caused and to resume her role as the Scarlet Temptress. Anything else was of scant importance.

Several hours later Jason woke to a pounding in his head. It felt as if someone had stuffed it with straw. Damn, that tea made him sluggish. What was in it? he wondered. He closed his eyes. Perhaps it was better that he didn't know.

A low growl and a gnawing ache in his stomach reminded him of his meager diet of late, and he looked around for something to appease his hunger. He saw nothing.

Reaching for the small bell on the bedside table, he gave it a quick shake, then winced as the tinkling sound echoed in his head. Lord, that was loud.

Falling back, he waited for someone to respond. Peevishly he hoped for Dahlia rather than the domineering Madeline. At least Dahlia wouldn't treat him like some helpless infant. Besides, with his old maid he could be himself. He clutched the bedsheet. Himself? Had he maintained his ruse while he was ill? Bits of the last few days flashed through his mind. Hell's breath. Before he received the nightshirt he'd been anything but the fop he was trying to portray.

He brought a hand to his temple. Would Madeline think his illness had caused the lapse? God, he hoped so. A few moments later he heard the sound of approaching footsteps. Then the door opened, and Lady Traynor's chunky figure filled the room. Jason gritted his teeth. Had luck deserted him altogether?

"Well. You've finally roused yourself. Good." She nodded. "I was just coming to wake you, since Dahlia is about to bring in your supper."

"Madam." Jason's mouth widened into a smile. "You must have intercepted my very thoughts. My stomach just reminded me of the neglect it's suffered."

She grinned.

His attention fastened on a small dimple that winked in her right cheek. Instantly another dimple came to mind— below a crimson mask, on smooth ivory flesh. Jason blinked. Good Lord. Now he was hallucinating, merging the Scarlet Temptress into Madeline's bulky frame. Had the sultry bandit obsessed him? Would he always see her in every woman he met? Giving an undignified snort, he focused his attention on Madeline's generous hips. No. There was no comparison.

Madeline moved closer.

He caught a flash of white as she removed a glove and brought her cool hand to his brow.

"Your fever has receded for the moment. That's a good sign, young man." Turning her back to him, she slipped on the glove again.

"Why do you wear those, Madam Traynor? Surely it's warm enough in here to discard them."

Seeing the way her body tensed, Jason realized he'd made a mistake.

With her back rigid, she walked to the fireplace. "It's not for comfort's sake, Montague." She turned to watch the flames leaping in the hearth. "I wear them . . . because of a disfigurement." Her gaze touched his, then quickly skittered away. "As a child, I, um, was severely burned by a cauldron of boiling water. I conceal them because of their grotesque appearance."

Jason cocked his head to one side. "Madam, if you fear I might be repulsed, I assure you that is not the case. I have always felt that one's outer appearance is mere window dressing for the soul." He looked down at her hands. Now clasped tightly together at her waist, they were small and slim, delicately shaped. "But your soul could never be concealed behind such shallow adornments. Your very presence here reveals the depth of your unrestrained compassion, your inner beauty that glows like sunshine through a delicate crystal prism." Hell, what made him say that? He darted a look at her face.

She turned away, but not before he caught a glimpse of her lips drawing down into a crestfallen bow. What had he said? Had he embarrassed her? "Forgive me, Madeline, I didn't mean to . . ." His voice trailed into a whisper. He hadn't meant to upset her. "I mean, they must have been quite lovely—your hands, that is."

He studied her profile, outlined by the golden glow flickering from the flames in the hearth. Her wide green eyes lured him into their depths, glistening emeralds brimming with youth in her seasoned face. He admired her lips, pale, yet shaped gently into full, dusty pink innocence. "As a matter of fact, I imagine *all* of you was quite lovely. You must have stopped the hearts of many a suitor," he said softly, his attention lingering on her perfect mouth.

Entranced, he watched her lips open in a tempting part. His chest tightened. For a moment he thought he saw a hint of timid elation flicker, but all too quickly she resumed her controlled visage.

"Young man." Her grating voice reverberated through the silent room. "I am much too old to listen to your inane flattery." She placed a hand on an ample hip and faced him fully. "Save your outlandish puffery for someone who will appreciate it." Turning for the door, she peeked back over her shoulder, the vulnerability in her eyes conflicting with her gruff voice. "Now if you'll excuse me, I'll see what's keeping Dahlia."

Jason shifted uneasily, wondering what on earth had possessed him to say those things to Madeline Traynor. What was it about her that unsettled him so? He had never, in his entire thirty years, found himself attracted to an older woman. Hell, Madeline wasn't just an older woman, she was an *old* woman. Still, every time she came near him he was entranced by the sound of her voice, her laughter, her clear green eyes, her full, soft mouth. . . . Damn! He was doing it again. If Nick ever found out about this, he'd never let Jason live it down.

After supper Samantha, needing time to herself, wandered outside to think on Montague's earlier words. That he'd likened her inner goodness, inner beauty, to a crystal prism had nearly destroyed her. Blast him for being so kind. She didn't feel flawless and pure. She felt more like a chunk of obsidian.

"Ah, there you are, Lady Traynor," Dahlia said from behind her. "His lordship's asking for you."

Samantha eyed the maid. "Oh? Why is that? Does he seek retaliation for his meager meal of crumpets and tea?"

Dahlia shook her head. "Oh no, milady. He wouldn't do that. He knows you're only doing what's best for him."

Samantha wished she could be as certain as Dahlia, but she had witnessed the lightning changes in Montague's personality too many times already not to be cautious. With wary intent she made her way into the house and entered the bedroom. She froze.

The scratchy horsehair chair had been covered with a soft flannel quilt. Three feather pillows lined its seat, and a large upholstered footstool sat between the bed and chair. The table that Dahlia had carried in earlier sat beside the chair with the chessboard and game pieces set up, ready for a match. The drapes had been opened to admit the last of the evening rays.

"Ah, madam. You have arrived at last." Montague waved his handkerchief. "Good, good. I am sorely in need of a diversion from this wretched boredom. Come along now. Let's have another game." He smiled wryly. "As I recall, the score is now about one to ten."

Samantha gestured toward the chair. "Who is responsible for this?"

Puzzled, he frowned. "Does it offend you? It certainly wasn't meant to."

"No, it doesn't. As a matter of fact, I'm very pleased. It's quite thoughtful."

He squared his shoulders and grinned broadly. "Well, then, it is *I* who has pleased you. I thought you might be more comfortable if you had cushions and a chair covering."

Samantha tried to conceal her pleasure. "I see." She straightened a fold in her skirt. "Thank you, Montague. In truth, that chair had begun to chafe. And as to a game of chess"—she sniffed—"I'd be delighted to trounce you once again."

He threw his head back and laughed, a deep, husky sound.

Settling herself into the now-cozy chair, Samantha moved aside the footstool and situated the table between them. With the slight improvement in Montague's health his cunning skills unfolded, and it took her nearly an hour to win the first game. She was certain that once he completely recovered he'd be a formidable foe.

"Well, young man, I see that you are indeed feeling a bit better. If you keep this up, you may yet offer me some competition."

He chuckled softly. "Spoken like a true sportswoman. Now quit lollygagging, woman. It's your turn to set up the board."

Another hour passed before Samantha triumphed again—but not without using every trick her father had taught her, and more. Montague wasn't just a good chess player, he was exceptional.

"I say, madam, I'm beginning to catch on to your game. You'd best watch your step, or I shall be the one doing the trouncing." He leaned his head to one side. "As a matter of fact, I feel a little wager might be appropriate."

Samantha arched a powdered brow. "What kind of wager?"

He pursed his lips. "Hmm. How about something simple?" He stared thoughtfully for a moment. "If you win, I'll drink that ghastly tea for the duration of my illness without complaint." His voice gentled. "And if I win, you'll take off your gloves."

Samantha swallowed. Did she dare? What if she lost? She couldn't take off her gloves! Don't be absurd, she told herself. The only game he'd ever won, she *let* him win. Drawing in a deep, steadying breath, she nodded. "Very well, I agree." Just as she reached to straighten the pieces a knock sounded.

"Enter," Montague responded.

The door opened, and Bromley's lanky frame filled the portal. "I's back, Massa." He lumbered across the room and laid a package on the bed next to Montague's hand. "I hopes I gots de right thing." He looked at Samantha and chuckled. "Yes, sah, I shorely do."

"I'm sure you did fine, Bromley." Montague smiled warmly at the servant, then winked. "Thank you."

Bromley beamed. "Yo' is mighty welcome, sah. Yes, indeedy, mighty welcome." Dipping his head, he backed out of the room, casting one last twinkling peek in Samantha's direction.

Montague lifted the package and handed it to Samantha. "For you, Lady Traynor."

"Me? Whatever for?"

"Because . . ." His voice lowered to a whisper. "You're . . . *very* special." He seemed to catch himself and added, "Besides, you gave *me* a gift, if you recall." He flicked an imaginary piece of lint from the mentioned nightshirt.

Samantha clutched the small package with a trembling hand. No one, other than her immediate family, had ever given her a present. She drew in a quivering breath. What kind of gift would Montague buy for a young lady? But then, to him she wasn't young. She was just an old, overbearing shrew. "Montague, I did not purchase your nightshirt with thoughts of gaining something in return." She smiled. "In truth, it was more for *my* benefit than yours." She considered the package. "I'm not certain I should accept this."

"Such falderal." He flicked a hand. "Of course you should. Now stop fussing and open it."

Samantha cast him a quick glance. Hesitantly she untied the twine and placed it neatly across the arm of the chair. Peeling back the brown paper, she caught her breath. Tears welled. Almost reverently she reached out a gloved finger to touch a flawless prism. The delicate crystal, cut in the shape of a heart, hung from a black velvet ribbon. "Oh, Montague. It's so beautiful. . . ."

Jason watched as she rose abruptly and turned her back to him, her slender shoulders quaking. He had purchased many a gift in his time, but no other woman had been so affected as Madeline. His throat tightened. He ached to pull her into his arms and hold her, comfort her. Realizing where his imagination was taking him, he clamped down on his wayward thoughts. "Madam, I assure you the present was not meant to make you unhappy. And if it continues to do so, then I'll throw the damned thing in the fireplace. Now come along, let's finish our game."

Samantha closed her hand over the prism and clutched it to her breast. Quelling her emotions, she took a settling breath and wiped moisture from her lashes. She turned and nodded stiffly. "Of course, Montague. Do forgive me for such a wretched display." She sat down and slipped the small heart into her skirt pocket. She would put it on later . . . when she was alone. Avoiding his tender regard, she lifted her chin and gestured toward the game. "Now then, I believe it's your turn to set up the men."

He shook his head. "Not until we've taken care of a small matter."

"What?"

He raised his hand. "Give me the prism."

She blinked. "Why?"

"Because I wish to put it on you."

"Montague, I don't believe—"

"Please?"

Samantha drew in a slow, shaky breath and removed the necklace from her pocket.

His eyes met hers and held them. "Come here."

Feeling like a blossom drawn to the sun's radiance, she rose and guardedly stepped to the side of the bed.

He opened his hand in silent command.

Carefully she placed the crystal in his palm and dropped the ribbon, letting it flutter onto his wrist.

Long, tanned fingers grasped the ends of the ribbon and separated the strands. Lifting the prism as if for inspection, he stared into the crystal a moment. "Bend closer."

His soothing voice melted over her like a warm, intoxicating balm, veiling her in its timbre of liquid velvet. Helplessly entranced, she leaned forward. Heat from his hands seared her skin as he slid his fingers beneath the hair of her wig. With every brush of his flesh against hers as he tied the ribbon, shivers raced up her spine. He was so close that she could feel his warm breath feathering her lips, smell the clean, musky scent of him.

His hands stilled suddenly, and his eyes darkened. Then slowly, methodically, his thumbs began to caress the sides of her throat with long, measured strokes that singed her flesh. As if lost in a dream, he stared at her lips, then pressed the back of her neck, urging her closer.

Her lips parted.

Suddenly he drew in a sharp breath. He tensed and jerked his hands away as if he'd been scorched. "There." His voice dripped icicles. "I believe the ribbon is secure."

Shattered, Samantha battled once again for composure. Her heart thundered in her chest. "Yes. Thank you." She straightened abruptly and returned to her seat.

Jason's mouth remained in a grim line as he set up the board and made the first move. What on earth was the matter with him? He had nearly kissed Madeline Traynor!

Samantha couldn't concentrate. Her thoughts were like a sack of spilled beans. Why had he given her such an intimate gift? Why did he arouse her passion, only to leave her unfulfilled? And why did she love it . . . love him? Oh, no. It couldn't be. She had wanted him to kiss her, to feel the firm pressure of his lips against hers, but she couldn't possibly be in love with him, could she? Stop this, Samantha, Stop.

"Checkmate," Jason announced suddenly.

"What?" Samantha scanned the board. She didn't even remember making any moves. Oh, heavens, he'd beaten her with the same three moves she'd used on him the day before. Her midsection tightened as the import of what had happened hit her. Oh, *God*. She'd lost the wager.

Jason, seeing her expression, knew a moment's guilt. He didn't feel he had won quite fairly. Her mind, he was aware, had not been on the game at all. Hell, he admitted, it was a wonder that *his* had been. But he wanted to prove to her that her disfigurement would not offend or repulse him. "Madam? I believe I've just won our wager." His gaze met hers, and his voice fell to a whisper. "Remove your gloves, Madeline."

Panic nearly strangled her. On trembling legs she rose. "Montague, please . . ."

Suddenly he grabbed for his handkerchief. A deep, bone-jarring cough racked his body. He struggled for breath. Frantically he sucked in air—only to cough it out again.

Samantha jerked the table out of the way, scattering chess pieces, and pulled him into a sitting position. She bent him over and thumped hard on his back.

His chest labored as he fought for oxygen.

With each strangled breath he took her own stopped. Each chest-splitting explosion tore at her breast.

It seemed like an eternity had passed before the attack subsided and he could breathe again. The aftereffects of the spasm showed in a tinge of blue around his mouth and in the way he collapsed back against the pillows, completely drained.

With an unsteady hand Samantha stroked his brow, then

reached for the damp cloth and bathed his face. Crooning softly, she spoke senseless murmurs to soothe and comfort him. She wanted to pull him into her arms and hold him, tell him how much he meant to her.

Still cradling his head, she leaned over and replaced the cloth on the bedside table. Lifting the decanter, she poured a cup of medicinal tea. "Drink this, Montague. Please."

He didn't argue. He merely nodded as his glazed stare fixed on hers. A shudder racked his body when he drained the cup. His strength spent, he slumped back.

Flooded with a sense of relief, Samantha bit down on her lower lip. She didn't realize she was crying until a salty tear stung the corner of her mouth.

CHAPTER 9

Nick Kincaid slid off of the back of his horse and led him into the stables behind Crystal Terrace. Sam Adams's leaflet, ready for reproduction, remained safely inside his bedroll. He wondered briefly if the coded message had anything to do with the rumors he'd heard. Was the king truly planning to punish the colonists for that silly tea party? Mercy. Didn't the man realize that if that happened, the colonists would retaliate? That it would mean war? Nick shook his head and turned his attention to the horse. "Mercy, Apollo. I hope the sovereign knows what he's about."

The large buckskin perked its ears and blinked a large eye.

Quietly, so as not to awaken Bromley, Nick unsaddled the stallion and stashed the bedroll under a mound of hay. He'd considered taking the horse to the hidden cave but was too tired to make the long walk back through that musky tunnel. Sighing, he removed Apollo's halter and tossed it over a rail.

That done, Nick led the horse outside and released him in the pasture. Shivering as February slid its cold hands up his back, he turned toward the rear of the house.

Creeping up the porch steps, he opened the door and sighed softly when he entered the warmth of the back hallway. He was frozen to the marrow, disgustingly dirty, and every part of his body ached. Unlike Jason, horseback riding was not Nick's forte. And why Jason was so set on breeding the surly beasts at Halcyon was beyond him.

The rarely used back stairway leading up to the master bedroom he knew Jason would be in seemed like a mountain to his sore limbs. But if he planned to see his brother this night, he had to climb those stairs. And he *had* to see Jason—had to know that he was all right.

The steps creaked, and Nick grabbed the banister to lighten his weight. He preferred not to wake Dahlia at this time of night and spend an hour explaining his presence.

Reaching Jason's room, he gently pressed the handle and slipped inside. Then, turning, he froze. An old woman slept in a quilt-covered chair next to his brother's bed. Something cold coiled through Nick's chest. Did his twin need constant attention? Was he *that* ill? With trembling hands Nick silently closed the door. He knew it was risky to enter the room with the old woman so close, but he had to know the truth of Jason's condition.

In the dim light cast by the low fire he readily made out his twin's sleeping form. Jason didn't look overly ill. His skin appeared a little paler than normal, though a bit flushed, but certainly unworthy of panic. His breathing seemed fairly normal in rhythm, with only a slight rasp.

Nick bent over, touching Jason's forehead with his palm. Barely feverish at all. What was going on here? Sighing, he removed his hand. There was only one way to find out. He shook his brother's shoulder.

Jason's lashes flew up. His lips parted as if to speak.

Nick silenced him with a finger to his own mouth and a jerk of his head in the direction of the sleeping woman.

Jason nodded.

Helping his brother from the bed, Nick led the way across the room and out into the hall. "Where can we speak privately?"

"In here," Jason whispered, moving in the direction of the vacant room next door.

Inside the spare bedroom Nick quickly crossed to light a candle. Turning to Jason, he smiled and embraced him heartily. Stepping back, he took mental inventory of his twin. It was like looking at a living statue of himself. Not one thing about their appearance differed, right down to that unruly curl that fell on their foreheads. There *was* a difference, of course. But few knew about it.

In the flickering candlelight Nick could see, too, that his brother wasn't as well as he'd first thought. Dark shadows smudged the area beneath Jason's eyes, and now that they were open, he could see they were streaked with red, their clear blue color glazed. Jason's cheeks had a hollow, sunken appearance. "Are you all right? Carl said you've been ill, but not this ill. May I get you something? Do you want to lie down?" Nick asked in a rush of excited questions. "What happened?"

Jason gave a weak smile and raised his hand. "Whoa. Slow down, little brother. One question at a time, please." A trembling hand rose to his hair, and he slid his fingers through the tumbled black curls. "In answer to all your questions—yes, I'm all right . . . *now*. This is not ill compared to what I *have* been. You can't get me anything, unless you have a storeroom of food in your pocket. I'll have to think about lying down. And as to what happened—I'd rather not talk about it."

Nick stared at Jason in disbelief for a moment, then relaxed. His brother was all right; a bit peaked, but all right. Jason was too cocky to be dying. Thank you, God.

Threading his fingers through his own hair, Nick felt the tenseness slip from his body, and he smiled. "Then what I heard at the Traveler's Inn last eve during supper must be true. A fair maiden has undone my big brother."

"Damn it, Nick, I wasn't *undone* by anyone. I merely had

a bout with the ague and am recovering nicely. And as for the fair maiden—she's about as *fair* as England's taxes, and as *maidenly* as the strumpets at Madame La Rue's."

Nick blinked. "Mercy, Jason. I've never known you to speak so abominably of a lady before. She must have set you back a pace."

Jason let out a long sigh. "More like twenty." He slowly crossed to the bed and sat down, leaning back against the pillows as the color drained from his face.

Nick felt his pulse begin to pound, and anger build to explosive proportions. "Who did this to you? Do you have any idea?"

Jason struggled to lift himself back into a sitting position. "No. Although I do have a couple of suspicions."

"Who—"

"But," Jason interrupted, "none that I want to discuss at the moment." He pulled a quilt from the foot of the bed and wrapped it around his trembling shoulders. "How did the meeting go?"

It took Nick a moment to gather his control. Jason looked atrocious. Then another, even more startling sight struck him. Jason was wearing a nightshirt. Who had managed that feat?

Jason eyed him, then clutched the quilt tighter and shifted uncomfortably. "Nick—the meeting?"

Nick shrugged. "It went as expected. The newest leaflets are ready. Parliament, too, I've heard, is upset over the Boston excursion and is considering retaliation against the colonists. It wouldn't surprise me if that wasn't what's in the pamphlet." He pulled off his gloves and tossed them on the chair. "I fear we're headed for war with the mother country."

"I know," Jason rasped weakly.

Nick examined Jason's pale features and felt stirrings of concern. "Come on, Jase. I think you need to go back to bed. We'll discuss this later. If you're up to it, we'll talk tomorrow. By the way, who is that old woman?"

"Madeline Traynor, a houseguest of Carl's. I think he sent her here to make my life miserable. Between her and Dahlia, you have no idea what I've been through in the last sennight. I've been strapped to that damned bed, flat on my back, suffering unimaginable atrocities I can't even begin to describe. If I ever get out of their clutches, I will personally strangle our beloved godfather."

Raising an eyebrow, Nick grinned. "She didn't look *that* bad, and Dahlia only does what she thinks is best."

"Humph. I'll gladly trade places with you. I could use a little uninterrupted rest." Jason's head came up, and a wicked smile touched his mouth.

"Oh, no, you don't." Nick laughed and backed away. "Don't get any ideas, big brother. And get that look off of your face. I am not changing places with you."

"*You're* well enough to withstand their ministrations," Jason pointed out. "*I*, on the other hand—"

"Absolutely not." Nick held up his palms.

Jason rose from the bed and wove slowly toward him.

Nick backed up another pace. He didn't think Jason was serious—at least he hoped not.

Nick stepped closer to the door. In his peripheral vision, he saw the door handle turn. He sucked in his breath.

Jason, too, saw the handle twist. Just as the door swung open he darted behind it, leaving Nick standing alone to face the intruder.

"Lord Windhall!" Samantha hissed. "Just what do you think you're doing? Why are you out of bed? And why are you dressed like—*you've been riding!* My heavens! Have you no sense at all? Has your illness addled your brain?" She braced her hands on her padded hips. "Well? What have you to say for yourself?"

Nick peeked over her shoulder at Jason's face grinning, around the edge of the door. I'll kill him. "Ah—er," Nick stammered. Mercy. What could he say?

"I don't believe this," Samantha railed. "I've spent days— and nights—nursing you back from the grave just so you could pull a trick like this. It wouldn't surprise me one bit if this tomfoolery didn't cost you your life. Blockhead! Idiot!"

Samantha wanted to kick him. And to think she'd worried herself sick over him. For what? The man was obviously a fool.

Nick noticed the old woman's hands balling into fists and tried to smooth things over before she had apoplexy. "I'm sorry, ah . . ." What was her name? Melba? No. Madeline. "I'm sorry, Madeline, truly I am." Putting on his best little-boy-lost look, he smiled cajolingly. "I know you're only concerned for my welfare. But—um—I just couldn't stand the confinement any longer. Please try to understand." Did her features soften just the slightest bit? "It got so bad that I started thinking death might be preferable to that bed." That should do it. Nick risked another glance at his brother.

Jason rolled his gaze toward the ceiling.

Samantha felt the anger drain from her body. She knew how he felt. Hadn't he only done what she herself had wanted to do so many times over the last few days? But *she* wasn't ill. Still, her anger slipped another notch. Did illness make confinement any easier to bear? No. If anything, it made it harder.

Sighing, and not completely unaffected by that innocent look, she softened her voice. "All right, Lord Windhall. Since the deed is done, I see no reason to harp on it. The only recourse now is to see that you're taken care of. Come along." She pinched the material on the arm of his coat, pulling him toward the hall. "I'll have Dahlia prepare a bath for you." She stopped and smiled. "And I will fix you an extra dose of Aunt Katherine's tea."

Aunt Katherine's tea? What was that? He'd never heard of it before. Mentally shrugging, Nick stepped toward the door, casting one last peek at his twin. Was something wrong with Jason? He looked like he was choking . . . or laughing.

Jason watched Nick leave the room through tears of mirth. Poor Nick. His little brother had no idea what he was in for. Madeline's coddling was enough to make him ill. And that tea! Lord, he wouldn't wish that on anyone. Well, except maybe . . . Nick.

"It's small recompense, little brother, for setting me up with two of your mistresses at the same time—in the same room." Jason's hand automatically rose to his jaw as if he could still feel those women's blows.

Crossing to the bed, he slipped under the quilt and pulled it up to his chin. Without a fire going the air in the guest room felt frigid. Snuggling deeper into the covers, he leaned against the headboard, a grin parting his lips. Good luck, little brother.

Then his thoughts turned to Madeline. He still couldn't believe that at one time he'd actually thought that *she* was the Scarlet Temptress in disguise. That first day when they'd laughed and played games he had been certain of it. Even that first night, in his fevered state, he could have sworn she was young and beautiful. In his vision her shiny black hair had swirled around smooth pink cheeks. He'd imagined her eyes to be a beautiful emerald green. Hell, he even thought he'd kissed the raven-haired beauty.

It had been a dream, of course. He knew that now. An erotic fantasy that even tonight left him longing to sample the taste of her lips, her tongue, sweet and . . . Stop it! he commanded. You're acting like a rutting boar over a damned apparition. What's the matter with you? First you moon over an outlaw, then a bloody mirage, and now a woman old enough to be your grandmother.

Pushing the unsettling thoughts from his mind, he slid lower beneath the quilt, enjoying his temporary solace. It wouldn't last, though. Nick would return the moment he had the chance. Jason had to get away from Crystal Terrace before being discovered—and before Nick came back. But where could he go?

There was no one in Lynch's Ferry that he could trust other than Carl. And Madeline Traynor was *his* houseguest. The only other person anywhere near was Jedediah Blackburn. And hell, he lived midway between Lynch's Ferry and Bedford County—a good half day's ride. Resigned, Jason sighed. He would go to Jed's. There was no place else. Besides, the scruffy old trapper was one of Jason's godfathers—and a loyal friend who wouldn't question Jason to death for appearing out of nowhere.

But how to get there? His damn body still didn't possess any strength. And in this freezing weather, even if he were able to ride, he'd probably have a relapse.

Getting away from Crystal Terrace would be no problem. Bromley had his head in the clouds most of the time, dreaming about one of the slave girls on the Wainwrights' plantation. Jason grinned. That boy definitely had a single-minded purpose in life. No, Bromley would give him no trouble. Jason could easily take a horse from the stables without being discovered—providing he was strong enough to mount it. But how would he manage the rest of the way? He damn sure wasn't well enough to ride all the way to Jed's. He needed a carriage. But how could he hire one without being seen?

A disguise? Yes, of course. That would work. But what could he use? He surveyed the room and tried to think. Rarely occupied, the chamber had sparse furnishings—just an armoire, a small dresser, a washstand, and a blue tapestry chair. Nothing for a ruse.

Jason visualized his own room. The armoire was filled with bright satin apparel belonging to his step-uncle, the real Montague Windhall, and Montague's hefty father, Leopold. On the chest next to the armoire sat several of the man's wigs in assorted lengths and a jar of white powder. Wigs? Powder? Leopold—that's it!

Jason sat up quickly—too quickly—and the room dipped crazily. He steadied himself and shook his head to clear it. The disguise would work, but how could he get into the room unobserved, without coming face to face with Nick? His twin would demand that they switch places again, and Jason wasn't about to do that. Oh, no, now that he was free of Madeline he intended to stay that way.

He leaned back against the pillows contemplating his

situation. He sensed that Nick was tired, very tired. Knowing his little brother, he'd probably fall asleep soon. And Nick slept like the dead.

Through the wall Jason could hear the murmur of voices and the occasional splash of water. He could almost visualize Dahlia stripping Nick and shoving him into the bath. Jason felt a trickle of apprehension. Would she notice the difference?

He let out his breath. Probably not. She would surely keep her eyes averted. Besides, what difference would it make if she did? She wouldn't tell anyone. Relaxing, he continued with his summation. After Nick's bath Dahlia would no doubt bring a tray of crumpets and tea-elixir. Jason's stomach coiled at the thought of that godawful tea. Oh, little brother, he thought, you're never going to forgive me for this one.

Although he had to admit the stuff did seem to help. "Rest," Madeline would tell him, "is what you need to recuperate." And within a few minutes after taking the horrid stuff he would indeed start to feel drowsy.

Jason blinked. The tea! All he had to do was wait until Nick drank the tea. Nick would go out like a snuffed candle. But how would he know when he'd taken it? A grin creased his cheeks. Oh, he'd know, all right. He closed his eyes and chuckled. Yes, he'd know. All he had to do was wait. . . .

Jason came awake to the sound of sputtering gasps and strangled curses. Instantly his thoughts flew to Nick, and he fought a chuckle. Without a doubt Nick had had the tea.

Lifting himself to a sitting position, he brought a hand to rub the back of his neck. If his calculations were correct, Nick should be asleep in less than thirty minutes. But what could he do to cause a diversion to get Madeline and Dahlia out of the room? Think, Jason. Think!

A few minutes later, his head aching from all the plans he'd considered and discarded, Jason heard voices coming from the hall. He shoved the quilt aside and made his way to the door, opening it just the slightest bit to peer out.

Dahlia and Madeline stood in the hall near the top of the stairs, conversing softly about Lord Windhall's condition.

"He's sleeping now," Madeline said. "I gave him two doses of the tea."

Jason flinched.

"That should stay any further riding expeditions for a while." Madeline laughed.

Jason couldn't argue with that.

"Let's hope it helps," Dahlia said.

"Yes, and if we're lucky, it will ward off any relapse this escapade might very well have caused. He should be pretty groggy for the next few hours." Madeline turned for the stairs. "And since we have a free moment, why don't we share a cup of tea and one of those delicious biscuits you baked this morning?"

Jason's stomach growled in appreciation, and he smiled as the housekeeper's face beamed proudly. She always had been easy to sway with compliments about her cooking.

As soon as the women disappeared from sight Jason slipped into the room where his brother slept peacefully. He smiled fondly down at his twin for a moment. Nick didn't realize what he was in for. "Sorry, little brother," Jason whispered softly before crossing to the chest.

An hour later, after gluing on whiskers and eyebrows, then donning a purple satin ensemble belonging to Leopold Windhall, the real Montague's father, Jason stuffed it with towels. Between stops to rest and catch his breath he managed to complete the disguise.

Satisfied with his appearance, Jason grabbed the remaining evidence of his ruse and shoved it under the bed. Now all he had to do was get away from Crystal Terrace without being seen.

Samantha sipped her tea slowly, enjoying the warm sweetness. Her elbows rested on the square oak table in the dining room, her thoughts on the man upstairs.

When she had awakened and found the bed empty her

heart had nearly stopped. She had been so frightened. . . . And then to find him in the guest room, dressed in filthy riding clothes—the blithering idiot! She shook her head. None of it made any sense. But one thing certainly did— Montague no longer needed her. Besides, she'd put off riding as the Scarlet Temptress long enough. She rose and looked longingly toward the stairs that led up to his room. A sigh left her chest. It was time for her to get back to work.

Jason sat in the common room of Merryman's Hotel in Lynch's Ferry. His neck itched beneath the wig, and powder kept dropping on his eyelashes. He felt terrible, and anger stirred him. The only carriage available to take him to Jed's was engaged until seven o'clock in the evening. Damn! He had hoped to reach the cabin before nightfall. Now it looked as though he wouldn't arrive until the early hours of morning, which was not the best time to approach the grumpy trapper.

A fitting end to a wretched day. Raising a tankard of ale to his lips, Jason noticed that his hand trembled. His head felt light and dizzy. Had he overdone it?

Downing the drink, he set the mug on the table and leaned back, closing his eyes. He felt very much like the old man he was trying to portray, and he wished he had someplace to lie down.

Jason's lashes flew up when someone nudged his arm.

"Sir? Sir? Your carriage is ready," the short, balding desk clerk announced.

Jason blinked, trying to focus. "What? Oh, yes. Yes, thank you." He nodded his head and rose slowly to his feet. The room spun. His legs felt weighted down. Cautiously, gripping the backs of chairs for support, he made his way across the hotel lobby to the front exit. His skin felt sticky, and his legs shook.

The carriage looked an impossible distance from the door. Gritting his teeth against a surge of weakness, Jason released the hotel door and stumbled to the awaiting coach.

Once inside he collapsed onto the cushion, letting his head fall back against the top of the seat. If he could just get rid of this blasted dizziness, he wouldn't feel so bad.

The carriage lurched forward, and Jason lowered his lashes, listening to the steady thud of the horse's hooves. His body swayed with the harsh rocking motion of the coach. Lord, he ached. And he was so tired.

Suddenly something startled him to awareness. What was wrong? He blinked and identified the source of his confusion. The coach wasn't moving. Had they reached Jed's? It seemed as if he'd just closed his eyes.

He gripped the window ledge and pulled himself up to push aside the curtain. His breath caught sharply. A blunderbuss was pointed threateningly at the driver.

Jason felt his pulse leap, quickly followed by a surge of impotency. He collapsed back against the seat. "Bloody hell. Not again . . ."

CHAPTER 10

From behind the red satin mask Samantha watched the old man climb from the carriage, his legs trembling as he lowered himself to the ground. Blast. Had fortune deserted her forever? Robbing the lordly British was one thing, but taking money from the elderly was entirely another.

The burden of frustration weighed heavily. She didn't want to rob him. But what could she do now? She couldn't just announce that she'd changed her mind and ride away. Heaving an inward sigh, she approached the old man, the gun held loosely in her hand. He wasn't a threat, of that she was certain. He looked too old and too ill for opposition.

As she stepped closer he turned, and sky-blue eyes met hers. She drew in a sharp breath. Instantly another pair of heart-stopping blue eyes came to mind. Was this man related to Montague?

Frowning, her gaze traveled over the elderly man's form. He was large like the viscount, and quite tall. He had the same broad shoulders, too. But his rump and belly protruded grotesquely. And those whiskers! Still, there *was* a strong resemblance. She searched his facial features closely but couldn't see much for all the hair. He looked quite ancient and was obviously suffering from some illness, if his glazed expression and the way he leaned against the carriage were anything to go by. Could he be a relative of Montague's? His father? His uncle? The resemblance was too striking.

So now what was she to do? She raised the blunderbuss. There was no help for it. She had to finish the deed . . . as gently as possible. "Your lordship. Please forgive my intrusion, but I must ask that you relinquish your purse."

Jason pressed his shoulder more firmly against the carriage to brace himself. He couldn't keep his legs from shaking or the ground from swaying. If he didn't get this confrontation over with quickly, he would very likely pass out at the woman's feet. And though he had often visualized himself in a prone position while in the company of this particular lady, he preferred that it be at a time when he could fully enjoy the encounter.

Reaching inside his pocket, he pulled out the few coins that he'd been given as change from the carriage fare and extended his hand toward her.

Samantha's heart cracked. The poor old dear. Those paltry coins were probably all the money he had. Then another thought struck her. Had Montague cast aside his elderly relative? Perhaps the old gentleman had come to seek a loan. Had the pompous viscount snubbed his aristocratic nose at the old dear?

No. Montague wouldn't do that, would he? He might be many things, but he had never struck her as cruel or unfeeling—unless this was yet another side of him that she'd never seen before. Giving herself a mental shake, she forced the thought back and pushed the old man's hand away, the money still in his grasp. "No, your lordship. The coins you offer are too meager for my efforts. I don't—"

"Madam," Jason interrupted in a raspy whisper, "if you'll not take my coins, then there is nothing for you. You will have to kill me to appropriate anything else from my person." He couldn't let her strip him again. His disguise would be exposed. And this time he knew he wouldn't survive the ordeal. If she was going to end his life, let her do it now and be done with it.

Samantha tried not to smile at his bluntness. What a proud old darling. Just like Grandfather Fleming. "I see." Clearing a chuckle from her throat, she nodded. "Then if that be the case, I guess 'tis nothing."

Through the slits in the mask her gaze met his for a moment before she turned to mount her horse. As she raised her foot to tap Starburst's hoof she caught a movement from the corner of her eye. She whirled swiftly.

The driver leapt from the top of the carriage. A knife blade flashed in the moonlight as he lunged toward her.

Shock paralyzed her limbs.

The old man muttered an oath, then shot forward. He grabbed her shoulders as if to shove her out of the way.

A sickening thud rent the stillness.

The old man's body jerked. His hands tightened on her shoulders as he sucked in a sharp breath. Then the pressure on her arms eased, and he closed his eyes before crumpling to the ground.

Samantha gasped and sprang back. She leveled the gun at the driver's chest. Fear quaked through her body, and she nearly pulled the trigger. Her heart pounded so hard she feared she might be sick.

The driver stepped back nervously.

Samantha fought for control. Never in her life had she felt such an overwhelming urge to kill another human.

Almost as if he envisioned her thoughts, the coachman dropped the knife and retreated another pace.

Did he realize how close she'd come to killing him? She

chanced a quick look down at the man who had risked his life for her. He lay on his back, his eyes closed, his mouth a tight line of pain. A hand clutched his side, and blood seeped from between his fingers.

Alarm shook her. How badly was he injured? What if he died? Dear God. Her actions had caused this tragedy. And the old man, uncaring of her part in this disaster, had saved her life!

Her stomach knotted, and her attention returned to the driver. "Get him in the carriage," she ordered, "and see that he's taken care of immediately. Your bungling actions may very well cost the man his life."

"My actions?" the driver spat, obviously having regained some of his bravado. "Weren't me who robbed the bloody coach, Scarlet *Strumpet*—were you. Too bad the old gent got in the way, though. Harlots like you deserve t' die." Squatting down, he roughly jerked the injured man to a sitting position.

"Be careful!"

The driver gave a disgruntled snort, but his actions gentled as he lifted the elderly man into the carriage. Closing the door, he turned to retrieve the knife lying on the ground.

"Leave it."

His outstretched hand froze, and he straightened to face her, hatred blazing from murky brown eyes.

Samantha narrowed hers. "Your name?" She stepped closer, her hand aching to squeeze the trigger. "I've learned that it's best to know the names of one's enemies"—she paused meaningfully—"before one buries them."

The frizzy-haired coachman, obviously unconcerned by her threat, faced her fully. His thick lips spread in a menacing smile over tobacco-stained teeth. "Rollie Parker." He dipped his head of bushy red hair. "Remember it, doxy. 'Cause it's me who's gonna put an end t' your shenanigans."

"Put an end to them later," Samantha snapped. "Right now, get that man to a physician." She moved back to Starburst and tapped his hoof. "Kneel."

After mounting she glared down at the red-haired man.

"Rest assured, Parker, I will check to see that you've done as I instructed." Her hands balled around the reins. "And if you have not, or if the old man dies"—her voice trailed off to a whisper—"then your life will be forfeit." She kicked the stallion into a gallop and raced toward the dense woods.

As soon as the forest closed around her Samantha reined the animal to a halt and climbed from the saddle. Choking sobs rose up to strangle her, and she fell to her knees. Hugging her stomach, she began to rock back and forth. Pain such as she'd never known burned through her like a trail of lava. Her shoulders sagged, and the knot tightened in her throat. "Oh, Papa, what have I done? What have I done?"

Jedediah Blackburn heard a carriage approaching down the lane and frowned at Hawk, who sat at the table. The half-breed shrugged and rose to stand by the door. That was one of the few things Jed liked about the Indian. He could always depend on Hawk's loyalty, if nothing else.

Turning, Jed grabbed a musket from its mount above the stone fireplace and crossed to the cabin door. When a body lived in the woods, folks didn't just come calling in the middle of the night—unless it was a damned half-breed escaping the husband of a lusty squaw.

Knowing Hawk would stay out of sight until he took stock of the situation, Jed stepped out onto the rough plank porch to await the arrival of the intruder.

A dingy black coach rolled to a stop near the porch step. "State your business," Jed demanded of the driver.

A red-haired man climbed down and opened the carriage door. "Got a hurt man inside." He gestured with a meaty hand. "Paid his fare t' be brung here. He needs fixin', but I ain't no damned medical man." He reached inside and pulled a bearded man into view. "If the old fool lives, it'll be up t' you. Don't matter t' me one way or the other."

Jed didn't move. Standing with his feet spread wide and the musket leveled across his chest, he squinted at the limp form. "Who is he?"

The driver shrugged. "Gave the name Windhall."

"Damn it!" Jed bellowed.

Hawk stepped through the door into view, his fists clenched.

Jed spoke to the Indian. "Help me get him inside."

They carried the unconscious form indoors and gently eased him onto a rope cot. Covering him with a quilt, Jed turned to face the coachman. "What happened to him?"

The driver hesitated and peered uncertainly at Hawk's deadly cold features. "Uh . . . that female outlaw run him through."

"What?" Jed's head snapped up.

Hawk stiffened, and his eyes narrowed into silver slits.

"When? How bad's he hurt?" Jed jerked the quilt back to inspect the wound, but seeing the protruding belly he knew had to be a disguise, he halted.

"'Bout twenty minutes ago," the driver answered nervously. "Don't know how bad, but he's spilt a bucket a blood. Inside my coach are a mess." He swung his hulking frame toward the door. "An' I got no more time for lallygaggin'. I got t' clean the blasted thing now, afore I can pick up another fare." With one last wary look at Hawk the burly man opened the door and hurried out.

As the door closed behind the driver Jed opened the front of his godson's garments and pulled out several towels. "Which one do ya suppose it is?"

"Jason," the half-breed returned without hesitation.

Jed had to agree. Nick was supposed to be in Williamsburg. Besides, Nick didn't get himself into these scrapes. Only Jason did that.

Grabbing one of the towels, Jed pressed it against the wound, then quickly removed the wig from his godson's head. Black hair tumbled over the younger man's brow, and Jed gently brushed it back, shaking his own graying head. How many times had he tended Jason's wounds? Too many to count, that was for sure. The boy was just too blasted daring for his own good.

Staring down into Jason's pale face, Jed sighed. "What'd

ya get yourself into this time, son?" He glanced up at Hawk. The Indian's head was turned toward the direction of the driver's departure, the harsh lines of his face tight with anger, those iron-gray eyes blazing.

Something cold and ugly snaked up Jed's spine. Either Hawk didn't believe the driver, or his thoughts were already calculating that female outlaw's execution. The half-breed wouldn't take Jason's mishap lightly. His devotion to the twins went too deep for that. Someone would pay for this deed. Jed didn't doubt that. But he couldn't help feeling relieved that *he* wasn't on the receiving end of Hawk's fury.

Rollie Parker slapped the reins of the team and drew in a steadying breath. Thank the moon for his quick thinkin'. That damned injun looked like he'd 'a' slit someone's throat if I'd 'a' tole him the truth about who done that old fool in. He shook his head, and a greasy strand of hair caught in the corner of his lips. Spitting it out, he wiped the slobber from his mouth with the back of his hand. Who'd 'a' thought the old buzzard woulda had an injun for a friend? A mean-looking injun at that. Rollie shuddered, feeling lucky that he'd escaped with his hair still intact. Couldn't trust those bloodthirsty redskins for a second.

Jerking his wool cape closer to ward off the cold, he sniffed and squinted into the darkness. Was that outlaw wench still out there somewhere? He hoped so. Langford said kill the bitch, and that's just what he'd do. "Hell, I already woulda done it if it hadn't been for that old buzzard Windhall. Now I'm goin' t' have t' keep on drivin' this lousy piece of junk they call a coach, just hopin' she'll stop me again. Next time, though, there ain't gonna be no interferin' old goat t' stop me from slittin' her purdy little throat." He laughed harshly. "She oughta knowed not t' mess with one o' Langford's kin. Blubberin' Bartholomew ain't much, but he's Langford's cousin, and that's all that counts."

CHAPTER 11

Samantha shoved herself into a sitting position on the bed and raised a hand to brush a thick tumble of hair out of her face. She couldn't remember ever feeling so tired, so drained. Suddenly the events of the previous night caved in on her. "Dear God."

The strain of her sleepless night made itself known. She had wandered through the forest until mere hours ago, when finally, exhausted and half frozen, she had returned to Riversedge and collapsed. But she had come to a decision. Never again would she risk another's life. Never. She would rather sell herself than go through this anguish again.

Firm in her resolve, she turned to the foot of the bed and retrieved her robe. Before she could devise a new plan to gain the money she needed she had to set her current circumstances to rights. It was time to face Carl. But just as she turned for the door the rattle of carriage wheels sounded out front. Her steps faltered, and she spun with a start. It was much too early for visitors.

Curious, she walked to the window that overlooked the drive and peered out. Below, Peter Hawksley's elaborate coach rolled to a stop before the front door. What in the world was he doing there at this hour?

Belting her robe tighter, Samantha hurried from the room, anxious to see what was afoot. Just as she reached the top of the stairs she saw Peter and Carl disappear into the parlor.

On silent feet she raced down the stairs and approached the now-closed door. Bending slightly, she placed her ear against the wood, listening. Their voices were low and hushed. She stepped closer, and her foot struck the leg of a small table. Her hand shot out to steady it.

For a long moment there was dead silence from inside the room. Then suddenly Peter's shrieky voice rose loudly.

"'Twas most upsetting, I must say. I merely stopped at the inn for a morning cuppa after a boorishly restless night and overheard that coachman. Imagine, that hoydenish outlaw actually stabbed an old man. A sickly old man who couldn't even begin to defend himself." He sniffed loudly. "They should hang the bloody wench, that's what I say."

"Who was he?" Carl asked, his voice sounding anxious.

"Can't say for sure, ol' man. But it seems to me as if someone mentioned the name Windhall." He laughed shrilly. "Of course, that's preposterous. Windhall isn't an old man. Why, he's barely a score and ten. Must be a mistake." Peter paused. "Unless Windhall has an elderly relative. I say, do you think that could be it? Do you think—"

Samantha didn't listen to any more. She turned from the door and fled back to her room, tears tumbling freely down her cheeks. Oh God, *she had been right*.

Carl couldn't believe his ears. Samantha was supposed to have stabbed some sickly old man named—Windhall? How? Wasn't she staying at Crystal Terrace? Wasn't Jason still abed with fever? Christ. What was going on?

Glancing again at the door, Carl faced the younger man. "I'm aghast at the entire story." Well, that much was true. "I certainly have no idea who the old man might be. And as much as I'd like to discuss it with you, Peter, you've caught me at a rather bad time. I was just on my way to an appointment, and if I don't leave momentarily, I'm sure to be late." He had to find out what had happened. And he wanted to know who was in the hall.

Carl strode to the door and opened it. Not a soul was in sight. Damn. "Effie," he bellowed, "fix Lord Hawksley some refreshment and bring it into the parlor." Turning back to Peter, he nodded. "There's no need to rush off, Hawksley.

Enjoy my hospitality, such as it is, and I'll stop by your plantation later this afternoon."

He met Peter's gaze for a solemn moment, then ducked out the door and raced to the stables. He had to get to the bottom of this quickly, before some overzealous fool put an end to Samantha's stunts—permanently.

Saddling his horse swiftly, he leapt astride the animal and reined to the west. He needed to see Jason. Somehow he knew Jason could cast light on this situation.

Realizing the earliness of the hour, Carl let himself into Crystal Terrace through the back door and silently mounted the stairs to Jason's room. Ever so quietly, just in case his godson was resting, Carl opened the bedchamber door.

The tall, dark-haired agent stood beside the window, leaning heavily on the frame, massaging his right side.

"Jason?" Carl said cautiously, not wanting to startle his cohort into a dangerous reaction.

The dark head swung toward Carl. "What's happened to my brother?" he demanded harshly, still rubbing his side.

Stepping into the room, Carl closed the door. "I don't know, Jase. Was Nick disguising himself as an old man for some reason?"

"You've got your twins mixed up, Carl. I'm Nick. And yes, Jason could very well be masquerading as an old man."

Nick? Carl blinked. He never would have believed it. At this moment the erect way he stood, the taut lines of his jaw, and the burning anger smoldering in those ice-blue eyes was every inch Jason. "Damn."

"What's happened to him? I know he's been hurt—I can feel that much. But how was he hurt? And how bad is it?"

"The carriage driver said the Scarlet Temptress stabbed him, but—"

"*What?*" Nick's voice dropped to a low, deadly whisper. "She stabbed my brother?"

"No! Damn it, Nick, there's got to be more to it than what the driver's telling. I'm sure of it."

Nick's mouth tightened, but he said nothing more. And

that frightened the hell out of Carl. Nick was an extremely dangerous man when angered. Unlike Jason, Nick didn't lose his temper. He calmly, coolly calculated every devastating move. And to think that that quiet fury was directed at Samantha. . . .

"Nick?" Carl said softly. "Before you do anything rash, let me find out what really happened."

Nick leaned against the window frame. "He's hurt, Carl. I've got to find him."

"I know." Carl's voice gentled. "But if you leave now, the masquerade will be exposed, and everything Jason did will be for nothing. I'll find him for you, Nick. You have my word on it."

Nick rubbed his side, lines of strain pulling down the corners of his mouth. *"One day."* Lifting his lashes, his cold stare raked Carl. "I'll give you *one day*. If you haven't found him by then, I'm going to." He pushed away from the window. "And if anything, *anything,* happens to my brother . . . I swear on my parents' graves, someone will pay for it with their life."

The glacial expression on Nick's face made Carl uneasy. He'd never looked more like Jason, and Carl didn't doubt for a moment that Nick meant every word he said. Fear for Samantha escalated. How could he protect her? Taking a deep breath, he nodded and turned to the door. "One day."

Nearly eight hours later Carl finally reined his horse down the narrow lane leading to Jed's cabin. Since he'd left Nick Carl hadn't found a trace of Samantha, Jason, or that coachman, Rollie Parker. He'd checked the hidden cave, Hawk's cabin, the tobacco shed, the hotel, everywhere. Jedediah Blackburn was Carl's last hope.

Nearing the log structure, he saw Jed step from the shadows of the porch, gun in hand.

"I figured ya'd show up sooner or later," Jed said, lowering the weapon to his side.

"Jason—"

"Is here." Jed nodded. "And alive."

Relief nearly toppled Carl from the saddle. "Thank God."

For the first time in hours he felt the tension leave his body, and he smiled into Jed's bristly face and warm brown eyes. "Got a glass of whiskey for an old friend?"

The returning smile on Jed's face peeled twenty years off of his age. "It's good to see ya, Carl."

Carl dismounted and shook Jed's hand. "It's good to see you, too, Jed." And it was. Carl had let too many months go by without visiting the trapper who'd taught him, Beau, and Derrick so much about survival. Providence had been with them the day they rescued the old reprobate from a bout with a hungry bear, and a friendship was born that would carry them through many years and many hard times. Without Jed's expert guidance the trio might very well have starved to death that first year in the savage splendor of the Blue Ridge mountains. They might have even perished at the hands of Indians if Jed hadn't been a friend of the chief, Flaming Wing, and convinced him to spare their lives. Yes. It was good to see his old friend.

Entering the cabin, Carl inspected the sparse but comfortable furnishings. Jed had never been one for luxuries. Then, seeing Jason lying on the cot, Carl turned to the old trapper. "How is he?"

Jed lifted a gnarled hand and gestured toward the cot. "See for yourself."

Carl approached the narrow bed and peered intently down at Jason. His cheeks were flushed, but his breathing was even, and he seemed to be sleeping quite soundly. Satisfied, Carl strode to a chair before the fireplace and sat down. "Have you learned what happened to him?"

"No. Jest what the driver tole us."

"Us?"

Jed nodded and handed Carl a glass of sour mash. "Hawk were here when that coachman brung the boy."

"Hawk?" Carl felt sick. "He knows about this?"

"Sure does."

"Damn." Carl knew without a doubt that Hawk would take it upon himself to avenge Jason. He didn't know which was worse—Nick out for Samantha's neck or Hawk out for her blood. Running his hand through his hair, Carl sighed. He had to talk to the half-breed. "Where's Hawk now?"

"Didn't say. But my guess is his papa's village. Knowing the breed, he's probably gone there to get some of them herbs he holds such store by."

"Has he said anything?" Carl gestured toward Jason. "About this, I mean?"

Jed shook his head. "No. But then, you know Hawk. He don't *have* to say nothin'." Jed swallowed a quick swig of his drink. "Anger were written on every muscle in that big, mean body of his."

Carl stared worriedly at Jed. "If I don't see Hawk before I go, make sure you tell him I must see him immediately."

Jed nodded. "Sure." He looked at Jason, then back to Carl. "How's Nick?"

"When I left him a few hours ago he was feeling pretty much like Jason."

Jed smiled. "Still hain't outgrowed them twin feelin's, huh?"

"Will they ever?"

"Prob'ly not." Jed shrugged. "I think that's one of a whole lot of thin's that keeps 'em so close." Jed tossed his drink back. "I heard Nick was in Willumsburg."

"He was. But I had to send him to Richmond in Jason's place when Jason became ill. Nick came back yesterday on his own. Hell, I knew he'd come, but I didn't realize he was already here until this morning."

"Ya never could tell 'em apart, could ya?"

Carl shook his head. "Not with their clothes on. And how you do it in a single glance is almost eerie."

"It's easy when you knowed 'em since birth. While you was in Boston I was there beside Beau the night they were born, pacin' right along next to him. Ya'd 'a' thought I was their papa 'stead of him. I was more shook."

"I'd like to have seen that," Carl teased. "I don't think I've ever seen you with your feathers ruffled."

"It weren't a pretty sight," Jed muttered. He rose and

refilled their glasses. "Has either of them two seen their mama lately?"

"Sybil is not their mother," Carl defended.

"Step-mama, then."

"I doubt if Jason has. But I think Nick did, shortly before she left for London."

"She went back? I thought her papa tossed her out on her tail."

"He did. Something about her being caught with some Frenchman. But word came that the old man died, and like a dutiful daughter she returned." Wanting to avoid the distasteful subject of Sybil Windhall-Kincaid, Carl rose and crossed to Jason's side, placing a hand on the younger man's forehead. "He still doesn't look well."

"I know," Jed said, rising. "But he's improvin'." He walked over to stand beside Carl, his gaze resting fondly on Jason. "And I intend to take real good care of this one. So you can stop worryin'."

"I never doubted it," Carl said, smiling. "And now that I'm sure Jason is in good hands, I'd better get back to Crystal Terrace and let Nick know his brother is safe—before he tears the walls of his room down."

CHAPTER 12

At the edge of the meadow encompassing Riversedge Hawk halted his horse and took in the changing scenery. As the moon rose and the sun receded behind the Allegheny mountains shades of dusk laced the forest with ribbons of blush gold and winter blue.

Winter . . . Hawk felt a tightness remembering the hours just passed. He had not meant to stay in his father's village long, but Winter Flower had beckoned him to her dwelling. Unbidden, his body stirred. She had been his teacher in the ways of a man and woman for many years, and even now, at thirty summers, she possessed the power to arouse him.

He shifted atop his buckskin, Kosh-ki. He would have enjoyed a few more hours on the woman's pallet. If his haste to return to Jason had not been so great, he would have. But Jason needed the *cohosh* herb to strengthen his body and heal the wound inflicted by that woman bandit.

Hawk's mouth drew taut with visions of revenge. No one, female or not, would escape punishment. Hawk would seek the one who had done this to his brother. She would pay. And if Jason died . . . if Jason died, Hawk would end the woman's life . . . very slowly . . . very painfully.

The sound of a rider approaching from the left brought his attention back to his surroundings. Quickly he wheeled his horse behind a spruce and waited silently.

The woman he had met in the glen rode past just a few feet from him, her long black hair swaying against her hips with the movement of her mount, her hand clutching a white bundle.

Intrigued, Hawk guided his horse through the trees, keeping a parallel course with her steed as it cantered toward the cave Jason used for Adversary.

She glanced up, and for a moment Hawk thought she looked directly at the hidden opening, but she then veered away—toward him. With this intimate view he could tell something disturbed her. Her cheeks were flushed, her mouth drawn into a tight line of anger. Or was it pain?

When she reined her stallion to a halt Hawk did the same, then dismounted and crept closer.

She jerked open the bundle and held up a red dress and mask.

His heartbeat quickened with anger. *She* was the one! Clamping down on his rising fury, he watched her every move.

"Never again!" she spat, lifting the gown in a stranglehold. "Because of you I nearly killed a man—may yet have killed him! An old, defenseless man . . ." A tear slid down her cheek.

Hawk frowned. Did she speak to the dress? Why did she cry?

She shook the garment as if it were a wayward child. "As of this day"—she raised the gown toward the heavens— "the Scarlet Temptress is dead."

Dropping to her knees, she frantically began clawing at the soft earth beneath the pine needles, obviously uncaring of the damage she did to her hands or nails. When the hole deepened to her satisfaction she plunged in the dress and mask, then covered the material with angry swipes at the dirt. Afterward she sat there for a moment with her head bowed, sobbing softly.

Hawk felt something tug at his heart. She looked so young, so alone. He cursed. This woman had injured Jason. He would not feel these things for her. He deliberately snapped a branch beneath his heel.

Suddenly her head jerked up, and she looked around wildly, searching the line of trees.

A wry smile twisted his lips. He shifted his weight to make another sound—to let her know she was being watched. But before he had the chance she sprang to her feet and mounted the stallion. Then, with a light kick to its sides, she galloped off toward Riversedge.

Hawk watched her retreat with mixed emotions. His stomach gnawed with a hunger to see this woman who had harmed Jason writhe in torture, but something held him back. Something was not as it should be.

Why would she cry and make those promises to the moon? And why did she seem so upset over her deed? Returning to Kosh-ki, he mounted and turned the horse. He would watch, follow, and learn about this woman. Then, when the time was right . . . he would take her.

When the woman rode up to the barn at Riversedge and dismounted a dark-skinned man came out to greet her, then led her horse into the shelter.

Hawk's fists knotted. The outlaw woman stayed with Carl.

So that is why Silver Hair had left word with Jed summoning Hawk. Hawk snorted and turned his horse around. He would not see Carl. He would not allow the man to sway him from his purpose.

Samantha's uneasiness lingered as she entered the house. She closed the door and drew in a long breath. How ridiculous, she assured herself. No one was out there.

Warding off the sensation, she turned for the hall. It was time to get her confrontation with Carl over. And it didn't take long to locate him and Christine in the parlor.

Carl sprang to his feet. "Where the hell have you been?" He crossed to her in angry strides and grabbed her by the shoulders. He shook her roughly. "Damn you, Samantha. I've been nearly out of my mind with worry. Where have you been? Why did you stab Ja—that old man?" He shook her again. "Damn you. I want some answers!"

Samantha had never seen Carl so livid. "I didn't—"

"Didn't *what?* Didn't stay out all night? Didn't rob that bloody coach? Didn't nearly kill a damn fine man?" He shoved her away from him and clenched his hands at his sides as if resisting the urge to strike her.

Christine stepped forward protectively. "Carl, wait. Please. Give her a chance to explain." Her eyes met Samantha's, silently begging her to justify her actions.

Samantha felt tears threaten to steal her composure. "It was all my fault, but I didn't stab him."

Carl sucked in his breath. "What?"

Samantha moved to stand before the settee. "The coach driver did. He was trying to kill me, but the old man jumped between us." Tears rolled freely down her cheeks. "He saved my life."

"Oh, Samantha." Christine reached out and took one of her sister's hands, squeezing it in understanding.

Carl's features softened a little, but his expression remained stern. "Then why didn't you come home?"

"I did. Then I overheard you and Peter, and I left. I

needed to be alone. I had to come to terms with what had happened." She looked at Carl. "How is he? Have you heard anything?"

"He'll live."

Samantha dropped down onto the settee. "Thank God." Swallowing, she turned back to Carl. "Who is he?"

Carl didn't answer for a moment. Then he shrugged. "A relative of Lord Windhall's."

She nodded slowly, not surprised by the news. "There's a striking resemblance."

Christine, still holding Samantha's hand, turned to Carl. "Can this conversation wait until tomorrow? Samantha needs to be abed. She does not look well."

Carl studied Samantha's face. "Yes, I can see that. Very well." He turned back to Christine. "Get her upstairs." His gaze swung to Samantha. "But rest assured, this episode will be discussed again—at length." Stiffly he turned to leave the room but stopped. "One more thing. Did you—ah—happen to see or hear anyone while you were meandering about?"

Samantha frowned. "No. I didn't *see* anyone."

"What's that supposed to mean?"

"It's foolish, really. But I could have sworn someone was following me. Even as I rode into the stables I felt it. Of course, I'm certain that it was only my imagination."

Carl paled.

Samantha looked at him curiously. "Is something wrong?"

He looked stricken. "Oh, sweet Lord, he *knows.*"

"Who knows? What are you talking about?"

Carl shook his head as if to clear it. "What? Oh, nothing. I—um—was thinking of something else. Listen, you go on up and get ready for bed. I've got an errand to run." He turned and grabbed his coat. "I may be gone for a few days." He glared at Samantha, then stilled. Blinking, he glanced worriedly at Christine. "Don't *either* of you leave this house . . . for *any* reason. And if I'm not back in time for

Peter's soiree, make my excuses." His expression hardened. "And yours." With one last troubled look he left the room.

Nick Kincaid paced before the window for the hundredth time. If he didn't get out of this room soon, he was going to become utterly deranged. Dahlia was determined to keep him a prisoner. Mercy. Couldn't she tell he wasn't Jason? That he was quite fit? Of course not. She hadn't seen him unclothed, so how could she? She'd never been able to tell them apart otherwise—especially if they didn't want her to.

He stared down at the sheet wrapped around his bare waist. After that other old woman, Madeline, had told Dahlia she'd found Jason returning from a ride, Dahlia had even taken the clothes from the room, just to make certain he didn't try anything so foolish again.

Nick gave a disgusted snort. You'd think after all these years the woman would be able to tell them apart. Lud. He was going to murder Jason for this—now that Carl had informed him that Jason was all right.

He moved to the window and brushed aside the curtain, which had become his habit during the last week of confinement. He'd thought about telling Dahlia his true identity, but he couldn't do it, not even for his own peace of mind. Dahlia would worry herself into an unscheduled grave over Jason if she knew the seriousness of his injuries. And Jason would kill him for upsetting her.

He dropped the curtain back into place. How many hours had he sat staring out the window, watching the deer and horses in the field? A hundred? It certainly felt like it. It was either that or read, and he'd already read until his vision nearly failed him. A couple of times he'd entertained ideas of escaping through the secret tunnel, but where could he go without clothes? The only ones awaiting him at the end of the tunnel were the Devilrider's. And *those* would most likely get him hanged.

He lifted the curtain . . . again. Well, he mused, perhaps today the ritual would end when John Falwick came—if he came—and pronounced Nick healthy. That shouldn't be too difficult, since he'd never been ill to begin with. And why hadn't the physician come sooner? That emergency trip to Five Forks shouldn't have taken him more than a few days, and it had already been over a week.

He looked back down at the horses, suppressing the urge to saddle a mount, to feel the leather beneath his legs, to smell the fresh—free—air. Shaking his head, he recalled how much he'd hated horseback riding . . . until now. Confinement obviously dulled the brain to the point of inertia.

Yesterday he had realized how bad off he'd truly become when he'd actually been delighted to accept an invitation—as Montague Windhall—to one of Peter Hawksley's atrociously dull parties at the week's end—if the physician ever returned to assure Dahlia her charge would survive.

Nick paced to the bed and back. How was Jason doing now? he wondered. He sensed that his brother felt better even though he was still very ill. And why had that woman outlaw stabbed him? What had his brother done to incite such a deed? And he didn't doubt for an instant that Jason *had* done something.

"Lord Windhall?" a man's voice said softly from the door. "How have you been feeling?"

Nick's head shot up, and a smile spread across his face. A short, round little man smiled gently. Strips of gray hair protruded above each ear, and small, square wire-rimmed glasses bordered his tiny brown eyes.

"Mister Falwick!" Nick's hand lunged forward in greeting. "You don't know how happy I am to see you. Dahlia just wouldn't believe me when I assured her I had quite recovered. Now perhaps you can convince her."

The older man chuckled. "Let me check you over first, son, then I'll give you my decision. How's that?"

"Yes. Yes, of course." Nick nodded vigorously, moving to the bed in long strides.

An hour later Nick took the reins from Bromley and jumped on Apollo's back. Kicking the horse's sides, Nick sped away from the stables as if the forks of Satan were after him.

It felt marvelous to be out in the open again. He was free. At last, he was totally free! No more sponge baths. No more of that punishing tea. No more tasteless, soft food. No more coddling!

He nudged Apollo into a full gallop and raced across the meadow with wild, reckless abandon. All he wanted to do was get into town and order the biggest, hottest meal the Merryman Hotel had to offer.

The snow, glaring from the sun's reflection, nearly blinded him. The wind, cold and biting, nipped his cheeks. But he felt great. Nothing could mar this perfect moment.

As he raced along the edge of a thick crop of pines another rider suddenly emerged directly in his path. Nick jerked back sharply on the reins. Apollo balked, sending Nick from the saddle like a wild arrow. He smacked against the base of a dead stump.

The other horse reared up, and its rider fell backward with a scream-filled flop.

Aghast, Nick leapt to his feet and ran to the lady's side, praying she hadn't been injured. But all he could see of her was a mound of lush yellow velvet and a pair of very shapely legs.

Shoving aside the material, he located a slim hand and pulled the woman to her feet. When her head came up and she looked into his face his breath caught somewhere in the region of his heart. He had never seen a more stunning, achingly beautiful woman.

Her smooth cheeks were streaked with snow. Gleaming raven-black curls had tumbled loose and fell in silken waves around her ivory face beneath a pert lopsided hat. The bodice of the riding habit had split, revealing the pearly swells of her full breasts. And her sweet lips formed such an adorable pout that he wanted to lean forward and kiss her.

Shocked by the scandalous thought, he shook his head and asked hurriedly, "Are you all right? Do you hurt anywhere? Would you like to sit down a moment?"

Christine Fleming peeked up at the strange man and nearly swooned. He was so devastatingly handsome he took her breath away. Pieces of bark clung to his thick black hair. His brown velvet coat was torn at the shoulder, as was his shirt, revealing smooth bronze muscles down his arm. He was so tall her head barely reached his shoulder. And those eyes! They were a startling pale blue against his dark skin, trimmed with the longest, thickest black lashes she'd ever seen.

Her gaze drifted to tight buff breeches, covered with grass and mud, that clung to his long legs and muscular thighs with such daring accuracy that she felt heat rise to her face. He was magnificent.

She swallowed before attempting to answer his questions. "Um—no, I do not think I need to sit down. I will be all right in a moment. I am not injured, just a little unsettled." And not just from the fall, she admitted to herself. She looked down at her severed bodice and quickly pulled the pieces together, her cheeks stinging with embarrassment.

Nick was held motionless by the color of her brilliant emerald eyes. He felt as if he were sliding down the side of a grassy knoll toward a shimmering green pool, knowing he was going to drown, and not caring in the least. "Ah—um, are you sure you're not injured?" Very good, Nick. That should impress her—if she likes idiots.

"Yes. Truly, I am fine. A little tattered, perhaps, but quite well." She smiled warmly.

Nick melted. "Good." He nodded, feeling himself grin stupidly, wondering if he looked as dumb as he felt.

"I am afraid it was my fault," Christine said. "I was not paying attention."

"Absolutely not," Nick corrected gently. "I am to blame. I should never have ridden at such a hectic pace, especially not in an area where other riders might be about."

Christine's left cheek dimpled.

Nick's knees nearly buckled.

She laughed softly at the expression of sheer chagrin on his face. "I suggest we share the blame equally and call it a stalemate."

Nick flashed her a smile. "Yes, milady." Suddenly a

thought occurred to him. "Where is your escort? Have you become separated?"

"Er—" Christine, having been blinded by that engaging smile, found herself groping for words. She could not tell him she was out alone. No lady would go anywhere unescorted. Darn Samantha for catching a chill, and darn that scrawny little man for bringing an urgent message to deliver to Carl's overseer, David Brown. And most of all, darn Samantha for pleading with her to deliver the message until she gave in. What could she tell this man? She certainly could not say she had been separated from her chaperon, or he would insist on taking her to the nonexistent woman. Oh, gracious. "Um—my companion and I were—um—experimenting with different routes through that small thatch of woods." She raised her hand, pointing to the forest she had emerged from moments ago. "I am supposed to meet her on the other side of that rise." She swung her hand to a small woody knoll.

"Then I'll ride with you to assure you arrive safely."

"No! I—um—mean, no thank you." She lowered her lashes. "You see, I would be severely reprimanded were I discovered in the company of a gentleman . . . unchaperoned."

Nick tried not to show his disappointment. "Of course. I understand. And I certainly wouldn't want to cause you any further distress."

Christine blushed and turned toward the horses. "Do you think I might prevail upon you to retrieve my mount? I really must be going before I am missed."

"Yes, yes, of course." Nick nodded and turned for the horses.

Christine watched the length of his long, graceful stride as he crossed the small glen. He was so tall, so finely built, so handsome. . . .

When he returned with her mare and extended his hand to help her mount she could not suppress a tremor as a tingle shot up her arm. Once in the saddle she stared down at him for a long moment, committing his face to memory. "Take care, milord," she said softly. "And watch out for any other careless riders."

Nick chuckled and nodded. "You, too, milady."

Watching her ride away, he sighed, then brought his foot up to the stirrup. Suddenly it hit him. "What a blithering fool! You meet the most beautiful woman in the world and *forget to ask her name.*"

CHAPTER 13

For several days Samantha wandered no farther than the river beside the house, pondering her feelings of guilt over that last fateful robbery and trying to discern another means to gain the money for her father. She seriously considered posing as Christine and playing chess for wagers but decided against it. There just wasn't enough time, and there was always the chance—slim though it might be—that she would lose. Hadn't Montague proven that?

The money she had saved thus far was perhaps a third of that required. If only there was some way to get the entire amount at one time. She frowned as something eluded her, then brightened when she recalled it. The shipment of tax money. The *reported* shipment, she corrected. But how would she find out for certain if there was one?

She rose and paced the room. Only one person in the territory would have access to that knowledge—Joshua Minter, the customs official. Peter's uncle.

Racing from her room as if the hounds were after her flesh, she charged into Christine's room. "What time is Peter's soiree tonight?"

Christine blinked at her twin's uncustomary entrance. "Why?"

"Because we're going to attend."

"But Carl said—"

"I know. But we have to go. It's urgent."

"Samantha, I do not think—"

"Please?"

Christine blinked again.

Samantha felt herself flinch, knowing Christine was shocked by the uncharacteristic plea. "Truly, twin, it's important. I may find the key to Father's dilemma tonight at the soiree."

Christine sighed in defeat. "Oh, very well. Although I have no idea how *you* are going to explain to Carl."

Samantha grinned. "I'll think of something. Now, what time does it begin?"

"Are you going as Madeline?"

"No. As you."

"Have you lost your senses? Both of us cannot appear at the same function."

"We won't. Now what time?"

"Eight o'clock."

"Good. I'll be ready by seven-thirty."

"But—"

Samantha didn't hear the rest of Christine's words as she left the room.

Four hours later Samantha joined her twin in the bed-chamber to dress.

Christine frowned as she slid her arms into the sleeves of a pink silk gown. "Are you certain you should be doing this?" she asked worriedly. "Not to mention that Carl is going to be livid when he finds we have disobeyed him."

Lacing the front of an identical pink gown, Samantha shrugged. "Carl won't find out if we can return early enough. And this is an opportunity too good to miss. If there's any truth to the tax shipment rumor, then the evidence should be in Peter's uncle's files."

"What if you are seen?"

"If I'm seen on the grounds, they'll just think I'm you." Samantha grinned. "And if I'm seen near Mr. Minter's office, whatever companion you're with at the moment can vouch for your whereabouts. Either way, you won't be implicated."

"I still do not like it. Suppose something goes wrong?"

"It won't. Relax, twin. Have a little faith in your big sister."

"Big sister? Samantha, eleven minutes hardly justifies that title."

Samantha's smile widened. "Minutes or a year, it makes no difference. I got here first, so I'm the elder."

"No wonder you continually lead me astray."

Samantha laughed at the truth of that statement. All their lives she had been the leader and Christine the follower. And of course, Christine had been quick to point out that fact to their father whenever they were caught in the act of a scandalous mishap.

"Have you heard anything more about the old gentleman you injured last week?"

Samantha grimaced. She wished Christine wouldn't put it that way. "Only that he's recovering. But I can tell you I nearly fainted when I learned the man was Lord Windhall's relative. I swear the Windhall family is out to plague me."

A knock sounded. "Yo' ready, chile?" Effie called through the door. "Dat skinny lord jest gots heah."

"Thank you, Effie," Christine answered, and she hurriedly tied the sash around her waist. "I will be down momentarily." Her fingers stilled, and she looked blankly at Samantha. "Lord Hawksley's coach? How ever did you manage that?"

Samantha grinned. "I sent him a message declining tonight's invitation . . . due to lack of transportation."

Christine chuckled. "Oh."

With Christine's toilet complete, she turned to Samantha. "What time will you arrive?"

"About an hour after you. I'm going to have to travel pretty slowly so I don't ruin my gown in that rickety old carriage out back. And I'll have to leave it some distance from Peter's house and walk the rest of the way. I'll come in through the garden. Keep an eye out for me so you'll know when to mingle with the guests."

Christine nodded and turned to the door. With her hand on the knob she stopped and looked back. "Be careful, Samantha."

"I always am," Samantha said lightly, hiding her trembling hands by jerking on white velvet gloves. She'd never attempted to break into someone's office before. But if there was any truth to the tax shipment, and she could get her hands on it, she'd have enough to send men after Father.

The evening passed with paralyzing boredom for Nick. He had arrived early at Peter's request to entertain the guests while Peter and Lady Millworth went to fetch someone named Christine Fleming.

Nick stood at one end of the elegant ballroom listening to the lifeless conversation of Minerva Carstairs and Lord Wainwright. Minerva, he had to admit, looked quite lovely. Gowned in jade silk, her pale curls piled high, she was indeed a becoming sight. Unfortunately, her wit suffered under the weight of those bulky curls. And her sultry sidelong glances made him decidedly uncomfortable.

It was obvious to anyone who had vision that the widow had her sights set on Montague Windhall. Nick smiled. How would Minerva react to the real Lord Windhall? Though well proportioned, the man had the wit of an imbecile. Nick's grin widened. What a delightful match.

Casting off thoughts of Minerva and the real Montague, Nick idly scanned the crowded room. The Hawksleys spared no expense when it came to entertaining, he noted dryly. Fine displays of crystal and china lined one long linen-covered table against the east wall. Beside that, at an angle, sat another with an array of food fit for George himself. On a raised platform before the curve of a glass alcove several musicians dressed completely in white murmured softly among themselves as they tuned their instruments.

Nick felt someone's hand touch his arm and turned, startled.

Minerva smiled invitingly. "I understand they play exceptionally well." She nodded toward the musicians. "I look quite forward to listening . . . and dancing"—she paused meaningfully, making a suggestive survey of his torso—"to their renowned melodies."

"Er—yes, of course, my dear," Nick whined, then he cleared his throat. Mercy. He hated this foppish ruse nearly as much as Jason. He looked around for a means of escape. At that moment he saw Peter emerge from the hallway, his head bent as he spoke to Lydia Millworth. Nick started to turn back to Minerva and excuse himself when he noticed a small woman on Peter's other arm. He went numb. It was she! The mysterious horsewoman from the meadow. Minerva ceased to exist.

Christine felt a steady, increasingly warm stare and, as if drawn by an invisible force, looked across the room. Her stomach fluttered. On the other side of the ballroom, next to Minerva, stood the man she had met in the glen a few days ago. Dressed in a braided jacket of gold velvet over brown satin breeches with tiny bows tied at the calves, he was pulse-stopping.

When her eyes met his and held across the laughter-filled room Christine felt an odd sensation spread through the nether region of her body, and she blushed profusely.

Nick's heart raced. She was even more beautiful than he remembered. Her silky upswept curls, piled fashionably high, glistened with soft white powder. Her long, slender throat was bare except for a pink velvet ribbon and a small ivory cameo. The bodice of the gown she wore dipped so low, he feared that she might overspill its bounds at any moment. He pulled in a strained breath.

Nick wasn't even consciously aware that he'd moved until he found himself standing in front of the magical creature, his hand extended. Mercy. Had he truly walked away from Minerva?

Christine, lost in the depths of those shattering blue eyes, placed her trembling hand in his warm brown one and curtsied. His hand tightened before he returned her greeting with a low bow and kissed her fingers. "Milady."

The haunting strains of the minuet began, and wordlessly, his gaze holding her prisoner, he led her toward the line of dancers.

Christine did not think her feet touched the floor during the entire set. She was only aware of the feel of his hand on hers. His tantalizing fragrance, a mixture of spice and another masculine scent she could not put a name to, teased her heightened senses. She felt intoxicated by his nearness.

But all too soon the music ended.

Nick didn't want to let her go. He felt he should have been stunned by his thoughts, but he wasn't. Deep down he'd always known that when he met his life-mate, as Hawk would call her, he would know it instantly. And he had. Nick had known the moment he pulled her from that bed of pine needles. Moisture beaded on his forehead. Mercy. Even the mere mention of the word "bed" in her presence nearly sent him into a state of apoplexy.

"Christine, my dear, I must say I wasn't aware that you and Lord Windhall had been introduced." Minerva's voice jerked Christine back to the crowded room. Lord Windhall? Was this the man her sister had disrobed? Oh, gracious. Her cheeks burned. Oh, my!

Lord Windhall smiled down at her, his sapphire eyes caressing her face. "Yes, Mrs. Carstairs," he said in a nasal lilt. "Christine and I are well acquainted. We met"—he paused and held her gaze with humor-filled eyes—"some time ago."

Christine blinked at the sound of his voice, then let out her breath and nodded quickly. "Oh, yes. Lord Windmill—*hall*—and I have known each other for simply ages." Her relieved look met his laughing one. How dare he make sport of her? Her mouth tightened. "That reminds me, Lord Windhall—"

"Christine, my dear," he interrupted, "how many times have I implored you to call me Montague?"

"Lord Windhall," she returned firmly, "how have you been feeling since that horrible ordeal with the bandit?"

"Very well, thank you. As a matter of fact, I feel better tonight than I have in years." He removed his handkerchief, gave it a flick, then dabbed his nose before returning it to his sleeve. Then his eyes locked with hers. "And, my dear, I'm afraid it's solely due to your presence."

Christine's cheeks felt as if they were on fire.

Minerva snorted. "Well, Montague, I see that you are quite occupied at the moment." She glared down at Christine. "Perhaps I'll speak to both of you later." With a disdainful sniff she turned regally and walked away.

Nick couldn't take his eyes off of Christine. Her cheeks were an adorable shade of pink. "You look overly warm," he said, inflecting just the right note of concern into his voice. "Perhaps a glass of punch and some cool air would not be amiss?"

"Yes, thank you." Christine felt very flattered by Lord Windhall's attention, yet confused by his manner. He did not seem at all like the man she had met in the glen. Yet he intrigued her. "I would like that very much."

Nick drew her arm through his and moved toward the doors leading to the gardens. He stopped momentarily beside a beverage table and appropriated two glasses of punch.

Outside he led her toward the end of the dormant flower beds. He set the goblets on a wooden bench and removed his coat to drape it around her shoulders. Then, retrieving the punch, he led her farther away from the house down a rock-lined gravel path. When they were well away from the other brave souls fording the February chill Nick turned to hand her one of the glasses.

When she reached for the crystal, light from the full moon bathed her in silver, and he found himself staring speechlessly. His hand shook, and punch trickled over his fingers.

Christine bit back a giggle.

"Sorry." He smiled crookedly, handing her the glass, then flicked his dripping fingers before rubbing them down his thigh. "I'm not usually so inept."

Nick took a sip from his own goblet. He needed to find another topic of conversation before he made a complete fool of himself. He lowered the goblet. "Peter mentioned your last name was Fleming."

She nodded and set her glass on a low stone wall.

"Hmm. Any relation to Derrick Fleming?"

Christine felt a wave of panic. What was she supposed to say? Samantha and she had never discussed the possibility that someone in the area might know their family. Heavens. What was she to do? Looking about quickly, she noticed they stood near a rosebush. What she needed was a diversion. "Well, I—" She reached out and touched the bush, deliberately pricking her finger. "Ouch!" She clutched the injured member, squeezing it hard until a droplet of blood seeped through the whiteness of her glove.

"What is it? What happened?"

Christine winced at the look of genuine concern on his face. "It is not severe. I merely pricked my finger on a thorn."

Nick set his glass down beside Christine's. "Here, let me look at it." He lifted her hand and removed the glove, causing a quiver to chase up her arm. He raised her hand to view the injury in the soft glow of a torch, then brushed away the speck of blood. "Truly it's not so severe." He smiled and brought it gently to his lips. "Save what it does to my heart."

When the moist warmth of his mouth closed over her bare fingertip Christine thought she might collapse at the deliciously wicked feelings that raced through her body. She lifted her gaze to his. Something intoxicating flared between them, and the world went still.

With aching slowness he released her finger and leaned forward, lowering his head, his lips a heartbeat from hers. A wave of unfamiliar sensations washed over her, frightening her with their intensity. Confused and a little anxious, she blushed and turned away. The movement caused her to catch a flash of pink over Lord Windhall's shoulder. *Samantha.*

Nick wanted to kick himself. He was having a devil of a time maintaining the Windhall ruse, just as he had that day in the glen. And he feared he was moving too fast. This is a woman of gentle breeding, for goodness sakes, not some trollop at Madame La Rue's. He backed up a step, needing to put some distance between himself and Christine's tempting little body.

"Perhaps we should go in now. It's getting rather chilly, don't you think?" He winced at his own words. He hadn't meant them as a pun. If he didn't get out of here soon, he was going to put his foot in his mouth—all the way up to his knee. He started to turn.

"No!" Christine cried. She had to keep him from seeing Samantha! Grabbing his shoulder, she pulled him back around and threw herself into his arms.

Nick was caught off guard by her forwardness. Then, as her small, warm body molded against his, sanity fled. With a moan he captured her lips.

Not ten feet away Samantha stood frozen in the shadows with her hands clasped over her mouth. A knife plunging into her heart couldn't be any more painful than the sight of her twin in Montague's arms. Visions that she'd never been able to clear from her mind rose. Images of his lean, dark body stretched out against white sheets, and the taste of his heated lips. Blast the man! Was he going to plague her forever? There hadn't been a day since that fateful robbery that she hadn't thought of him. She turned away from the painful sight.

Lowering her hands, she took a deep, steadying breath. She wouldn't look at them again. She would continue as if she hadn't seen them. With her heart lying in the pit of her stomach she kept her eyes averted until she heard them leave, then waited a few more minutes before making her way around the gardens and entering the house through the servants' entrance. She couldn't let thoughts of Christine and Montague distract her. Not now.

Hurrying through the maid's quarters and up the back stairs before she was seen, Samantha slipped into the upper hall, thankful that Carl had once mentioned Mr. Minter's study was located on the top floor.

There were only three rooms on the upper level. Moving to the nearest one, she tried the latch. It was the room set aside for the ladies' use—and fortunately unoccupied. The next was locked. Samantha gnashed her teeth and walked to the last. Behind that she found a storage room. Obviously the locked one was the study. Suddenly her hopes soared. Were the rooms connected? Possibly by a balcony? Smiling, she slipped inside the dusty room and closed the door. Blackness claimed her surroundings.

Though edging very slowly across the chamber, she still managed to bump into several pieces of furniture and a wooden crate before she found the door to the private veranda.

She expelled her breath and slipped outside to check the balcony. It was not connected as she had hoped. At least four feet separated it from the other one. Peering down at the billowing gown she wore, she shook her head. She couldn't possibly jump that distance in this dress.

Retreating back inside, she raised her skirt and untied the layers of full petticoats, sliding them down over her hips. Still the gown was too cumbersome.

Sighing, she removed the rest of her clothing, then her shoes. She gathered the gown, petticoats, and slippers and placed them in an empty crate near a sheet-covered chair. It didn't matter if they wrinkled. As soon as she completed her search she would sneak out the way she'd come in.

Wearing only her chemise, she inched out the balcony door and walked over to the wood baluster, then looked down. A hedge ran the length of the house just below. She drew back, and a knot grew in her stomach. The ground looked so far. But there was no other way to reach the study.

Summoning all her courage, she climbed up on the rail and stood, keeping her balance by placing her hand on the side of the building.

She shook off the anxiety that challenged her resolve and gauged the distance to the other balcony again. It looked even farther than it had moments ago. This is insane. Only a fool would attempt something of this nature. Then visions of her father's gentle face, thin and drawn behind cold black bars, rose to haunt her.

She clamped her chattering teeth together and took a deep breath. Looking straight ahead, not daring to glance down again, she let go of the wall and lunged.

She grabbed the opposite railing with both hands. Her body swung out. Her stockinged feet dangled in midair. She bit her lip to keep from crying out. Her heart beat at a frantic pace. Good Lord!

With her fingers in a death grip around the banister she slowly raised her leg and brought her knee to the outside edge of the veranda floor. Pulling herself up, she hugged the rail until she was able to roll over the top.

She slid to the floor and lay on her back, her heart slamming against her chest, her breath coming in short, painful gasps.

Slowly her heart rate began to settle, and her stomach started to vibrate with uncontrollable laughter. That had to be the craziest thing she had ever done. No one with a drop of sense would do something like that.

Rising, she pressed the latch and opened the door. Relieved, she quickly slipped inside and made her way to the fireplace. She located a small taper and flint on the mantel, then, after lighting it, moved to the desk and sat down. She rifled through the papers on its top first, but they made little sense to her. They seemed to deal with a cargo of some sort.

Delving further, she opened the drawers. They contained two ledgers and several receipts. Two ledgers? How odd. She placed them side by side and compared them. They revealed the same information, but the recorded amounts varied. She leaned back in the chair. Why would anyone keep two ledgers? And why would they record different amounts for the same expenditures?

After searching the room thoroughly and finding nothing she walked over to the fireplace and leaned against it. There was no place left to look. She stared down at the intricately patterned carpet in the center of the floor. If she had information she wanted to keep to herself, what would she do with it? Burn it? Dropping to her knees before the fireplace, she dug through a mound of ashes. Still nothing. She started to rise when she noticed a charred wad of paper in the far back corner.

Carefully extracting it, she straightened and moved closer to the light. It was only partially destroyed.

With gentle tugs she untangled the papers and spread the scraps across the desk. They looked to be parts of a bill of sale. There was a piece of a note with just the words "Raleigh Tavern" written on it. And what looked like a receipt for . . . what was that word? Weapons? Still, nothing concerning any tax shipment.

Deciding to keep the scraps until she had more time to examine them, she shoved them into the bodice of her chemise, then turned for the door. She'd pressed her luck far enough tonight; it was time to go.

Suddenly voices penetrated the heavy oak door. *Close* voices. Someone was coming!

"Oh, no." Panic gripped her by the throat. She had to get out of there. Blood racing, she fled toward her only escape—the balcony.

She didn't stop to think, she merely leapt onto the railing and dived for the opposite veranda. Her hands groped for the opposite banister—but caught only air.

Hawk stood, arms crossed, leaning against the trunk of a towering pine near the edge of the garden, still stunned by what he had seen.

For the last week he had watched the black-haired woman. He had seen her leave Riversedge each morning and walk down to the river. Her lovely face had been drawn into a frown, her eyes rimmed with red as if she had been crying.

He had watched her sit for hours on the bank, staring at nothing, twisting a blade of grass between her fingers. At those times he had fought the urge to go to her, to ease her pain. But because of Jason he could not.

He had followed her here tonight, stayed back, hidden in the trees. Though his vision of the gardens had been impaired, he had seen her sneak along the hedge-trimmed border, then later observed her outrageous antics on the terrace. He could not help but admire her courage.

His attention drifted back to the balcony, and suddenly he saw her burst from the door. He jerked upright. She was not going to stop!

Without hesitation she jumped on the rail and dived for the other veranda.

He sucked in his breath and watched helplessly as she fell. Damn! Instantly his legs were in motion as he raced toward her unconscious figure lying in the shadows.

When he reached her side he knelt and gently brushed aside the heavy curls at her temple. Blood seeped from a thin cut near her hairline. Her head had struck a stone.

Swearing beneath his breath, Hawk scooped her up into his arms and hurried toward the forest where his horse was tied. He knew enough about the white man's laws to realize that if she were captured, she would hang. His gaze lowered to the woman's face. He could not let that happen. He had other plans for her.

CHAPTER 14

As Hawk headed back to the trees carrying his slight burden he passed close to the gardens and saw Nick emerge from the house with a woman in a pink dress. Hawk's stride faltered. The woman looked familiar.

Stepping behind the shelter of a spruce, he watched through a part in the branches as Nick placed his arms around the woman in a protective gesture. Her head rested against his shoulder, a hand raised to her temple. They stood silently together for a moment, then the woman lifted her face and looked up at Nick.

Hawk inhaled. His gaze flew to the face of the woman he held in his arms, then back to the woman with Nick. A low rumble began in his chest and rose to a soft, deep laugh. "Damn."

Still smiling, Hawk pulled his burden close to his chest and turned to Kosh-ki, then lithely swung onto the stallion's back. He did not quite understand why, but perhaps it was not good to take the woman now. No. He would wait to see what transpired when Jason recovered. Besides, he now knew where to find the girl—when he wanted her.

That he had unwillingly come to admire the woman and her bravery Hawk tried not to think about. Nor did he choose to consider the fact that, were she an Indian, he would have taken her to his mat—to his heart. She would make a worthy life-mate.

Hawk snorted at his wayward thoughts and shifted his delicate load to a more comfortable position. No *white* woman was worthy of anything. His own mother—*white* mother—had taught him that.

He looked down at the dark-haired beauty. Still, this

woman *was* different. She was fearless . . . and gentle. He did not know her motives, but he knew her actions had been prompted by something important to her.

After retrieving the old carriage he had seen the woman leave in the forest, Hawk headed for Riversedge. As the back of the plantation came into view he slowed the buckskin and team. He knew where to take the woman. He had seen her pacing before an upstairs window several times. At least he thought it was her.

Leading the horses behind the stables, he eased from the saddle and quickly scanned the area. No one was in sight. Silver Hair could not afford many servants, and at the moment this pleased Hawk. It would be difficult to battle an enemy with a woman in his arms.

All remained silent as he slipped inside the house and carried her up the stairs. After locating the bedroom he assumed was hers he turned back the bedcovers and gently laid her down.

Just as he pulled the sheet over her she moaned and lifted her lashes. She stared at him curiously, yet showed no sign of fear. "Hawk," she whispered, then she frowned as if confused. "Who *are* you?"

"No one special, little outlaw," he answered in a hushed voice. He brought his hand up and lightly stroked her pale cheek. For a long moment he watched her, enchanted by the outlaw woman's exquisite features. He explored her loveliness, then focused on her full, soft lips that dared a man to taste their sweetness.

Shocked by his thoughts, he tightened his mouth and forced himself to remember the pain of his mother's rejection. White women were not to be trusted.

Though his thoughts were bitter, his senses were not. Unconsciously he slowly examined her slim body, outlined by the apple-green quilt, lingering on the swell of her tempting breasts. He felt desire stir and, aware of the potential danger of the situation, turned for the door.

"Please." Samantha raised a slim hand. "Won't you tell me why you're here?" She could not explain the easy, almost familiar companionship she felt with this man, and her gaze roamed over his face as if the secret would unfold from there. His skin was dark and framed by thick black hair that was tied at the back of his strong neck. Extravagantly long, straight lashes rimmed deep-set silver-gray eyes. Candlelight wavered on the hollows along his hard jawline and firmly sculptured mouth.

"I intended to punish you," Hawk answered, surprising himself by revealing his aim.

By the time the import of his words sank in he was gone, and Samantha lowered her hand to the covers. Punish her? What had she done to warrant such a thing from an— Indian? Her heart started to pound. Yes. He *was* an Indian. She had seen a likeness of one at the fall fair last year.

She closed her eyes and gently rubbed the tiny cut on her temple, her thoughts tumbling chaotically. Why would an Indian want to punish her?

"Samantha?" Christine's voice called anxiously from the hall. "Are you here?"

She sat up, flinching from the pain in her head as she clutched the covers to her chest. "I'm upstairs."

Footsteps sounded in the corridor, then the door burst open and Christine hurried inside, her face flushed, her expression tight with concern. "Oh, Samantha, what happened? Are you all right? When I felt that pain in my head I thought you were d-dying. . . ." Her lips trembled, and tears began to gather.

Samantha winced, realizing how distraught her sister felt, and she opened her arms.

Christine crumpled against her, tears streaming down her cheeks. "Oh, sweet heaven, Sam. If anything happened to you, I could not go on. I was so frightened, so afraid that you had been killed."

"Shh," Samantha soothed. "I'm all right, and so are you. Now come on, you'll make yourself sick if you keep this up."

Sniffing, Christine raised her head. "What happened?"

"I was nearly discovered in Mr. Minter's study, and I

tried to escape rather hurriedly. Unfortunately, my timing was off when I attempted to jump from the balcony."

"Jump! Are you insane?" Christine looked horrified. "You *could* have been killed!" A fresh surge of tears erupted. "I cannot take any more of this. It has to stop. Please, Sam, I have already lost Father. Do not let me lose you, too."

"Father isn't lost. And don't ever let me hear you say that again!" Samantha snapped, shaking Christine roughly. "I won't allow him to rot in that prison. No matter what we have to do, no matter what *I* have to do, Father will escape and return to us."

"You mean return to the *one* of us who still breathes, do you not?" Christine said stiffly.

"No," Samantha answered with gentle insistence. "I promise you, twin, we will both be on hand to greet our father." Feeling the small cut on her head begin to throb, Samantha leaned back against the pillows. "But things had better start improving soon if I'm going to see that end."

"Did you not find anything of value in Mr. Minter's office?"

"No. Nothing." She frowned, then reached into the bodice of her chemise. "At least I think it's nothing." She withdrew the charred papers. "I did find these, but I'm not certain what they represent." She tossed them on the bedside table. "And right now my head hurts too much to think about them."

Christine looked concerned. "Effie has already retired, but if you like I will fix you a cup of tea."

Samantha smiled weakly, knowing what a magnanimous gesture Christine was making by offering to lower her station long enough to complete the disgracing task of preparing tea. "That would be fine, twin. Thank you."

Samantha's thoughts turned back to the strange Indian when Christine had departed to the kitchen. He had saved her yet intended to punish her. Why? She brought a hand to her brow. Her head ached. She couldn't think properly. But tomorrow, she thought, she would try to sort it out.

Christine returned with the tea and poured Samantha a cup. The steaming, sweet brew did help relieve the ache and clear her thoughts. She looked at Christine sitting in the tapestry chair next to the bed and remembered the scene she'd witnessed earlier. "Christine? Were those Lord Windhall's arms I saw you in?"

Christine blushed to her toes, then straightened her shoulders and sat up stiffly. "Yes. And it was all your fault."

"What?"

"Well, it was. You were right behind him, and he was about to turn around. He would have seen you if I had not done *something.*"

"My compliments on your ingenuity, twin. But did you truly have to kiss him?"

Color flooded Christine's cheeks. "Well, no. That was his idea." She rose from the bed and paced to the fireplace and back again. "But how could I blame him? Why, I literally attacked the poor man." Her hands twisted the pink folds of her gown. "He must think I am a . . . a . . ."

"Wanton? Harlot?"

Christine paled. "Oh, no. Do you imagine he does?"

Samantha chuckled. "No, twin. I was merely attempting humor. He probably enjoyed the encounter immensely and is counting his blessings at this very moment."

"Do you truly believe so?"

Samantha mentally rolled her eyes. Christine's life had been much too conventional. And Samantha didn't have the heart to tell her sister that her first summation had probably been correct. The man undoubtedly thought Christine a loose woman. Samantha smiled inwardly. Well, if she knew her twin, Lord Windhall would soon find out how inaccurate he'd been. "I'm certain of it," Samantha answered. "But don't be surprised if he comes calling on the morrow."

Christine looked stricken. "Tomorrow? Oh, no. Whatever shall I do? How can I face him?" She collapsed back into the chair. "I cannot face him. I will never be able to face him again."

"Yes, you will. All you have to do is give him a good sound

reason for throwing yourself in his arms." Samantha hesitated. "Other than the real one, that is."

"Oh? And what might that possibly be?"

"Tell him . . . you saw an Indian, and it scared you."

"What?"

"An Indian," Samantha repeated. "You know, a red man with buckskins. Tell him that it scared you so much you nearly fainted."

"That is the most absurd thing I have ever heard."

Samantha arched a brow but didn't mention her visitor. "If you can think of anything better, I'd like to hear it."

"All right," Christine agreed with a heavy sigh. "After all, I would rather have Lord Windhall think I am a lunatic than a tainted woman." Christine rose and crossed to the door, then looked back. "Are you sure you are all right?"

Samantha nodded.

"Good. Because tomorrow, if Lord Windhall makes an appearance, I will expect Aunt Madeline to be there as chaperon."

"I don't care what Hawk told you," Jason spat, whirling on Jedediah. "I am *not* going to eat any more of those damned leaves!"

"Ya mule-headed—"

"No," Jason grated firmly. He clutched the baggy satin breeches to his waist and stomped across the cabin to where Jed sat at the table. Jason's hand slammed down on the surface. "In the last fortnight I've swallowed enough medicine to last me a bloody lifetime! And furthermore, tonight I am returning to Crystal Terrace, where I can get some peace and . . . decent food."

"Boy, ya ain't got the brains God gave a grasshopper."

"You could be right," Jason said tiredly. "But I've taken all the coddling I'm going to. I feel all right now. Damn it, why can't you accept that?"

"Fine. Go ahead. Go back to that fancy house and them cold-eyed servants. Don't make me no never mind."

"I'm not trying to hurt your feelings. I'm just tired of

being fussed over. Come on, Jed," he cajoled. "Let's not part with angry words between us."

"Wouldn't be the first time."

Jason smiled. "No, it wouldn't. But I'd feel better about it."

"Humph. I still don't see how ya can go back with Nick there anyway."

"I'll dress as the old man, and if I meet anyone on the road, I'll introduce myself as Leopold, Lord Windhall's father."

"That ain't very respec'ful of your step-grandpa."

"I don't think he'll mind." Having never met his stepmother's deceased father, Jason wasn't overly concerned one way or the other. "Besides, it won't be for long. Just until Nick and I can switch places again."

"Will Nick go back to Willumsburg?"

"Yes."

"What's he doin' up there, anyway?"

"Smuggling goods." Jason grinned. "Silk and fine lace, I believe."

"Them sounds like real necess'ties."

"Evidently the wealthy think so. And the profits are used to fund the minutemen." Crossing to the cot, Jason sat down and pulled on his stockings. "Do you have a horse I can borrow?"

"Ol' Molly. But send her back as quick as ya can. I need her fer haulin' pelts."

"I'll send Hawk back with her as soon as possible." Jason rose, shoving towels down the front of his breeches and buttoning them. He watched Jed shake his head in unconcealed disgust as Jason made his transformation into an old man.

It wasn't an easy trip. He started out late, and the wound in his side, though rapidly healing, still ached. Molly's plodding gait jolted over the frozen, rocky hillside, jarring him so much that he had to clench his teeth in order to bear the pain.

Ironically, by the time he reached Crystal Terrace Jason closely felt like the old man he appeared to be. He could feel the deep lines etched into his forehead, and his hands trembled from cold.

Dahlia wasn't surprised by the tired, elderly gentleman who appeared on the doorstep at three o'clock in the morning. It took her all of fifteen seconds to realize it was Jason. But, she didn't chastise him, and within moments she had ushered him into the parlor and had a steaming cup of tea laced with brandy sitting before him.

Maybe it was a good thing he looked so ghastly. Perhaps his twin wouldn't be so apt to fly into a rage over the little switch Jason had pulled on him. Of course, if Nick did start fuming, Jason could always remind his brother of that time he'd sent Jason to Lorelei Whitcomb's dinner party, knowing that two of Nick's mistresses were going to be in attendance.

Swallowing some of the soothing tea, he leaned his head against the back of the settee. He didn't doubt Nick was going to be a little upset—or very upset—but with his head pounding the way it was, he just hoped his little brother would wait until morning to reproach him.

"Jason?"

At the sound of his name Jason swung toward Nick, who stared anxiously from the doorway. He was dressed in a long wine-colored dressing robe tied at the waist, and furry drawstring slippers peeked from beneath the hem.

"That is *you* behind those whiskers, isn't it?"

"Yes, little brother. Although I must admit, I doubt if anyone other than yourself would be able to tell."

Nick smiled and shoved his hands in the pockets of the robe. "I probably wouldn't have been able to either, if Carl hadn't forewarned me of your disguise. You look positively horrid."

Squirming against the uncomfortable padding lining his hips and stomach, Jason brushed a glob of powder from his eyelash. He wished he were in bed right now—naked and free of these encumbrances. He could certainly do with a night of uninterrupted sleep . . . without medicine. "I probably feel worse than I look. So if you plan to chastise me, I beg you wait until tomorrow. I'll be able to handle it better then."

"Chastise you? Whatever for?"

Had Nick been hit on the head? He couldn't be serious. "Don't play games with me, little brother. I'm not in the mood for it. I know you're angry about my switching places with you, and I'll be happy to listen to your views on the subject after I've had a good night's rest."

"Oh, that. Yes, I was put out at first, but now—well, I can see that you actually did me a favor."

"What?" Jason straightened in his seat. "What favor?"

Nick crossed to the fireplace and leaned against the mantel. "If you hadn't switched places with me, then I wouldn't have met Christine Fleming."

Jason frowned. He'd heard that name somewhere before. "Who the hell is Christine Fleming?"

"Only the most beautiful woman God ever put on this earth." Nick grinned. "She's Madeline Traynor's niece."

Jason groaned. *That's* where he'd heard the name. "And you're thanking me? Now I know you've injured your head."

"My head? What are you talking about?"

"Nothing." Jason waved his hand. "Continue."

"Anyway, it's a long story, so I won't go into it tonight, but I want you to meet her tomorrow. I'm going to call on her at two o'clock."

"Not a chance, little brother. I plan to catch up on some sleep before you return to Williamsburg."

"No."

"No? What do you mean, no?"

"I'm not leaving."

"Damn it, Nick, you have to go back. I don't know anything about the smuggling operation in Williamsburg."

"There isn't anything pressing right now. The blockade has just about halted all activities, except Clayton Cordell's ship, and it was crippled by some pirates." Nick withdrew a hand from his pocket, giving it a flick. "I'm staying."

Jason choked back a string of curses. What in the hell was the matter with Nick? Jason studied him closely, then stifled a low moan. He had seen that look on Nick's face too many times not to recognize it. Nick was in love . . . again.

Rising slowly to his feet, Jason removed the wig and tried to tame his tousled hair. He'd been through this a thousand times. And from past experience he knew there was only one way to handle Nick's dalliance and get him back to Williamsburg where he belonged.

Jason had done it before, and he would do it again. All it took was a few well-chosen words—and actions—to convince the lady in question that Nick—Montague Windhall —was a rake of the first water and totally undesirable. Of course, convincing Madeline might be a little tougher, since she knew Montague well. But he'd pull it off.

Moving toward the door, Jason stopped and glanced back over his shoulder. "What time did you say *we* are going to call on Christine Fleming?"

CHAPTER 15

As Samantha had predicted, a note from Montague arrived the next morning declaring his intention to call on Christine at two o'clock that afternoon. Tarrying over her toilet, Christine was not ready when Effie announced his arrival, so it was left up to Samantha, dressed as Madeline, to entertain him until her twin made an appearance.

Samantha hadn't seen Montague up close since the morning she surprised him in dirty riding clothes, standing in the guest room at Crystal Terrace, so she wasn't prepared for the change in him.

Today he was dressed in pale blue satin, nearly the same color as his eyes. His hard masculine features, softened by rice powder, appeared somehow less threatening.

He was still undoubtedly one of the best-looking men she'd ever seen, but something was different. His carriage was more erect and formal, rather than the lithe grace she'd noticed the night she'd robbed him. His movements seemed more refined. But the most startling change was his mouth. Before she had noticed a hard, almost cynical curve to it, a dangerous slant, whereas now it tilted up in a gentle bow.

The viscount handed his cloak to Effie and turned to speak to someone behind him. Samantha swallowed a gasp of surprise when she saw the old man who had saved her life. What was he doing here?

Montague turned back to her and smiled as he approached her. "Lady Traynor, how are you?" he asked in that awful high-pitched voice. Then, lifting her hand, he kissed it.

Samantha frowned down at his bent head. Why was he being so formal? She studied the elderly bearded man, and her confusion increased. He seemed to be scowling about something. Mentally shrugging, she turned to Montague as he rose. "I'm quite well, young man. And I can see that you are doing equally as well," she announced in her scruffy cadence.

"Yes, yes. I truly am." The creases in his cheeks deepened. "And I've brought someone to meet you." He gestured to the older man. "Lady Traynor, may I present my br—father, Leopold Windhall."

Father? Oh, Lord. "How do you do?" Samantha nodded as Leopold, too, kissed her hand. Then, turning back to Montague, she frowned. "Your father, you say?" She looked into the older man's eyes, and something tightened around her heart. "Yes, I can see the resemblance."

"I've heard a lot about you, Lady Traynor," Leopold grated in a raspy voice. "I hear you took good care of my boy."

"Actually, it was Dahlia who did all the work. I merely sat

up with him a few nights." She swung her hand in the direction of the settee. "Would you gentlemen care to have a seat? Christine won't be joining us for a few minutes yet."

Montague nodded and sat on the settee indicated, but Leopold chose a chair near the fireplace. His movements, she noted with surprise, were oddly fluid and graceful as he lowered himself onto the feather cushion. How could that be? He must be nearing sixty. And the last time she saw him he certainly didn't walk that well.

Shaking off the thought, she moved near the door. "Would either of you care for some tea?"

"What kind?" both men blurted in unison.

Samantha checked a smile. "Mint, I believe."

Montague looked embarrassed at the sudden outburst, but Leopold merely looked relieved. Why? He had never tasted Aunt Katherine's tea, had he? She grinned inwardly. His son had probably told him about it.

Montague smiled sheepishly. "That would be fine."

Leopold's eyes held hers as he nodded.

Suppressing an odd shiver caused by that knowing stare, Samantha excused herself long enough to inform Effie, then returned to take the chair opposite the elderly lord. "I understand that you were i-injured in a mishap with a highwayman recently."

"Woman," Leopold corrected. "Highway*woman*. And yes, I was wounded."

"If I ever get my hands on the bloody wretch who did it, I'll see her hang," Montague injected heatedly.

Leopold's head swung toward his son. "The Scarlet Temptress didn't accost me. The driver of the coach did."

Montague stammered. "But I thought—mercy. Everyone believes the outlaw did it."

Samantha felt her insides quiver.

Leopold looked stricken. "Who the hell started that rumor? Do you realize half the imbeciles in Lynch's Ferry will be out to do her harm? The next time she robs a coach she could bloody well be killed."

"Good riddance, I say."

Leopold tensed and looked as if he wanted to strike his son.

"Um—I understand, Leopold, that you just arrived in Lynch's Ferry." She directed the conversation to a safer subject, one that didn't turn her insides to jelly. "Where are you from—originally?"

"England, then later Shenandoah," he snapped, his attention still on Montague. "I have a plantation called Halcyon there."

"Halcyon? What a strange name. What does it mean?"

He shrugged. "Peaceful or calm. Mythology claims the Halcyon was a legendary bird who supposedly calmed the wind and sea at the winter solstice."

"And is it peaceful there?"

The white beard stretched into a smile. "Very."

"I've never been to Shenandoah myself, but I hear it's quite lovely. Isn't that somewhere near the southern Allegheny mountains?"

"Yes," Montague answered for his father. "And it's much more than that. It's beyond lovely—it's majestic. Just standing on the balcony of Halcyon overlooking the paddocks is enough to inspire one to take up painting. Or poetry."

"It sounds as if you love your home very much."

"I do."

"Why do you stay here then? Especially in winter?"

"Er . . ." He looked helplessly at Leopold.

"We've just recently purchased Crystal Terrace," Leopold spoke up. "My son is here to oversee the spring planting of the tobacco. Right now he's trying to procure a taskmaster and several field slaves."

The rustle of satin brought everyone's attention to the parlor door.

"I am sorry to be so late," Christine said shyly from the archway.

Christine, Samantha noted proudly, had never looked lovelier. Her raven hair was left unpowdered, flowing in shimmering waves to her waist and held loosely away from her face by a pale green satin ribbon.

The dress she had chosen was of the latest Paris fashion. Yards of ivory petticoats flowed from the open front of the skirt, flanked by draping layers of lime and forest green. But the square neckline of the gown gave Samantha cause for concern. It plunged scandalously low, and Christine's dusky pink crests perched daringly near the lace trim. One wrong move and Samantha feared her twin would pop out of the bodice.

She glanced at Montague and clenched her teeth. Small beads of moisture had formed on his forehead. She turned to Leopold. He looked pale, almost as if he'd seen a ghost. His eyes were wide with shock, his jaw agape, and his gaze glued to Christine. Lecherous old fool.

Samantha rose, as did the men. "Christine, I'm sure you know Montague Windhall."

Christine nodded but stared at the floor.

"And this"—Samantha gestured to the bearded man—" is his father, Leopold."

Christine raised her head and smiled. "I'm pleased to make your acquaintance, your lordship." She extended her hand and curtsied low.

Only momentarily speechless, Leopold seemed to regain his composure quickly, and he placed a kiss on the back of Christine's hand. "Not nearly as pleased as I am, milady."

Samantha could have sworn she heard a husky overtone in the older man's deep voice.

Turning back to Montague, Christine offered her hand. "It's nice to see you again."

The look on the younger man's face reminded Samantha of an adoring puppy whose master had just patted his head. Her heart sagged. Obviously the man was awed by her beautiful sister. For the second time in her life Samantha felt the tearing bite of jealousy.

Samantha's hands drew into fists. What was the matter with her? He had kissed her two times—in a feverish delirium—and she was acting like a love-bitten schoolgirl. This must cease. The man meant nothing to her. But try as she might, she couldn't stop the memory of his hands in her hair, or the feel of his long, hard body hot against her flesh, or of his mouth, hungry and demanding on hers.

In an attempt to repress the memory she looked at Leopold. His attention was on Christine's and Montague's clasped hands, his lips drawn tightly together, almost as if he were angry. Didn't he approve of Christine?

"Er, Christine, why don't you go see what's keeping Effie while I show the gentlemen the gardens?" She turned to Leopold. "If that meets with your approval."

He pulled his attention from the pair and nodded stiffly.

Montague, though, looked perplexed as he watched Christine depart. "Um, perhaps I'd better wait inside. I've—er—still not fully recovered from my bout with the chill." He smiled. "You two go ahead."

Leopold hesitated. Then, releasing a slow breath, he, too, nodded. "As you wish." He extended his elbow to Samantha.

She laced her hand through his arm and was shocked by the feel of hard, taut muscles beneath her fingers. Her gloved hand trembled, and Leopold's came up to cover it. The heat from his palm seared all the way to her toes, and her gaze flew to his. Their eyes met and held. Something intoxicating swirled through the air. His hand jerked almost as if he was as stunned by the encounter as she.

Samantha recovered first and gestured toward the glass doors leading to the veranda. "This way, your lordship." Why did her voice sound as if she'd been running?

"Won't you need a wrap?"

Samantha knew she should wear one. After all, elderly ladies never went out in chilly weather without a shawl, but the way her pulse drummed and warmth rose to her face, she'd probably break out in a heat rash.

"No. I'm not likely to expire from a little cool weather."

"Very well, madam, lead the way."

Once they reached the gravel path that led through a

winding maze of hedges Samantha stopped abruptly and faced the old man. "Why don't you care for my niece?"

"What makes you think I don't?"

"Leopold, we are too old to play children's games. Why don't you just tell me the problem? Perhaps we can resolve the situation."

He looked thoughtful for a moment, then nodded. "Perhaps you're right, Lady Traynor." He touched a leaf on the hedge with his gloved finger. "My son is a fine man. Unfortunately, he loses his heart quite frequently, shall we say, to beautiful, wide-eyed young ladies such as your niece. He has a job to do—at Crystal Terrace—and it's presently being neglected."

"And you think my niece is the cause of this neglect?"

"Not entirely, no. But as I'm sure you've witnessed, her lovely presence is definitely distracting him from his purpose." He frowned suddenly. "Speaking of your niece, did she by chance help you when you cared for my son during his illness?"

"Why do you ask?"

He shrugged, and his belly rose with the movement. "Montague mentioned something about seeing a beautiful apparition with black hair and green eyes. She certainly fits the description."

Samantha swallowed. Visions of the times Leopold referred to rose to taunt her. She could still feel the strength of Montague's arms around her, his lips caressing. She removed her hand from Leopold's sleeve and hugged her upper arms. "I believe she did sit with him once or twice while I ran an errand," she lied smoothly.

"I see." He stared thoughtfully at a row of winter crocus, then reached down and picked a small white bud, twirling it between his gloved fingers. "How old is she?"

"Eighteen."

"That young?"

Samantha smiled. "Well, to you and I certainly. But I don't think your son thinks she's too young."

"No, I don't suppose he does." Suddenly his expression

hardened, and he turned abruptly. "I think we should go in now, before they—er, I mean—I'm starting to feel chilled."

Samantha watched him curiously, then nodded in agreement and started back down the path. Her foot caught on a root protruding through the gravel, and she pitched forward.

Leopold grabbed for her, but his big belly got in the way. Overbalanced as he was, they both went sprawling into the hedge.

Samantha's hands flew to her face to stop a shout of laughter. The way Leopold was spread out in the hedge beside her, on his back with his stomach bubbled skyward, looked utterly ridiculous.

Recovering instantly, he sprang to his feet and reached to assist her. She kept her face covered lest he see her mirth.

Evidently he mistook her quivering shoulders for tremors, for he pulled her gently to her feet, then into his arms as far as his belly would allow. "Are you all right, Madeline? Please don't cry." His hand stroked up and down her back in a soothing gesture. It felt so wonderful and so warm that she pressed closer, her breasts flattening against the solid wall of his chest, his soft belly curving beneath her bosom, cushioning her stomach. His hand stilled, and he moved back to look down into her face. His forehead creased; sky-blue eyes locked with hers, searching, probing. Then, as if remembering where he was, he released her abruptly.

Fear spiraled through her. His hands had been on her back, one part of her that wasn't padded. Had he guessed her secret? Oh, please, no.

"Are you all right?" he asked coldly.

She nodded.

"Let us go inside, then."

His stilted manner worried her. Had his hands told him she wasn't the old woman he believed her to be? Or was he appalled by the fact that he had held her so close? Neither prospect was very appealing.

Stepping back through the still-open glass doors, Samantha nearly crashed into Leopold's back when he came to an abrupt stop. "What?" She darted a look into the room.

Christine was in Montague's arms in what could only be interpreted as a searingly passionate kiss.

Samantha felt the blood drain from her face.

Leopold balled his hands into deadly fists, and when he spoke his voice was so low, so dangerous that a tingling of fear snaked up Samantha's spine.

"Release her at once, Montague."

The couple jumped apart.

Christine blushed profusely and stared at the floor.

Montague, on the other hand, smiled brightly. He didn't seem in the least contrite. Didn't he fear his father?

Samantha peeked quickly at Leopold's face. He was furious. His eyes were blazing slits, his lips a tight line. If she hadn't known better, she would have sworn Leopold was jealous of Montague.

Intrigued, she watched as he slowly unfurled his hands. For just an instant something ugly flickered in his expression, then receded behind a wall of cold blue ice. When at last he spoke his voice held all the reassuring warmth of an avalanche. "We're leaving—*now,* Montague."

As soon as the two men departed Samantha turned on Christine. "What was all that about? Christine, don't you have a bit of sense? I can understand you wanting to kiss Montague. He's very attractive. But with his father here? Have you lost your senses?"

Christine flounced down onto the settee. "I have truly made a muddle of it now, have I not? Oh, Samantha, I do not know how it happened. One moment I was standing there talking to him, and the next I was in his arms." She stared down at her tightly clasped hands. "It was not something I planned. It just happened." Her lower lip trembled. "Now his father is going to think I am a . . . a strumpet." She whispered the despicable word.

With a sigh Samantha sat beside her sister and pried her hands apart. How could she blame Christine when she herself had fallen under Montague's irresistible spell? "I doubt that," she tried reassuring Christine. "He hasn't lived to his great age without experiencing a good deal of life.

Besides, he's probably seen his son's charm at work more times than we can count. I doubt if he'll blame you. If anything, he'll probably horsewhip his son for corrupting an innocent."

"Oh, no! I could not bear it if Montague were harmed because of me." She scrambled to her feet. "I must speak with his father at once."

"Leopold? Oh, no, Christine. You'll only make matters worse. I'll go. The last time you tried to explain your way out of something Father locked you in your room for two days."

"I doubt if he will listen even to you, Aunt Madeline. He was terribly angry when he left."

"I'm not going as Madeline. I'm going as Christine. Now come upstairs and help me change."

"You'll never make me believe that," Nick stormed at his twin.

Jason sighed and tossed his wig on the bed. "Damn it, Nick. I *saw* the Temptress. I saw her mouth, her chin, and her breasts above the crimson gown. I tell you Christine is the same woman." He turned furiously on his brother. "God's teeth! She even came to see me when I was ill— probably to examine her handiwork. I kissed her, held her. Do you think I wouldn't know the same woman I caressed so intimately? Do you think I wouldn't recognize that taunting laugh she has? Well, I do. I'm telling you, Nick, Lady Christine Fleming is the Scarlet Temptress. And by damn, I'll prove it to you."

Nick shook his dark head. "It must have been someone who looked like her. She's too genteel, Jason. She would never be able to do something like that. You don't know her like I do. She's a true lady. I would stake my life on that."

"Not if I could help it," Jason shot back. "Because you'd lose, little brother. She *is* the Scarlet Temptress."

"You wouldn't want to place a little wager on that, would you?"

"Name it."

"A thousand pounds against Adversary."

168

Jason faltered. Adversary? His stallion? "Name something else."

"Not so sure now, are you, big brother?"

Jason gritted his teeth. He couldn't let Nick get the better of him. Besides, Jason knew he was right. "Done." He spun on his heels and moved toward the door. "I can use the extra cash. Now if you'll excuse me, little brother, I intend to spend the next hour"—he pulled at the fake beard—"in the bath, getting rid of Leopold."

Nick laughed. "Too bad. I was beginning to like the old gent." He straightened the lace cuffs below the sleeves of his satin redingote. "While you're about that, I am going to call on Peter. I'd like to know what information he might have to impart. I heard a rumor this morning that last eve Hawksley manor was set upon by thieves."

Jason's hands stilled on the beard. "The devil you say. By all means, find out the particulars. It should prove most interesting."

After Nick left Jason sought the bath, but his mind was on the incident at Hawksley's. Was the Scarlet Temptress involved? Hadn't Christine been at Hawksley's last night?

An hour later Jason slipped on his buff breeches and a flowing white shirt, his black hair still damp and gleaming from its recent scrubbing. Lord, it felt good to wear his own clothes again.

"Your lordship?" Dahlia said from the other side of the bedroom door. "You've got a caller—says her name's Lady Fleming."

Jason started. What in Providence did *she* want? Damn. He didn't have time to dress as Leopold. Then he smiled. Perhaps this was his chance to learn more about the oh-so-proper Lady Christine . . . and perhaps give him an edge toward winning his wager with Nick. "Thank you, Dahlia," he called back. "Go on about your business. I'll see to the lady."

Standing in the spacious red-tiled entry, Samantha waited for Dahlia to summon Leopold while idly fingering the skirt of the gown she wore—Christine's green satin.

"Lady Fleming?" a deep voice said from behind her. "You wanted to see me?"

Samantha whirled sharply and came to an abrupt halt. In her wildest imaginings she hadn't expected to see Montague— *this* Montague—facing her in the hall. "No. I wanted to see your father."

"Why?"

Samantha stared at the floor. It was either that or devour that gorgeous chest. Why was he dressed like that? "I—um— wanted to explain. I don't want him taking his ire out on you over what happened at Riversedge. It was my fault. I should never have allowed you to k-kiss me."

Jason moved to stand in front of her. Then his eyes lowered to her mouth. "I enjoyed kissing you," he said gently, truthfully, remembering the night of his fever.

Samantha glanced about nervously. Why did his husky tone do such strange things to her? Heavens, she could drown in that voice. "Well, I"—she swallowed—"enjoyed kissing you, too. But I don't want your father angry because of it."

Jason edged his finger beneath her chin and tilted her face up to his. "My father isn't here—nor is he the ogre you believe him to be. I'm quite certain he still remembers what it was like to be young"—his gaze captured hers—"and in love."

Samantha's heart tripped. She hastened to change the subject. "He was angry when you left. I just assumed . . ."

Jason brushed his thumb over the curve of her lower lip. "Shh." He didn't want her to speak. Besides, he was having trouble concentrating on her words. Every movement of that sweet mouth pulled him closer. God. He had never wanted to kiss a woman so badly.

Samantha stared dumbly up at him, desperately wanting to feel the warmth of his lips.

Jason slid his hand along her cheek, caressing a path to the back of her neck. Slowly he inched her forward until her breasts touched his chest. Minor explosions erupted in his body, and with a groan of deep, voracious need he lowered his mouth to hers.

Samantha felt as if she'd turned to liquid. Pleasure trembled through her at the gentle, erotic movement of his lips on hers. Without her realizing, her hands moved to stroke his wide shoulders and tight muscles before slipping higher to encircle his neck. Her movement brought their bodies fully together, and she felt a shudder reverberate through him. With a low, almost pained animal growl he molded her to him and parted her lips.

Her gasp was silenced by the gentle brush of his tongue as it slowly entered her mouth. Desire spread through her with the swiftness of a flame as he continued the delicious assault, his hands sensuously massaging her shoulders, his chest firm against her tingling breasts. Hesitantly her tongue touched his. With a mixture of terror and excitement she felt the hardening of his lower body against her belly.

For the first time in his life Jason was completely ruled by his emotions. This woman affected him in a way that no other woman ever had—perhaps ever would. He knew he should halt this insanity, but he couldn't. Of its own volition his hand rose and closed over her firm breast. A jolt of urgency tore through him as her nipple hardened against his palm. She trembled, and a hot ache of desire shot to his loins. He slid his other hand down to her hip and pulled her hard against his burning arousal.

Genuine fear—whether from him or herself she couldn't be certain—brought her back to sanity. She had to stop this madness *now*. "Montague, cease this, I beg you."

Jason was too lost to hear, much less comprehend, her plea. He took her mouth again and again.

Dear Lord, she prayed, he must stop. Samantha's thoughts tumbled frantically for a solution. Then, summoning all her strength, she placed her hands against the front of his shoulders and gave a hard shove. "Stop this at once!"

Coming out of a fog, Jason blinked. "What?"

"How dare you maul me in such a manner?"

"*Maul* you?" He sounded shocked.

"It certainly appeared that way."

"Why, you little Jezebel." His eyes flashed angrily, and he stepped closer. "Just who do you think you're trying to fool? You enjoyed that little skirmish every bit as much as I did."

Samantha felt the blood rush to her cheeks at the truth of his words and drew on her anger. "Skirmish? *Skirmish.* How dare you? Why, you oafish clod, your touch leaves me cold," she lied defensively.

A muscle along his jaw began to throb, and Samantha backed up.

"Shall I show you how my touch truly leaves you?" he asked ever so softly, advancing a pace closer.

She knew she couldn't withstand another assault on her senses. Dragging in a deep, fortifying breath, she lifted her chin. "You, *sir,* are quite incapable of showing me anything of interest." With as much hauteur as she could manage she whirled to the door and jerked it open. "Good day, your lordship."

Retreating as quickly as she could while still maintaining her dignity, she scampered into the carriage, her pulse pounding, her hands shaking. How dare he say those hateful things? How *dare* he! She had only sought to stop the kiss before it got out of hand. But for him to call her a Jezebel—and to call that beautiful kiss a mere skirmish! Of all the nerve. She flounced back against the velvet upholstery. The womanizing blackguard! And she'd felt guilty for the way the Scarlet Temptress had treated him. Ha! The swine deserved everything he got—and more.

Suddenly an idea flared, and her lips spread into a slow, wicked smile. Her hands relaxed, and she smoothed the folds of Christine's gown. She chuckled low. Perhaps it was time for the Scarlet Temptress to arise from the dead—and make another scandalous appearance.

CHAPTER 16

When Samantha arrived home she was in such a hurry to reach her room that she nearly collided with Effie.

"Whoa, girl, slow down. Yo' sista ain't up deh. She went with dat Pamela girl." Effie handed her a sealed parchment. "I was jus' takin' dis to yo' room 'fo yo' 'bout run me down."

Samantha smiled as she recognized Nichole Heatherton's handwriting. "Thank you." Grasping the envelope, she ripped open the letter from her very best friend, anxious for the latest word from England.

Dear Samantha,

I have been trying to keep up with all the news concerning your father. And, in doing so, I have learned that he is to be brought to trial in midsummer. As you know, the magistrate has strong proof against your father for treason. And it may be enough to convict him.

The sheriff was furious when he could not find you or Christine. I think he had hopes of bringing the two of you in for questioning. He probably thought one of you might say something to implicate your father. But then, he does not know you like I do.

My own papa has been raving for the last fortnight about the injustices your father and several others have suffered at the hands of the king's men.

I heard him talking to Maman just this morning. Samantha, he is actually making plans to move to the colonies. He said my Uncle Arthur has a small plantation near Bedford County, in the Augusta lands, that he has offered to my papa for a piddling sum. As I understand it, the plantation is very near Riversedge. Won't it be wonderful to live close to each other again?

Do they truly have Indians there? I . . .

Still grinning, Samantha hurried upstairs and placed Nichole's letter in her cedar chest along with the others. She didn't know whether to be happy or worried that her father wouldn't be brought before the magistrate until summer. It gave her more time to gather the funds for his rescue. But it also gave her a time limit. What if she couldn't acquire the money before then?

Sitting down at her dressing table, she removed the ribbon from her hair and drew a brush through her thick curls. Perhaps her vengeful plans for Montague weren't so far-fetched after all. Her father must be freed. And for that she needed money—lots of money.

Montague was the perfect victim. The womanizing fool has more money than brains—or so she'd heard. She set the brush down. As soon as she changed she would need to reclaim her crimson costume and set her plan into motion.

For an instant she hesitated, recalling what had happened when she'd last worn the dress. And what about her vow? She clamped down on her feelings of guilt and the sting of her conscience. She had to do it. But nothing would go wrong. She wouldn't let it. And this time she would get her due.

Jason still mumbled to himself as he strode into his study and poured a healthy shot of whiskey. Damn the woman. Why did she infuriate him so? God's teeth! He'd never been one to lose control. In his line of business one had to have a clear head. So why was she able to unsettle him as no other?

A knock sounded at the door.

"Jason?" Dahlia called through the closed portal. "Hawk's waiting for you down by the river."

Hawk? What in the world was he doing here at this hour? Jason wondered. "Thank you, Dahlia." He grinned as he pulled on a light coat. He was a hell of a lot more comfortable dressed as himself while at home.

Remembering Hawk, Jason shook off thoughts of comfort and raced down the stairs, then out the back door. As he neared the river's edge he didn't see Hawk. But then he hadn't expected to. The man could blend into the woods like raindrops into a stream.

"Hawk?"

Like an apparition the half-breed suddenly appeared in front of him. "Greetings, brother."

Jason smiled and clasped his hands. "Good to see you, my friend. But why have you come here?"

Hawk studied Jason solemnly. "I bring news of the one called David Brown. He has been taken by soldiers. They boast how they would torture him to find the location of the iron machine."

"Bloody hell! Do you know where they're keeping him? Does Carl know about this?"

"I doubt it. He rode along the north trail earlier. I do not think he has returned yet. As for where the printer is held . . ." Hawk shrugged.

Jason frowned distractedly and again extended his hand. "As always, brother, your news is appreciated. I just hope the Devilrider is able to find and free the man before it's too late."

"I will come with you."

"No. I don't want you involved in this. If I'm captured, I'd just as soon hang alone."

A black brow climbed Hawk's forehead. "I would just as soon you did not hang at all."

Jason grinned. "Now *that* we can both agree on. Take care, my brother. And thank you. Oh, and when you get a chance, could you take Molly back to Jed?"

Hawk nodded, raised his hand in farewell, and slid into the trees.

Jason turned and strode toward the house, but just as he approached, Dahlia came out the door carrying a folded parchment.

"Carl's servant Hadley just brought this." She extended the note.

Jason took the missive and opened it quickly. The deep, bold strokes of Iron Sword leapt from the page.

My friend,

David Brown has been placed under arrest by the king's men. Should you wish to alleviate this situation, he is being held in the cellar at Hawksley's.

It is my understanding that there is to be a small supper party there this evening. But the odds are not in your favor. Four soldiers occupy the barn, and Captain Harvey Langford is a guest in the main house. Fortunately, only one guard has been assigned to watch David Brown.

Jason crumpled the note. "I've got to go out."

Dahlia's concern couldn't be concealed. "Be careful, son."

He reached out a hand and squeezed her elderly one. "I will, Dahlia. Don't worry." Then, brightening to ease her fears, he asked, "Aren't you supposed to go to evening services tonight?"

"Yes."

He smiled and winked. "Then just for good measure, remember me in your prayers." Planting a light kiss on the aged cheek, he bounded into the house and dashed up the stairs. He wanted to get changed and be gone before Nick returned. His little brother might want to assist, and Jason had enough problems worrying about himself and David.

Retrieving his black costume from the cedar trunk and realizing at once that Dahlia had cleaned it, he smiled, then quickly picked up a lighted candle from the mantel. Turning, he slipped behind the wall tapestry and opened the concealed door to the tunnel.

Within minutes he'd passed through the damp corridor and emerged into the trees just below the hidden cave. As he approached the crevice Adversary gave a soft, low snicker.

With only quick stopovers from Carl to feed Addy while Jason was ill, and Jason's limited visits since, he knew the stallion would be eager to escape his stall.

Half an hour later, as he approached Hawksley Manor from the stretch of forest that bordered the east side, Jason saw the sentry posted near the root cellar door. Hatred flared at the sight of the man's uniform. Could he be the one who had killed Father? Instantly Jason berated himself. The man wasn't old enough. Relaxing his curled fists, Jason's thoughts turned to Iron Sword. So far his information had been correct. But then it always was. Now all Jason had to do was figure out a way to get rid of the guard—preferably without killing him. Maybe if he clubbed him with the hilt of his knife . . .

Leaving Adversary in the woods, Jason stealthily made his way to the edge of the trees. Seeing his path was clear, he bolted for the side of the mansion. In the shadows he flattened himself against the outside wall and inched toward a nearby window. He could hear the tinkling of glasses, music, and boisterous laughter coming from inside.

Slipping the knife from the waist of his breeches, Jason crept silently toward the back of the building. Just as he passed the protruding brick of the main fireplace he heard the front door open. Concealing himself in the small shadow afforded by the bricks, he held his breath and waited.

Light footsteps tapped against the veranda walk board, coming closer to where he stood. Jason risked a quick peek around the edge of the bricks. Virginia Hawksley headed straight for him. God's blood! What the hell was she doing out there? Automatically he shot a look to the back of the house. A tryst with the guard? A slow smile spread across his face. Well, well. Virginia had a little more spunk than he'd given her credit for.

An idea took form, and Jason slid his knife back into place, then pressed himself flat against the wall. The footsteps drew closer, and he readied himself. As Virginia strolled past he shot forward. One hand clasped over her mouth while the other encircled her waist.

Her sparse body went rigid.

"Don't make a sound," he grated in her ear. Stepping backward, he made his way down the side steps, pulling her along with him.

Free from the lights, he marched her toward the woods. He could feel her terror rising, and he was tempted to tell her she would come to no harm. But for his plan to work, she had to be frightened enough to obey him.

As they entered the forest he stopped next to a pine tree and bent his lips to her ear. "I'm going to remove my hand. If you scream, I'll be forced to silence you. Do you understand?"

She nodded jerkily.

Jason removed his hand and reached for the sash tied around her waist.

"Oh, please," Virginia whimpered. "What do you want from me?"

Jason knew what she feared. "Don't worry, milady," he rasped gently. "Your virtue is not at risk. I merely have need of your sash."

He could almost feel her relief.

Removing the gold satin, he positioned her closer to the base of the tree. "I'm going to tie you. But rest assured, no harm will befall you—if you do as I say."

Virginia bit her trembling lower lip and nodded.

After tying her loosely Jason stepped back. It bothered him to frighten her so. Damn it, she didn't have any part in this. Wanting to relieve her anxiety, he flashed her a bright smile. "If I wasn't so pressed for time, milady, I wouldn't be so quick to release your lovely body." He explored her rail-thin frame, stopping to linger on a chest that closely resembled his own. Well, hell, what did one little lie hurt?

Virginia trembled, but Jason could tell she was pleased by his remark. "Now I want you to count slowly to one hundred, then start screaming. If you try to make a sound before that time I might be forced to do something we'll both regret. Do you understand?"

"Oh, yes," she whispered.

"Good girl. Start counting. Now."

Jason raced through the trees until he stood where he could see the guard. He crouched down, knees bent, fingers braced on the ground. Timing was going to mean everything. He hadn't seen any of the other soldiers, so he could only hope that they were being entertained in the slave quarters.

Virginia's scream sliced through the silence.

The sentry jerked upright and swung toward the sound. He stepped forward, obviously torn between duty and chivalry. When Virginia screamed again chivalry won out. The guard clutched his rifle and raced toward the trees.

Jason bolted across the lawn to the side of the house and glanced through the window to make sure those inside hadn't heard Virginia. Peter stood next to an officer, his hand raised in animated conversation. Joshua Minter sat close by, his head tilted as if listening to their discussion. Several others milled around with drinks in their hands. Obviously Virginia's cry had gone undetected.

Relieved, Jason raced to the back of the house and lifted the heavy bar over the cellar door. Grasping the iron handle, he heaved the door upward.

David Brown's surprised face stared up at him.

Jason placed a silencing finger against his own lips, then motioned for David to hurry.

David nodded mutely and scrambled out of the cellar.

They ran full speed back across the lawn toward the woods. Jason quickly mounted Adversary and pulled David up behind him, then kicked the stallion into a gallop and charged deep into the forest.

Since the new location of Carl's press was less than a mile away, Jason decided to take David there. Carl should be back by now, and it would be up to him to get the man to safety.

After delivering the grateful printer to the shed Jason headed back to Crystal Terrace. He stayed in the shadows of the trees, knowing that the small detachment of soldiers would soon be searching for their escaped prisoner.

Using this precaution, it took him well over an hour to cover the four-mile distance. Wanting to get back to the house in case the soldiers came asking questions, he didn't take the time to remove his costume. Instead he quickly stabled Adversary, grabbed the candle, and hurried through the narrow tunnel.

As he opened the door behind the tapestry an uneasy tremor tickled up his spine. He tensed. Someone was in his room. Not daring to rustle the woven barrier, he backed up a pace and snuffed the candle between his gloved fingers. Setting the holder down near his feet, he claimed his knife and slowly brushed aside the tapestry.

The room was in total darkness, and he crouched, ready for the attack.

"I wouldn't if I were you," a low, sultry voice advised.

Recognizing the voice instantly, he clamped his teeth together and lowered his hand. What in the hell was *she* doing here?

He heard a flint strike, and the flare of a flame illuminated the room as the Scarlet Temptress lit a candle.

Unbidden, he stared at her body. God, she was something. Then his thoughts turned. What was she doing there? Had she discovered his ruse? God's teeth. Was he now to be blackmailed by the wench?

"Well, well, what do we have here?" she asked, aiming the blunderbuss at his chest as she flicked a curious look toward the tapestry. "Another bandit?" She relaxed and lowered the gun. "I see you've found a better way into the house than I have, but I'm afraid you'll have to concentrate your efforts elsewhere, sir. Lord Windhall's assets are currently under siege. By me."

His gaze rose to her masked face, and relief poured over him. She hadn't discovered his secret. She assumed he was another bandit, like herself, out to rob the viscount. He smiled at the absurdity. "We could always share."

Samantha was taken aback by the straight white teeth that gleamed brightly against his tanned skin. "Who are you?"

Jason sheathed his knife and bowed gallantly. "The Devilrider at your service, milady."

Something in his manner touched a familiar chord, but she dismissed it instantly. She had never met the man before, she was certain of it. "Well, Mr. Devilrider, I do not share. And as you can plainly see, I take precedence." She gestured toward the concealed door. "Now, if you would kindly leave me to my business . . ."

Jason's attention fastened on her mouth below the crimson mask. He was positive it was Christine's mouth, the mouth he'd sampled so thoroughly just hours before. His attention lowered to the swell of creamy flesh exposed above the low-cut scarlet gown. He could again feel the smoothness, the firmness beneath his palm.

He felt a curl of revenge slither through his midsection. He'd waited a long time to meet this woman again. He had a score to settle. And he knew just how to do it. "I'm afraid I can't do that, madam—"

Footsteps sounded in the hall.

Jason swung sharply. Instinctively he stepped in front of the Temptress and drew his knife. He dropped into a crouch just as the door opened.

CHAPTER 17

Nick bit back a sputter of surprise when he opened the door to Jason's room. He had called on Christine and been there when the soldiers came. They had ruthlessly questioned the servants, himself, and Christine, wanting to know if they'd seen a masked man dressed all in black. They hadn't, of course, but Nick knew they were searching for his brother, so he hastened to return home to warn Jason of the house-to-house search.

But he had not expected to find his brother—and a woman dressed in scarlet—in the bedroom. Mercy. What was Jason up to now? And how was Nick supposed to react? Looking to the woman, Nick swallowed. She was stunning.

The long, curly white wig she wore was a little out of fashion, but it looked highly becoming, he noted before focusing on her lips. Mother Mary! She has Christine's mouth! No wonder Jason was so adamant that Christine was the Scarlet Temptress. If Nick hadn't just left her himself, he would agree. But Christine was at Riversedge. And unless she'd grown wings, she could not possibly have beaten him to Crystal Terrace. His spirits soared. *Jason was wrong.*

"What is the meaning of this?" Nick said finally, trying to inflect outrage into his voice while fighting the urge to smile at his twin.

Jason straightened from his crouched position and shot Nick a warning look. If Nick didn't control that quirk at the corner of his mouth, the game would be lost. "Step inside and shut the door," Jason demanded sharply.

Nick did as instructed. Should he act surprised? Frightened? Outraged? Mercy. "What do you want?"

The woman stepped from behind Jason and raised the blunderbuss. "That which was denied me on our last encounter, Lord Windhall—your fat purse . . . and any other valuables that might be about. And do make haste, for I grow impatient."

Had Jason set this up? No. Jason would have told him. Nick peeked at his twin, then crossed his arms. "Absolutely not. You ruffians will soon learn that the gentry will no longer bow to your outrageous demands."

The Temptress's hand tightened on the gun. "You fool."

Jason edged closer to the woman to stay any sudden move she might make toward his brother. "You heard the lady." He waved the knife. "The loss of your finances surely wouldn't be as painful as the alternative."

Nick opened his mouth to protest, but the stern look on Jason's face stopped him. Knowing Jason wanted him to play along, Nick reached inside his coat and withdrew his purse. He tossed it to his twin. "I'll have your head for this." He scowled for the benefit of the outlaw.

Jason caught the purse and, ignoring his brother's poor acting abilities, slipped the knife away and turned to the woman. "Let's be off." He wanted to get her alone.

"No." She stepped forward, glaring at the purse. "That looks disgustingly light. He cheated me out of my take the last time. This time I'll have my due." She turned toward Nick. "I want more."

Jason swore beneath his breath. Bloody hell. Now what? Meeting his twin's gaze, Jason shrugged. "You heard the lady."

Nick tried not to look surprised. What in the world was Jason doing? He hesitated. Then, seeing the nearly imperceptible nod of Jason's head, Nick sighed. "I have a strongbox in the study."

Now Jason hesitated. The one with Sam Adams's missive? No. Nick wasn't that witless. Was he? Uneasy now, Jason motioned toward the door. "Lead on."

Noticing the way Jason placed himself between Nick and the Temptress as they descended the stairs caused Nick to smile at his brother's unconscious protective gesture.

Inside the study Nick walked over to the fireplace mantel and lit a candle. He surely hoped Jason knew what he was about. Removing a row of books from the shelf, he withdrew a metal box from behind. "You'll pay for this," he grated, hoping to sound threatening as he handed the box to his brother.

Jason winked at the Temptress, then grinned cockily at Nick. "You'll have to catch me first."

"Open the box!" Samantha demanded.

Nick's gaze flew to his twin.

"We haven't time," Jason cautioned. "We've tarried long enough as it is. There's too many soldiers about."

Samantha gritted her teeth. She didn't trust Lord

Windhall for an instant. Ignoring the Devilrider's advice, she repeated, "Open it."

Nick glanced at Jason. His twin was staring at the floor. Shrugging, Nick reached inside his fob pocket and withdrew the key. "You'll be sorry for this," he muttered. *Or I will.* He inserted the key into the lock. How on earth was he going to explain the contents?

"I said we don't have time for this," Jason snapped. He turned to the Temptress. "Let's go. *Now!*"

Samantha swung toward the masked man. Just who did he think he was, giving *her* orders? "Stay out of my business."

Jason knew he couldn't allow the box to be opened there. Turning abruptly, he snatched it and stormed out of the room.

Samantha stared furiously at his retreating back. Raising the gun, she scowled at Lord Windhall as she edged out of the door behind the arrogant outlaw.

Nick chuckled, watching the stiff set of the Temptress's shoulders as she retreated. Mercy. Jason was going to have a hard time with that one.

The Devilrider was walking toward the stables when Samantha stepped out the side entrance. Blast the man. Who was he? And just who did he think he was to take her booty? She'd show him. Striding quickly after his tall frame, she raised the gun. "Hand them over."

Jason stopped at the entrance to the stables and spun back to face her. He admired her spunk. Stepping inside the building, he backed into the shadows. "You may have the spoils for a price."

"Oh? And what might that be? Your life?"

"A kiss."

"What?" She cleared her throat. "Don't be absurd."

"What's so absurd about wanting to kiss a beautiful woman?"

"How do you know I *am* beautiful?" she challenged. "I might wear this mask to conceal hideous features."

Jason chuckled. "I'll take my chances."

His soft laugh did funny things to her stomach. "And what about you? Is your mask covering something offensive?" Why was she feeling breathless?

Jason shrugged. "I've had no complaints thus far." He moved closer. "Now, madam, I demand my due."

Samantha knew she had only two choices—either shoot the man or submit. She studied his powerfully built chest. She had never injured another human being in her life—at least not intentionally. Watching the even rise and fall of the fabric against his muscles, she knew she couldn't shoot him. Her gaze rose to his firm mouth, revealed below the black silk mask. But dared she kiss him? Lowering the gun, she stepped toward him. "Why a kiss?"

Jason slipped his arm around her waist and pulled her against him. "Because I must," he answered softly, lowering his head.

The strongbox fell to the ground, and the blunderbuss dropped beside it.

Samantha's world swayed. His mouth was so warm, so gentle, moving expertly against her lips. There was something familiar about the way this man's mouth caressed hers. Did all colonial men kiss like this? With this searing, soul-stripping passion that weakened the knees? Unable to stop, she slid her hands up his chest.

He pulled her fully against his hard length and deepened the kiss by parting her lips with his tongue. Her hands slid into the silky tendrils of his hair beneath the hood while her traitorous mouth admitted entrance to his probing warmth. He tasted of brandy, tobacco, and mint, a heady blend that left her dizzy.

"You are mine, Temptress," he murmured softly against her mouth. "Mine . . ." His tongue traced the outline of her lips before again slipping between her teeth.

She could feel the silk of his mask caressing her cheek, reminding her that he was an outlaw. This man had no right to kiss her. None at all. Yet despite her misgivings, she couldn't stop the heat blazing through her body or the erratic beat of her heart. What was he doing to her? She had no idea that a kiss could be so sensual, that she could feel this savage need to be closer, to want to absorb him completely within her.

There was no thought of holding back. She welcomed the heat of his hand as he caressed her breast. Tremors of pleasure shook her so hard that even the ground seemed to vibrate beneath her feet. She stiffened. The ground *was* vibrating.

Jason shoved her from him. "Someone's coming." He grabbed her hand and raced through the stable to the opposite end, then out the other side. He looked around for a means to get her safely away. Relief slid through him when he saw her hunter standing docilely by a tree near the rear entrance. "Go on, get out of here." When she didn't move immediately Jason grasped her by the waist and tossed her onto the animal's back. "Damn it, woman. It could be soldiers. Now get the hell out of here."

She tightened the gray's reins. "Not without my due."

The thunder of hooves rumbled closer.

God's teeth! Jason wanted to shake her. "Later. Now go!" He slapped the hunter on the rump. As much as he wanted to murder the infuriating woman, he couldn't risk her being captured by the king's men.

Samantha gasped as the horse lurched beneath her. Hearing the thunder of hoofbeats behind her, she quickly guided Starburst deep into the thickest part of the forest.

A shot rang out.

Something cut across her arm. Pain sliced up to her shoulder, and she cried out.

Starburst reared up, pawing the air.

A soldier burst from the trees, tossing aside his smoking pistol to raise a musket. "Halt, Temptress! You've been found out."

Frightened, Starburst reared.

Panic gripped Samantha as she flew from the saddle. Her

186

ribs slammed into a rock when she hit the ground. Gulping for air, terrified, she clawed at the soil, trying to crawl in an effort to escape.

The soldier climbed from the saddle, his musket leveled threateningly. "Get up," he commanded.

The coil of terror tightened. She tried to stand, but pain ripped through her chest, and the ground spun crazily. "I can't." She clutched her ribs.

The soldier reached out to grab her by the hair. Her wig came off in his hand, and her long curls tumbled free.

At that moment another rider burst into the clearing.

The soldier swung the musket and fired.

The Devilrider ducked and turned his horse sharply, then dived at the soldier.

Both men crashed to the ground. They tumbled and rolled. The sickening thud of flesh against flesh echoed through the stillness. Their breaths rasped harshly as each struggled to gain the advantage.

The Devilrider sprang to his feet. He drew back a deadly fist and drove it into the soldier's jaw. The man fell unconscious.

The Devilrider dropped to Samantha's side. "Are you all right? Did he hit you?"

She nodded. "It's just a graze." She stopped to clutch at her ribs. "It's my—"

He grabbed the material of her sleeve and ripped it down her arm, exposing a bleeding gash. "God damn that sniveling redcoat!"

"It's not deep," she assured him. "Please, just help me onto my horse. I must get out of here before more of them arrive."

He seemed to hesitate. Then, glancing around the clearing, he nodded and scooped her up into his arms.

Samantha couldn't stifle a small cry.

Immediately his hold loosened. "God, I'm sorry." With long, graceful strides he carried her to where Starburst stood pawing the ground.

Lifting her gently, he eased her into the saddle and wrapped the reins around her palm. Then, hurrying to his own horse, he grabbed the blunderbuss she'd dropped on the stable floor from his saddle and shoved it into her hand. "You might need this."

As she reached for the weapon pain shot through her arm.

"Are you certain you can ride?"

She nodded. Then hearing the thunder of several more horses' hooves rumbling across the clearing, she felt fear spiral up her spine.

The Devilrider looked toward the sound. "Take the quickest route home. I'll stay behind to throw the soldiers off of your trail."

"No. I'll be all right. Just get out of here." Holding the gun close to her ribs, she tightened her grip on the reins. "Thank you," she whispered before nudging the hunter forward.

Jason clenched his fists as he watched her leave. She had nearly been killed! As long as he lived he would never forget the gut-tightening fear he had felt when he heard that shot. And when he had seen her lying on the ground! He took a deep breath, forcing the painful picture from his mind.

Glaring back at the soldier, he felt a burning urge to kill the man. But the approaching hoofbeats reminded him of his precarious position. He ran to where his horse stood in the clearing.

Suddenly a thought struck him, and he stopped. Black hair? She had long black hair! And so did Christine Fleming.

When Jason entered his bedroom at Crystal Terrace a short time later Nick was seated in the chair, picking at lint on his gold satin breeches. He bolted to his feet. "What happened? I heard a shot."

Jason tore off his mask, then flung it and the strongbox he'd retrieved from the stables onto the bed. "She was injured, Nick. A ball grazed her left arm. Then that bastard soldier pulled off her wig." His eyes met his twin's steadily. "She has black hair. *Long* black hair. And if I had any doubts that Christine was the Temptress, I don't now."

Nick opened his mouth to protest.

Jason raised his hand. "Damn it, Nick, I know it was her. And now I can prove it to you."

"How?"

Jason smiled. "Tomorrow you are going to call on Lady Fleming." He moved to the bed and sat down. "I never thought I'd see the day I would encourage you to—er— fondle a lady, but, in order to prove to you that she *is* the Scarlet Temptress, it's necessary."

"You can't possibly mean that."

"Of course I mean it. It's the only way to prove her true identity."

"No," Nick said firmly. "I will not debase a young lady's honor just to prove that my thoughtless brother is wrong."

Jason grinned roguishly. "All right, little brother, then I'll do the honors."

"No!"

Jason chuckled. "I didn't think so."

Nick paced to the bed. "What if you're mistaken?"

"I'm not. The gash is just below her left shoulder."

"But what if you *are* wrong?"

Jason didn't answer but lifted a confident brow as he unlaced the ties of his shirt.

Nick stared thoughtfully at the carpet for a moment, then sat down. "All right, Jason." Something calculating flared in his eyes for a moment. "It's against my better judgment, but I'll do it."

Jason watched Nick suspiciously. He'd seen that look too many times not to recognize it for what it was—trouble. Nick was up to no good. He'd probably try to conceal what he found on Christine's arm. But Jason was way ahead of him. "Fine." He removed his boots and set them aside. "But I'm going with you." Rising, he pulled off the black shirt and tossed it to Nick.

"What?" Nick caught the garment, his expression revealing distress. "Why?"

Jason suppressed a smile. He wouldn't let Nick know he was on to him. "Because, little brother, someone has to keep Lady Fleming's chaperon entertained."

CHAPTER 18

Samantha glanced across the bedroom at Christine. Her twin hummed happily to herself while selecting the gown she planned to wear for Montague's visit that afternoon. Samantha was still stunned by the encounters she'd had the night before first with that arrogant bandit the Devilrider, then with Montague, and finally with the soldier.

She rubbed her bandaged arm and pressed a hand to her bound ribs. A grimace pulled at her lips when she remembered the ugly bruises left by her mishap with the stump and the soldier's pistol. Thank goodness Carl hadn't yet returned from another mysterious "few days" jaunt and learned of this. He would have strangled her.

Still, she had been surprised to discover that Montague had been to visit Christine in her absence. Samantha smiled as she recalled Christine's embarrassment. Christine had told Montague that Madeline was upstairs, abed with gout, and had spent the entire evening alone with him. She feared if anyone found out, her reputation would be in ruin. Of course, Samantha had pointed out, it must not have bothered her too much, or she'd have sent the rogue packing.

And now Samantha was forced once again to pose as Madeline to chaperone Christine and Montague shortly after midday tea. As her twin so graciously put it, she couldn't chance another meeting with Montague without proper escort.

Samantha sighed and shifted her shoulders. Her arm hurt like the devil, and her ribs ached every time she breathed. The last thing in the world she wanted to do was entertain Montague Windhall.

"What happened here last night?" Samantha asked, wondering why her sister was in such a spirited mood.

"Nothing," Christine replied. "Well, not much, anyway. But as you know, Montague called last evening, and—well, I think he really cares for me." Her lashes lowered. "At least that is the impression he gives."

"And how do you feel about the pompous lord?"

Christine carefully placed the burgundy-colored gown she'd selected on the bed and turned to face Samantha, her mouth set in a stubborn line. "He is not pompous. He is a very gentle, very kind man." She crossed the bedroom to where Samantha sat in a chair. Stopping in front of her, Christine placed her hands on her hips. "You would see that if you would stop robbing him long enough to look!"

Samantha frowned at her twin. Standing there in only her thin chemise, black hair tumbling over her shoulders, green eyes flashing, she looked like an avenging angel. Suddenly struck by something she'd never noticed before, Samantha frowned. Christine looked different. A rosy glow touched her smooth complexion. And there was a new boldness about her, a new depth to her manner. "You're in *love* with him!"

Christine flipped her hair over her shoulder and swung back to the bed. "That is none of your concern."

Samantha rose. "Come, twin, this is *me* you're talking to. Don't play your prim games now. I want to know." She bent her head to look into Christine's eyes. "Well?"

Christine smiled shyly. "Well . . . yes."

A series of emotions tumbled over Samantha at once: anger, hurt, and a sense of betrayal, all mixed up with happiness for her sister. The feel of Montague's lips on her own came back to taunt her. The warm timbre of his voice lulled her senses. Why him? Why couldn't Christine have fallen in love with someone else—*anyone else?* Taking a deep breath, Samantha nodded. "I see." She cleared her throat. "Does he know?"

Christine shook her head. "I cannot tell him—at least not yet. Not until I know how he feels about me."

Samantha's thoughts drifted back to the previous afternoon, when she'd seen Montague at Crystal Terrace—when he'd kissed her. Pain tore at her heart. Montague had indeed kissed her like a man desperately in love. She had only stopped him because she'd feared her own lack of control. But to think that glorious kiss had been meant for Christine sent slivers of torment through her soul. "I hope for your sake that he does care and is not merely using you as a distraction."

"Do not be obtuse." Christine giggled. "He is not a bounder." Turning back to the bed, she lifted the gown. "Now, if you will help me get dressed . . ." She walked over to the armoire, retrieved a brown wool ensemble, and looked back at Samantha, grinning. "I will help you."

An hour later Samantha settled her padded hips down onto the striped settee and looked around the empty parlor, then to the scones, jams, mince pie, and fresh mint tea that was set out neatly on the low marble table before the hearth. Christine had gone all out in an effort to impress her guests, right down to using Carl's best china.

Samantha didn't rise when Hadley escorted Montague into the parlor. Seeing Leopold with him, she swore inwardly. Blast. What was he doing there? Knowing she should make an effort to rise, she tried, but she hurt too much to move. Her ribs were throbbing, and her arm stung painfully. Under the pasty disguise her skin felt pale and clammy.

"Good afternoon, gentlemen." Samantha greeted the men with a nod. "Please excuse me for not rising, but my gout is giving me trouble today." She gestured with her good arm. "Won't you be seated? Christine will be down momentarily."

Montague took a seat on the settee across from her, and Leopold again chose the chair.

"Would you care for a cup of . . . mint tea?"

Montague chuckled. "Yes, thank you."

"None for me," Leopold replied, obviously not amused by her attempt at humor.

Leaning forward very slowly, Samantha poured the tea into a cup. "Sugar? Milk?"

Montague nodded. "Both, please."

"Where is Lady Fleming?" Leopold grated.

Samantha blinked in surprise. Why should he care? "Putting on her shoes, the last time I saw her."

"No, I am not. I am right here," Christine said lightly from the archway.

Both men swung in her direction. They made a hurried but thorough inspection of her person.

Samantha frowned. They seemed to be anxious about her twin's appearance for some reason.

The men rose to their feet.

"You look ravishing," Montague exclaimed a bit breathlessly, crossing to Christine's side. He lifted her hand and placed a kiss on her fingers.

"Quite ravishing," Leopold added, following his son's lead. His attention, Samantha noticed, lingered on Christine's left sleeve. Why? Her lashes lowered thoughtfully. Had someone informed the Windhalls of the soldier's encounter with the Scarlet Temptress? Had he described her and told of her injury? Did they suspect Christine? How intriguing, she mused. "Montague and I were just about to have some tea, Christine. Would you care for some?" Samantha asked cheerfully.

Christine looked surprised. "Yes, I would, Aunt Madeline. Thank you."

Samantha filled her twin's cup, careful not to show any sign of pain.

"Have you heard the news?" Leopold drawled slowly as he reclaimed his seat before the fireplace. "My son was set upon last evening—by that Scarlet Temptress again."

"Oh, no!" Christine exclaimed. "How awful for you." She turned and glared at Samantha.

"Yes, it was," Montague said, nodding. "But it seems that wasn't all that happened. As I understand it, a soldier came very close to capturing her. As a matter of fact, he claimed she was wounded."

Christine's hand instinctively rose to her left arm. "My word. How frightening."

Both men looked down at Christine's arm, encircled by her hand.

Samantha could have kicked her. She knew Christine remembered the echo of pain she'd suffered when Samantha had been shot. Searching for something to say to ward off the men's suspicion, Samantha asked, "Was she badly injured? Perhaps even killed?"

Leopold's gaze swung to meet hers. "No. It was just a graze." He looked pointedly at Christine's arm. "On her left arm."

Guiltily, Christine lowered her hand, her smooth cheeks coloring. "How terrible—for you, I mean. Too bad the soldier did not capture her." Christine leered at Samantha. "But perhaps the hoyden will now think twice before plundering another innocent victim." She smiled at Montague. "And scandalizing the good gentlemen of our community."

"I quite agree," Montague returned.

"I also understand that a woman's garment was found at Peter Hawksley's," Leopold inserted. "They believe it may belong to the Temptress." He smiled at Christine. "After they found Mr. Minter's office in shambles and unearthed a woman's gown, Langford surmised that it was the work of our sultry outlaw. Obviously she disguised herself to gain entrance to the soiree." His eyes narrowed fractionally. "I've been told that the gown very closely resembled the one you wore that night."

"The pink one?" Christine asked innocently.

"Yes," Montague answered. "But I've assured them, my dear, that you were wearing the gown when I brought you home that night. You do still have it, don't you? I mean, just in case the king's men should ask?"

Christine smiled weakly and clasped her hands. "Yes." She lowered her lashes and her voice. "Although I would not wish to show it to anyone."

Nor I, Samantha thought worriedly. How would they be

able to explain two identically made gowns? Christine was going to have to add some lace or something to make the gown appear slightly different.

"Why not?" Leopold asked, seeming to have leapt to some conclusion as he leaned forward.

Christine's color rose. "It is torn."

Torn? Samantha frowned. Christine had never said anything about it. And why was she having difficulty meeting Montague's eyes? What had happened to the gown?

Montague, too, Samantha noticed, looked decidedly uncomfortable. What was going on?

"Well, you may not be able to avoid it," Leopold rasped. "Captain Langford may demand to see the garment."

"If the officials wish to see the gown, then Christine will show it to them," Samantha snapped, wanting to put an end to a conversation that was obviously upsetting her sister. She rose slowly to her feet. "I am beginning to feel rather stifled in here." She turned to Leopold. "Would you care for a short stroll?"

He looked as if he were about to refuse; then, glancing at Montague, Leopold nodded. "Yes, of course, Madam Traynor. I'd be delighted."

"Please excuse us," Samantha directed to Montague. "We shouldn't be long."

As they walked toward the river sunlight sparkled on the waves of the James like scattered flecks of gold. The heat of the sun had melted the previous night's frost, leaving the ground damp and springy. Samantha stepped carefully, not wanting to jar herself by slipping.

Leopold slowed his pace to match hers.

It was a good thing, too. Her ribs felt as if they were poking into her lungs. Every breath was becoming more and more painful. The way she'd landed when she fell from the horse, it was a miracle she hadn't broken something.

Reaching the bank of the river, Samantha led Leopold downstream toward the gazebo. She knew she had to sit down—and soon.

"Where is Carl?" he asked suddenly.

"Away on business."

Leopold tightened his hold on her uninjured arm as she stepped over a fallen branch. "When do you expect him back?"

"Soon. Did you wish to see him?"

Reaching the steps of the gazebo, he helped her to a gold-cushioned bench along the inside wall; then, taking a seat beside her, he leaned back. "No." He turned abruptly. "How long have you and your niece been in Lynch's Ferry?"

"A little over six months. Why?"

"Just curious."

Why all the questions? And why did she have the feeling he was mentally calculating something? Had he learned when the Temptress began her siege? Was he making a comparison? "It seems like so much longer," Samantha said gruffly. "At times the colonists are so lacking in proper decorum, I'm tempted to return to England early."

"Early? When are you supposed to return?"

"At the end of summer. Christine's father wanted her to see some of the world before she settled down to marry," Samantha lied. "We spent last year in France."

"Does her father have someone in mind for her to wed?"

"Yes," Samantha answered, half truthfully. Actually, her father had harbored plans for Samantha to marry. "Our neighbor's son, William Bucknell."

Leopold frowned. "Is she in love with him?"

Samantha thought of William's kind, gentle nature. He had always been like the brother she and Christine never had. Smiling with warm fondness for her endearing neighbor, she nodded. "Yes, I'm certain she is." Was it her imagination, or did Leopold suddenly look angry?

"I think we should be going in now." Rising, he extended his hand. "It grows quite chilly out. And I'm sure this isn't doing your gout any good."

Samantha allowed him to help her to her feet. Pain shot through her side, and she grimaced. She smiled weakly. "I quite agree. I hope I haven't overdone it already."

Leopold was silent on the return trip to the house, and Samantha wondered what direction his thoughts had taken. Was he still considering Christine as the outlaw? Smiling at the absurdity of that, she led the way into the house through the dining room and crossed to the parlor. The door, Samantha noticed with surprise, was now closed.

When Leopold opened it the scene that met them caused Samantha to gasp out loud.

The sleeve of Christine's low-necked gown was pulled off her left shoulder and down her arm. Montague's head was bent, his mouth against her throat, his arms around her waist, holding her close.

"God damn you, Windhall!"

All four heads swung toward the entry archway.

Carl Malderon towered in the opening, his face nearly purple with rage. The veins in his temples bulged as if they were about to burst, his hands clenched into angry fists. "This time you've gone too far!"

Montague straightened stiffly.

Christine cried out.

Fleetingly, Samantha noticed that Leopold explored Christine's naked arm, and the blood left his face.

Christine jerked up the sleeve of her gown.

Carl took a threatening step forward.

Leopold moved with remarkable speed, placing himself between Carl and Montague. "Take it easy, Carl," he warned softly.

Distantly, Samantha noticed that Leopold's voice had lost its raspiness.

Carl bristled. "Get out of my way."

Leopold didn't move.

Everyone seemed to stop breathing as the two men faced each other.

"In private," Leopold grated firmly.

Carl's fists tightened, and for a moment he looked as if he might refuse, but something in Leopold's manner must have changed his mind, for he nodded. "My study." He glared damningly at Montague. "Right now."

Montague rose to his feet, smiling apprehensively down at Christine.

Christine's gaze shot past him to the archway, and she burst into tears.

Samantha swung around and looked back to Carl, and beyond. Peter Hawksley stood in the spacious doorway with his mouth hanging open.

Jason, too, became aware at that moment of Peter's presence and swore softly beneath his breath. Damn, what a mess. Now that Peter Hawksley had witnessed Christine's compromise, there would be no easy solution. Either Carl would have to call Nick out for a duel, or Nick—or *someone*—would have to marry Christine.

Moments later Nick joined them in the study and closed the door behind him. Then, turning to face Carl, he lifted his chin. "Before you say anything, I want you to know that I am prepared to marry Christine."

"No!" Jason burst out. He swung to Carl. "This is all my fault. I was so blasted sure she was the Scarlet Temptress that I encouraged Nick to disrobe her to verify my suspicions. I knew the Temptress was injured last night and was certain that Nick would find the wound." Jason shook his head. "As we all saw, I was wrong. This whole thing is my fault." He turned to Nick. "I'll marry her."

"Jason," Nick interrupted, "I know you're only saying that to protect me. But the truth is, I *want* to marry Christine. Even if this had never happened I would have asked her." He looked at Carl, then back to his brother. "I love her, Jase. *Really* love her."

Jason felt as if something had punctured his heart. His little brother was going to marry the woman Jason loved. *Loved?* His stomach clenched. He didn't love Christine, he loved the Scarlet Temptress! Then visions rose of the kiss he and Christine had shared in the entry at Crystal Terrace. He could still feel the way she trembled in his arms, the way she responded so passionately—the way *he* went up in flames. Good God. Was he in love with both women?

Carl laced his fingers through his thick gray hair, the lines in his face softening. "Bloody hell, I wish this had never happened." He moved to his desk and sat down. "But short of killing Nick, or sending Christine back to England to escape the scandal, there's nothing else to be done."

"Shall we schedule the wedding for the middle of next month?" Nick asked. "I know it's short notice, but under the circumstances, I believe it's necessary."

Jason dropped into a chair. He felt as if his throat had closed up on him. "Yes. And for your sake, I'm damn glad she wasn't the Scarlet Temptress."

"What is this obsession you two have with the Scarlet Temptress?" Carl blurted angrily.

"It's not the *two* of us," Jason offered. "It's me. I'm the one who wants her . . . caught."

"Because of what she did to you?"

"Among other things."

"Jason," Nick said softly, "I know this may not be the time to bring this up, but I believe I've just won our wager."

Jason paled.

"But don't worry, big brother, you can keep Adversary." Nick smiled. "For I've gained something far more valuable."

CHAPTER 19

The March winds had gentled to a soft breeze, almost as if in appreciation of the wedding planned at Riversedge. As Samantha strolled out into the garden to make a last-minute inspection of the elegant setting she noticed early roses blooming along the gravel pathway in an array of reds, pinks, whites, and yellows. Perfect.

She moved to one of the several rows of chairs and sat down before a hastily built lattice arch. Her gaze traveled over the wide walkway that divided the chairs down the center, leaving them in two neatly arrayed sections, then slid to the thin streamers of pink and burgundy satin draped from row to row on either side of the aisle.

Fingering one of the streamers, she looked back at the white wooden curvature woven through with alternating strands of pink, burgundy, and silver before white roses had been added in delicate clusters—Christine's touch.

Christine. Her baby sister was getting married. She swallowed back a tightness and channeled her thoughts in another direction. It wouldn't do to start crying and ruin her Madeline face.

She looked down at her gloved hands and let her thoughts roam over the last four weeks. Montague, of course, had paid constant court to Christine. So much so that her twin was in a continuous state of euphoria. Leopold had remained conspicuously absent, although Montague had explained by saying the elder man had been called away on business.

Of Hawk Samantha had seen nothing since their encounter the night of Peter's soiree. She glanced toward the forest. Would she ever see him again? Did she want to? No. Hawk was much too intense for her peace of mind.

Peace of mind? Her lips tightened. She hadn't had much of that over the last weeks, not with Captain Langford coming by every few days, wanting to question Christine about the pink gown—which, much to Christine's chagrin, she had been unable to repair. A smile touched the corner of Samantha's mouth when she thought of all the excuses Carl and Madeline had given the pompous officer. They had informed him on each visit that Christine was away shopping for her trousseau, out with Montague, or indisposed. And the man was becoming positively flustered.

Christine and Montague, of course, had attended numerous parties and teas in their honor, while the Scarlet Temptress had all but disappeared. Carl's mysterious outings had increased in frequency, and he was gone a good deal of the time. That left Samantha to post all the invitations, take care of the banns, and arrange the minister, the flowers, the menu, and a thousand other incidentals.

She turned back to the house. Weddings tended to be quite tedious . . . and this one would be a turning point in Christine's and Samantha's lives. In the four weeks since that ghastly scene in the parlor she had not left the house. But today, after the wedding, that would change. Christine and Montague planned to take a short honeymoon in Williamsburg. And because summer—and her father's trial—grew nearer, the Scarlet Temptress must ride again.

This definitely upset her guardian. Carl had been furious when Samantha told him of her intentions to resume her dangerous role, but there was little he could do unless he locked her in the bedroom. He had no doubt considered that, but she wouldn't be swayed. The need was too critical. That she was going back on her word to never rob another carriage, she determinedly shoved aside. Her father's life meant more than a mere vow. She would be careful to see that no one came to harm, but it must be done.

Samantha shifted the padding on her hips to a more comfortable position and reached for the banister bordering the covered veranda. She hated to have to wear the disguise all day, but several guests had traveled great distances and arrived at Riversedge a day early.

"Missy?" Effie called, stepping out onto the portico. "Dis jest come fo' ya." Effie extended a white envelope.

"Thank you," Samantha returned, taking the letter from the woman's brown hand. She broke the seal and read the missive. Bartholomew Dungworth requested he be allowed to bring a guest to the affair—his esteemed cousin, Captain Harvey Langford.

Samantha swallowed her despair and turned to the maid. "Please arrange another setting for dinner, Effie. And have Hadley deliver a note of acceptance to the Dungworths."

"Yessum, I shorely will," Effie said, nodding vigorously as she bustled back into the house.

Samantha glanced back down at the parchment. This was going to be one wretched evening with the arrogant officer in attendance.

Her spirits sagged. Lifting the hem of her skirts, she plodded up the steps to the house. She didn't have time to think about it now. The wedding was only hours away, and Christine was still in the blasted tub.

Two hours later Samantha descended the stairs dressed in a bulging gray satin gown. Today more than ever she hated the Madeline disguise. She hated the paste and wig, and above all the dowdy, matronly gown. The desire to strip off her masquerade and scrub her face was nearly overwhelming. How long had it been since she'd worn a lovely ball gown—that she could be seen in? How long had it been since she'd danced? Since gentlemen had vied for her attention? It seemed like forever.

As she ambled into the ballroom she found Carl nursing a glass of brandy. He looked quite grand. The deep wine-colored satin redingote and breeches hugged his large, lean frame to perfection. "My, don't you look striking. And here I thought Lord Windhall was to be the groom."

Carl laughed and crossed the room to her side. Taking her hand, he squeezed warmly. "Ah, Samantha, you do my old heart good."

Samantha smiled and returned the gesture. "There's nothing old about you, Carl."

"Flatterer." Releasing her hand, he moved back to the elaborate bar he'd had constructed for the wedding party. "Would you care for a brandy? A sherry?"

"No, thank you," she said, smiling. "I need to keep a clear head today."

Carl's grin faded. "Damn it, Samantha, I wish you'd give up this notion. You could be killed. Or someone else could."

"Stop it, Carl. Don't try to make me feel guilty. It won't work. This is something I have to do, and no amount of emotional blackmail is going to change that. About the only thing that would is the date and time of the tax shipment."

"Tax shipment," Carl scoffed. "I've heard that rumor,

too, but I don't believe it." He turned back to the bar. "You didn't find anything in Joshua Minter's office. And if there *was* to be a transport, he would've had the information. Nothing goes on around here that Joshua doesn't know about."

"Oh, I'd say there's one thing Mr. Minter's unaware of." Her cheek dimpled. "Me."

Carl opened his mouth as if to retort, then quickly closed it. Turning, he tossed back his drink and set the glass on the bar. "The guests should be arriving soon. Let's go wait in the entry hall."

Minerva Carstairs and Peter Hawksley were the first to arrive. Minerva, dressed in a bright pink gown, tugged the material of her full skirt through the open double doors. Peter wore forest-green satin. Standing side by side, they resembled a giant pink mum with one thin leaf.

"Well, well, Madame Traynor," Minerva cooed, "don't you look stunning. I do believe this is the first time I've seen you wear anything but those drab woolen gowns. Really, my dear, you should wear satin more often. It so improves your, er, rather sallow complexion." She smiled smugly at Peter and raised her pink lace fan. "Don't you agree, Peter?"

Peter cleared his throat and looked uncomfortable.

Samantha lowered her lashes and smiled tightly. "Thank you. I'll try to remember that." Raising her gloved hand, she summoned Hadley. "Won't you have some refreshments while we await the other guests?"

Carl nodded to Peter and Minerva but said nothing as Hadley escorted the pair through an arched entrance that led to the main ballroom.

Sally Blankenship and her brother Westly appeared next, followed by Virginia Hawksley and Joshua Minter. Samantha felt a twinge of guilt for the way she'd ransacked his office a few weeks ago. As far as customs officials went, he wasn't a bad sort.

The Millworths, their daughter Pamela, and the Wainwrights arrived soon after Virginia and Joshua. Then followed an overwhelming entourage of visitors from Lynch's

Ferry. Samantha and Carl had no time for anything but greeting the new arrivals.

Half an hour later Lord Bartholomew Dungworth's huge, flabby frame filled the doorway. Behind him stood a tall, well-built man in military uniform. About Carl's age, Harvey Langford struck a handsome pose. But pitted pockmarks on his lean cheeks gave him a dangerous, sinister look.

"Carl, Lady Traynor," Bartholomew gargled, "I'd like for you to meet my cousin, Captain Harvey Langford."

"We've met." Samantha smiled wryly. "Isn't that so, Captain?"

Langford stared coldly down at her. "Yes, madam. On several occasions." His black eyes gleamed. "But I trust *this time* Lady Fleming is not out or . . . indisposed."

Samantha felt her lips crinkle with laughter. "No, not this time." She turned toward the crowd of guests milling about the main hall. "Won't you gentlemen help yourselves to some refreshments?"

Langford's gaze followed hers. He nodded distractedly while he scanned the room. Stepping forward, he brushed past Samantha. "Which way to the refreshment table?"

Carl showed no sign of reaction as he motioned to Hadley. "My man will direct you."

Samantha breathed a sigh of relief when Bartholomew and his cousin disappeared into the crowd.

When the last of the guests had been shown into the ballroom Samantha turned to Carl with a worried frown. "Where is the groom? He should have been here by now."

Carl smiled. "Don't worry. Montague will be here in plenty of time. He'd never leave a lady standing at the altar."

"Especially not *this* lady," Montague said from the door behind them.

Samantha spun sharply. Montague stood before her, looking so handsome her heart gave a wild kick. White breeches hugged his muscular thighs, and a dark wine velvet coat stretched tautly over his broad shoulders. His black hair was left unpowdered and swept into a queue, revealing the strong lines of his lean features. Only that disgusting layer of white powder and those awful black patches lessened his masculine beauty.

A dead weight settled in Samantha's stomach. Her sister was going to marry Montague Windhall, and there was nothing Samantha could—or would—do about it.

Behind Montague Leopold stood silently, wearing a dark blue velvet ensemble with a silver waistcoat. His wig, like others he had worn, curled closely around his bearded face.

"Come in," Carl said. Then to Montague he added, "The minister is waiting. Last-minute instructions, I believe."

Samantha watched Carl and Montague saunter off toward the study, then turned back to Leopold. For an instant she could have sworn she saw a flash of pain, but if so, it vanished quickly.

"Well, madam," he said, raising his arm, "shall we join the rest of the guests?"

Samantha took Leopold's arm. "Of course, your lordship. After all the greetings I've grown quite parched."

An air of gaiety buzzed around the ballroom, but Samantha didn't feel it. Her heart hurt. Her sister was going to marry Montague, and Samantha would spend the rest of her life coveting her twin's husband.

Leopold led her over to the bar. "Sherry?" he asked, lifting a decanter. At her nod he poured the amber liquid into a glass. After fixing a brandy for himself he guided her to a seat by the fireplace. "To the unity of our families," he said solemnly, raising his crystal goblet in a toast.

Why did she get the feeling he was unhappy about the union? She took a sip and lowered the glass. "You don't like Christine much, do you?"

He looked surprised. "What? Of course I like her. Why would you ask that?"

"It's just a feeling I get."

"Well, madam, I fear your feelings have led you astray this time. I couldn't be happier for Montague. Your niece is a lovely young woman, and I'll be honored to call her sis—

daughter." He took a quick drink, almost as if to swallow his words.

From outside the strains of the orchestra rose, announcing the beginning of the wedding. Samantha tensed.

Leopold looked bereaved, then, controlling his features, he extended his hand to help her rise. "Shall I escort you, Madam Traynor?"

Samantha set the glass aside and placed her palm in his. She noticed a small, nearly imperceptible tremor when his hand closed around hers as she rose. With a mixture of confusion and distress she allowed him to usher her to the chair designated for her. With a long look at Montague Leopold sat down beside her, his lips drawn tight.

When the last guest was seated Montague took his place in front of the arch along with the minister.

The slow, lumbering tempo of the wedding march began, and all heads turned in the direction of the house.

Hadley, dressed in a splendid array of black and white satin, approached the double doors and in one fluid movement turned the knob and swung them open.

A gasp of awed surprise echoed through the audience.

Christine stood in the center of the doorway, her dark head bowed, holding a flowing bouquet of white roses woven through with burgundy lace and pearls.

Samantha cast a quick peek at Leopold. His sky-blue eyes reflected tortured anguish. What was happening? Was Leopold in love with her sister? Impossible. Or was it?

Discarding the inconceivable thought, Samantha turned her attention back to Christine. Her twin was so beautiful. The white silk gown that had put the seamstress in a frantic tizzy for days was absolutely breathtaking. Sheer lace sleeves hugged slender arms from shoulder to wrist. The square neckline, trimmed in pearls, forced her full breasts up and out, barely concealing their crests. A pearl necklace adorned with a single amethyst rested in the valley of her bosom.

The tight bodice of the gown molded her small rib cage and even smaller waist before flaring out in yards of layered silk that flowed into a twelve-foot train. Then a pearl and amethyst tiara held in place a frothy veil that would soften her radiant features until Montague—her husband—lifted it.

Samantha quickly brought a handkerchief to her eyes to stem the flow of tears that would jeopardize her disguise.

Carl escorted Christine down the aisle and placed her hand in Montague's. The bride and groom locked gazes, then turned and approached the minister.

Samantha fought against the pain rising in her chest, but a small sob escaped.

"Don't," Leopold commanded softly. His hand found hers and squeezed gently.

Her gaze rose to meet his, and suddenly everything was all right. His grasp gave her the strength she needed to watch the rest of the ceremony without weeping.

But when Montague slowly raised the veil and gazed into his bride's eyes, then kissed her tenderly, Samantha couldn't control the ache that squeezed her heart.

At the same moment Leopold's hand tightened on hers, and he let out a slow, heavy breath, almost as if he had had the same reaction. But she had no time to ponder the thought, for at that moment the guests rose and gathered around the newlyweds.

When Montague drew her into his arms and hugged her warmly Samantha's chest tightened. The only man she'd ever allowed close to her heart was now her brother-in-law.

Leopold seemed reluctant to kiss the bride, but he did so quickly, then stepped back, puzzled.

Samantha leaned close. "Is something amiss?"

He blinked and pulled his gaze from Christine. "What?" His eyes settled on Samantha's mouth, and he blinked again and looked even more confused. "No. No. Nothing."

Frowning, she stared at him a moment, then returned her attention to the newlyweds. Montague and Christine accepted several rounds of kisses and boisterous congratulations before retreating indoors to open their gifts.

Samantha and the older viscount hung back, neither in a hurry to join the festivities. They moved to allow some guests to pass and ended up by the lattice arch.

Leopold picked off a cluster of white roses and stared down at them sadly for a moment, rolling them between his fingers. Then, abruptly, he tossed the roses aside.

Excusing himself, Leopold sauntered over to the refreshment table. Samantha watched him closely. Something troubled him. He seemed to be hurting. Was he ill?

"Who is that gentleman?" a voice said from directly behind her shoulder.

Samantha turned and found herself face to face with Harvey Langford. "The bridegroom's father," she answered stiffly.

"Introduce me," Captain Langford commanded.

She pursed her lips to keep from telling the arrogant man to introduce himself. "Of course."

They approached Leopold from behind. "Your lordship?" Samantha called softly.

Leopold turned, looking first at her, then at the officer. "Yes?"

"This gentleman would like to make your acquaintance." She motioned toward the captain. "Lord Windhall, this is Captain Harvey Langford."

The sudden blaze of undisguised hatred that crossed Leopold's features shocked Samantha. What on earth?

As if by sheer force of will the older man slowly relaxed his taut features and lowered his drink. "How do you do?" His voice sounded brittle.

"Lord Windhall," Langford acknowledged with a nod. "I want to speak to you in private." He indicated the newlyweds. "It's concerning your son. Unless, of course, you'd prefer I summon the groom from the arms of his bride."

"In the study," Leopold rasped, gesturing toward the hall. He turned and set the glass down on the table, then spoke to Samantha. "Excuse me, Madam Traynor, I won't be long." His lips thinned as he faced the officer once again. "Shall we?"

Samantha watched the two men make their way across the crowded room to the hall. What was going on here? What did Leopold have against the captain? Had they met before? Of course not. The captain wouldn't have asked for an introduction if that were the case. Shaking her head at Leopold's odd behavior, she went to find Effie. She wanted to make sure the housekeeper hadn't seated the captain next to Leopold Windhall.

Jason closed the door to the study and took a moment to compose himself before turning to face the king's puppet. As always, a flame of burning hatred seared his chest, and for the thousandth time he posed the question to himself: Could this be the soldier who killed my father? Shaking off the unanswerable question, he glared at the man. Harvey Langford. This was the arrogant bastard whose assumption concerning the Scarlet Temptress and Christine mirrored Jason's—or had done so before Nick disclosed the fact that Christine couldn't possibly be the bandit. What did he want? And why here, at the wedding? "You wished to speak to me?"

Langford ambled over to the chair behind Carl's desk and sat down. "I understand that your son was put through a rather tedious ordeal by the Scarlet Temptress." He folded his hands on the desk. "Tell me about it."

Jason leered at the soldier's unbending, pitted features. "What's to tell? She robbed him, stripped him of his clothing, and left him to walk home."

"Naked?"

Jason focused on the dancing flames in the hearth. "Yes."

"Did he describe her to you?"

Jason shrugged. "He didn't have to. I met her for myself a few days later."

"Where?"

"On the road to Bedford County."

"I heard about that." Langford leaned back in the chair. "Weren't you injured that night? By the Temptress?"

"No. I was unfortunate enough to step forward at the

wrong moment. I didn't realize the driver was going to lunge with his knife."

Langford's brow knitted. "The driver injured you?"

"That's correct."

"Was he her accomplice?"

"Not to my knowledge."

The captain's expression turned thoughtful. "Nevertheless, I'd like to question him. What's his name?"

"Rollie Parker."

Langford seemed to relax. "I see." He lowered his gaze to the polished surface of the desk. "Describe the Temptress."

"Tall, heavyset, thin-lipped."

The officer's head whipped up. "That's strange. I heard she was small and comely." His nostrils flared. "As a matter of fact, Private Baylor, the soldier who nearly captured her last month, said she was quite stunning, and that she had long black hair." He smiled coldly. "Much like that of your son's esteemed bride."

"I can assure you that in my estimation Christine does not resemble the Temptress in the least. Besides, the day after the outlaw sustained the shot in the arm Christine was found in a rather compromising position, and I can vouch for the fact that she had no injury."

"Indeed?" A sudden flash of triumph glinted in the captain's eyes before he quickly suppressed it.

Jason could have bitten off his tongue. No one, other than the Devilrider and the soldier, could have known where the injury was located. Damnation.

Langford leaned forward. "Injuries can be concealed."

Jason wasn't fooled or amused by the captain's game, and he'd had enough of the hated soldier. "Then why don't you summon Christine and have her remove her gown?"

"An intriguing idea, but hardly proper—or necessary." He rose and crossed to the door. Opening it, he stepped into the hall. His mouth twisted into a complacent smile. "I have a much better way of dealing with the situation." He looked toward the ballroom. "Who knows, perhaps I can even beat the Scarlet Temptress at her own game."

CHAPTER 20

As the first rays of dawn slid through a part in the drapes at the Traveler's Inn Nick eased from the bed and glanced down at his sleeping wife. Her lips, soft and slightly parted, tempted him to once again sample their nectar. Mercy! Had he married a siren? He smiled. No, Christine was no siren. She was real. She was a lovely, passionate woman who had inflamed the male animal in him—several times, he remembered wickedly. Mercy. He'd never expected her to respond so wantonly as she had last eve. The mere memory caused him to grow taut, and he had to fight the urge to take her again. Take her now.

Get hold of yourself, old man. Do you want the woman to think she married a rutting goat? Disgusted with himself, he moved away from the bed and dressed quietly. After one last longing glimpse of his bride he slipped out of the room, determined to cool his ardor.

Very few people were about in the common room of the Traveler's Inn at this time of the morning, Nick noticed as his footsteps echoed hollowly through the empty hall.

Finding a chair near the window, he sat down and waited for the proprietor to bring the cup of chocolate he'd requested. He picked up a week-old publication from the seat beside him, and with forced concentration he studied the latest issue of Dixon and Hunter's *Virginia Gazette*, trying to keep his mind off of Christine.

"Massa Kincaid, sah?"

Nick's head snapped up. He glanced around quickly to see if anyone had heard the young Negro call him by his true name. The common room was empty. Thank heavens. "Yes?"

The boy pulled something from the inside of his shirt. "A man axed me t' give yo' dis heh papah." He extended a sealed note.

"Thank you." Nick took it and dropped a coin into the boy's palm, then waited for the youngster to leave before he broke the wax seal. A frown pulled across his brow as he read.

> N.K.
>   Meet me behind the stables. Ten minutes.
>
>   P.H.

Nick folded the note and slipped it inside his pocket. Why in the world was Patrick Henry here? And what did he want? Closing the publication, Nick tossed it back on the chair and rose from the table.

Stopping at the front desk, he made arrangements for Christine's breakfast, and as an afterthought he ordered another bouquet of flowers sent to his wife—since she'd obviously appreciated them so much the night before. Then he penned a quick note to be delivered with them. He smiled as he thought of how Christine would respond to his gesture when he returned.

The town of Bent Creek was nearly deserted as Nick walked toward the livery stable. A slight breeze lapped at the aged wood of the smithy's sign hanging overhead. When Nick reached the corner of the building he skirted the structure and slipped into the shadows at the back. Immediately he felt a presence beside him.

"Kincaid."

He couldn't see the man's face, but he recognized Patrick Henry's voice. "What's this all about?"

"In a minute," Patrick returned. "Come on. We'll use the shed."

Nick followed Patrick across the cluttered area behind the stables into a large, dilapidated building where they made their way to a tiny office in the back.

Inside Patrick lit a candle and turned to face Nick.

Patrick's thin features looked pale in the flickering candle-light. Small wire-rimmed glasses balanced precariously on his long, straight nose, and his brown hair was left unpowdered and tied back with a black ribbon. His usually mobile mouth was drawn into a narrow line.

Nick blinked at the angry set of Henry's jaw. Although he knew Patrick could be a formidable opponent, his friend usually maintained a gentle demeanor.

"What is it, Patrick? What's this all about?"

The younger man eased down in a chair behind the desk. "It's Parliament, Nick. They've sent a garrison of men to Williamsburg in an effort to control the smuggling. It seems that if we refuse English goods, we get nothing." He removed a parchment from his coat. "This whole situation with England is getting out of hand. Half the Crown-appointed governors in the colonies have never set foot on American soil! Yet they sit behind their grand desks and proclaim intolerable laws." He ran a slender hand through his hair. "Well, we're not taking any more. We're gathering a group of men at this very moment for a convention. I want you there, Nick. But until then I need you back in Williamsburg to deal with the privateers. Those soldiers have them frightened. If something isn't done soon, we're going to lose our only stand against the Crown." As if suddenly remembering something, he smiled lopsidedly. "Oh, by the way, congratulations on your marriage. And I'm truly sorry to ask this of you on your honeymoon." He shrugged. "And you know I wouldn't if it weren't impor-tant."

Nick nodded, but inside he was falling apart. Did Henry truly expect Nick to leave his bride of a few hours?

"Clayton Cordell's ship will attempt the blockade three days hence. He's carrying weapons for our militia. We need at least twenty men to unload the cargo and store it in the caves just south of the inlet. You're the only person who can gather men we can trust. Only you. And I don't have to tell you how vital this operation is. It could mean life or death to our country."

Nick let out a slow breath. Mercy. What was he to do? He brought his hand up to rub at the back of his neck. "Patrick, my wife is here with me."

"Send her back."

It seemed like a harsh command coming from Patrick Henry, but Nick knew his friend wasn't trying to be offensive. He merely stated the solution in as few words as possible. Still . . ."Patrick, I've only been married for one day. I can't just send my wife home. I'll take her with me. She'll be fine at the Raleigh Tavern."

Patrick smiled gently. "Nick, I know how you feel, and under any other circumstances I would agree with you. But not this time. It's much too dangerous." He leaned forward. "If you're caught, they'll torture you to death, and you'll never reveal a thing. I know that, and you know it. But can you truthfully say that you could withstand the torment if they persecuted your wife before your eyes? Could you sit there calmly while they defiled her?" His look was intent. "Or, to protect her, would you tell them what they wanted to know?"

Nick tried to banish the vivid picture Patrick drew. Dear God. He'd never be able to sit by and watch Christine suffer.

"You're only human, Nick. You couldn't stand to see someone you love tortured any more than I could. That's why it's imperative that she remain beyond their reach. They're capable of any atrocity at this point. And believe me, abusing a beautiful woman is the least of their concerns."

Something ugly coiled inside Nick's stomach. He couldn't take a chance with Christine's life. Still, it didn't make the situation any easier. Just what kind of explanation was he supposed to give his bride?

Nick lowered his hand. There was only one workable solution. He wouldn't tell her. Mercy. He *couldn't* tell her. He would summon Jason to take Christine home. She would never know the difference, and he knew his twin was the only person he could trust with Christine's safety . . . and her tempting little body.

Jason shifted in the saddle atop Adversary and glanced toward the line of trees on his left. Where the hell was Nick, and why had he sent for him? What could possibly be so urgent that his brother would forfeit time from his honeymoon? "If I were in Christine's bed," he said aloud, "I damn sure wouldn't leave it for any reason."

Adversary's ears perked up. The stallion snorted and shook its black head, almost as if scolding Jason for the dishonorable thought he'd voiced.

Jason reached out and patted the sleek neck.

Suddenly Adversary jerked his head upward and whinnied, then sidestepped nervously.

Jason swung his attention back toward the trees.

Nick emerged from the forest on the back of a bay horse.

As his twin rode toward him Jason studied him closely. He looked like hell. The lines of his face were drawn taut, his brow creased into a deep, heavy scowl—definitely not the glowing figure of a bridegroom Jason had expected to see.

Reining his horse to a halt, Nick nodded. "Thank you for coming so promptly, Jason. I appreciate it."

Something crimped Jason's midsection. What was wrong? Nick looked tired. No, more than tired. He looked frustrated. "What is it? What's happened?"

"I need your help," Nick said wearily. "You have to switch places with me and take Christine home to Crystal Terrace."

Jason stared at his twin as if he'd lost the top of his head. He wasn't serious. He *couldn't* be. "All right. What's the true reason you wanted to see me?"

Nick's hands tightened on the reins. "That *is* the reason. And believe me, it's not something I wish to do. If there was someone who could take my place in Williamsburg, I'd certainly let him."

Jason felt as if he'd stepped into the middle of a nightmare. What was Nick talking about? What did

Williamsburg have to do with any of this? Jason brought his hand to his neck. "Nick, you're not making sense. Why don't you start from the beginning?"

As Nick retold his conversation with Patrick Henry Jason's heart beat steadily louder. Oh, no. God, please don't. You above of all know I'm not up to this test of willpower. But as Nick's words droned on Jason felt himself slipping deeper into the realm of defeat.

". . . and that's why you have to switch places with me. I can't take her with me, and I can't send her home alone." He sucked in a strained breath. "Besides, it's best she doesn't know of my activities just yet."

Jason felt nauseated. "God damn it, Nick! Have you lost your senses? I can't switch places with you on the morning after your *wedding night.*"

"Christine's life depends on it, and possibly my own as well, Jase, or I wouldn't ask."

Jason groaned. Please, God, he repeated silently, I don't deserve this.

"A detachment of soldiers has been sent to Williamsburg to disband the smuggling operation, or so they hope. If I'm caught, or even if they merely suspect me, they may try to use Christine to get to me." He drew in a tortured breath. "Mercy, Jason, I can't put my wife through that. I can't risk her. You're my only hope."

"Why can't I go to Williamsburg in your place?"

"I only wish you could. So help me I do. But you don't know the contacts. You don't know whom to trust. Unfortunately, I'm the only one privy to that. And I wish to heaven I wasn't!" He kneaded his temples. "Do you truly believe I want to hand my bride over to another man? Even if he is my brother?" He shook his head and laughed harshly. "Not very likely."

Despair oozed over Jason like sour milk. "Won't she be able to tell the difference between us?" He felt heat burn the back of his neck. Lord, he was acting like a callow youth. "I mean now that you've . . . ."

Nick's features blazed with anger. "The only way she'd be

216

able to do that is if she saw *you* without your clothing." His eyes narrowed. "I love you, Jason. You're my brother—a part of me. But so help me, if you touch my wife, I'll cut your heart out . . . along with any other part you hold dear."

A muscle twitched in Jason's jaw as he felt his own anger rise. "Don't jump to conclusions, little brother. My only concern was that she might see me emerge from the bath or something and see my scar. Damn it, we'd be living in the same house."

Nick let out a slow breath and laced his fingers through his hair. "Mercy. I'm sorry, Jason. Of course that's what you meant. This whole mess has me at my wits' end. You know without my saying that I trust you."

It's a good thing *one* of us does, Jason thought. Feeling the grievous weight of his brother's words and knowing Nick to be truly upset, Jason tried to assuage the guilt of his betraying heart. "What can I say to make you reconsider? What can I do?"

"Nothing. Just take Christine home—and keep her safe. That's all I ask. I love her, Jase, more than mere words could ever express. Just protect her for me."

Jason felt sick. There was no way out; he had to do it. And may God have mercy on us all. "With my life," Jason promised, wondering if that might not in truth be the final price.

"We're to make the switch at the back of the livery, inside the old smithy's shed. I've already informed Christine of our return. I gave her some feeble excuse about receiving a message for an urgent interview with a potential overseer for Crystal Terrace." Nick lowered his hand and gripped the reins. "I'm going to change into buff breeches and a white shirt when I get back to the inn. I know you carry similar attire in your saddlebags, so change and wait for me. I'll leave Christine on the pretense of bringing the carriage around. But of course, you will return with it."

"How long will you be gone?"

Nick shook his head. "A week, possibly two."

Jason grimaced inwardly. It sounded like a lifetime. Knowing that Nick had enough problems on his mind, and not wanting his little brother to know how unsettled he felt, Jason strove for nonchalance as he dipped his head in agreement. "When do we make the switch?"

The corner of Nick's eye jumped. "In an hour."

Jason watched the stiff set of his twin's spine as he turned the horse and rode back toward the trees. At the tortured look on his brother's face Jason wanted to bellow out his own frustration. How was he going to pretend to be Christine's husband—new husband—and not touch her? Not make love to her? He shook his head. "I'll never survive."

Adversary snorted.

By the time Nick returned to the inn and changed into the buff breeches and white shirt Christine had supervised the packing, then had the luggage carried downstairs.

Nick gave their room one last inspection before studying his wife.

She sat primly on the side of the bed, her hands folded in her lap, looking for all the world like a schoolgirl. Nick's throat bunched as he remembered the night just past. She was no schoolgirl. She was a woman now—*his* woman— and he was pushing her into the arms of another man. Oh, Lord, please let Jason be as honorable as I believe he is. He moved closer to his wife. He didn't know how Jason planned to avoid Christine's bed without causing suspicion, but he prayed Jason would think of something that wouldn't cause Nick too many problems when he returned. He explored Christine's beautiful face. But in the meantime he needed to say good-bye to his bride—even if she didn't know they were parting.

He crossed to the bed and stood before her, memorizing her delicate features and the silky black hair that hung loose to her waist. A tiny yellow hat that matched her traveling outfit held the tresses away from her face, revealing the fragile line of her jaw. She looked up curiously. Her soft, pink mouth, still slightly swollen from his lovemaking, drew his attention, and his stomach tightened. He ached to take her again, to imprint his soul on hers. But time grew short.

Leaning forward, he drew her up to her feet and pulled her into his arms. He just wanted to hold her for a moment. "I love you, angel," he whispered, brushing his lips against her temple. "Don't ever forget that." His mouth slid to hers with a need born of desperation.

He felt her tremble, and his arms closed around her tiny body. How was he going to let her go? He nuzzled her neck and felt her nipples harden against his chest. His body responded violently, and he drew in a ragged breath. He had to stop this now—or he wasn't going to be able to.

Easing her away from him, he chuckled and leaned his forehead against hers. "Love, if we don't leave immediately, I'm going to miss my appointment"—he touched his lips to hers—"by a fortnight."

The color in Christine's cheeks deepened.

Nick laughed softly, then sobered. "I'll go get the carriage." He swallowed. "Wait here for me."

"I will not go anywhere."

Nick knew he should leave. Jason surely awaited him in the smithy's shed by now. But his attention returned to Christine, and, unable to resist, he again claimed her mouth.

Passion exploded in his veins, and he moaned against her moist lips. His hands slid to her bottom, pulling her hard against him. His body throbbed to life, and his senses took flight. He couldn't let her go. Mercy. He just couldn't let her go right now. His hand trembled as it moved up to her breast.

Christine slid her fingers through his hair, her lips parting for his exploration.

For an instant Nick's thoughts fluttered to his brother waiting in the shed, then he deepened the kiss. To hell with it. Jason could wait.

CHAPTER 21

Jason paced the littered floor of the smithy's shed. Where was Nick? What the hell was keeping him? Jason's teeth clamped together, and he strode away from the door. He knew *exactly* what was keeping his brother.

Kicking a piece of broken chain across the floor, he glared damningly at an empty barrel. Why did the thought of Christine in Nick's arms make Jason hurt so much?

The door creaked as it opened, and Jason whirled around.

Nick sauntered into the building looking so damned pleased that Jason felt the unholy urge to throttle his own twin. Immediately he felt the sting of guilt. Jealousy was an emotion Jason had never felt before—never thought he'd feel at all. And that it was directed at his own brother made his stomach churn. Shifting uncomfortably, he forced lightness into his voice. "All set?"

Nick nodded silently, then raised a hand to the back of his neck. "As ready as I can be, under the circumstances." He grasped the horse's reins and mounted. "I've arranged for the smithy's son to return Adversary for you." He couldn't look at Jason; his expression was pained. "I know how lost you'd be without him."

"Yes," Jason said softly, feeling Nick's pain as if it were his own. On leaden feet he approached Nick and reached up to clasp his hand. "Godspeed, little brother, and don't worry over your bride. I'll see to her safety."

Nick closed his eyes for a moment, then dipped his head and quickly rode out of the shed.

Breathing deeply to rid himself of the knot of pain in his chest, Jason massaged his temples, then made his way to the livery stable. He retrieved the carriage and climbed inside for the short ride. He didn't want to think about the trip back to Crystal Terrace . . . or the night to come.

The sun was high, nearing noon, when the carriage rolled into the drive at the Windhall mansion. Jason reined the team to a halt, then sprang from the seat as if it burned him. Reluctantly he held out his hand and helped Christine from the carriage. Stiffening at the warmth of her hand in his, he quickly escorted her into the house.

Dahlia stood openmouthed in the entryway. "What is it? Has something happened?"

"No, Dahlia." He shook his head. "I merely returned on an urgent matter of business." He smiled down at Christine. "My bride has been most congenial about it, I must say."

Christine blushed and glanced away.

He returned his attention to the older woman. "Have Bromley bring in the luggage, then send him to the study. I want a message delivered."

Dahlia blinked at him curiously, then nodded and bustled toward the back of the house.

Jason felt awkward as he turned to Christine. "Um, if you'll excuse me, l-love"—he swallowed—"I need to check the ledgers before I meet with the overseer."

"Of course, Montague. I will attend to the unpacking and discuss supper arrangements with Dahlia."

Jason nodded. "Plan on an extra guest. I'll be sending a note to Carl requesting that he join us this evening."

Christine looked shocked. "This evening?" Then, schooling her features but unable to hide the downward pull of her mouth, she raised her chin. "As you wish." She pivoted toward the stairs, then hesitated. Turning back to him, she silently raised her face to him as if for a kiss.

Jason felt the blood freeze in his veins. Lord, he didn't want to kiss her! "Ah . . ." He sighed. Hell, there was nothing he could do to get out of it.

He lowered his head and quickly pecked her pursed lips, then jerked back. "Until later, my dear."

Before she could say anything he spun on his heels and

marched into the study, closing the door firmly behind him. Letting out his breath, he slumped against the panel. "Damn," he said, "I'll never survive this." Pushing away from the door, he tromped across the room, grabbed a piece of parchment and a quill from the desk, then rapidly penned a note to Carl asking—no, begging—his godfather to join him as soon as possible.

Moments later, when Bromley arrived, Jason thrust the missive in the servant's hand and hastened him on his way.

That done, Jason bounded for the stables and saddled a mount. He would pretend to go for a ride to meet with the supposed overseer, then return, he hoped, about the same time as Carl. For Christine's benefit Jason would make up a tale about finding the overseer unsatisfactory, then close himself and Carl in the study, where they could sort out what to do about this quandary.

An hour later Jason rode back into the stables and breathed a sigh of relief when he saw Bromley tending Carl's horse. Jason quickly handed over the reins and hurried to the house to join his godfather.

He found Carl situated in the parlor. Unfortunately Christine, too, was in attendance.

Jason forced a smile as he entered the spacious room. "Well, Carl, I see my bride has kept you appropriately entertained while I saw to my dreary business," Jason said lightly as he crossed to Christine's side and patted her hand.

Carl's cheeks creased. "She has always done a much better job of entertaining than you ever did."

"Alas, you are probably correct."

Carl nodded. "How did your meeting with the overseer go?"

Jason feigned indifference. "Poorly, I'm afraid. The man's qualifications weren't up to par at all. He would never do." He gave Christine a small smile. "It seems our honeymoon has been interrupted for nothing."

"You could always continue it," Carl supplied helpfully.

Jason gritted his teeth and cast his godfather a murderous

222

glare. What was he about? Carl knew that Jason and Nick had switched places. Jason had put that much in the note. Had Carl decided on a course of retaliation for all the pranks Jason and Nick had pulled on him over the years? "A heartwarming suggestion, Carl. But I fear I'm totally exhausted from the tedious ride this morning and that dreadful meeting this afternoon. Besides, I'm equally certain that my sweet wife could use the rest." He grinned at Christine. "Isn't that right, dearest?"

Christine looked crestfallen.

Jason swore beneath his breath.

Carl smiled.

Clenching his teeth, Jason scowled at his grinning godfather. "Won't you join me in the study for a brandy?"

"Certainly, Montague. I'd be delighted." Carl rose. "If you'll excuse us, Christine?"

"Of course."

Carl strolled out of the room toward the entry hall.

Jason dipped his head in Christine's direction, not daring to meet her eyes, and followed Carl out of the room.

Christine watched her husband's broad shoulders disappear through the archway. What was troubling Montague? she wondered uneasily. In the morning he had been so passionate, but this afternoon and tonight he almost seemed like a different person. Had she done something inappropriate? Could he be upset over her wanton behavior earlier? Did ladies not behave so even after marriage? She felt the blood creeping to her cheeks at the memory of her shameless abandonment.

Reaching up to twist the end of a black curl draped over her shoulder, she tried to think of a way to redeem herself. Mayhap she could apologize openly and ask him how he preferred her to act. She swallowed. No. That would never do. Such words would not pass her throat. She traced her fingers along the arm of the high-backed chair. But if she did not speak to him about his obvious displeasure, how was she ever to learn what he expected?

Drawing in a fortifying breath, she squared her shoulders and turned for the study. She would tell him she wished to speak to him when he and Carl were through.

On silent feet she moved down the tiled entry hall and approached the study door. The men's voices, she noticed, carried quite clearly through the thin panel. A frown drew her eyebrows into peaks as she heard Montague's voice raise in anger.

"Damn it, Carl, I've got to have some help. How in the hell am I supposed to avoid Christine's bed? I'm supposed to be a newlywed, for Christ's sake!"

Christine's hand flew to her mouth.

"Calm down, Jason," Carl ordered. "We'll think of something. Did Nick say how long he'd be gone?"

"A fortnight, possibly more. He left for Williamsburg when we made the switch." The younger man's voice lowered. "He's going back to his original cover in the governor's office. Evidently there is a shipment of weapons attempting the blockade that will need to be transported to Concord."

Christine's eyes grew wide with incredulity. Switch? Cover? Who was Nick? Who was Jason? Why would Montague want to avoid her bed? And what did he mean he was *supposed* to be a newlywed?

Her husband's voice rose again.

"You know, I blame this whole mess on the Scarlet Temptress. It's just another of many debts the woman will have to pay."

Carl laughed. "Why?"

"Because if she hadn't robbed me, I wouldn't have gotten sick. Nick would have stayed in Williamsburg instead of coming to Crystal Terrace. We wouldn't have switched places. My twin wouldn't have pretended to be Montague Windhall and married Christine. *And I wouldn't be in this predicament!*"

Christine choked back a strangled cry.

Carl chuckled again. "I never thought of it that way, but of course, you're correct. Though if it's any consolation, I believe I have a solution to at least one of your problems."

"I'm listening."

Christine leaned closer, her mouth drawn tight.

"Well," Carl began, "you could fake a couple of broken ribs." His laughter sounded evil through the door. "No woman would expect you to make love if you were in pain."

The one called Jason laughed, too. "Carl, you're a genius!"

Christine clenched her teeth and swung from the door. Her mind whirled with the vast amount of information she had just heard. So there were two of them, hmm? Twins. *How dare they?* How dare this Nick and Jason—whoever they were—toy with her affections?

A ball of guilt rolled across her stomach. Had she and Samantha not done the same thing? Christine moved toward the staircase. But that was different, she thought. *She* had at least used her true name. Her hand clutched her throat. Heavens! If there was no Montague Windhall, then was she married to this—this Nick person or not?

A coil of anger tightened in her chest, and she brushed aside the question. Twins! He—they—would not get away with this. No one made a fool of Christine Fleming!

Raising her chin, she marched toward the bedroom. She needed time to think. With just a little time she would come up with a fair settlement for the heartless bounders.

Closing the bedroom door quietly behind her, she crossed the room and sat in a chair, her fingers drumming on the quilt-covered arms.

Mont—Nick—was in Williamsburg, supposedly under yet another guise in the governor's office. Was he in danger? Would his life be threatened if his masquerade should be discovered? A tremor rippled through her at the mere thought of his being in peril. She might be angry with him, but she truly did love him and did not want to see him harmed.

Still . . . he did deserve to be taught a lesson. She brought a hand to her mouth and nibbled her fingertip. Williamsburg. She had heard of the place many times, but she had never been there—since they did not reach their honeymoon destination. A slow smile crept across her face. What if she were to go there? No. Her grin widened. Not as Christine, but as . . . the Scarlet Temptress?

Excitement swelled as she remembered Montague—Nick—mentioning a bolt of red velvet he had recently purchased. On the trip to Williamsburg she could occupy her time by making a satisfactory copy of her sister's scarlet gown.

After spending the night in the man's arms she did not doubt that she possessed the attributes required to entice him. She flicked a curl over her shoulder. How would Nick manage the fiery Scarlet Temptress? Would he remain true to his beloved wife? Or would he succumb to the lusty outlaw's charms?

Her finger tapped against her lip. What delicious revenge. Now all she had to do was convince Samantha to switch places with her—without telling her sister why. She might be furious with Nick, she reasoned, but she would not see him jeopardized by her actions. No. She would have to make up a plausible excuse to convince Samantha to switch places on the day after the wedding.

Rising, she crossed to the bookshelves. What could she say? She knew she would not have to worry about her twin's virtue where this Jason person was concerned. He had avoided her touch like the plague all afternoon. He would not try to entice Samantha into his bed. Still, Samantha was not going to be easy to persuade.

Christine reached for a book and withdrew it from the shelf. As she flipped through the pages the word "dispatch" caught her attention. Dispatch? A monumental plan began to form in her mind. She would not have to invent an excuse for Samantha. All that would be required was a short dispatch to her twin summoning her to Crystal Terrace. Christine smiled in earnest. Of course, upon her arrival

Samantha would find a second missive that would simply read:

Assume my position as Montague's wife. I will explain upon my return a fortnight hence.

CHAPTER 22

Samantha felt numb as she stood back and surveyed her Christine–like appearance in the gold-framed mirror. She still couldn't believe that she was at Crystal Terrace posing as Montague's wife. Why had Christine and Montague returned? Why did Christine want Samantha to switch places with her?

Heaving a great sigh, she smoothed the flowing folds of the silvery lilac gown she'd donned. The questions had tumbled over and over in her mind for the last hour, ever since she'd answered her twin's summons and found the other note. What could Christine possibly be thinking?

Shaking her head, Samantha moved toward the door. Her sister never practiced such foolishness—well, almost never. She was much too sensible for that. Casting off the troublesome thought, she opened the door. Whatever her twin's reason was, Samantha would learn it upon her sister's return. In the meantime she had enough problems worrying about her first encounter with her new brother-in-law.

Lifting her skirt, she straightened the bandage on her right knee; then, dropping the hem, she sauntered out the door, hoping the fake injury would forestall any advances from her twin's husband. As she reached the top of the stairs and placed her hand on the banister another thought struck her. What if Montague could tell them apart? She relaxed. No.

He hadn't been married to Christine long enough to know about her little quirks. But she couldn't help wondering how he would react the first time Christine refused to eat for days because she'd found one of her gowns had grown too snug. Or how he'd accept one of her temper tantrums when she stomped off and disappeared for hours.

Well, she decided, that was Montague's problem now. Trailing her fingers on the banister as she descended the stairs, Samantha practiced limping.

With Montague and Carl away she had little to do. And why on earth were they checking the drying sheds anyway? Those wouldn't be needed until next fall. Shrugging at the oddity, she crossed the entry to Montague's study and grabbed the first leather-bound volume within her reach, then carried it into the drawing room.

Pulling a small ottoman in front of a striped chair, she sat down and braced her leg on the cushion, then raised her skirt above her knee, revealing the bareness of her calf and the white bandage.

For the first time she glanced down at the book she'd taken from the study. Laughter bubbled up the back of her throat. Oh, well, perhaps the art of skinning bears might be interesting.

"Lady Windhall! What has happened?" Dahlia entered the room and bustled to Samantha's side, concern marring the older woman's pleasant face.

Lowering the book, Samantha fought back a wave of guilt. She hated to deceive Dahlia. Drawing in a slow breath, she forced a brave smile as she knew Christine would. "It is nothing, Dahlia. Do not worry. I was such an imbecile." She lowered her lashes as if embarrassed. "I missed a step on the staircase and took a slight tumble." She gestured toward the bandage. "I twisted my knee."

"Oh, you poor child."

Samantha winced at the housekeeper's sincere distress. "I am afraid Montague is going to be terribly angry with me for such a foolish mishap." She lowered her lashes. "I mean, it *is* our honeymoon and all."

228

"Now don't you worry about that." Dahlia crooned and patted Samantha's hand. "His lordship won't be angry. Only worried." Her features softened. "Are you sure you're all right? Has Bromley gone for the physician? Can I get you anything?"

Samantha smiled and squeezed Dahlia's hand. She was such a dear person. "I am quite well, Dahlia. And I have no need of a physician. Now stop fussing so." She released the older woman's hand and folded her own in her lap. "But please, when my husband comes home, would you ask him to join me?"

Dahlia's gaze drifted to Samantha's right cheek for a moment, then she nodded. "Of course. But I'll not leave you on your own in here," she said firmly, turning for the door. "Just let me get the mending, and I'll keep you company."

"What about supper?"

The housekeeper smiled. "It's just stew and corn cakes tonight. And it's already cooking. Since I didn't expect you and the master back today, I'd planned on having a simple meal. I hope it's all right."

"Oh, yes. That is a splendid choice—one of my favorites." Samantha flinched when she realized that for as long as she could remember Christine had detested stew, referring to it as the meager repast of commoners. Samantha mentally shrugged. It would be up to Christine to set Dahlia straight about her preferences when she returned.

Dahlia disappeared through the doorway, then returned shortly with a bundle of clothing and a sewing basket.

Samantha spied one of the shirts she'd seen Montague wear. "Do you mind if I help?"

The older woman looked surprised, then grinned. "Not at all." Evidently seeing where Samantha's attention was drawn, Dahlia picked up the white silk shirt and handed it to her. "This one's missing a button."

Samantha didn't want to examine her reasons for feeling pleased about the intimate chore, nor how she ached to raise the shirt to her nose and breathe in the scent of his body that surely lingered on the material.

With her head bent and her fingers working awkwardly at the unfamiliar task Samantha didn't know of her brother-in-law's arrival until Dahlia jumped up.

"Good heavens!" the older woman cried. "What's wrong with *you?*"

Samantha's head snapped up.

Montague stood in the doorway, leaning heavily on Carl. He didn't answer Dahlia's question. Instead he explored the length of Samantha's exposed leg, his expression troubled. "Christine? What happened to your leg? Are you hurt?" He started to move forward, but Carl reached out a hand to stay him.

"Sit down, Montague, before you do yourself more damage. I'll see to your wife."

Carl led Montague to a chair opposite Samantha. Turning, he dropped down on one knee before her. "How did this happen?" he asked, reaching out to brush her skirt away from the wrapping.

Hoping to sound like Christine, Samantha injected a tiny whimper into her voice. "I fell down the stairs."

"What?" Montague exploded, rising halfway out of his seat. But Carl shot him a hard look, and he sank back down.

"It was nothing." Samantha wanted to ease Montague's concern. "Truly. I just twisted my knee." She flashed him a warm smile. "It should be back to normal . . . in a fortnight or so." Still smiling, she looked at Carl.

He was staring at her right cheek.

Samantha stifled a groan. Oh, no. Carl had seen her dimple. She cast a quick peek at Montague, but fortunately his gaze remained focused on her bandaged leg. Returning her attention to Carl, she offered him a small, tremulous smile, praying that he wouldn't give her away.

Carl blinked, then something humorous altered his expression. He turned toward Montague, then back to her again. All at once his face broke into a broad grin. "Yes, Christine, I'm sure your knee will mend just fine." He turned to the younger man. "Montague, though, may take a while longer."

Samantha frowned and looked at her brother-in-law, noticing for the first time that his shirt was unbuttoned, the beginnings of a wrapping visible through a part down the front. "Montague? What happened to you?"

He cast her a lopsided grin. "I'm afraid, sweetheart, that I had a disagreement with my horse and—"

"His horse won." Carl laughed. "He's cracked a couple of ribs."

"Oh, no!" Samantha's hand flew to her throat. "Are you in pain? Shouldn't you be lying down?" She turned to the housekeeper. "Dahlia, have Bromley fetch the physician at once."

"No!" Jason countered. "I—um—this has happened before. I see no need to inconvenience Mr. Falwick." He frowned and looked back down at her knee. "But perhaps he should see to your injury."

"No. I—er—please, no. I am embarrassed enough without having the physician witness my silly clumsiness." She mentally pleaded with him to understand.

Montague's gaze softened and lowered to her mouth. "All right, sweetheart. But I warn you, if your knee does not improve in a few days, or if there is too much swelling, the physician will be summoned immediately."

Relieved, Samantha nodded.

Carl chuckled.

"Humph." Dahlia sniffed. "Neither one of you has any sense." She turned to Carl. "If you'll help these two into the dining room, I'll see to setting the table."

"Of course." Carl nodded.

As soon as Dahlia left the room Carl rose and lifted Samantha up in his arms. He grinned at Montague. "Do you think you can make it on your own? Or shall I come back and carry you in, too?"

Montague's jaw clenched. "I think I can manage on my own. But thank you anyway." Scowling, he rose slowly to his feet and followed them into the formal eating area.

Montague sat at the head of the table, leaving Carl and Samantha flanking him.

Dahlia placed a steaming cauldron of stew on the table along with corn cakes and freshly churned butter. When she'd finished Jason requested a bottle of wine.

Within moments Dahlia returned, but it was Carl who reached for the port.

"In consideration of your injury, Montague, do let me fill the goblets." The burgundy liquid sloshed into the glasses, then Carl raised his in a toast. "To the newlyweds. May your injuries not cripple your desire for each other."

Montague sputtered and coughed.

Samantha swallowed a large gulp, her face feeling as if it were on fire. She lowered her lashes and watched Montague dab at his lips, his stare setting flame to Carl's countenance. Lowering his napkin, he clenched his hand around the stem of the goblet. "I'm certain that it won't, Carl." Montague's words hissed from between his teeth. "But thank you for the gesture."

Carl smiled down into his glass.

Samantha took another sip and raised her head. Was she going to blush like a silly child every time someone mentioned the intimacies her supposed marital status entailed? She squared her shoulders and raised her chin. "Yes, Carl. Thank you. But as my husband has pointed out, the injuries won't cripple our—er—feelings for each other."

Carl raised his goblet. "Hear, hear."

Samantha slowly brought her own glass to her lips, noticing as she did so that Montague did not drink from his. Instead his tormented gaze remained fixed on the table. "Montague? Are your ribs hurting?" Samantha asked softly.

His eyes met hers and lingered. "No, sweetheart. I was just thinking of what a wretched honeymoon you're having to endure." He flicked a glance at Carl. "As soon as these bloody injuries heal, perhaps you can enjoy a proper one."

Samantha didn't know what to say, yet she couldn't help but envy her twin for the fulfillment of such a promise. She instantly felt a stab of guilt and lowered her head. During the balance of the meal she occasionally cast a scathing look at Carl and an anxious one at Montague, but she finished in silence.

Carl, who seemed to be enjoying himself immensely, kept up a constant bout of conversation throughout supper. And if he noticed that Samantha and Montague replied only in monosyllables, he never mentioned it.

Finally, the repast at an end, Montague suggested they adjourn to the parlor for a brandy.

Rising, Carl came around the table to Samantha's side and, with a gallant flourish, scooped her up into his arms. He grinned down at her and winked. "I've been meaning to ask you, Christine, where is Madeline? I haven't been able to locate her for some time now."

Montague's attention snapped to Carl. "What? Madeline is missing?" He stepped forward, his features darkening with concern. "How long? Who was the last person to see her?"

"No!" Samantha clamped her teeth together. Blast Carl. What was he trying to do? "I mean—um—Madeline is not missing." She searched frantically for an excuse. "She went to . . . Boston."

Montague's features relaxed.

Carl frowned. "Boston? Why would she go there? She doesn't know anyone in that part of the country."

Samantha dug her nails into the back of his neck, and a feeling of satisfaction swept over her when he winced. "I believe she's returning to England." She peeked over Carl's shoulder at Montague.

He looked as if he were fighting the urge to reveal distress. "Will she return to Lynch's Ferry?"

"I'm not certain," Samantha said gently, remembering the bond she and Montague had shared while she portrayed Madeline.

At his crestfallen look Samantha wanted to swear out loud. Blast Carl Malderon! "But I am quite certain that she will write soon and let us know of her plans."

Montague inhaled deeply. "Yes. Of course she will."

Carl carried Samantha into the parlor and lowered her onto a settee. Turning, he met Montague coming in the doorway and guided him to the seat beside Samantha. "Sit here," Carl chortled. "And enjoy your wife's company while I pour us a draught." He smiled down at Samantha. "Would you like a sherry? Or, if you prefer, I'll ask Dahlia to brew you a cup of tea."

"Sherry is fine." Samantha smiled, but Carl would have had to be blind not to notice the lacerating look she cut in his direction. She would see that Carl got his just reward. He could stake his impoverished plantation on that.

Carl must have intercepted her thoughts, for he suddenly looked very uncomfortable. He turned quickly to prepare their drinks.

Montague eased down onto the settee beside Samantha, and she instantly became aware of their close proximity. His clean, manly scent rose up to entice her. His thigh brushed against hers, and even through the layers of petticoats she felt the tautness of his muscles. Feeling his shoulder press against hers, she fought the urge to lean into him.

She glared damningly at the small seat that forced her and Montague to share such an intimate cocoon. Someone really should make these things larger,.

Montague pulled back from her and slipped his arm onto the back of the seat, directly behind her shoulders. He shifted slightly so as to face her. The movement caused his chest to brush her arm. A warm tingle raced up the assaulted limb, and she shivered. She immediately looked at Montague to see if he'd noticed.

He had. Tortured blue eyes penetrated her composure as sweet stabs of desire lanced her breast. She swallowed tightly and gave him a weak smile. The air thickened around her as she watched his gaze slide to her mouth. With a will of its own her body swayed forward. Her lips parted unconsciously, and his mouth drew nearer . . . or was it hers?

Suddenly a drink was thrust in front of her. "Your sherry, Christine." Carl's voice jerked her to her senses.

With a trembling hand she took the proffered glass and

quickly brought it to her lips, hoping the sherry would soothe her frayed nerves.

Carl took a chair near them and crossed his legs. He looked so smug that Samantha felt the urge to flatten his nose.

Not trusting herself to refrain from doing just that, she leaned back as well, being very careful not to touch Montague in any way. Her shaky composure couldn't take another encounter with his potent masculinity.

When Samantha finished her drink Carl abruptly rose and extended his hand. Now what? She could tell by the gleam in his eye that he had something up his sleeve.

"It's getting late," Carl said, grasping her hand and pulling her to her feet. "I'm sure you and Montague are quite ready to retire. I'll carry you up so Dahlia can help you prepare for bed." He turned to her brother-in-law. "Then I'll come back to help you."

Montague's features hardened.

Carl smiled, then he lifted Samantha into his arms. As he neared the doorway Dahlia came into the room.

"Ah, good." Carl nodded. "I was just going to summon you. Lady Windhall needs assistance in order to retire."

"I thought she might." Dahlia nodded as she fell into step behind Carl.

Samantha peered over Carl's shoulder at Montague and frowned. His hands were balled into fists, and he stared damningly at Carl's back. Then his gaze rose to meet hers and softened. Something unreadable flicked in their blue depths for a moment before his lashes lowered, almost as if it pained him to look at her.

When Carl deposited Samantha on the bed Dahlia bustled to the chest-on-chest to rummage through the drawers.

"I'll bring Montague up in about fifteen minutes," Carl announced. Then, with a mock salute, he hurried out the door.

Samantha ground her teeth together. Blast. *Blast.*

Dahlia walked to the bed carrying a white garment over her arm. Reaching for Samantha's hand, the older woman carefully helped Samantha to her feet and placed the clothing on the bed.

Aged fingers began to work on the lacing of Samantha's gown. "We'd better hurry if we're going to have you decent by the time your husband arrives."

Samantha sighed and gave herself up to Dahlia's ministrations.

With her skin refreshed by a vigorous scrubbing in lilac-scented water, Samantha felt Dahlia draw the last stroke of the brush down the back of her hair before turning to lift the filmy white garment from the bed. The housekeeper held it up and shook it gently, allowing the gauzy folds to unfurl. It was a bedrobe, one so sheer that Samantha might as well don nothing at all. The woman didn't truly expect her to wear that—did she? Oh, Lord.

Samantha lifted her arms, but just as the garment slipped over her head a knock sounded at the door.

"Are you decent?" Carl's voice drifted through the closed panel.

"Just a moment," Dahlia called out before pulling back the covers on the bed and motioning Samantha with a quick wave of her hand.

Barely remembering her ruse in time, Samantha checked the urge to run and hobbled to the bed, then climbed beneath the welcome barrier as Dahlia crossed to open the door.

Montague walked into the room beside Carl, and the color seemed to leave his face. He quickly looked away.

Samantha swung her attention to Carl. The blackguard seemed quite pleased with himself about something. What?

"If you'll excuse us, Dahlia"—Carl motioned to the door—"I'll help Montague disrobe, then leave the lovebirds to their nest."

Samantha gasped.

Montague went rigid.

Dahlia scurried from the room.

Oh, Lord, Samantha muttered inwardly, then she flicked an anxious glance at Montague.

He looked angry about something as Carl guided him to the side of the bed and began to unbutton his waistcoat.

Montague brushed the intruding hands aside. "I'll do it," he said in a constricted voice.

Carl stepped back, a smirk on his face as he waited.

With quick, jerky movements Montague shrugged out of the brown satin coat and threw it at Carl. The waistcoat followed swiftly.

Carl smiled about something.

Samantha pressed back into her pillow and clutched the quilt to her breast, enthralled by the ripple of muscles down her brother-in-law's back beneath fine silk. When he tore the shirt from his broad shoulders and flung it in Carl's direction he revealed the glorious bronze of his back, contrasting with the white bandage. She blinked and tried to gather her scattered thoughts.

Montague's anger seemed to increase as he sat down on the edge of the bed and tore off his shoes and stockings. Then, rising slowly, he glared at Carl and reached for the buttons on his breeches.

CHAPTER 23

Samantha drew the blanket closer to her breast and pushed even farther back into the bed pillows as Montague's hands moved with deliberate slowness to the fasteners of his breeches. Her gaze flew frantically to Carl for some sign of rescue.

"Er, Montague?" Carl's voice sounded hoarse. "Since it's—um—so late, perhaps I could prevail upon you for a bed for the night."

Montague's features settled into an oddly satisfied expression. "Of course you may."

Carl's chest deflated with a whoosh of breath. "Good. Will you show me to my room?"

Montague glanced at Samantha. He winked wickedly before turning back to Carl and flicking a hand toward the door. "Just use the guest room—next door on the right." He smiled smugly. "Good night, my friend."

Carl hesitated. He opened his mouth as if to say something, then closed it and nodded. "Yes, yes. Good night, then." His face creased with concern before he stalked out of the room.

Samantha felt a nervous tremor creep along her spine. Now what? Blast it! Her sister's husband was just about to join her in bed. She cast Montague a fearful look. At the sight of his near-naked form she swallowed and searched wildly about for some means of deliverance. Nothing. She swung back to Montague and was surprised to see something akin to anxiety in his features before he quickly turned around.

"Er, perhaps I should go check to see if Carl needs anything."

Relief flooded her senses. "Yes, perhaps you should."

Montague grabbed his shirt and headed for the door. Then, opening it, he halted. "I might have a drink with Carl before he retires. Don't wait up for me, l-love. You need your rest."

As Jason closed the door to his brother's bedchamber he let out a pent-up breath and turned to find Carl leaning calmly against the wall.

The older man removed his watch from the fob pocket of his waistcoat and checked the time. "I'd have given you at least five more minutes."

Jason clenched his fists, wanting desperately to wrap his fingers around his godfather's neck. "What kind of game are you playing? Do you truly feel the need to test my honor? Damn it, Carl, I could throttle you for pulling such an idiotic prank."

Obviously unconcerned with Jason's anger, Carl swung toward the stairs. "Consider it retaliation for all the pranks you and Nick have played on me in the past." He peered over his shoulder and flashed a smile. "Now how about offering me a tot?" He studied the closed door of Nick's bedchamber. "It looks to be a long night."

Silently vowing to level vengeance on Carl's silver head, Jason led the way down to the study. Once inside he poured two glasses of port. "I wonder if Nick realizes the position he's put me in."

Carl accepted a glass and took a sip. "Only if he knows that you're attracted to Christine."

Jason shrugged. "I may have made mention of it, but not to any great extent."

"Perhaps you should have. Then he might have found another way to handle the situation."

"How?" Jason snarled. "By taking her with him and risking both their lives? Not very likely." He strode to the chair behind the desk and sat down. "Besides, he trusts me."

"Then what's the problem?"

Jason sat his glass on the oak surface before him and stared thoughtfully into the amber liquid. "I'm not sure I can trust myself. Oh, not that I'd deliberately betray my brother. I wouldn't. But I find it exceedingly difficult to maintain control of my baser instincts in my sister-in-law's beguiling presence."

Carl chuckled. "I think you're worrying overmuch. Your honesty is too deeply ingrained to allow the situation to get out of hand."

"I pray you're right, Carl. I truly do." He leaned back in the chair and met the older man's gaze. "But just as a precautionary measure I'm going to spend as little time here as possible. I trust I can depend on you to look after her welfare during my frequent absences?"

Carl took a chair opposite Jason. "Of course. Well, as long as I'm able to, anyway. I'm soon to make a trip to Bent Creek for a day or so, but I won't know the date until I receive word from Patrick. If you're away at that time, I'll ask Iron Sword to watch out for her."

"Who is Iron Sword?"

Carl lowered the goblet. "Jason, we've been over this before. I can't and won't tell you that."

Jason's thoughts drifted to the woman lying upstairs in his brother's bed. Was Iron Sword a ladies' man? Would he tempt Christine in Jason's absence? The thought froze. He realized he was acting just like her husband. God's teeth! He didn't care what she did.

"Ever the protector, hmm, Carl?" Jason stood and retrieved the bottle from the sideboard, refilled his own glass, then the older man's. "Very well, then, how about a game of chess to while away the hours till dawn?" Jason chuckled at Carl's confused look. "My dear godfather, you don't expect me to return to Christine's bed, do you?"

"No. Of course not. But I didn't plan on staying awake the entire night, either." Carl downed the port and rose to his feet. "If you're going to make yourself scarce on the morrow, then you're going to need some rest tonight." He flashed a broad smile. "Come along, godson. You can share the room with me."

Jason stifled a curse, unwilling to attempt to share the single bed in the guest room. "You go ahead. I'll make do in here." He nodded toward the richly stuffed leather chair near the fireplace.

Carl shrugged but said nothing as he sauntered out the door.

At the first light of dawn Jason slipped quietly back into his brother's bedchamber, praying fervently that he wouldn't disturb Christine. He didn't like the idea of lying beside the woman. He loathed the idea, in fact, but he had to make it appear as if he'd spent the night with her.

He padded softly to the side of the big, inviting bed. His heart's pace picked up. All he had to do was take off his clothes and slide in . . . beside her. His hands trembled and paused on the buttons of his silk shirt. Slide into bed with her! Ha! He didn't trust himself that far.

Moving to the chair, he sat down. No. They'd both be considerably safer if he kept his distance. When she awakened she would find him in the chair. He'd make up some excuse about his ribs hurting too much to lie down.

He pulled his shirt out of the waist of his breeches and ran his fingers through his hair. He didn't have to simulate the effects of a sleepless night. He'd most assuredly had one in the study, but he wanted Christine to awaken and find him looking as though he'd tried to sleep beside her bed during the night. He twisted his mouth. Quite the ardent, if incapacitated, bridegroom. Leaning back, he yawned and lolled his head against the seat, then closed his eyes. God, he was tired.

A small mewling sound came from the bed.

His eyes snapped open, and he stared wonderingly over at the woman tossing restlessly amid the flannel bedcovers. The quilts had slipped down to her waist, revealing the sheer bodice of the white gown she wore.

A flame coiled through his belly, and he feasted on the perfect shape of her full breasts. Firm and high, their coral tips strained wantonly against the thin material.

Jason drew in a deep breath and tried to ignore the temptation. She was Nick's wife. His brother's wife.

When he lifted his lashes again it was to find her standing before him, her arms outstretched in invitation.

Christ! he swore silently. He gripped the arms of the chair to keep from moving toward her. But he wanted to. Oh, God, how he wanted to. He made a valiant effort not to look at her body, so temptingly displayed through the gossamer folds, but his traitorous stare would not waver. Forcing his attention upward, he met the naked desire smoldering in her eyes. Heaven help him.

"Jason?" Her throaty voice was like a caress. "Come to bed."

Jason squeezed his eyes shut. Go away, temptress . . . go away. I'm not strong enough to resist.

Then he was lying in the immense bed, naked. How the hell had that happened? Trying to regain his senses, he shifted and attempted to rise. But something moved beside him. Immediately he became aware of the small, delicate body cuddled in his arms. Oh, no. He cursed the soft bottom pressing against his hardening length, stirring emotions he had no business feeling.

Then he noticed the position of his arm. It was draped over her shoulder, his fingers cupped around her breast. For a moment he allowed himself to enjoy the warm weight in his palm, to inhale her intoxicating fragrance and nuzzle the creamy flesh exposed above the neckline at the back of her gown. Of their own will his lips caressed her velvety skin, and his body leapt in response.

The air around him thickened. Desire claimed his composure. Ever so slowly his thumb rose to stroke the stiff little bud teasing his palm. But when she moaned in her sleep and stirred, his hand immediately stilled. Please, God, don't let her wake up.

Evidently God expected him to save himself, for she turned toward him and buried her face in the hollow of his neck, her hands rising to slide up his chest. Sweet fire scorched through his body. Feathery strands of silky hair teased his chin as she brushed her lips back and forth across the wildly throbbing pulse at the base of his throat. She murmured something, and her sweet breath seared his flesh. He ached to become one with her, to bury himself inside her.

Her arm slipped around his waist, drawing him closer as she pressed her thighs against his. Jason's body sprang to life. His manhood tightened in exquisite torture.

Unable to stop himself, his lips brushed her hair, then slid lower to tease her temples. Tauntingly she lifted her lips, and his mouth trailed down her smooth cheek to claim their moistness.

Jason's resistance collapsed. Hungrily he devoured the softness presented to him, reveled in the heat of her soul-stripping kiss. His tongue slid between her teeth, and when she gave an odd little sound of pleasure, then touched her tongue to his, he nearly exploded.

Desire so intense it bordered on pain knifed through him with piercing jabs. From somewhere in the shadowed area at the back of his brain his conscience tried to interfere, tried to tell him this was wrong. But he closed his mind to the warnings, and his arms tightened around her, seeking to absorb her soul into his.

Long fingernails dug into the flesh of his back as she returned his kiss with a passion that neared violence. His hands trembled as they slid down to cup her bottom and pull her closer to his aching loins.

His mouth drank again and again from the sweetness of her lips as he floundered in a sea of breath-stealing desire. He moved down her satin curves to sample one tight pink crest through the material of her gown.

She thrust her hips against his throbbing manhood. Her nails raked furrows in his back, and she arched her spine to press closer. Unable to help himself, he gently tugged at the tight bud so boldly offered to him.

The barrier between them became an obstacle he couldn't tolerate. He tore at the gown, carelessly flinging it from her body. The need to feel her warmth against his naked flesh consumed him.

A whimper escaped her lips when he slid his hand down to cover the nest of soft curls that shielded her most intimate secret.

Jason's conscience screamed at him.

His eyes flew open. Frantically he blinked. He was still sitting in the chair. His heart slammed against the walls of his chest. Perspiration beaded his forehead. It was only a dream, he realized. Thank God. It was only a dream.

Yanking his shirt together, he sprang to his feet and nearly ran across the room in his haste to leave. He stormed into the room where Carl slept and angrily slammed the door.

Carl lurched up in the bed. "What the hell?"

"Get up," Jason said through gritted teeth.

Carl blinked wildly and shook his head. "What's happened?"

"I just made love to my brother's wife!" Jason roared.

"What?" Carl bolted from the bed, his face a mask of fury.

Undaunted, Jason waved him away. "Don't panic, Carl.

Fortunately, the unholy performance took place in my dreams." He glared at the older man. "This time."

Carl sagged back down onto the bed. "Damn you, Jason. You nearly took a decade off of my life."

Jason moved to the fireplace and gripped the mantel. "It didn't do me a hell of a lot of good either."

Carl shook his head and slid his fingers through his silver hair. "I'm too old for this."

Jason shot him a scathing look and threw himself into a chair. He banged his fist down on the arm. "I wish to hell I could understand why this is happening to me. Ever since the night I was robbed by the Scarlet Temptress I haven't been the same. First I find myself infatuated with a woman I should want to see hanged. Then I become enamored of an old woman. And now this. I've never in my life had a problem with self-control. And I've damn sure never betrayed another's trust." He rose and paced to the fireplace. "But there's something about her, something that draws me to her. I lose my senses when I'm in the same room with her—and my sanity if that room happens to be a bedroom."

Carl began to chuckle. "You sound like a man in love."

"No." Jason whirled around. "God's blood! I must be losing my mind." He turned to the door and jerked it open, then stomped out into the hall.

Carl rose to his feet and followed. "Jason, wait. There's something I think you should know. The woman in—"

"No more!" Jason held up his palm. "I'm going for a ride. A *long* ride." He lowered his hand and drew it into a fist. "And you, my dear godfather, can plan on remaining at Crystal Terrace as a buffer until my brother returns."

CHAPTER 24

For the hundredth time in the last ten days Jason rode away from Crystal Terrace. Even the fact that Nick had finally sent a man back with Adversary did not ease his spirit. The constant ruse and his close proximity to Christine were wearing him down. He had to get away. He could no longer trust himself with Nick's wife. He'd tried avoiding her for the last week and a half, yet even in Carl's presence Jason couldn't keep his hands or thoughts from her—and each day grew worse.

Reining Adversary to a halt at the cave, he dismounted and led the stallion inside. It was a long walk across the fields to Crystal Terrace, but maybe it would give him enough time to come up with a reason he could give Christine for leaving. And he would leave. Tomorrow.

As he started down the hill his step faltered. But what about today? his mind asked. Carl was expecting a message at home. He had to go. How would Jason make it through the day confined inside that house—with Christine? Suddenly he smiled, and his pace quickened. That one was simple—he wouldn't.

Samantha stared at Montague. A tour? Alone with him? Good Lord, that was much too tempting. In his presence her resistance melted like wax over a flame. No. She didn't trust herself to be alone with him. Not now . . . not *ever*. The last week and a half had stretched her control to the limit. She perused his strong profile, outlined against the parlor fireplace. Then again, she mused, what possible trouble could she get into just going on a short tour? Wasn't it better than being closeted inside with him?

Carl coughed. "Montague? I thought you still had business to attend today."

"I do," her brother-in-law answered quietly. "But I've decided it can wait until tomorrow."

"Is that wise?" Carl looked concerned.

Montague held the older man's gaze steadily. "Probably not. But then, as I'm certain you recall, I don't always exercise prudence."

"Perhaps this time you should."

Montague stared down at his long fingers as they curled around his teacup. The fragile vessel looked as if it might crumble beneath the pressure of his grip. Was the business that vital? "Montague, if you'd rather not, I—"

"Be ready in half an hour." Montague straightened and set his cup on the low table between them. "And wear something warm. We'll be on horseback." He hesitated. "That is, if you think your injury can withstand a ride."

Samantha shot a look from Montague to Carl. Carl looked unhappy about something. Men! Who could understand them? "I'm certain it won't pain me too much—as long as I do not overdo it," she added quickly. Rising, she crossed to the doorway. "Are you sure *you're* up to it?"

He nodded. "I'll manage."

"Then give me a moment to change into my riding habit and put up my hair."

"Leave it down," Montague ordered, his gaze caressing the length of her curls. Then, as if catching himself, he added, "I'm anxious to be off, and it will save time."

Once out of the man's sight Samantha raced to her room and dressed in her green velvet riding habit and small matching plume hat. When she returned to the drawing room minutes later she found Montague alone. "Has Carl gone?"

"Yes." Obviously not wanting to discuss Carl further, Montague took her arm and guided her toward the stables.

Atop their mounts they cantered slowly across the open fields toward the woods. Trailing behind Montague, she was hard put not to notice the ease with which he rode, or the way his muscles rippled as he effortlessly controlled the powerful roan he'd chosen.

Did he have any idea what his slightest movement did to her insides? Stop this, she ordered. Montague is beyond your reach, and he always will be. A heaviness settled in her chest.

"I've often wondered how a tobacco plantation operates," Samantha offered as they neared one of the drying sheds.

Jason stared at his sister-in-law. He wished he knew something about the operation himself. Hell, he raised horses, not tobacco. That was Nick's area of expertise. Hoping he could bluff his way through, he drew the roan to a halt in front of the shed and dismounted. "I'm not truly that informed myself," he admitted. "I rely a great deal on the overseer." Well, that much was true. His hands encircled her waist and tightened as he helped her dismount. He fought the urge to crush her against him and kiss her soundly. "I mainly deal with the accounts and the sale of the crops."

Samantha quickly eased away. "Have you any new prospects for an overseer?"

Jason shrugged, peering out across the fields. He couldn't tell her that there would be no overseer, no crops. As soon as Nick returned Jason would go home to Halcyon, and his twin would return to Williamsburg. Jason's eyes slid back to hers and held. "None."

Samantha shifted her feet, suddenly anxious about their isolation. There wasn't even a field hand in sight.

The old gray wood building before her looked inviting and warm. Perhaps a bit *too* warm. She moved back another step. "I do not think I would care to go inside," she stated truthfully. "It looks quite spooky."

Jason smiled and took her hand. "It's not as bad as it seems. Come on, I'll show you." He pulled her forward and raised the latch. The hinges squeaked as the heavy wooden door swung open.

Samantha immediately became aware of the warmth of

his hand wrapped around hers. Her throat constricted, and she forced herself to concentrate on something else. She glanced about the dank room. Sunlight filtered in through the cracks in the walls, illuminating the dirt floor strewn with withered tobacco leaves. Several burlap-covered barrels sat against one wall. Balls of twine were piled haphazardly, their loose ends snaking out in all directions. Row after row of hooks hung from the ceiling near the massive fireplace and enormous bellows.

"I can imagine how they dry the leaves," Samantha offered. "They must hang the tobacco on the hooks and build a great fire to hurry the process."

Jason nodded. Hell, it sounded reasonable to him. "Yes. After that they tie the tobacco into bundles and pack it in barrels for shipment." At least he was fairly certain that was how it was done.

Samantha tilted her head to one side and studied him. Somehow he seemed distant from his life's work. Why? Was he so wealthy that the plantation was just a secondary income and of little importance? "Is there a great deal of profit in tobacco?"

"Yes. Like myself, many men of title and little else came from England in hopes of amassing their own fortune." His voice turned bitter. "The ones that survived found indigo and tobacco the most profitable." Then, as if shaking himself from a painful reverie, he cleared his expression, but his voice remained brittle. "Come along. I'll show you where we store and dry the seeds."

She hated it when he behaved in that stilted manner. She knew the warmth and humor he possessed—had seen it many times while posing as her fictitious aunt—and she wanted to see it again. "I understand that you came to know my Aunt Madeline well during your illness," Samantha prompted, hoping to lighten his mood.

His features softened as he helped her mount, then carefully swung up into his own saddle. "Yes, I did. She's a fine lady. A fine woman indeed."

Samantha couldn't suppress the little thrill that shot through her. "She spoke highly of you, too."

"Did she?"

Samantha couldn't pull her stare from his face. "Yes," she half whispered. "She showed me the lovely prism you gave her." Her hand rose to her own chest, secretly feeling the outline of the crystal heart beneath the blouse of her riding habit. "It meant a lot to her." *More than you'll ever know.*

Montague cleared his throat and looked away, almost as if embarrassed. "Yes. Well, it was meager recompense for the time she spent tending to my needs."

Samantha's hand tightened on the prism. "Is that why you gave it to her? As payment for services rendered?" She couldn't control the iciness in her voice.

Montague's startled gaze met hers. "Of course not. I gave it to Madeline because"—his voice gentled—"it reminded me of her brightness and wit, of her inner warmth and compassion."

Suddenly his mouth clamped shut, and he straightened in the saddle. "We're wasting time. If we're to see more of the plantation, we'd better be off."

Samantha hid a satisfied smile as she reined the horse around to follow. She had only seen a small glimpse of the real man, but it was enough.

The tour of the plantation and its operation had been sketchy to say the least. Montague seemed tense and preoccupied—so distant Samantha came away with no more knowledge of how tobacco was raised than she'd started with.

When the sun reached its peak he lead them to the edge of the James River, and they dismounted. Pale spring grass grew thick beneath the shelter of an umbrellalike evergreen that overlooked the swiftly moving water.

Montague pulled leather saddlebags from his horse's back and revealed the makings of a picnic lunch. He looked up as he spread a blanket he'd retrieved from behind his saddle and smiled. With a swing of his hand toward the chicken, bread, and apple pie he was setting out, he announced, "With Dahlia's compliments." He reached back into the saddlebags and withdrew a bottle of French wine, a grin teasing his lips. "And mine."

Samantha chuckled and spread her skirts as she sat on the blanket beside him. "Why, Montague, how positively gallant of you. If we weren't already married, I'd accuse you of courting."

His eyes met hers seriously. "Marriage is no reason to stop pampering the woman you love." His attention moved to her lips. "I'd devote my life to courting you, if I could."

His words had the effect of a storm on her senses. "And I would enjoy every minute of it," she said softly, knowing how true those words were. Glancing away, trying to arrest her wayward thoughts, she removed a chicken leg from the basket and brought it to her lips, then sought to ease the seriousness of their conversation. "What woman wouldn't? It would be like having her own knight in shining armor."

A dark brow arched, but there was an unmistakable twinkle in those blue eyes. "A knight? You seek to have a knight in attendance?" At her nod he rose to his knees and bent forward in a mock bow. "Then by all means, milady, let me do my knightly deed." He took the chicken from her hand, wielding it like a sword, and with a flourish he tore off a small piece of meat.

She looked at him questioningly.

He smiled and promptly popped the morsel into her mouth. "A damsel should never have to tarry with the task of feeding herself. Nay. Never when there is an able-bodied knight about."

Samantha tried to ignore the way her lips had tingled when he touched them with his fingers and primly chewed on the chicken, then shot him a teasing grin. "It could get rather messy when you feed me the pie."

He sighed and sat back on his heels. "Alas, the chivalrous man must suffer overmuch to insure the pleasure of his lady fair."

Samantha laughed and grabbed the chicken leg. "Enough. If you keep this up, I won't be able to swallow my food. Now eat your own meal, Sir Buffoon."

The lighthearted mood remained throughout the repast. At last, her stomach filled to the limit, Samantha moaned and leaned back on her elbows. "I don't think this was such a good idea after all. Now I'm too sleepy to ride." Lying down, she lowered her lashes. "You'll just have to continue on without me."

Montague chuckled and clasped his hands behind his head as he stretched out beside her. "No. I'll force myself to wait until you've rested."

Samantha raised one lid and peered over at him. He had closed his eyes. "Sir, I think you play me false. Had I not suggested a rest, you most assuredly would have."

"Only for your own well-being. Now be quiet, wench, and let me renew my strength. There may be dragons yet to slay."

"Dragons?" Samantha laughed softly, then lowered her lashes and tried to do as he suggested. But it was impossible. How could she rest with him so near? Her ears picked up the slightest sound of movement, the rhythm of his breathing, even the erratic beating of her own heart.

Visions of Montague reaching out to her, pulling her body against his, were so vivid that her breath stopped. Suddenly something touched her lips, and her eyes shot open. Her stare locked on Montague's intent face as his finger traced the outline of her mouth. She blinked. "Montague?"

His finger stilled. "It's getting late, sweetheart. We'd better go."

Samantha nodded numbly, wishing he weren't so close. "Yes. Of course. I didn't realize the time."

Jason straightened and withdrew his hand. "It's all right, there's little left to see."

Samantha gathered the remains of the food while Montague folded the blanket and tied it to the roan's saddle.

As the sun pinkened the western horizon they turned their

mounts back toward the manor. Uneasiness settled around Samantha. She had spent the day basking in Montague's company, but now her situation came back full force.

When they arrived they learned that Carl would not be returning that eve. Except for the servants, she and Montague were alone. An anxious tremor skittered along her spine. Oh, she didn't worry about his taking her to bed; her injury—and his—safeguarded her from that. At least she hoped it did. His injury? Her hand shook as Montague helped her dismount. From what she could remember, he hadn't flinched with discomfort one time all afternoon. Come to think of it, she hadn't limped either. She had enjoyed herself so much, she'd completely forgotten the ruse. Had he noticed? And what about his ribs? Were they healing already? Oh, Lord, if that were so, she was in serious trouble.

After handing over the reins to Bromley, Montague walked Samantha into the house. She retreated to her bedroom to freshen up and change. Selecting an outfit was a problem she hadn't thought of—until now. She wanted to wear something feminine, yet something that wouldn't entice. She had enough problems without intentionally fanning the flames of Montague's desire.

She wasn't sure how much protection his injured ribs offered, or her own supposed injury. And she certainly didn't want to find out.

Searching through the armoire, she was surprised to find a rather plain yellow gown amid Christine's wardrobe. Perhaps Providence was with her after all. Smiling, Samantha quickly stepped into the dress. But just as she pulled up the bodice Dahlia strolled into the room. "Ah, I see I'm in time to help." The older woman moved behind Samantha and began fastening the back of the gown. "I should have allowed his lordship in to do this," Dahlia teased familiarly, "but supper is nearly ready, and I found myself with a bit of time." She turned Samantha around and nodded approvingly. "My, don't you look stunning."

Samantha frowned. Stunning? She swung toward the

gilded mirror against the wall behind the dressing screen and nearly fainted. Was this the plain gown she'd taken from the wardrobe? Good Lord! The bodice seemed almost inadequate. And what about the tiny lacings down the front? They didn't draw the bodice entirely together. Instead they left a tantalizing expanse of flesh visible beneath the thin yellow strings. Blast. She couldn't have chosen a worse dress—and it was too late to change.

Montague stood at the foot of the stairs when she began her descent. As she drew closer his head came up, and the color left his face. Something dangerous flared in his expression for an instant, then a cold, shuttered mask fell into place.

"You look beautiful." He took her hand and held it for a moment, his attention lingering on her bodice. "Too beautiful." Suddenly he seemed angry about something and abruptly released her. "Shall we go in to supper? I'm certain Dahlia has prepared a superb meal."

Confused by his brusque behavior, she nodded.

He held the chair for her while she sat, then took his own place at the head of the table.

"Did Carl's message say when he would return?" Samantha asked, desperate to rid herself of the strange tension that seemed to weight the very air around her.

"No." Montague's voice was clipped as he reached for the platter of pheasant Dahlia had set before him. "But I imagine he'll call around tomorrow. Why? Is something pressing?"

"No. I just thought he might return, since he failed to bid me good-bye."

"He's less than an hour's ride away. It's not as if you weren't going to see him for months."

Once more Samantha felt the heat of embarrassment touch her cheeks. Put that way, her comment had sounded inane. "I—I—you must try to forgive me, Montague. This is the first time I've ever been away from my loved ones, and I'm not certain how I should act."

Montague's eyes met hers with a warmth that singed her

petticoats. "You're not away from those who love you." He focused on her mouth. "Not by any means."

Samantha drew in a halting breath and shifted nervously in her chair. How she envied Christine. How she wished she *were* Christine. Then it would be so easy to reach out and take Montague's hand . . . to lead him up that staircase to their bedroom . . . to lose herself in the heat of his hungry kisses . . . to dissolve beneath the fire of his molten passion.

His fork hit the side of his plate, startling her. She blinked.

His jaw had tightened. A muscle drummed wildly near his temple. "Damn it. Stop looking at me like that."

Samantha paled. "What? I don't know what you mean."

"The hell you don't," he fairly shouted. "You sit there making love to me with your eyes, tempting me with that damnable dress and provocative mouth. You know I can't do anything . . . with my ribs like this. God's teeth! Stop making it harder on me." The chair scraped back as he stood abruptly. "I'm going out." He spun toward the door. "Don't wait up for me."

Samantha felt Montague's tortured words all the way to the center of her heart. Slowly she set her own fork down, her appetite suddenly gone. Making love to him with her eyes? Had she done that? She hadn't meant to. If anything, she'd intended just the opposite.

She rose and walked out onto the back veranda. Things were getting out of hand, and the situation could destroy not only her and Montague but Christine as well. No matter what the provocation, she must avoid him.

Uncaring that she was without a cloak, Samantha left the veranda and wandered down to the stables. Inside, the big roan that Montague had ridden stood regally in his stall, his beautiful head tilted as he seemed to study her.

Samantha had to quell the unladylike urge to leap astride the beast and bolt from the stables. She frowned. Why not take a ride on the roan? Montague was gone. Probably in the carriage, since his horse was still there. All day she'd played the prim and proper lady of the manor, sitting atop that sweet old mare that didn't possess an ounce of fire. Why not ride the spirited beast? Perhaps it would help rid her of the demons.

Without thought to the dress she wore she stepped up onto the rail and slid onto the horse's bare back. Because of the cumbersome folds of the gown she couldn't ride astride, but it didn't matter. She could handle the stallion.

The roan pranced nervously and snorted.

Samantha soothed him with soft words and a gentle stroke before she bent to unlatch the stall.

As if released after months of confinement the steed sprang forward, his nostrils flaring.

Once out of the barn Samantha grabbed the flowing mane and let the horse have his head. She gloried in the great animal's speed, giving little thought to what Montague would say if he found her out. Her only thoughts were of the horse's smooth rhythm and the freedom of the moment.

Cold nipped at her cheeks. The wind whipped her unbound hair wildly. The roan's hooves thundered as he labored toward the distant forest. The speed, the darkness, the serenity—they were like magic.

More than an hour had passed before the chill finally made itself known and Samantha turned the horse back toward Crystal Terrace.

She hadn't ridden very far in her homeward trek when a fox suddenly darted in front of the roan. He veered sharply to the left. Unprepared for the abrupt turn, Samantha lost her seat and plummeted to the ground. The frightened horse, now riderless, reared up and bolted across the field.

Samantha sat on the grass for a moment catching her breath. She knew she was fortunate not to have injured herself.

She glared at the retreating animal. Blast the beast. Now she would have to walk back. Brushing the hair from her forehead, she looked toward the manor. It was nowhere in sight. She must have ridden farther than she thought. Sighing, she rose to her feet.

Trudging back toward Crystal Terrace, she peered down at the ground. "Lord," she mumbled. "As if Montague isn't already enraged enough. If I don't get to the roan and stable him before—" She shuddered to think of what he might say. Lifting the pale skirt, she picked up her pace. He will be positively livid, she thought. She was so intent on her troubles that she didn't see the rider blocking her path until she nearly collided with his horse.

Jerking her head upward, she gasped. Her stomach fluttered with excitement. Unnerving night-lit eyes glittered down at her from behind a mask of smooth black silk.

CHAPTER 25

Jason stared down at his brother's wife from behind the mask of the Devilrider's costume. He tried not to notice how beautiful she was, or how her silky dark hair shimmered in the moonlight. Damnation! he cursed. What was she doing out here? When he left her he had assumed she would retire. Why the hell hadn't she? He had deliberately stayed away. Even gone to Carl's in an attempt to avoid her. And Carl, the grinning idiot, had put Jason to work.

"What are you doing here?" she asked suddenly, startling Jason.

"It doesn't matter," he returned a bit too sharply. Even if she didn't realize the position she'd put him in, *he* did. No matter how much he would like to, he couldn't leave her out there alone to walk home in the dark. He would have to take her back. Something leapt in his chest at the thought. Damn it! "Where's your mount?"

At first she looked surprised at his knowledge, then she shrugged. "He threw me and bolted."

"What? Were you injured?"

She shook her head. "Not physically."

Relaxing his curled fingers, he looked away. He knew he should turn his horse around and leave that very instant; that escorting her home, placing her on the saddle before him, would be a mistake—an enormous mistake.

Furrowing his brow, he tried to concentrate on another means, and it surprised even him when he realized his own traitorous hand had reached out to her. "May I offer assistance, milady?"

She stared down at his extended palm for a long moment. "Yes. Thank you," she said quietly, slipping her hand into his.

Jason felt a jolt tingle up his arm. God's teeth! What was the matter with her? Why didn't she fear him? He was *supposed* to be a ruthless outlaw, wasn't he? Blithering fool. How do you always manage to get yourself into these messes? Releasing a quiet moan he bent down and lifted her onto the saddle in front of him. He immediately regretted the action when her soft thigh brushed against his sensitive loins.

Adversary lurched forward, and Jason's hand automatically tightened around her waist to keep her from slipping. With no small amount of disgust he felt his fingers tremble against the firmness of her stomach.

Samantha felt the tremor in his hand, and it caused her own body to shiver in response. She couldn't still the racing beat of her heart or stop the flood of memories as her mind surged backward in time, back to the moment she'd first met the Devilrider in Montague's bedroom, to the passion they'd shared minutes later in the stable. Thank goodness she'd been dressed as the Scarlet Temptress then, and that the man now holding her had no idea of the intimacies they'd shared.

But she knew. And it was causing a monumental upheaval in her senses. She tried to hold herself stiff, not wanting to touch him, but the jolting gait of the black stallion kept rocking her against the rogue's solid chest, playing havoc with her already strained nerves, and by the time they reached the plantation she was a quivering mass.

When he finally drew the horse to a halt he dismounted smoothly and reached up to help her down. "Safe and sound, milady." His teeth flashed gleaming white in the darkness.

Something in his manner seemed familiar as she felt his strong fingers curl around the sides of her waist. He stood close to the horse, and as he lowered her from the saddle her breasts brushed against his chest. His body tensed, and his fingers dug into her flesh as he slowly slid her down his powerful length. From behind the mask his eyes burned brightly into hers, charging the air with excitement. Sweet sounds of night enfolded them, and almost reluctantly, as if he couldn't stop himself, he bent his head to her.

Samantha was startled by the heated touch of his lips, but she didn't attempt to pull back. She couldn't. For the first time she willingly kissed him without reservation. Something about him reminded her of Montague—a Montague that was not married to her sister; a Montague that she was free to love without reservation; a Montague that was hers alone.

She pressed closer, her arms sliding around his neck.

Jason felt a shock wave ripple through his body. What in the name of heaven was he doing? his conscience demanded. God's blood! Jerking his mouth from hers, he set her away from him. "I don't imagine your husband would appreciate this, Lady Windhall."

Samantha gasped. "Who *are* you?"

Jason felt the muscle in his jaw throb. I'm your brother-in-law, he wanted to shout, and you have no business enticing me. He wanted to shake her, but one look into those huge green eyes drained his anger, and his betraying hand rose to touch her cheek. "Someone who wishes you didn't belong to another."

Her shaky indrawn breath was nearly his undoing. Knowing he had to get away that very instant or disgrace his family, he dipped his head sharply in a mock salute and mounted. "Another time, milady." He wheeled the stallion around and rode swiftly toward the forest. Only he knew it was to place distance between himself and temptation.

"I should have told him I wasn't Christine," Samantha whispered as she stared into the darkness. But she knew her decision had been the right one. She didn't know him— didn't even know his true name. And to reveal her own identity could cost not only *her* life, but her father's as well.

"You blithering fool," Jason grumbled as he rode into the hidden stable at the base of the mountain. What was the matter with him? Never in his entire life had he had such a problem with control. And with his twin's wife! For God's sake, was he losing his sanity?

Dismounting, he leaned against the side of the stall. He knew he couldn't take much more of this. Christine was seeping into his blood like a murderous plague. He had to get away. Now. This very moment.

Changing into his own clothing again, he leapt back onto Adversary and jerked the reins toward Jed's cabin. He would stay with the trapper that night and leave for Halcyon at first light. Carl could send Jason's things. He didn't trust himself anywhere near Crystal Terrace. But a twinge of guilt caused him to rein the stallion to a halt. He couldn't disappear like this. Not without telling Christine.

Samantha dressed in one of Christine's revealing nightgowns and slipped into bed. Her nerves weren't up to another encounter with anyone of the masculine gender. But it seemed that she had just lowered her lashes when the bedroom door suddenly opened and Montague strolled into the room.

Surprised, and without giving thought to her attire, she sat up. "Montague?"

He stopped midstride, his stare slipping down the front of her sheer gown. His mouth tightened, and he abruptly turned away. "I'm sorry I awakened you. But an urgent matter has arisen, and I must leave for my other plantation immediately."

Samantha jerked the covers up to her chin and watched him toss some clothing into a satchel. "Halcyon?"

He didn't look at her. "Yes. And before you suggest accompanying me, I must tell you that it's going to be an uncomfortable trip. You're not feeling up to it . . . with your injury and all."

Samantha swallowed. She wasn't going to suggest *that*. She was glad he was going, glad that his tempting presence would be beyond her reach. So why did she feel such emptiness? "How long will you be gone?"

He seemed to take a moment to consider it. "A few days, possibly less."

A few days. By that time Christine would have returned to her rightful place as Montague's wife. A heaviness settled in Samantha's chest, and she watched the rippling line of his back as he packed his clothes. She knew this was the last time she would see him. When Christine returned, Samantha would leave.

She bit her lower lip as a thought formed in her mind. As soon as Montague left, the Scarlet Temptress would ride again—diligently. Her father's freedom came first, then her own. And she would never be free until she left Virginia and the shattering presence of her sister's husband. "I'll miss you," she whispered softly.

Montague's hands stilled, and he turned slowly, his eyes dark with pain. "And I'll miss you, sweetheart, more than you'll ever know."

Her chest tightened unbearably. She blinked back the tears. She couldn't let him see what his departure was doing to her. "Godspeed, Montague. And when you r-return"— she cleared her throat—"you can be certain that your wife will be waiting with open arms." Sudden visions of Christine rushing into those powerful arms burned a trail through her mind. She was unable to contain the pain, and a tear slid down her cheek.

"Don't," Montague whispered raggedly, crossing quickly to her side. He sat on the edge of the bed and covered her hands with his. "I can't bear to see you unhappy." He studied her face hungrily, almost as if committing it to memory. "Things will be different when I return. I promise you." His deep voice gave an odd little lurch. "My wound will be healed, and so will yours." His gaze lowered to her mouth. "Then nothing will keep us apart."

"Yes," she managed through trembling lips.

His hands tightened on hers. Then, as if surrendering to defeat in a well-fought battle, he bent forward and covered her mouth with his.

Knowing it would be the last kiss she and Montague would ever share, Samantha held nothing back. Every feeling, every measure of her love went into the kiss, and her lips parted willingly for his intimate invasion.

A low rumble sounded from deep within his chest, and his hands slid behind her back, pulling her fully against him with a savagery that took her breath away. The pleasing weight of his body pressed her down against the bed. His moist tongue thrust fervently into her mouth, and she welcomed it greedily, knowing she would have only these last few precious moments to carry her through a lifetime.

She felt the shudder that racked his body, and her whole being responded to the sensation of his hand covering her breast. The air left her lungs when his thumb stroked the tender peak that had hardened beneath his touch.

"I want you," he groaned. "God, Christine. How I need to feel you beneath me."

Samantha stiffened at the sound of her sister's name. He wasn't making love to her. He thought he was making love to his wife. Pain stabbed her heart, and she turned her face away. "We can't, M-Montague. My leg, your ribs."

Suddenly he jerked up and released her. His hand shook as he raked it through the thickness of his hair. "God, I'm sorry, sweetheart. I nearly forgot your injury—and mine," he added quickly. "I'm afraid you have a way of distorting a man's better judgment."

He rose from the bed and retrieved his satchel before returning to her side. For a long moment he stared down at her. Then, as if unable to control the impulse, he bent forward again and brushed his lips across hers. "Good-bye, sweetheart." Pulling back, he searched her face. Then, in a low, constricted voice, he whispered softly, "I love you."

Abruptly he straightened. Then, without looking back, he left the room.

Samantha clamped a hand to her mouth and let the tears fall freely. He was gone from her life. Forever.

CHAPTER 26

Jason cast one last pain-filled look at Crystal Terrace and tugged Adversary's reins, directing the animal toward the river. His mouth still tingled from the warmth of Christine's lips, and he ached to feel the softness of her body against his. He knew the decision to leave her had been the right one, yet it didn't stop the ache. No one had ever warned him that loving a woman could hurt so damned much. Sick with despair, he nudged the stallion. "Come on, Addy, let's get out of here."

Hours later, emerging from the last stand of trees, Jason saw the bristly-haired Jed step from the shadows of his rough-planked porch, musket in hand.

The aging eyes squinted, then widened as he lowered the weapon. "Whatcha doin' here this time o' mornin', boy?" The corners of his heavily whiskered mouth pulled down into a frown. "Ain't nothin' happened to Nick, has it?"

"No, Jed. As far as I know, my little brother is perfectly fine." He studied the comforting face. "But I could do with a cup of that tar you call coffee."

"Tar!" Jed snorted and turned to go inside. "Ha! Ya insult a man's offerin's, then 'spect him to be neighborly."

"When that man's one of your godfathers you do," Jason teased, even though he'd never felt less like doing so.

"Humph." Jed lifted the door latch. "Biggest mistake I ever made."

Jason dismounted and tied the horse, then followed the older man into the warmth of the shelter. The familiar smell of pine smoke wafting from the fireplace assailed Jason with a hundred childhood memories of times he'd spent inside these log walls. It reminded him of summers he, Nick, and Hawk had spent hunting under Jed's expert guidance; of times they'd teased Hawk, telling him that Jed knew more about hunting than an Indian brave. Which, now that he thought about it, was probably true.

He glanced at the skin of a black bear spread out before the fireplace and smiled, recalling the story of Father and Cousin Derrick's daring rescue.

The warping floorboards creaked as Jed strode over to a flimsy plank table in the center of the room and retrieved two tin cups, then moved to the hearth and filled them from a dented metal pot. Returning, he handed one to Jason, then sat in one of two chairs placed before the wavering embers.

Silently Jason took the opposite seat and sipped the coffee, wincing at the strong taste. "What do you use to make this stuff? Tree bark?"

Jed harrumphed and shifted against a burlap cushion. "Young upstart."

Staring down into his cup, Jason was reminded of another vile brew. "You know, I think you and Madeline Traynor would make quite a pair."

"Who's she?"

Staring thoughtfully into the flames, Jason reflected on touching memories of Madeline. "Just a woman."

"What is it, boy? What ails ya?"

"I'm going home to Halcyon."

"Why? I thought ya was doin' work for them rebels."

"I was. I still am. But I have to leave here, Jed. I'm up against a situation I can't manage."

"What? You? Naw. What kind of sitiation?"

Jason set his cup down on the floor and raised a hand to

knead the back of his neck. "It's not something I want to talk about."

"Keepin' it festerin' inside ya ain't gonna help." The trapper's tone softened. "Why don't ya tell ol' Jed?"

Slowly Jason met his godfather's eyes, then released a long, painful breath. "I think . . . I . . . oh, hell. I'm in love with my brother's wife."

"Nick's married?"

"Ten days ago." Jason offered a small apologetic smile. "We would've invited you, but we know how you feel about getting dressed up and leaving the mountain."

"Ya done right, boy. I ain't usin' my store-bought breeches till they carry me out in a pine box. 'Preciate the thought, though." He furrowed his brow. "Who'd he marry?"

"Cousin Derrick's daughter."

Jed's bushy eyebrows shot upward. "Which one?"

Which one? Jason turned, puzzled. "He has more than one daughter?"

"O' course. Don't ya 'member your pa tellin' ya?"

Jason frowned as he searched his memory. "I have a vague recollection of his mentioning something about the birth of Cousin Derrick's child in one of his letters when I was at boarding school, but I don't recall the details. Hell, I couldn't have been more than twelve at the time."

Jed chuckled. "Well, I 'member. Had a big whoop-de-do over it. Tied one on for days, we did. Your pa was so proud for Derrick gettin' hisself a set o' mirror twins, jest like you an' Nick. 'Cept, o' course, Derrick's was gals."

"Twins?" Jason stiffened. The thought flashed: Christine has a twin. Images of the Scarlet Temptress rose, then visions of Christine—the Christine he had been so certain was the sultry bandit. "Twins?" Like the ball of a musket, it struck him. Blood pounded in his ears. "Twins! They're bloody twins!" He bolted to his feet. White-hot rage seared through his veins. All this time, all the torture he'd been through. And there were *two* of them!

His eyes narrowed. "Carl. That bloody bastard! He knew all along!" Even that night he'd insisted on helping Jason prepare for bed with—with—which one? A muscle jerked wildly in Jason's temple. He paced. His fists opened and closed. "Carl . . ."

Swinging toward the door, he grabbed for the latch.

"What's wrong, boy? Where ya goin'?"

Jason's blood surged like the James River at flood stage. "To see that son of a strumpet I used to call godfather." He nearly tore the latch off in his haste to open it.

"Son, ya better calm down some first," Jed said gently.

Jason clenched his teeth. His chest heaved. "After what that bloody bastard did to me, I may never be calm again." He drew in a breath and turned back to the trapper. "Don't worry, Jed, I won't do Carl *much* damage."

"I ain't worried 'bout Carl. I'm worried 'bout you." Jed stared at him somberly. "I guess by the way ya been hollerin' that Carl done somethin', and it has to do with Derrick's gals. Maybe if ya told me about it, I could help."

"Thanks, but I won't need any help," he clipped harshly. "I've been played for a fool. And you can forget what I said about being in love with Nick's wife. It seems I don't know *whom* I'm in love with." His fingers bit into the latch. "But Carl does."

"Do ya want me to go with ya?"

"No. I'm all right, Jed. And I won't do anything I might later regret."

The trip to Riversedge passed in a blur as Jason raced the stallion through the woods. His emotions swung like a pendulum from humor to anger, from intense joy to fear of how Carl's words might affect the rest of Jason's life.

"Damn you, Carl," Jason swore aloud. "You bloody bastard. You'd better have the proper answers."

As he neared the back of Riversedge around midday he saw Hadley leading Carl's mount toward the house. Was Carl leaving? Jason scowled. Not yet, he wasn't.

Leaping from the saddle before Adversary had slid to a

stop, Jason strode furiously across the yard and took the veranda steps three at a time. When he reached the door he didn't bother to knock. Instead he banged it open with a resounding crash. His gaze darted from room to room as he stomped through the lower house. "Where the hell are you?" he bellowed for Carl.

"What's all the commotion?" Carl called from overhead.

Jason raced up the steps and met Carl just as the older man emerged from his room.

Carl's hands froze in the act of pulling on his coat. "What is it? What's wrong?"

Jason didn't give him the benefit of an answer. Instead he drew back his fist and slammed it squarely into Carl's jaw.

The older man staggered back against the wall, his eyes wide with surprise.

"Which one is married to my brother?" Jason hissed, his anger not in the least abated by the slight reddening of Carl's chin.

A hand rose to rub the injury as Carl pushed away from the wall. "So that's what this is all about." His lips quirked. "How did you find out?"

"It doesn't matter," Jason snapped. "Damn it, Carl, tell me. Which one is married to my twin?"

"Christine."

Jason felt another rush of anger. "Which one is Christine?"

"The one married to Nick."

"Goddamn it!"

Carl raised his hand. "All right, Jason. Calm down. I'll give you your answers, but I'm pressed for time. I was just leaving when you came storming in here. Patrick Henry's message just arrived. I've got to go."

"I don't give a damn about Patrick Henry!"

Carl sighed. "Let's go to the study." He walked toward the staircase. "I think we could both use a quick drink."

Jason glared daggers at his godfather's back as he followed him down the stairs. He felt a moment's remorse for the way

266

he'd punched Carl but quickly discarded the feeling. After all that Carl had put Jason through, he deserved it.

Carl poured two glasses of whiskey and handed one to Jason. "To begin with, their names are Christine and Samantha. Christine really is married to Nick," Carl said softly. "But Samantha is the Scarlet Temptress." He leaned against the desk and swirled the liquid in his glass. "When Derrick's ship was searched in the harbor last year the authorities found gunpowder on board. The magistrate had him arrested and sent to London Tower. Samantha is trying to gather funds to effect his rescue before he goes to trial. She fears, as we all do, that he'll be hanged for treason. And of course, until the outcome of the trial is known, all of Derrick's funds have been seized."

Jason was momentarily speechless. Cousin Derrick was in prison? Samantha was the Scarlet Temptress? Christine was Nick's wife? Jason heaved a long sigh. So which one was he in love with? Samantha was the beautiful bandit who'd disrupted his entire life. But was the woman he'd held in his arms just hours ago Christine or Samantha? "How do I tell them apart?"

"Massa Malderon, suh?" Hadley's voice called from just beyond the study door as he knocked. "Dat friend o' yours is heah. He be waitin' out in de yawd."

"Thank you, Hadley. Tell him I'll be there momentarily." Carl glanced at Jason. "I've got to go, Jason. I have a friend waiting. He's going to Bent Creek with me." He offered a half smile. "He's always wanted to meet Patrick Henry."

Jason ground his teeth. "Carl, I won't let you get away with this. Damn it, how do I tell them apart?"

Carl shrugged as he crossed to the door and opened it. Then he winked. "Samantha's dimple is on the right." Chuckling softly, he closed the door.

Dimple? Jason wanted to shout. What has that to do—

His eyes widened. *Dimple?* How clearly he could see the Scarlet Temptress's smile—or, more precisely, the dimple in her *right* cheek when she smiled. And Christine on the day she married Nick. When she looked up at him for the first time as his wife she had given him a dazzling smile—and her *left* cheek had dimpled.

Elation grew, then suddenly plummeted. He searched frantically for the memory of the woman he'd left at Crystal Terrace. He closed his eyes, again picturing her smile as they bantered during the picnic. Her dimple was on the *right*. Jason's knees nearly buckled with relief. She was Samantha —*his* Samantha. But why had she switched places with the real Christine? And where *was* Christine? He shook his head and swung toward the door, then halted suddenly. Did they know about him and Nick?

He lowered his gaze to the floor. The pained look on Samantha's face the night before had been real. His leaving had hurt her deeply, but she hadn't tried to stop him. Was it because she thought he was her sister's husband? A wry grin tipped the corners of his lips. Of course it was.

"Samantha." He tasted the name. "The Scarlet Temptress." A growl escaped between his teeth, and he turned for the door. "Samantha. The beautiful bandit who forced me to strip, then left me to walk home . . . naked." A flash of remembered fury sparked, and revenge reared its head. "I told you, vixen, that you wouldn't escape my wrath."

Reaching for the door latch, he paused. But what about her father? Damn it. He had to do something to help Cousin Derrick. Jason's own father would haunt him from the coffin if he didn't. He lowered his hand and tried to think. At any other time he would merely have advanced the funds to Captain Cordell and had him handle the arrangements. But he'd contributed most of his ready cash to Patrick Henry. Of course, there were considerable assets he could sell at Halcyon, but that could take months. Jason opened the door. He would think of something to help Cousin Derrick. He had to.

Riding away from Riversedge, he fought the turmoil churning within him. He wanted to go back to Crystal Terrace and see Samantha—to look at her with new insight. But what he had planned for *that* young lady would take time. And the problem of Cousin Derrick needed to be resolved immediately. After all, the man would soon be his father-in-law . . . providing Jason didn't strangle Samantha first. No. Cousin Derrick's dilemma took priority.

A plan began to form, and Jason smiled, slowly, devilishly. He knew exactly where to get the money—and who was going to help him. David Brown. After all, the man did owe him a small favor.

Then afterward . . . Samantha.

CHAPTER 27

Samantha awoke to the sound of excited voices. Blinking away sleep, she brushed back a thick lock of hair and sat up in bed.

The voices came again. Dahlia's voice . . . and Bromley's. What in heaven's name? She rose quickly, then slipped on her robe and crossed to the door.

Dahlia and Bromley, standing at the top of the stairs, halted their conversation and turned in her direction.

"What is it?" Samantha asked as she stepped into the hallway.

Bromley opened his mouth as if to speak, but Dahlia silenced him with a glower. Then, turning to Samantha, the older woman shrugged. "It's nothing, milady. Bromley's just excited because the soldiers captured that heathenish outlaw they call the Devilrider."

Blood drained from Samantha's face. "What?" Her hand shot to the banister for support. Dear God.

"Dey's gwine t' hang him, missy," Bromley blurted, his dark eyes sparkling with excitement. "Dey caught him robbin' de Wainwrights. Dey's buildin' de platfo'm right dis minute—in de middle o' town. Gwine t' do it soon as dat captain gets heah. Dem soldiers is jest waitin' fo' dere boss man so dey can take off dat outlaw's black mask."

Samantha closed her eyes and tried to gather her composure. They're going to hang him. No! Her eyes snapped open. "Bromley, saddle my horse."

Her gaze met Dahlia's for an instant. The older woman's features reflected a deep inner fear.

Samantha dressed hurriedly, then threw on a long, dark cape and raced to the stables. While she waited for Bromley to saddle the mare her thoughts churned for a plan to rescue the Devilrider. She needed help. Desperately. But who? She bit her lower lip in concentration. There was no one she could trust. Other than Christine and Carl, no one knew of her disguise, of her excursions . . . except Hawk. Hawk? That's it! Exhilaration rose, instantly followed by anxiety. Could she find him? And would he help if she did?

Grinding her teeth at Bromley's slow movements, she waited for him to finish, then she stepped close. "Quick, Bromley. Give me a hand up."

Digging her heels into the animal's sides, she leaned low over the saddle as the horse shot forward. Before she could look for Hawk, she must go to Riversedge and change her clothing. It wouldn't do for Lady Windhall to be seen traipsing across the countryside in search of an Indian. But she must hurry. Merciful God, she silently prayed, protect the rogue with your mighty hand.

After changing at Riversedge and tossing her mask in a satchel, she raced Starburst toward Carl's back field, where she'd first met Hawk. Finally, an eternity later, she broke through the last of the trees, and the small green meadow came into view.

She looked around frantically. There was no sign of another human. "God, no! Please. He has to be here." She leapt from the saddle and spun around hurriedly, making an intimate survey of every tree, every branch. Nothing. "Hawk!" Her hollow voice echoed in the silence. "Oh, Hawk, please. I need you!"

No answer.

A tear slipped down her cheek. Without Hawk she had no hope of saving the Devilrider. Pain, breathtaking in its intensity, carved into her breast, and she bowed her head. "Please," she whispered raggedly. "God, help me. I can't let him die." Another tear slipped warmly down her jaw.

"You are breaking my heart, little outlaw," a deep voice grated from beside her. "Why do you cry?"

Samantha's head whipped up. "Hawk! Oh, thank God!" She clutched at his arms, reassuring herself that he was truly there. "I need you."

Hawk's eyes widened fractionally, then a smile touched his firm lips. His hands rose to close around her waist, pulling her close. "Then our needs are mutual."

"No!" Samantha gasped, leaping back. "I didn't mean it that way. I need your *help*. A f-friend of mine is in trouble. He's been captured by the soldiers, and they're going to hang him." She stepped forward again, grasping his hand. "Please, Hawk. You have to help me rescue him."

Hawk frowned. "Who is this friend?"

Samantha shook her head. "I don't know his name, but the soldiers call him the Devilrider."

Hawk's body went rigid. "The Devilrider?" His hands clamped around her upper arms. "Where is he? Damn it, woman, answer me!"

Surprised by his sudden severity, she pulled out of his grasp and drew her cloak closer together. "I-In town. Bromley said they were building a—"

Hawk turned away. Placing his fingers to his lips, he whistled. An instant later a pinto charged into the glen. Without preamble Hawk grasped Samantha around the waist and tossed her onto her saddle. Then, turning to his own mount, he leapt astride the large horse. "Let's go."

The pace Hawk set taxed both their horses to the limit, but fear for the Devilrider's life took precedence over the animals' discomfort.

When at last they neared the edge of town Hawk reined

his stallion to a halt and dismounted. "I'm going in," he ground out as he reached up to help her down. "Could you manage a distraction while I free the Devilrider?"

What was the Devilrider to Hawk? She didn't have time to think about it now. Nodding in answer to Hawk's question, she untied her satchel and lowered it to the ground. When she opened it she lifted out the crimson mask. Then, flinging off the dark cape, she turned to Hawk and smiled. "Will this suffice?"

Hawk didn't seem in the least surprised. Instead he merely stared at her for a long moment, then stared toward town. "You take great risk with your own life in that costume." His gaze returned to her face. "But it should cause its share of chaos." He placed his hand against her cheek. "Give me ten minutes." His thumb traced the outline of her lower lip. "And take care, little outlaw. I would not wish to rescue you also."

"I'll be very careful," Samantha agreed softly. Then, on impulse, she raised up on her toes and placed her lips lightly against his.

Hawk's body tensed. Slowly his hand lowered to her waist and drew her to him. The pressure of his mouth increased, and he tilted his head to kiss her fully. It was a strange kiss, warm and gentle yet laced with firmly controlled passion and . . . remorse?

When he finally lifted his head his eyes met hers for a long, silent moment. Then, releasing his breath, he offered a small smile. "I will save this man for the sake of us all. But in doing so, know that I forfeit my own desires."

Turning abruptly, he swung up into his saddle.

Samantha frowned. What a strange thing to say. And what exactly did he mean by "the sake of us all"? Shaking the thought aside, she glanced up at Hawk as he wheeled the pinto around. An idea struck her. "Wait, Hawk. I just thought of a better plan."

"Oh, Nick, I've truly done it this time," Jason murmured as he looked out at the crowd of people from his slightly spread-legged stance on the gallows. Raised, excited faces stared back. The bloody bastards couldn't wait to see him hang. He twisted his hands against the leather bindings ensnaring his wrists behind his back. Hang. The word sent chills up his spine. He stared up at the noose swinging loosely above his head. He could almost feel the rope tightening around his neck, choking, suffocating.

He drew in a deep, stabilizing breath. Damn it. He wouldn't give those vultures the satisfaction of witnessing his fear. He'd concentrate on something else. His thoughts staggered to the bungled robbery he'd attempted at the Wainwrights' last eve. Well, at least he'd gotten the money away, if nothing else, thanks to David. Since Wainwright's safe was in his study on the second floor, David had suggested he wait outside so Jason could toss the money down. It had been a good plan and had gone well until Jason tried to escape back through the house. If only he'd—

Suddenly the crowd's attention shifted to something behind them, and Jason looked toward the street. Langford and his men rode through town toward the gallows. Panic bounced through Jason's stomach. Langford would unmask him now, and moments later . . .

Chest-tightening fear—not only for himself, but for Nick —gripped him. When they revealed Jason's face, what would happen to his little brother? And what would happen to Christine . . . to Samantha? Oh, Lord in heaven, what have I done to them?

A movement off to the right caught his notice, and Jason turned his head to see a tall, hooded figure in black slowly climb the steps toward him. A wave of cold terror washed through Jason's body. The hangman. He closed his eyes against the blood-freezing sight and said a swift prayer for the salvation of those he loved.

He momentarily thought of all that he would miss. His brother, Halcyon, children . . . a wife. Samantha. He would never see her again, never hold her, kiss her . . . make love to her. A grievous weight pressed down on his heart. She would never know how much he loved her.

At the sound of horses reining to a halt Jason raised his lashes and watched Langford dismount. The captain had won. Jason, and probably Nick, would die by his hand.

A junior officer patted Langford on the back as he made his way toward the steps. The captain stopped and smiled at the lieutenant, then tilted his head and spoke.

At that moment Jason felt something cold touch his hands. His gaze flew to the hangman now standing close beside him.

"When I give the word—move," a familiar voice whispered.

Relief flooded Jason's senses, and he couldn't stop a grin from spreading. "Hawk."

A sudden scream rent the air. All eyes swung to a red-clad woman racing her horse through the crowded street. People scampered out of the way to keep from being trampled beneath dangerous hooves as the Scarlet Temptress cleaved a frenzied path to the gallows.

Jason felt the leather at his hands snap as Hawk severed the restraints with a blade.

"Now!" the half-breed bellowed, and he dived off the platform.

The Scarlet Temptress slid her horse to a halt. It reared up. "Here!" she yelled, extending her hand to Jason.

Jason didn't hesitate. He grasped her wrist and swung up behind her.

The horse gave a wild whinny, then bolted forward.

An echo of excited voices mingled with harsh commands. A volley of gunshots exploded.

Something seared the flesh of Jason's upper arm, but he didn't loosen his hold on Samantha's waist. He leaned forward, his lips touching her ear. "What about Hawk?"

"He's going to lay a false trail for the soldiers."

Jason winced against the pain in his arm. "Then head for the river. There's a place we can hide."

Samantha gave a jerky nod and reined the horse into the woods, toward the James. Undergrowth tore at her skirt, and low branches jabbed her arms. But it mattered not. Nothing mattered . . . as long as he was safe.

When they reached the river he directed her to the south, then into a portion of woods that looked totally impenetrable. For what seemed like hours they edged their way through the dense maze of trees until they finally came to a tiny clearing and a small structure.

"It's Hawk's," he told her as they neared the cabin.

"So you do know him! I wondered why he was so quick to leap to your rescue at the mere mention of your name."

"My name?" His gaze swung sharply to hers. "You know my name?"

"Only that you are called Devilrider, and that you support the colonists' cause." And most importantly, she added silently, you're not my brother-in-law. Even though she'd suspected him at first, she knew he couldn't be. She'd been in the room with both of them at the same time. "How did you come by that title anyway?"

He seemed to relax, then gestured to his attire. "Why? Am I not deserving of the appellation?"

She turned in the saddle to study him more closely. He *did* have the appearance of a devil. "Yes. But I can't help wondering if you're truly as evil as proclaimed."

He seemed to consider her words for a moment, then smiled. "Perhaps." He slowly assessed the curves revealed by the daring scarlet gown, then fastened his attention on her lips. "But I imagine it depends on one's interpretation of evil."

Samantha blushed at the blatant appraisal. "How do you know Hawk?" she asked, seeking to change the subject.

As if he'd read her thoughts, the Devilrider chuckled. "'Tis safer grounds you seek, hmm, milady?"

She felt her cheeks redden.

"But in answer to your question," he continued, "we grew up together. Hawk is like a brother." He slid from the saddle, then reached for her.

She placed her hands on his shoulders as he lowered her to

the ground, keeping her eyes downcast. He'd grown up with Indians? With savages? Or had Hawk been reared in the white man's world? Frowning, her gaze drifted to the sleeve of the Devilrider's shirt. A blotch of fresh blood stained the material. "You're hurt!"

"It's just a graze, angel. Don't concern yourself."

A finger of warmth caressed her spine at the endearment, but she brushed it aside. "I'm not concerned," she said firmly, "but I intend to examine this." She reached to inspect the area. "I didn't save you from the hangman so you could bleed to death."

He laughed softly. "Remind me to thank you for that." Bowing, he motioned toward the door. "And if you insist, milady, then I'm at your mercy."

Entering the cabin, she stopped, surprised by its furnishings. She wasn't certain what she'd expected to find inside Hawk's domain, but it most surely hadn't been hand-carved furniture, heavy linen curtains, and a brass bed.

"I believe you'll find a bucket of water near the stove, and a stack of clean rags on that sideboard," the Devilrider said from directly behind her—so close that his arm encircled her as he raised it to indicate an enclosed shelf.

Samantha felt the warmth of his breath feather her ear, and she suddenly became aware of their intimate surroundings. The cabin, nestled deep within the woods, was miles from civilization. They were entirely alone.

Stepping quickly toward the cupboard, she took a deep breath, then swung back to him. "Sit at the table while I gather the things needed for your arm."

He turned, paused as if to consider it, then walked to the bed. "I think I need to lie down." A smile played about his lips as he stretched out his length on the feather tick.

Samantha's heart tripped wildly against her chest, and she whirled back to the cabinet.

Deliberately she waited several minutes before approaching the bed, the clean cloths tucked under her arm and a bowl of water in her hands. Peering down, she noticed that his eyes were closed behind the mask, his breathing deep

276

and even. Was he asleep? She set the bowl on a bedside table, then leaned over to study her patient.

Slowly his lashes lifted, and their gazes locked for a long, silent moment. His lips curved into an inviting, sensuous smile. "You're very beautiful."

"Let me see your injury," Samantha commanded firmly, trying to control the erratic leap of her pulse.

The Devilrider smiled, showing strong white teeth, and his hands rose to the front of his shirt. Slowly, erotically, he inched the material up his powerful chest, revealing a rippling expanse of muscles before slipping it off.

Samantha drew back. "What are you doing?"

"It might be a bit less cumbersome to tend the wound without my shirt."

His perfectly logical explanation spawned a surge of skin-tingling apprehension. And the sight of that wide virile chest sent odd little quivers through the nether region of her body. "Perhaps you should remove your mask also," she said stiffly, hoping to divert attention from his near nakedness. "After all, by now you must realize you have nothing to fear from me."

He intimately explored the contours of her own masked face. "In truth, I have more to fear from you than from any other."

What did he mean? And why was he looking at her like that? Lowering her lashes, she stared at his bare torso. Memories of the other times she'd been held against that wall of maleness rose to haunt her, and she yearned to slide her hands over the hard planes of his exposed flesh, to feel those soft dark hairs beneath her palms.

"Milady, you're laying torch to my senses."

The sound of the man's throaty tone captured her attention. She blinked. "W-What?" Her voice trembled softly. She cleared her throat. "What did you say?"

A mocking smile curved his mouth below black silk as he continued to study her features. He seemed to peer through her crimson disguise to somewhere deep within. "I understand now why you are called . . . Temptress."

Samantha shifted uneasily beneath his penetrating stare, offering him a nervous smile. "Why, sir, do you say that?"

He raised a finger, gently tracing the crease of her dimple. "Could it be that even you are unaware of the charms you possess and . . . the effect they have on me?"

Her heartbeat quickened. It was a heady feeling to think she could truly entice him. Swallowing tightly, she tried to divert the topic to safer issues. But before she could utter a sound his fingers slid behind her neck, gripping the powdered wig that concealed her hair. He tugged until it slipped from her head, releasing her thick hair. "Then again," he murmured softly, "perhaps you *are* aware." He eased off her mask, then slowly explored her features.

His eyes captured hers and held them prisoner while the hand at her nape exerted an unyielding pressure, drawing her forward, dangerously close.

The heat of his mouth touched hers, and awareness flared across her soul like a torch set to gunpowder. His firm yet pliant mouth nibbled, explored, ravished with agonizing thoroughness. Her mind reeled and ceased to function as his tongue pressed gently against her lips, seeking entrance, then eased between her teeth to glide suggestively against her own in an erotic dance of seduction.

Blood pounded in her ears as she tasted a lingering trace of ale and mint. The silk of the domino caressed her cheek while she inhaled the intoxicating scents of pine, leather, and a heady muskiness that destroyed her logic.

Intuitively she brought her hands up, threading her fingers under the edge of his hood and into the vibrant thickness of his hair, unaware, uncaring what happened to the cloths she'd held moments before. The tips of her breasts tingled when she pressed anxiously against the solid heat of his chest. Her world spun crazily, then ceased to exist altogether as she lost herself in his ravenous possession.

A low, beastly growl rumbled from his throat, setting flame to Samantha's smoldering desire. He turned her in his arms and pressed her into the bed's softness. The hammering of his heart thundered against her breast, and the strength of his thighs molded to hers. Like a man long denied nourishment he feasted on her mouth again and again.

When he finally pulled away a small cry of protest escaped her lips, and she opened her eyes. He wavered above her a moment, his gaze piercing the black mask in a blaze of impassioned sapphire. Then, groaning, he pressed fevered kisses down the column of her throat, stopping to taste the wildly beating pulse at its base before searing a path to the rise of her barely concealed bosom.

In a whisper-soft caress his hand at her waist massaged slowly up her side until it molded around the under-swell of her breast. His thumb stroked back and forth lazily, taunting, teasing, methodically inching its way upward.

Anticipation coursed through her, and she drew in an unstable breath . . . waiting.

His tongue touched the flesh above her bodice at the same instant his thumb brushed the tip of her nipple.

A jolt of pure pleasure raced to the juncture of her thighs. Clutching him to her, she arched against his hand, wanting, needing . . . what?

After several long, delicious moments his hand left her breast and roamed to the buttons of her gown. One by one he unfastened each until the last slipped from its notch below her waist. He brushed aside the red velvet and fingered the laces of her chemise. Ever so slowly he pulled at the ties until the material parted, exposing her naked breasts.

Hearing his sharp intake of breath, Samantha opened her eyes and through lowered lashes watched his hungry perusal.

"The reality of your beauty far surpasses my meager fantasies," he whispered thickly, nuzzling her softness. His lips trailed slowly down her neck and along the rise of her quivering breast to sample a tight pink bud. With tormenting leisure he teased and circled the sensitive peak before lovingly sucking it into his mouth.

Samantha's spine arched into a curve. She strained upward, wanting to absorb the heat of his mouth. Her fingers tightened, pulling him closer. His mouth increased its amorous assault, and the light rasp of his tongue sent a scorching blaze of desire straight to the apex of her thighs. A delicious pulsating warmth drummed to life in her secret, unexplored region. It built in intensity. Her body trembled with the force of a craving she couldn't begin to understand.

As if he sensed her frustration, his hand edged inside the folds of her gown and eased downward, lingering momentarily to knead the silken flesh of her abdomen before gliding lower to slip between her legs. "Sweet Jesus, Samantha," he whispered, his mouth returning to hers with savage insistence, "I want you." Lightly, almost reverently, he stroked her. "I want to feel myself here, deep inside you."

Pleasure so intense it bordered on pain sliced through her with the swiftness of a thrusting rapier, and her eyes sprang open.

Light flooded the room.

Her gaze flew to the door, and she strangled on a scream.

The Devilrider stiffened, and his head whipped to the side. Instantly he shielded her body with his.

Samantha stared at the doorway in wide-eyed horror.

A man stood silhouetted against the sunlight, arms folded, watching.

CHAPTER 28

The Devilrider glowered at the figure standing in the doorway. A low, violent curse erupted, and he moved away from Samantha, still shielding her from view. "Cover yourself," he grated harshly before turning on the intruder. "What the hell are you doing here?"

The man stepped from the glare of light into full view. "I

live here," Hawk said severely, not attempting to hide his displeasure.

Samantha fought waves of embarrassment. She felt she would surely die of shame. For Hawk to see her and the Devilrider together like this! Her cheeks flamed. She would never be able to face either of them again.

"Damn it, Hawk. You knew we were in here. You could have *knocked,*" the Devilrider snarled hotly.

"I saw no need to announce entrance at my own door." Hawk's stare leveled on Samantha. "Nor did I expect to . . . interrupt such an engaging scene."

"Enough!" The Devilrider's tone lowered dangerously. "Our actions, whether correct or improper, are none of y—"

Grabbing her mask and the cloak, Samantha hugged them to her naked chest. Shame coursed through every vein in her body. She couldn't, *wouldn't,* listen to any more. Fighting back tears, she sprang from the bed and bolted past the two men.

Outside she found Starburst standing beside a wide, gnarled stump. She jumped on it and mounted him. In a frenzy she jerked the reins and wheeled the startled animal around, then kicked his flanks and headed for Crystal Terrace, scalding tears spilling down her cheeks, humiliation leaving her mortified by her own wantonness.

In her room she slammed the door and tromped to the cold hearth of the fireplace. Running a trembling hand down the side of her gown, she tried to understand what had caused her to fling her morals aside and behave in such a promiscuous manner. Never before had she shown such disgraceful tendencies. So why now?

Then another thought struck her. Samantha. He had called her by name! How had he known? Would he give her away? Would she be the next victim for the gallows? She bit her lower lip and slammed her hand down on the mantel. "Carl! He must know Carl." She rubbed her stinging palm. "Damnation! Why did the blasted rogue come into my life?"

Disturbed by the thought, she flung the cape and mask on the bed. Unconsciously her hand rose to remove the white hairpiece. Silky tendrils of her own hair slid beneath her fingers. The wig. Blast! She'd left it in Hawk's cabin.

Her hand dropped to her side and curled into a fist. She fought the urge to stomp her foot. Well, it could just stay there. Not for all the rubies in India would she return to that—that—den of the devil. Devilrider indeed. The man was Satan himself.

Stripping off the crimson gown, she tossed it over the back of a chair and quickly dressed in one of Christine's silk wrappers, then sat on a low stool before the dressing mirror. She placed her elbows on the dresser and massaged her temples. Her head ached, and there was an odd, rather empty feeling in the pit of her stomach. Remembered excitement flared. Blast! She had to get a hold of herself. Releasing a breath, she straightened. No, she reasoned, she didn't need to get hold of herself—she needed to get away from here. She needed money for her father, and money to get herself out of Virginia. And there was only one way to accomplish that. But first she'd have to find out when the next elite gathering would occur.

Sally Blankenship was just setting down her needlework when Samantha arrived. Seemingly pleased with her visitor's company, Sally escorted Samantha into the parlor, where they sat before the fireplace and enjoyed a cup of hot cider.

"It's good to see you, Christine," Sally said quietly. "I haven't seen you since the wedding. How have you been? How's your aunt?"

Samantha hid a wince. "I'm doing quite well. And Aunt Madeline is fine. As a matter of fact, she's away at the moment."

"Truly? Where?"

Samantha shrugged. "Visiting some acquaintants in Boston. She hasn't let us know for certain yet, but she may be considering a return trip to England now that Montague and I are married."

Sally looked genuinely sad. "I shall miss her. She always had a way of brightening my day."

Warmth surrounded Samantha's heart. "I know she's quite fond of you as well."

Sally blushed, then waved her hand. "Enough of this." She leaned forward in the seat. "Tell me how you like being married."

Samantha thought about how she would truly feel if she were married to Montague. Her heart raced. "I love it."

"Spoken like a true bride."

Heat stung Samantha's cheeks. Were her emotions that transparent? Trying to appear unruffled, she flicked a lock of hair over her shoulder. "Sally, you're embarrassing me."

The redhead pressed her lips together, but the laughter remained in her violet eyes. "Sorry."

Samantha shifted uncomfortably. "Um—so tell me, what has been happening in the last couple of weeks? I—um—have been too preoccupied to hear any of the latest gossip."

Leaning back, Sally folded her hands primly in her lap, her features still marked with humor. "Well, let me see. Two weeks, you say? Hmm. It was about that time that Virginia had a small dinner party, and I met Captain Langford again." Her eyes met Samantha's. "There is something about that man that frightens me." She shrugged. "Anyway, shortly after that Maybelle Dungworth had a birthday party for Bartholomew. He's twenty-seven now."

Samantha nearly choked on her cider. "What? He's only twenty-seven? Good heavens. I thought he was much older."

"So did I," Sally agreed. Then, setting her cup aside, she straightened her skirt. "That's about all the news I can recall—oh! I did hear something quite exciting the night I met Captain Langford again." She grinned. "It seems he's going to outsmart that female outlaw."

Samantha's interest peaked. "Oh? How is that?"

Sally frowned. "Let me think. What were his exact words?

Oh, yes, I have it. He feared the outlaw might have gotten word of the tax shipment that's to pass through the area. He was going to see to it that she never learned of its true route, that the shipment was going to be transported by way of Hawksley's field, without military escort, and disguised as a simple hay wagon. Isn't that ingenious? Who would think of a hay wagon carrying money?"

No one, Samantha silently concluded. "Hmm. So when is this monumental ruse supposed to take place?"

Sally's brow furrowed in concentration. "Well, that was two weeks ago Friday. And the shipment was supposed to pass on the day before the Sabbath, a fortnight from then." Her jaw gaped. "Why, that's this evening. Heavens, where has the time gone?"

Samantha sat frozen in the chair. The tax shipment was being transported through Hawksley's field tonight. It was unguarded. And there was enough money in that one shipment to pay for her father's rescue—and her own.

A tingle of premonition shook her. Or was it fear? Could she do it just one more time? The only time she'd ever have to do it again? The breath slid slowly from her lungs.

Yes.

Jason eased out of the saddle in front of the cave, then led Adversary inside. As he changed clothes the conversation he'd just had with Hawk at the cabin tumbled around in his head. He'd explained to his friend about Samantha. About how he planned to marry her. He'd even asked Hawk to be his best man. Pain etched his heart when he recalled Hawk's reply.

"I cannot, Jason."

"Why?"

"I am leaving for England."

"What?"

Hawk shrugged. "I had not thought to tell you in this manner." He reached inside his shirt and withdrew a folded parchment, then handed it to Jason. "I received this three days ago."

Jason read it quickly, surprised by the contents. "You're going to see your mother? After the way she walked out on you and your father?"

Hawk's expression hardened. "Yes."

"Why now? Why not after the wedding?"

A long silence revealed Hawk's answer before he spoke. "I think you know why, Jason."

Hurt for his red brother tightened his stomach. Hawk was in love with Samantha. "Yes, I think I do." Jason leaned closer, his voice soft with understanding. "I wish it could have been different."

Hawk's solemn gray eyes met Jason's. "No, you do not. And neither would I if I were going to marry her."

The truth of Hawk's words settled on his chest like a heavy weight. Shifting uncomfortably, he changed the subject. "When do you leave?"

"Two days."

Adversary snorted, yanking Jason back to the present. Damn, he was going to miss Hawk. Finishing with the buttons on his white shirt, Jason headed toward Crystal Terrace.

"Christine?" he called as he entered the house. When he received no reply he walked into the parlor.

Samantha sat primly on the edge of the settee. "Whatever are you shouting about?"

Jason's steps halted. He stared down at her upturned face, then drew back, feeling as if he'd been struck in the stomach. This wasn't Samantha. "Where is my brother?"

Christine jolted in surprise. "Oh! *Jason.* Oh, good heavens." Her hand fluttered nervously. "Mont—Nick is upstairs changing. Do forgive me, I thought you were he." A dimple creased her left cheek. "Perhaps I should introduce myself." She extended her hand. "Madam Christine Fleming-Windhall—soon to be Kincaid."

Jason couldn't help but smile. She was adorable. Perfect . . . for Nick.

"Jase?" Nick's voice sounded from behind.

Startled, Jason spun sharply to face his twin. Nick looked

great. Obviously marriage suited him. But at the moment Jason had more pressing matters to consider. "Where is Samantha?"

Nick turned to Christine. "You told him?"

"No, I did not."

Nick swung back to his brother. "How?"

Jason shrugged. "It's a long story. One I'll gladly explain later. But at the moment I need to find the vixen."

Christine chuckled softly, and Jason felt a warmth steal over him. She sounded just like Samantha.

"She was not here when we arrived, Jason," Christine offered quietly.

"God's teeth—oh, excuse me." Jason felt his neck warm. "I didn't mean to offend you."

Christine laughed. "Having Samantha for a sister, I doubt there is much in the way of profanity that I have yet to hear."

"Massa?"

All three occupants of the parlor turned at the sound of Bromley's voice.

Jason and Nick stepped forward simultaneously.

Bromley's mouth fell open. "Oh, Lawdy me. Dere be mo' dan one o' you. Lawd. Oh, Lawd!"

Jason looked at Nick, then turned back to the servant. "It's all right, Bromley. We're twins." Then, more seriously, "But I'd appreciate it if you wouldn't let that fact become common knowledge."

"No, sah, I shorely won't." He shook his curly head, his wary gaze still flitting from one brother to the next.

Jason nodded. "Good. Now what was it you wanted?"

"Oh!" Bromley stepped forward. "A man done brung dis heah note fo' yo'." He extended a piece of parchment, then hesitated. "I—a—don' know which one it be fo'."

"I'll take it." Jason waved a dismissing hand. "Thank you."

As Bromley left the room Jason tore open the seal on the parchment. He skipped to the signature. Iron Sword. Returning to the body of the message, he felt the strength drain from his body.

My friend,

Of late I have learned that our good captain, one Harvey Langford, has set a trap for the Scarlet Temptress. He has passed word of a false tax shipment supposedly disguised as a mere hay wagon.

The information was given to Davidson Millworth by the captain, which leads me to believe, knowing Millworth's penchant for gossip, that it was done intentionally so the Temptress would learn of the shipment supposedly passing through Hawksley's field this afternoon.

If you know the lady in question, and I'm certain you do, you might want to warn her of the impending danger.

Jason's fingers curled around the note. So that was where Samantha had gone. The damned fool. She was going to get herself caught—or worse!

CHAPTER 29

Samantha watched the slow movement of the hay wagon as it made its way through the waves of flourishing indigo. She had been watching its progress for some time, making certain that no soldiers were near. The whole situation seemed most odd. What if it was a trap? Her wary, logical side warned. And what if it wasn't? her more daring side countered.

Blast. She was going to have to make up her mind one way

or the other. Sighing, she perched her mask on her nose, then tied it before reining Starburst toward the trees at the end of the field. From that position she could surprise the driver.

Holding tightly to the gun, she waited until the wagon was scarcely twenty feet from the trees. Then she rode forward, her gun raised threateningly. "Hold there!"

The driver's head jerked up.

Samantha's breath stopped, and panic swirled up her spine. Rollie Parker!

His red, craggy beard widened into a leering smile, and his small eyes shifted to something behind her.

Samantha felt the cold threat of danger. But even as the sensation took form she knew it was already too late.

"Well, well. Hello, Madam Temptress," Harvey Langford snarled, triumph filling his voice.

Jason whipped wildly at Adversary, urging him to greater speed. His heart beat frantically in his chest. Samantha was in grave danger. He could *feel* it. Please, God, let me be in time.

The shortcut through the woods brought him to Hawksley's field from the south side, and he drew Adversary to a halt to inspect the area before entering it. His chest constricted. Less than a hundred feet away from him Samantha sat atop her horse disguised as the Scarlet Temptress—and Harvey Langford had a musket pointed at her back.

Fear sliced through Jason's belly, but he forced it back. He would deal with fear later. Samantha needed him. Quietly he slid out of the saddle and edged around the trees, moving toward the captain.

"Drop the weapon," Langford commanded.

Samantha hesitated, then allowed the blunderbuss to slip to the ground.

"Remove your mask," Langford continued in a harsh voice, jamming the barrel of his musket into Samantha's spine.

Jason's steps halted, then quickened to a fevered pace.

Samantha turned her head and brought her hand to the edge of her mask. She caught a slight movement in the trees a few yards back. Her pulse quickened. A black-clad form darted from one tree to another. The Devilrider! She released the breath she hadn't even known she was holding. She had to give him time to reach the fray.

She turned to Harvey Langford. "Why, Captain? You already *believe* you know who I am. Or so I've been told. Are you so anxious to prove the truth of it?"

"Enough! I'll listen to none of your prattle. Remove the mask *now.*"

"Afraid of me, are you?" she taunted.

He grabbed her by the arm, jerking her from the saddle. "Bitch! Take it off, or I will!" His breath, so close to her face, was sour and heavy with stale tobacco. He twisted her arm behind her back and wrenched her up against him. "You've caused me more trouble than ten miscreants. But this time"—his cold eyes bored into her—"you—are—mine."

She jerked frantically, trying to dislodge his grip and escape. When his hand moved she thought she'd succeeded. But his fingers rose to her mask. A strangled cry pierced her throat.

At that moment the Devilrider dived at Langford's back. They all sprawled to the ground. "Get out of here!" he bellowed, struggling with the soldier.

An enraged growl erupted from Rollie Parker just as he leapt from the wagon.

Samantha turned. Oh, God! She looked around rapidly for some assistance. To her right she caught sight of a stout broken tree branch. She dived for it and swung just as Parker lunged. It caught him on the side of the head, and he crumpled into a heap.

Her gaze darted to the Devilrider as he drew back a fist. His power connected soundly with Langford's jaw. The man crashed to the ground, and the Devilrider sprang to his feet. "Come on," he ordered, grasping Samantha's hand and jerking on her arm so hard it nearly pulled from its socket.

He didn't bother to shorten his strides to match her smaller ones as he relentlessly yanked her along behind him.

When they reached his stallion he angrily tossed her into the saddle, then mounted behind her, jerking her back against his chest, his arm a steel band around her waist.

"Thank yo—"

"Shut up!" he roared. "Don't say one damned word!"

Samantha clamped her teeth together. What was the matter with him?

The black horse's hooves pounded heavily as they raced through the trees. She held on to the Devilrider's tense arm, her thoughts a maze of confusion. What had angered him so? Surely not his forced rescue.

As they drew abreast of a cave he reined the stallion to a halt and jumped from the saddle, then yanked her down and shoved her inside.

"You damned little fool! You nearly got yourself killed! Do you wish for death? Is that it? You risk your life needlessly because you seek execution?"

"Don't be ridicu—"

"Silence! I've had enough of your excuses." He grabbed her by the shoulders and shook her, then slammed her up against him, his fingers biting cruelly into her flesh. "Don't ever, *ever* do that to me again."

"What are you—"

His lips ground down on hers.

Samantha's heart nearly exploded. Good God, what was the matter with him? She shoved at his chest, but it was like trying to move a boulder. The angry kiss went on and on. A dizziness clouded her senses as she fought for breath. He can't do this to me, she told herself. She kicked at his booted shin only to wince at the pain she inflicted on herself. Impotent tears threatened to strip away her dignity. The savagery of his lips hurt her more than his angry words.

She was falling. No, not falling—being lowered. She felt the softness of the hay mound at her back, then his hard length pressing down on top of her. There was no doubt of the raging desire flaring through the hard contours of his body. Lord!

Finally she managed to twist her head to one side, avoiding his lips. She pressed back into the hay and looked up, barely able to make out his masked features in the darkness of the cave. A muscle throbbed wildly against his tight-set jaw. His lips were drawn into a narrow line, his eyes blazing behind the impervious slits. "What have I done to enrage you so?"

He recoiled, his body tense. "What have you done? You don't know? God's blood, Samantha. Do you have any idea what it did to me to see Langford's hands on you? To know what that bastard would have done after he unmasked you?" He drew in a jagged breath. "And I'm not just talking about hanging. No, Langford would have . . . taken you first. Hell, why shouldn't he? In his mind you're nothing but a lowly outlaw. He would have raped you viciously. When he finished he would more than likely have slit your pretty little throat to save the magistrate the trouble of enlisting a hangman." A deep shudder rumbled through him. "I wanted to kill the bastard with my bare hands—and you for allowing it to happen."

He studied her silently for a moment. "No. That's not true. I could never hurt you." He lowered his head, his mouth a breath away from hers. "I love you, Samantha," he whispered painfully. "I couldn't bear it if something happened to you." He captured her lips in a tormented kiss.

Samantha sought to thwart his advances, but his fervid words echoed in her ears. I love you, Samantha. Her heart leapt, and she slid into a scalding, sensuous pool, drowning in his kiss. Her body was aflame with need as his lips melded to hers. Perhaps if he'd ravaged her mouth as he'd done before she could have resisted. But this sweet, slow, gentle invasion was more than she could endure. Her arms closed around his neck, and her lips parted.

Desire arrowed through Jason, piercing his reason. Raw hunger clawed at his loins. He couldn't let this happen, not yet. First he had to explain, to identify himself. Placing his hands against the hay on either side of her head, he attempted to rise, but she whimpered softly, tightening her grasp as her tongue entered his mouth. All Jason's intentions vanished beneath a wave of pleasure. Time stood still. There was only the taste and feel of her mouth working magic on his, of her lush little body writhing beneath his own.

Lost in the fever of her kiss, his hands sought the softness of her hair but met the stiff curls of another white wig. Impatiently he pulled it from her head and slid his hands into her silken strands.

She pressed closer, her fingers trailing his shoulders to dig deeply into his flesh. The fire in his loins ignited. He needed to feel those hands against his bare skin. Pulling away, he tore the shirt off, then again seized her mouth.

Like a tiny tigress she raked her nails down his back while gently biting his lower lip.

The assault on his senses was more than he could bear. He was lost in a maelstrom of swirling emotions as his hands sought the firmness of her breasts. He teased and fondled rigid peaks through the thin material of her dress. Losing patience, he unhooked the bodice.

The last of the evening light filtered through the cave opening and cast golden shadows over the delicate fullness of her perfectly proportioned breasts. Her skin, the texture of the finest silk, quivered beneath his touch, then leapt in response when his mouth closed over a jutting pink tip.

Her hands shot to his hair, gripping tightly as she tried to press closer to his mouth.

Savoring the taste of her, his hands made free with her smooth curves, caressing, kneading the pliant flesh. But when that ceased to be enough his fingers massaged slowly down her quivering belly.

Her cry of pleasure nearly sent him over the edge. He sucked in a shallow breath, then began a slow, sensuous stroking motion while his body screamed in agonizing need. He couldn't take much more.

"Oh, sweetheart, I want you." He lifted his hand and pulled the mask away, wishing he could see her better in the darkened cave.

Her hand rose as his had done and pulled the domino from his head, then her fingers gently traced the outlines of his face. "I wager you're quite comely," she teased softly.

"Temptress," he whispered as his mouth again closed over hers.

She moaned and thrust her hips against his throbbing manhood, teasing, tempting.

The breath lodged in his chest. He couldn't endure this torture any longer. His need of her was too great. He had waited too long. If he didn't take her now, he was certain to disgrace himself.

He reached for the buttons on the front of his breeches but stilled when he felt her small hand press against the material covering his swollen shaft.

Jason's breath caught. He clamped his hand over hers to stay her movement. "God, sweetheart. Don't touch me. Not now."

A soft, wicked little laugh escaped her, and she cupped her fingers, squeezing his firm flesh. For one awful moment Jason feared it was all over for him. Gulping for air, he grabbed her hand and placed it against his chest. "Vixen," he was at last able to murmur. "You're merciless." Then, in retaliation, his mouth sought hers in a violent, searing kiss.

When he had taken his fill of her mouth he hungrily trailed fiery kisses down her throat to reclaim her breast.

"Yes," she whispered raggedly, arching to meet his lips.

Her impassioned plea sent shards of desire slicing into his control. With shaking hands he fumbled with the remaining material of her gown and chemise until he had them fully apart. "This time," he rasped hoarsely, "nothing—not even you—will stop me."

He heard her sharp intake of breath an instant before her fingers sought the buttons of his breeches and freed the restrictive clothing from his body. Then her hands were on him, touching, caressing.

Jason's restraint reached its limit. He couldn't bear another moment. He grasped her hands and yanked them above her head, pinning them as he fitted himself between her thighs. She inhaled an expectant breath.

Entering her moist warmth just the slightest bit, he paused, then leaned forward, placing his lips against hers. He thrust sharply and absorbed her pained cry with his mouth.

Her tightness nearly destroyed his control. He wanted to move, to savor the delicious motion he knew would bring them fulfillment. But he hesitated, allowing her a moment to relax, to accept the pressure deep inside her.

Finally, when his body's restraint crumbled, he withdrew and then plunged forward. She arched, trembling, her mouth moving hotly on his, her legs holding him to her.

Trying to stall the exquisite pain, he began a slow, sensuous maneuver. He withdrew, then thrust, then retreated again.

Her stomach tightened beneath his, and her hips arched in violent urgency. Jason almost cried out in relief when he felt her stiffen as she tumbled over the sensual abyss of their unity. Only then did he plunge a final time, his body shuddering with the force of its own powerful release.

For several long minutes they lay silent, each struggling to breathe normally.

A warm, contented glow enfolded Samantha. Never had she thought anything could be so magnificent. Tears formed beneath her lids and slid from the corners.

Jason tasted a salty drop and kissed it away. "Don't cry, angel. Truly, I tried not to hurt you."

Samantha hugged him to her. "It's not from the pain. It was just so beautiful, so wonderful, I never dreamed . . ."

He laughed softly against her throat. "Nor did I." He nibbled a trail up her neck to her swollen lips. "And this time . . . it will be even better."

When she next opened her eyes the amber rays of dawn had brightened the cave with their saffron luster. Samantha couldn't remember when she'd last slept so hard, so soundly, without worry or fear. She snuggled deeper into the warmth of the body beside her. A smile curved her lips as she lay there for a moment, listening to the deep, even sound of his breathing.

Suddenly she snapped alert. She'd never seen his face, she realized—didn't know his name. Good heavens. She'd spent an incredible night in his arms and knew nothing about him.

Her fingers touched the silky hairs on his chest, then trailed down his side. Easing back, she pushed herself up on an elbow and brushed the hair from her cheek, then looked down.

Horror-stricken, she stared at the sleeping face of her sister's husband.

CHAPTER 30

Samantha's hand flew to her mouth. Her fingers dug into the hay and soil beneath her palm. Pain such as she'd never experienced tore into her with the fierceness of a rabid wolf. Dear God. Her brother-in-law! The man she'd just spent the night with was her brother-in-law. She sprang to her feet, searching blindly for her garments.

The bastard! He had said he loved her—Samantha. He had known all along! Tears blurred her vision as she grabbed the velvet gown and hurriedly dressed.

Her mind ceased to function as killing pain paralyzed her very thoughts. She wouldn't allow herself to think about what she'd done—couldn't. She had to get away from here.

Swiftly leaving the hidden aperture, she looked around for a mount and was relieved when she spotted the stallion only a few feet away, still saddled from the night before. Without giving thought to the consequences she approached the spirited animal. Lifting the reins, she led him to a low boulder and mounted.

He shifted nervously and flung his head upward.

"Easy, boy," she soothed in a quivering voice, leaning forward to stroke the satiny neck. "I need you. Please don't cause mischief. I have enough concerns to bear for the moment."

Almost as if he understood her, the horse gave a soft nicker, then lowered his head docilely.

Settling her tense limbs in the saddle, she urged him forward in a slow walk until she was certain the sound of his hooves would not be heard by Montague, then nudged him into a gallop.

The wind slapped wildly at her face as she guided the animal through the trees and beyond Crystal Terrace, but it couldn't stop the guilt from stealing into her reason or the nausea from rolling in her stomach. She had made love with her sister's husband. Her brother-in-law. It was a fact she would live with for the rest of her life. Fleetingly it occurred to her that she'd seen Montague and the Devil-rider together. Who was the other man? The one she'd responded to so feverishly in the stables? God. Was she truly a wanton who would melt beneath any man's touch? And what about Christine? She'd betrayed her twin —herself—over the lustful urges of her own traitorous body.

Tears slid down her cheeks, and her throat tightened. She could never face Christine again. Never. A knot of breath-stealing pain twisted in her breast. She had to flee. It was the only solution. She would leave the country she'd come to love as her own, leave her sister and—who? The Devilrider? Montague? A disgusted laugh clenched her chest. She didn't even know. Closing her thoughts to the tormented musings, she nudged the stallion to greater speed.

When she at last reached Riversedge she climbed from the saddle and tied the horse to a front railing. Across the yard she saw Hadley wave, but she didn't respond. Her insides felt as if they'd been carved out.

She climbed the stairs to her room on stiff legs and walked straight to the armoire to grab a satchel. After laying it open on the bed she haphazardly snatched dresses, undergarments, and brushes, tossing them into the brown portmanteau. For a long moment she stared at the array of Madeline gowns still lining the clothes cupboard; deciding she might need them later, she shoved those, too, into the bag.

After adding a couple of the gray wigs, she changed from the tattered scarlet gown into a day dress, then gathered her things and hurried from the room.

You're taking the coward's way out, a little voice reminded her, but she ignored it. It didn't matter anymore. She was a trollop and betrayer, so what did the mere title coward signify? Besides, was it cowardice to refuse to hurt Christine by telling her of the mishap? No. Her sister didn't deserve that kind of pain. Samantha had enough for both of them.

Reaching the bottom of the stairs, she rushed through the entry to the hidden storage room behind the closet and retrieved the coin she'd been saving to free her father. Her father. Another not-so-different pain cut into her heart. She'd failed even him.

Striding through the parlor, she headed for the door leading to where the stallion was tethered. She didn't know where she would go, but at the moment it didn't matter. Nothing concerned her but fleeing the hurt and betrayal she'd inflicted upon herself.

Just as she reached for the latch it turned, and the door swung open to reveal Carl's lanky form. "What in the world—" His voice broke off as he spied the satchel in her hand. "What's this? Where are you going?"

Samantha opened her mouth, but the words cramped in her chest.

Carl's expression softened. "What is it?"

His tone and gentle understanding were her undoing. Racking sobs broke from her throat, and the next she knew, she was held firmly against his strong chest, her shoulders heaving with all the torment she felt.

She didn't know how long she stood there, how long he held her, before the sobs finally subsided into hiccuping breaths.

Carl removed his handkerchief from his pocket and dried her eyes. He bent his head and looked into her face. "What happened?"

The words spilled free like the rush of a waterfall. She told him everything—what had happened with Montague and the Devilrider, how she had fallen in love with Christine's husband.

"And last night . . ." She hesitated, for the first time feeling the true weight of her actions. Tears filled her eyes anew. "Oh, Carl," she whispered shakily, "I made love to my sister's husband, believing him to be another." She waited silently for the censure she was sure to receive. But for an endless moment Carl remained speechless.

Finally he slipped his arm around her waist and led her into the parlor. There he eased her down into a chair, then strode to the fireplace. "Do you remember tales of your father's cousin, Beau Kincaid?"

She sniffed and nodded, confused by the direction of his thoughts.

"Do you also know that Beau had two sons?"

Samantha frowned. "I recall Father mentioning them, but I don't understand what this has to do with me."

"Everything."

"What?"

"Samantha, Beau's sons, Jason and Nick, are twins. And they're posing as Montague Windhall—and the Devilrider." He knelt down before her and grasped her hands. "Believe me when I tell you that you were not with Christine's husband, Nick, last eve. Both Nick and Christine were with me. You were with Jason." He went on to explain everything from the beginning.

For an instant, overwhelming joy surged through her.

Then her spine stiffened at the import of his words. "Twins? Montague? Nick? Jason? The *Devilrider?*" Her hands clamped into trembling fists. Blood swirled furiously through her veins. The bastards!

"What a fool I must have looked to them. How they must have laughed."

"No. No, they didn't do that. Jason has been as upset as you over this whole thing."

Now why didn't she believe him? And what did it matter? Jason had lied to her. Deceived her. Made a fool of her. Inch by inch an icy calmness claimed her, and she rose slowly to her feet. "I see."

Every muscle in her body felt frozen as she walked silently into the hall to retrieve her satchel. Staring at it thoughtfully, she turned and saw that Carl had followed. She nodded stiffly. "Thank you for telling me."

He opened his mouth to say something more, but she turned her back on him and mounted the stairs. She'd heard enough for now. The need to reach her room was urgent. At any moment she would shatter into a million fragments . . . and she'd rather do that in solitude.

As she entered the bedchamber and deposited the satchel on the tapestry chair some of the frigid numbness wore off, and elation flickered again before being replaced by searing, white-hot anger. Although, in truth, she didn't know to whom it was directed. There were two of them—twins. Her blood raced furiously. They were distant relatives. Her hands clenched. And they had made a fool of her. She kicked the leg of the chair. "Ow! Blast it!"

Limping to the bed, she sat down and grasped her foot to massage her throbbing toe. But the pain acted as a solvent, infusing her anger with reason. She couldn't blame them. They had done nothing more than she and Christine. But, an impish little voice urged, she couldn't run to Jason with open arms. Not yet. He deserved something for all he'd put her through—some small penance. She studied the portmanteau, and an idea took form.

Rising, she crossed to the satchel and opened it, then lifted out the gray satin gown she'd worn so often as Madeline. Her fingers stroked the fine material. Jason—and she was now sure it *was* him after what Carl said—had often shown his attraction to Madeline, though he'd tried very hard to conceal it. She smiled slowly. How would he react if Madeline attempted to seduce him?

With her spirits lightened she sauntered to the dressing mirror and held the gown up before her. She inspected the fabric, then met the emerald shimmer reflecting from her eyes. And suddenly she knew she couldn't do it. There had been enough games. She loved Jason.

An hour later Samantha halted the black horse before the wide double doors of Crystal Terrace. She mounted the stairs, then raised her hand to knock, but the door jerked open. Jason's tormented eyes met hers. For a long moment they stared at each other. Then a slow, melting smile graced his mouth, and he took her hand. "We need to talk."

"Um. Excuse me."

Jason swung around.

Samantha, too, turned to see Jason's exact replica standing in the drawing room doorway. Stunned, she stepped aside to appraise the two men. Seeing them together, she could see the slight differences. Jason's features were a little harsher, his jaw just the tiniest bit more arrogant. "You must be Nick."

"Yes. I—"

"Not now," Jason interrupted. He squeezed her fingers. "Later."

She followed him outside, across the field and up the incline to the cave. Neither spoke. Not yet. When they reached the darkened crevice Jason turned to face her.

He explored her face intimately, then he led her to the mound of hay where they'd spent the night. He stared for a moment, as if in fond memory, then turned to her. "Sit here."

Heat seared her cheeks. She could well imagine just where

the rogue's thoughts had wandered. Blast the man. He made her feel positively giddy. Lowering herself onto the fodder, she primly spread her skirt about her.

Jason watched the action with a spark of amusement, then joined her. But he didn't touch her. Instead he leaned back and laced his fingers behind his head. "Thirteen years ago my father was killed by two men. There were three witnesses to the deed, but two of them met with untimely deaths.

"The third, Luke August, was killed a week later. I was in Italy at the time, in school, though I did return the moment I received word. After locating Luke August's brother Charlie, I questioned the man. All Charlie told me was that Luke came home that night, packed abruptly, and left. The only thing Luke had mentioned about the murder was that he and his friends had seen a scarred soldier kill a lord of the realm and dump his body from the wharf. The murderers had seen Luke and his friends, too, and they feared for their lives."

Jason drew in a heavy breath, as if the telling brought raw pain to the surface. "When I related the information to Carl"—Jason paused—"he's my godfather, by the way." Focusing again on the ceiling, he continued. "When I told Carl what I'd learned, and that Nick and I planned to look for Father's murderer, he ordered Nick and me back to Italy. He probably feared what we might do, especially since we knew one of the bastards was a soldier. Being under age and completely within Carl's authority, we had no choice but to obey."

He rubbed the back of his neck and rolled his head as if it ached. "When we completed our schooling and returned Nick wanted to stay close to Williamsburg, close to the docks, in the event someone else had witnessed the deed. While there Nick became involved with Patrick Henry and the forming of the Continental Congress—which, I've just learned, will meet for the first time in September."

He straightened to a sitting position. "Anyway, I set out to find a scarred soldier." He laughed harshly. "Do you have any idea how many soldiers have scars on their faces?" He shook his head. "Nearly all of them. I won't go into the details of my long and fruitless search, but while I was about it I became involved with the rebels—hence my disguise as the Devilrider."

"Did you ever find him? The soldier, I mean?"

A muscle jerked in Jason's jaw. "No."

She felt his pain. "Jason, I'm so sorry."

He shrugged. "I'll find him someday." His lips tightened. "Someday . . ."

"I'll help."

Jason's body jerked. "What?" Then comprehension dawned. "No! God, no. Samantha, you are undoubtedly the most scatterbrained, irresponsible hoyden I've ever known. You help me? Ha. You'd probably end up getting yourself killed."

Samantha's back stiffened. "You're right, of course." She rose to leave.

Jason's hand snaked out and grasped hers. "Samantha, wait. I didn't mean that the way it sounded." His tone softened. "The truth is, I fear for your life. You have no idea what I went through when I saw Langford holding that gun on you." His grip tightened. "No idea at all."

Samantha felt her anger drain. "I only sought to help."

"I know that, sweetheart. But for my own peace of mind, promise me you won't attempt to find out anything about my father's death."

"I promise I will not seek information concerning your father's death. There. Does that do it?"

He eyed her skeptically. There was something about the way she had said that that made him uneasy. "I suppose." He pulled her down to him. "Now, madam. There is another matter that needs to be settled between us."

"Oh? What might that be?"

"The date of our wedding. I was thinking that tomorrow might be appropriate. Wouldn't you agree?"

Samantha's heart took a giant leap. "What?"

He raised his fingers to brush her jaw lightly. "I just asked you to marry me—tomorrow."

"That's impossible."

"That I proposed to you?"

Samantha smiled and planted a soft kiss on his lips. "No. It's just that tomorrow is too soon. I would have to have a dress, post the banns, contact the clergyman—"

"Samantha, we can't have a proper wedding. At least not here. Remember, Lord Windhall is already married to Christine Fleming." He bent close and slid his tongue over her lips. "And I, milady, do not intend to wait any longer to share your bed." He brushed his mouth across hers, then retreated a space. "Please, Samantha, in the interest of our future family"—his hand moved to rest over her stomach—"which may already have begun, let's marry posthaste."

Samantha's hand covered his. A babe? Was it possible that last night— "Of course, Jason. We must consider our future heirs." She chuckled suddenly as her true relationship to Jason struck her. "Tell me, dear cousin. Since dual births obviously run in our family, do you suppose we may have created another set of twins last night?"

Jason pulled her to him, then lowered her to the hay. "If not then, perhaps now . . ."

Nick and Christine were in the drawing room when Jason and Samantha finally made their way back to the house.

Christine seemed wary. "Is everything settled? And am I forgiven for duping you into switching places with me?"

Samantha hugged her sister. "Yes, twin." Then, turning to Nick, she embraced him. "Welcome to the family, my dearest brother-in-law."

Jason stepped up behind her. "And I'd like to be the first to invite you to attend our wedding in Bedford County tomorrow."

"Not only yours," Nick commented softly.

Jason tilted his head, his expression revealing mild confusion. "What?"

Nick lifted Christine's hand. "In case you've forgotten, big brother, I married Christine under a false name. And if it's all the same to you, I would prefer to marry her again, lawfully this time."

Christine blushed. "You had better. Especially after Williamsburg."

Jason looked curiously at his brother.

Nick shrugged. "You have no idea what I've been through in the past fortnight. I tell you I nearly collapsed when I entered my room at the Raleigh Tavern and found the Scarlet Temptress awaiting me."

"What?" Samantha blurted.

Christine raised her chin defiantly. "Well, I merely took on the ruse because I had just learned of Nicholas's duplicity and was in quite a temper. I sought to teach the bounder a lesson." Her left cheek dimpled. "And I did."

Jason laughed. "I would like to have seen that." Then more seriously, "But back to the wedding plans. I think we should proceed with haste." He winked at Samantha. "We have our future heirs to think about."

Christine turned fiery red before she hid her face against Nick's chest.

Nick burst out laughing. "I never thought of that. But I do believe you have a valid point. Tomorrow would suit us all."

"Shall we invite Leopold?" Samantha asked.

Jason coughed. "Um, Samantha? About Leopold . . ."

Rollie Parker cast Harvey an angry scowl. "Why me? Why don't you go down there and spy in them windas? If they catch me, they'll probably slit my throat."

"Quit caterwauling, Parker. Just do it. That blunderbuss was identified as belonging to Carl Malderon, and I don't have to remind you that Lady Christine is, or was, his ward until she married Windhall. And I myself have seen the gray in the stables at Riversedge." He glanced at the horse tethered behind him. "The Windhalls are up to their stiff white necks in this, and I intend to prove it." He squinted, peering through the line of trees bordering Crystal Terrace. "Now get down there."

Casting Harvey a look of bitter loathing, Rollie jerked his tricorn down over his brow and walked off in a huff. "Stupid bastard's too lordly t' do his own dirty work. Afraid he might muss them snappy white gloves o' his. If he weren't so free with his coin, the uppity swine would be lookin' for some other poor cat's-paw t' be doin' his biddin'. Just 'cause he helped me out when the army give me the boot don't mean the bastard owns my soul."

Slapping a low-hanging branch out of his way, Rollie swung his big girth around the final barrier surrounding Crystal Terrace and looked nervously about. Stepping as lightly as a man his size could, he darted from side to side across the yard until he neared the garden. He stopped behind the hedges and gave the area another quick survey. Seeing no one, he raced to the side of the building and flattened himself against it. Stealthily he edged toward a window. Hearing voices, he froze; then, after a moment, he inched closer and peeked through the open drapes.

"And I'd like to be the first to invite you . . ."

Stunned, Rollie kept his attention on the two Lord Windhalls, then the two Lady Christines. Backing carefully away, he nearly tripped over his own feet as he hurried back to Langford.

Samantha still couldn't believe that Jason and Leopold were the same person, or how relieved he'd been when he found out *she* was Madeline. To think that he'd loved her even as an old woman.

Filled with warmth, Samantha followed Christine upstairs to help her undress before seeking her own bed and contented dreams. But when Samantha opened the door to Nick and Christine's room, she jerked to a halt.

"What happened to the candle? Did it go out?" Christine asked warily.

"I don't know." Samantha stepped forward, inching her

way across the darkened room. "But stay behind *mmm*—"
A gloved hand covered her mouth. An arm encircled her
waist. Fear choked her. She kicked and twisted, thrashing
and struggling with all her strength. Panic clawed her throat.
Something slammed hard against her jaw. The floor swayed.
Then all swirled into blackness.

CHAPTER 31

Jason rose from the settee and placed his empty glass of
whiskey on the low table. "Well, I don't know about you,
Nick, but I'm bushed."

Nick frowned. "Where are you going to sleep tonight?"

A flicker of humor entered Jason's eyes. "Don't worry,
little brother. I can wait until tomorrow night to share
Samantha's bed."

Relief flooded Nick's features. "I'm truly happy for your
sense of decency, Jase. I was not looking forward to playing
the heavy-handed in-law."

Jason pinned Nick with a hard look. "Just for the record,
little brother, if I wanted to bed Samantha tonight, I would.
And nothing you or anyone else said would stop me."

"I didn't mean—"

The door burst open, and Bromley stumbled into the
room. Blood ran down the side of his face from a wound on
his head. "Massa!" he cried out. "Two men done took yo'
hoss—and de womenfolk."

Jason's blood froze. "What?" He clamped his hand on the
boy's arm and helped him sit down. "What men? What are
you talking about?" Jason swung fearfully toward his brother, but Nick was already bounding up the stairs.

"Damn it, Bromley, speak up. *What* men?"

The boy shook his head. "I don' know 'em. I never seed 'em afore."

"What did they look like?" Jason urged, panic rising.

"One's big an' hairy—de other a soldier."

Slivers of ice slid through Jason's veins, and he released his hold. "Langford."

Nick charged down the stairs, his expression frantic. "They're gone, Jase. God in heaven, they're gone!"

"Let's go." Jason felt a numbness steal over him as he hurried to the barn. What would Langford do to Samantha? A knot twisted in his stomach. He knew exactly what the bastard would do—when he finished with her. Sucking in a shallow breath, Jason forced back the terror threatening to consume him.

Inside the stable they quickly saddled horses. Then, gathering two lanterns and lighting them, Nick handed one to his brother.

As Jason took the lamp and mounted he turned to his twin. "He'll head for Richmond. His men are there. I'm going in that direction. See if you can pick up their trail on this end in case I'm wrong."

"No." Nick swung atop Apollo. "He won't go to Richmond, Jase. Langford doesn't have enough proof. For heaven's sake, they're ladies of the realm. The magistrate won't arrest either of them on the word of a mere captain—and Langford knows that." Nick's throat worked as he gripped Apollo's reins. "He'll kill them, Jase. He has to."

Fear raked his spine. But no matter how much he wished it to be different, he knew Nick spoke the truth.

Nick nudged his horse forward. "I believe he took them to lure us. I think he'll leave a trail, then pick his vantage point and leisurely await our arrival."

Jason's back straightened. "Then let's not disappoint him." He dug his heels into Adversary's hide.

Within moments they found the trail a child could have followed. As they rode through the misting rain horrible visions conjured in Jason's mind. In one he could see the captain savagely violating Samantha and Christine; in the next he could hear a demented laugh as Langford slit first one ivory throat, then the other.

The pain in Jason's chest was like none he'd ever felt before; killing in its intensity, every breath hurt, every muscle around his heart was a tight band. "Oh, sweetheart, just hold on," he whispered into the night. A chill shook him, and he tightened his knees against the saddle. If Langford harmed Samantha, he'd cut the bastard's heart out and feed it to him.

An hour later the brothers crested the top of a small knoll and drew their horses to a halt.

Jason studied the tracks leading from the trees to a deserted plantation. Its barren range fanned out from the edge of the woods to envelop dormant fields. He surveyed the boarded windows of the house, then the caving roof of the barn.

He saw a movement from the corner of the structure. His pulse leapt. "There's Samantha's horse," he whispered. "I'll check the barn first." Without waiting for Nick's response Jason snuffed the lantern and slid off Adversary. He raced into the line of trees and edged close to the dull gray building, then stepped out into the open.

Just as he neared the structure something lying on the ground grabbed his attention. His hand trembled as he reached down and picked up the black velvet ribbon and crystal. He lifted his gaze to the barn door, and a cold hand gripped his heart. What would he find inside?

"What is it?" Nick asked, coming up behind him.

"The necklace I gave Samantha. She must be—"

A hoarse cry echoed from beyond the door.

Nick tensed. "Oh, God!"

Without a second thought both men charged into the barn.

Samantha watched Harvey Langford smile as he stood by a second-story window in the plantation house, moonlight reflecting on his hated features. Her stomach heaved from the filthy rag tied tightly across her mouth, the dust nearly choking her. She twisted her hands against the bindings at her back and shifted her legs on the tattered quilt covering the tick beneath her. Why was he keeping her in this vacant, dusty bedroom? What had the animal done with Christine? Where had he taken her?

Suddenly Langford spun around and crossed to the only piece of furniture in the room—the bed where she lay. His hand snaked out and gripped her upper arm, jerking her to her feet. "I've got something to show you," he grated smugly as he hauled her to the window.

She looked out at the barn and surrounding yard below, illuminated brightly in the silvery light.

Langford pointed toward the barn. "See that door? That's the only way in—or out. Parker has lined the back wall and both sides with a trail of gunpowder, then sprinkled hay atop it." His hold on her tightened. "Your sister is inside—and soon your saviors will be, also." His breath blew foully against her ear as he gestured to a line of pines beyond the ravaged barn. "Look toward the trees on the left. Ah, yes, see that flash of white? There are your champions."

She stared at the two forms darting among the trees, moving steadily toward the barn. After the barest hesitation they walked out into the open. Suddenly one of them bent and picked up something from the ground. He seemed to study it for a moment, then looked toward the barn door. He said something to the other. Both men studied the structure. A faint feminine cry caused their heads to whip up. Almost instantly they charged into the barn.

Langford laughed delightedly as Rollie Parker leapt from the side of the building and slammed the barn door shut behind them, quickly dropping a heavy bar into place. The bearded man withdrew something from his pocket and sprinkled it across the front of the building. Then, disappearing around the side once more, he returned a moment later and tossed hay over the new line of gunpowder.

Samantha's heart began to pound as she realized Parker's intent. He was going to set fire to the barn. He would burn them alive! She began to struggle hysterically, but Langford's hold tightened. "Be still." His eyes took on a rabid gleam. "Look."

Horrified, Samantha watched as Parker struck a flint and lit the hay. Gunpowder exploded in a luminous flare. Flames quickly spread to encircle the building and lap hungrily at the sides.

Christine's terrified scream pierced the night. The flames shot higher. Bellows and frantic pounding against aged wood mingled with Christine's cries.

Samantha began to struggle wildly. Oh, God, help them! Somebody help them! She swung her head from side to side in torment.

Langford slapped her. "Watch, bitch."

But Samantha couldn't heed his words. She drew her head back and slammed it forward into the captain's jaw.

He staggered backward. Their feet tangled, and he tripped, taking her down with him.

The breath nearly burst from her lungs when she hit the floor, Langford landing on top of her. She kicked and fought, screaming her hatred through the folds of the gag. She would *kill* him.

The soldier jumped to his feet. He viciously grabbed her by the hair and jerked her up, then shoved her face against the window. His chest heaving, he rasped, "I said *watch.*"

She tried to close her eyes to the building now fully ablaze but couldn't. She was paralyzed. She knew nothing could possibly live through that fire. Tears tumbled down her cheeks. Scalding pain seared her soul. Then, through a dazed blur, she watched the roof of the barn collapse in an explosion of flames.

Langford laughed harshly, then released her.

She slid silently to the floor. They were dead. All of them . . . dead.

The officer crossed the room and lit a candle, then placed it in a wall sconce and turned back to her, his pitted face aglow with triumph.

Fleetingly she realized that she would probably die soon, too. But she didn't care. With her loved ones gone, nothing mattered anymore. Nothing. Let Langford do his worst. He couldn't hurt her. She was beyond feeling, beyond pain.

She was dimly aware of the soldier pulling her to her feet, then removing the gag and bindings. When he swung her up into his arms and carried her to the bed she didn't resist. Inside she was dead, too.

She lay motionless as Langford unbuttoned her bodice. Somewhere in the farthest reaches of her mind she knew that he was going to rape her, but it didn't matter. Closing her eyes, she prayed it would be over swiftly—and he would kill her.

A hand touched her breast, then brushed the chemise aside, but she didn't move, didn't resist. A wet mouth covered her nipple and bit sharply. She didn't flinch. Almost as if from outside herself she felt the mouth move up to cover hers, its tongue plunging deeply, sickeningly between her passive lips.

Suddenly it was gone, and she felt the sting of a blow across her cheek.

"Snap out of it, bitch. I want you to know what I'm doing to you."

Through blurred vision she saw the hand raise to strike again, and she waited for the blow. But it never came. She blinked and tried to focus.

Langford stood frozen, his attention on something across the room.

She followed his line of vision to the door, and her pulse jumped. Life surged through her veins. Jason.

"You're a dead man," Jason said in a cold, lethal voice, a pistol pointed at the captain.

Langford grabbed Samantha by the hair and jerked her in front of him. A knife flashed in his hand. He forced it hard against her throat. "One move, Windhall, and she dies. Now drop the pistol."

For a moment Jason hesitated, then he studied the blade

at her throat. Defeat flickered briefly in his eyes as he lowered his weapon.

Keeping the knife at her throat, Langford cinched her waist with his other arm. "So this one is *yours*. I knew she had to be the Scarlet Temptress because of her haughty defiance, but without your black garb I didn't know you were the Devilrider—until now. You rescued her one time too many, Windhall." He pressed the knife deeper. "How do you tell them apart?"

"I can't," Jason said matter-of-factly. "But then, I've never had to. One of them was always available to help me make a fool of you."

The soldier straightened upright.

Samantha realized instantly what Jason intended. He sought to distract him.

Crystal-blue eyes flared with hatred. "Oh, not that she distributed the pamphlets that made you look like an imbecile to your major." He shook his head and began to pace, his hands clasped behind his back. Each turn inched him closer. "No, that was strictly my doing—as was the rescue of McDaniels and Brown."

Samantha could feel Langford's heart pounding hard at her back.

"Nor did she help me relieve the Wainwrights of that goodly sum, or cut my binding on the gallows. For those deeds I had another accomplice." He smiled tauntingly. "Wouldn't you like to know who it was?"

Before the captain could answer Jason pushed on. "Then, of course, there was the Scarlet Temptress"—he flicked a glance to Samantha, then back to Langford—"whichever one she really is, who was responsible for making you look the buffoon you truly are before the entire town. They thought her quite daring when she boldly rode through your detachment of men—and snatched me from beneath your very nose."

"Enough!" Langford roared.

Jason turned on the soldier and studied him for a long

moment, then suddenly narrowed his eyes. "Tell me, Langford, why did you kill Beau Kincaid?"

Samantha felt the captain's involuntary jerk. "What?"

Jason's hands clenched. "Surely you remember the night thirteen years ago when you and Parker killed the nobleman on the wharf—when you threw his body into the bay? Or is it such a common practice with you that you can't remember such a menial deed?"

Langford's hold on her slackened just the slightest. "How could you know about that?"

Jason's forward step faltered. His hands unfurled, then tightened again. "Beau Kincaid was my father."

Samantha felt a prick at her throat as a jolt passed through Langford.

"You're related to that lowlife son of a whore?" He snorted harshly. "I should have known."

"Why, Langford?" Jason advanced another step, his voice dangerously calm, his features stiffly controlled. "Why did you kill him?"

Though he asked the question casually enough, Samantha could sense the barely restrained fury behind the soft-spoken words.

"Why?" Langford snapped. "The filthy whoremonger killed my sister—*that's* why."

"What?"

Langford laughed curtly. "Not the paragon you believe, eh, Windhall—oh, excuse me—Kincaid."

"You're lying."

Langford ignored him. "He took her like a common harlot. My sister, Mary Elizabeth Langford, the daughter of one of the queen's own knights—and your father bedded her without care to her station." His fingers dug into Samantha's side. "He ruined her. I begged her then to tell me his name, but she refused. She said they loved each other, but he was bound by the church to his second wife. Oh, supposedly he would have divorced the woman, but Mary didn't want him to lose all for her. The cur didn't even know of the babe he'd planted in her belly. Toward the end my Mary ran away to have Kincaid's bastard in some hovel near Richmond. Only after the girl was born and my sister lay dying from childbed fever did she reveal the name of the blighter responsible." His fingers bit deeper into Samantha's flesh. "She knew she was dying and begged the midwife to take the child to its father—Beau Kincaid."

Jason had paled with each of Langford's words. "Where is the child?"

"At the bottom of the sea, for all I know—or care. I gave her to the old woman and told her to get rid of the squalling brat."

An enraged growl erupted from Jason. He charged forward.

Langford shoved Samantha into him. The knife pricked her jaw, then clattered to the floor.

Jumping back, Langford drew his pistol.

Jason straightened immediately and shoved Samantha behind him. "You've only one shot, Captain." His voice became soft, almost gentle. "Make certain you aim well."

The pistol fired. A ball slammed into Jason's shoulder. His body jerked. He gasped and fell to his knees.

For a long moment complete silence filled the room. Then slowly Jason raised his head, watching the blood seep from his shoulder. A cynical smile twisted his lips as crystalline eyes blazing with malice lifted to the officer's.

Langford looked around nervously. Beads of moisture popped out on his brow. His hands shook as he backed toward the door.

Jason rose to his feet. A deadly smile curved his mouth. He withdrew his knife from the waistband of his breeches and stepped forward. He kicked the blade lying on the floor toward the soldier. "Pick it up, Langford. I'll give you more of a chance than you gave my father."

The soldier retrieved the knife.

Warily the two men circled the bedroom, each seeming to measure the other's abilities.

Langford lunged.

Jason sidestepped and spun away, his knife leaving a deep trail of crimson to darken the sleeve of Langford's shirt.

Like a crazed animal Langford attacked again, swinging his knife wildly.

Jason dodged. A cold smile twisted his mouth as he sliced a gash across Langford's other arm.

Knowledge of certain defeat twisted Langford's features. He feigned an assault to the right, then changed directions, tripping Jason.

Caught off guard, Jason stumbled.

Langford pounced on him, slamming Jason's injured shoulder onto the floor.

The knife slashed toward Jason's throat. His hand came up, holding Langford's wrist. By sheer strength Jason kept the blade just inches from its target.

Langford levered all his strength against the upraised arm, his knee pinning Jason's other shoulder.

Blood gushed from Jason's wound, and his arm began to tremble.

Samantha felt terror rise. Jason couldn't hold on much longer. She leapt to her feet.

The knife inched lower.

She searched frantically for something to stop Langford.

The blade pressed against Jason's throat.

Samantha screamed and dived at the captain. The force of her body knocked him sideways.

A furious bellow exploded. Langford sprang to his feet and swung the knife.

She spun quickly and parried the thrust.

Jason tried to rise but fell back against the floor, his face deathly pale.

Langford advanced, his cold expression a promise of death.

As she retreated Samantha hit the backs of her knees on the edge of the bed.

Langford's knife rose—her heart the target.

"Nooo!" Jason cried out.

The blade arched. A sickening thud froze the movement.

Langford jerked. He whimpered. His back curved grotesquely. Wildly he clawed at something behind him. His eyes glazed, then closed as he slumped to the floor.

Samantha gaped in shock at the dagger embedded in his back. Then her gaze flew to Jason.

He lay on his side, the knife still in his upraised hand as if he meant to throw it, his attention on the doorway.

Warily Samantha turned.

Standing in the threshold, Hawk stared coldly down at Langford's body.

CHAPTER 32

Stunned silence filled the vacant bedroom. Then Hawk finally spoke. "I stopped by Crystal Terrace to say good-bye and found Bromley and Dahlia near hysteria." He shrugged. "I thought you could use some help."

Almost immediately another form appeared in the open door. "Good God," Nick blurted, his gaze going from one person to the next, finally coming to rest on his brother. "Are you all right, Jase?"

Jason nodded, then eased to a sitting position.

Samantha jerked her bodice together and raced to his side. Then, tearing a strip from her petticoat, she pressed the wad against his bleeding shoulder. How close she'd come to losing him. "Where's Rollie Parker?" she asked Nick.

"Dead."

"You killed him?"

Nick shook his head. "Hawk did. That's how we got out of the barn."

He crossed to his brother and dropped to his knees, then he reached for the front of Jason's shirt.

"Be careful, he's been shot."

Nick's hands stilled, then he carefully lifted the material and peered at the wound. "It's quite ugly, but I imagine he'll live." He rose to his feet. "Make yourselves comfortable for a few minutes. I'll send Christine up." He grinned. "I left her with the horses and threatened her with a sound thrashing if she attempted to interfere." He winked at Samantha, then turned to his twin. "You might consider my method, big brother." Chuckling, he motioned to Hawk. "Come along, friend. I have need of your expertise. I've no idea how to make a litter for my brother's transport."

Late that night, when the tired travelers arrived at Crystal Terrace, Hawk and Nick carried Jason's litter into the house while Christine and Samantha followed close behind.

As they entered the drawing room Nick, who led the entourage, came to an abrupt halt, nearly causing Samantha to crash into Hawk's back.

"What's wrong?" she asked curiously. She skirted around Hawk and the litter to stand beside her brother-in-law. A cold wave of panic surged through her. Three faces stared back at her from the drawing room: Carl Malderon and Peter and Virginia Hawksley. Samantha's heart sank. Defeat robbed her of breath. To have come so far, only to be found out now.

Christine came up beside her. "Oh, no."

"What the hell's going on?" Jason snarled from his prone position.

Samantha reached out a hand and slipped it into his. She squeezed tightly, her fingers trembling. "We have company."

"What?" He tried to rise.

Carl stood and crossed to the entry. He studied each of them, the last being Jason. "What happened?"

"Langford," Jason offered simply.

Carl nodded. "That's what I was afraid of. Where is he now?"

"Dead. So is Parker."

Carl's features seemed to relax. "Thank God you're all safe."

Samantha eyed the other two people in the room, then returned her attention to Carl. "Are we?"

The older man's glance flicked to the guests, then back to her. He smiled fondly. "Yes, Samantha, you are." He motioned for Nick and Hawk to carry Jason on into the drawing room and lay him on one of the settees.

Cautiously Samantha entered the room behind the others, still uncertain.

When Jason was situated Carl raised his hand as if to make an announcement. "After all the trouble I caused everyone"—he looked pointedly at Samantha—"I decided I'd better let everyone know who was who to avoid further mishaps." His hand swung toward Peter. "May I present my fellow cohort, known to you all as Iron Sword."

Hawk snorted.

Jason choked back a strangled cough.

Nick let out a heartfelt "Mercy."

Samantha moved next to Jason and simply stared at Carl as if he'd lost his senses.

"How ever did you come by that name?" Christine blurted.

Peter elevated his chin, his beaklike nose held at a lofty angle. "I chose it myself. Rather dashing, don't you think?"

Jason quivered with laughter beside Samantha, and she pinched him. "It's quite a grand name, Peter."

Peter smiled. "Thank you." Then, gesturing toward Virginia, he added, "You all know my sister, but what you do not yet know is that she is my right arm and helpmate." He grinned fondly at the thin woman, then turned back to Jason. "You see, Lord Kincaid, our father was one of those killed in the riot in Philadelphia. Virginia and I have very strong animosities toward the British, which is why we joined the Daughters and Sons of Liberty—respectively."

He looked at Samantha. "Uncle Joshua, too, is one of us. And if the maid hadn't found your dress, the captain would

318

have never learned of the mishap at Hawksley Manor nor tried to question Christine."

Samantha grinned. "Well, tell your Uncle Joshua that I have some scraps of paper in my bedroom that I found in the fireplace that night."

Peter began to chuckle. "'Tis quite fortunate that you secured them."

"Why?"

"After the so-called robbery was reported, Langford had his men search the room for clues to the thief's means of entry and escape. I'm certain that had the scraps been in place, they would have been found."

"Then I'm glad I did something right that night." She frowned suddenly. "Why were the soldiers staying at your manor? I thought they were going to stay at the Millworths'."

Peter shrugged. "The ones to be sent by the governor to guard the real tax shipment will. Langford and his men were sent by the magistrate—at the request of the captain and Bartholomew Dungworth—to capture the Scarlet Temptress."

"I see." She glanced up at the faces of those around her. "You're all in on this. And that being the case, I'd like to return the items I've taken from each of you at one time or another—and apologize."

Peter shook his head, and without the wig and powder he looked almost handsome. "No, Samantha. We have no need of them. Besides, by relieving us of those few trinkets you truly strengthened our own charades as upstanding and quite outraged loyal subjects."

Jason spoke up. "There is one item you confiscated from me that I wish returned."

Samantha's eyes softened as she stared down at him. "What?"

"My pistol." His gaze drifted to Nick. "Nick and I each received one for our sixteenth birthday. It was the last gift Father ever gave us."

"Oh, Jason. I'm so sorry."

He smiled and squeezed her hand.

Dahlia entered the room at that moment bearing a silver tray laden with teacups and a steaming pot. "Well, I see you all made it back." Her red-rimmed eyes belied her gruff tone as she scanned Nick, then Jason for injury. She frowned at the latter. "You're hurt."

Jason waved a hand. "Just a scratch, nothing to worry about." He reached up and took Samantha's hand. "And I have an excellent nurse to see me to a speedy recovery."

Dahlia chuckled. "She didn't do too badly the last time either."

Samantha gaped at the older woman. "You knew?"

Dahlia nodded. "From the first. I was anxious about Jason's condition and peeked in on him during the night. I saw you sleeping in the chair without your wig and makeup. It wasn't hard to put things together after that." She grinned. "Although I admit that when I first saw you and Christine together at the wedding it threw me. Later I figured you had to be twins, too. After the wedding I lost track of which one was which until I figured out your dimples were on opposite sides."

Samantha shook her head. "Did I have anyone fooled?"

Jason tugged on her hand. "I can think of one."

Samantha chuckled. "Hawk?" she asked innocently, glancing at the half-breed.

The pressure of Jason's hand increased.

"No," Hawk said softly. "I knew. Jason remained blind to your deception."

Carl let out a disgusted breath. "And to think I spent weeks looking for you, scared to death you'd find Samantha and do her harm."

"I could not have harmed her." Hawk's eyes met Samantha's and softened. "It would have only served to harm myself." As if his words had somehow given something away, he stiffened. "And now that I know all my friends are safe I will say good-bye." He looked at Samantha, then Jason. "May I?"

With a solemn nod Jason released Samantha's hand.

Samantha frowned. What?

Hawk closed the distance between them, then pulled Samantha to him. Slowly he bent his head and kissed her. The tenderness in his lips brought on a sting of tears. In a tight voice he whispered for her alone, "If you ever need me, I will come."

With one last look he raised his hand in farewell and slipped out the door.

"Where is he going?" Samantha asked.

"England."

"Why?"

Jason's eyes met Samantha's. He studied her for a moment, then let out a slow breath. "I'm afraid, sweetheart, that Hawk, like myself, fell hopelessly in love with you."

Samantha's legs folded, and she sank to the floor. "Will he ever return?"

"He didn't say, but I think he will—once he comes to terms with his feelings."

Samantha laid her head on Jason's shoulder. "It seems I've caused nothing but heartache." She smiled halfheartedly at Christine, who stood silently beside her husband. "Even to my own sister." She raised a hand toward her twin. "Did I ever apologize to you for the way I behaved the night I robbed Lord Windhall—the first time?"

Christine's left cheek dimpled. "Not in so many words, but I knew when you stomped out of the house, vowing to rob the governor, that you did not mean to be brusque. You were merely overwrought."

Samantha grinned, then looked back to Jason.

His beautiful row of white teeth flashed. "That reminds me, madam. Did *I* ever thank *you* for rescuing me from the gallows?"

"No."

He pulled her down to him. "Thank you," he murmured against her lips. "But don't ever jeopardize your life like that again."

"Ah-hem." Carl set his teacup aside. "Don't you think Jason should be in bed having his wound tended? Besides, I think we could all use some rest."

Samantha pulled back from Jason's embrace, feeling warm with desire. "Yes. I do believe Jason should be in bed."

Several chuckles echoed around the room as the men moved to help Jason.

After he was situated and the guests had departed Samantha carried a cup of tea to Jason's bedchamber and set it on the bedside table. Hiding a smile, she opened a bottle of Aunt Katherine's medicinal tea, then poured a generous portion into the cup.

"God's blood, Samantha. Do I have to drink that again?"

"Yes, milord."

His hand snaked out and caught her wrist. "Come here, vixen."

Willingly Samantha set the bottle aside and went into his arms. Without shyness her lips met his in a hungry kiss that sought to absorb him.

Breathing hard, Jason pulled his mouth from hers. "Woman, I wish you'd wait until I'm capable of recompense before you shower me with such passion."

Samantha chuckled and returned to her task. "Then by all means drink this, milord. It will surely hasten you to a speedy recovery."

Jason eyed the cup skeptically, then smiled suddenly. "A speedy recovery, you say?"

She nodded.

He took the cup and downed the contents in one gulp. After a wheezing curse he set it aside to reach for her again. "I do believe you're correct. I feel much better already," he murmured as he pulled her mouth to his.

The warmth of his lips moving against hers sparked a surge of joy that knew no restraints. This devilishly handsome rogue was hers . . . forever. And he loved her. He had proven that again and again. Her lips parted as he drew her closer, deepening the kiss. Desire rushed through her veins, and her pulse quickened. Blast. Jason was in no condition for this—not now. Easing back from his embrace, she sighed. "You aren't up to this." Before he could argue she changed the subject. "How did you know the captain killed your father?"

Jason's mouth tightened. "I didn't. I merely sought to distract him. I was as shocked as he when he confessed."

Samantha shuddered in remembrance. "Do you think your father truly loved the captain's sister?"

Relaxing his hold, Jason caressed her back. "Yes, Samantha, I do. My father wouldn't have bedded her while married to another if he didn't."

"What do you think happened to the child?"

He raised his lashes and stared at the gold overhead canopy. "I don't know. But I intend to find out as soon as I'm able to travel." He pulled her back to him. "Now, vixen, where were we?" His lips sought hers.

"Mercy, Samantha. Have you no consideration? Jason is much too weak for that kind of foolishness," Nick scolded playfully from the doorway.

"Hell's breath. Isn't a man allowed any privacy around here?"

Nick chuckled. "In due time, sibling. In due time." He turned to Samantha. "Now, my dearest sister-in-law-to-be, I came to inform your amorous patient that someone just delivered a message."

"From who?" Samantha asked.

"None of your business, little sister."

Jason's tone lowered threateningly. "Nick . . ."

"Relax, Jase. It's just a missive—from David Brown."

Jason glanced quickly at Samantha, then back to Nick. "Let me see it." He took the note from his brother's hand and carefully opened it. As he read his eyes grew bright, then he handed the parchment to Samantha.

"What is it?" Christine asked suddenly from the doorway behind Nick.

Tears rolled down Samantha's cheeks, and the letter fluttered to the floor. "Papa."

"What has happened?" Christine's voice quivered, and she paled. "He is not—"

"No!" Jason quickly assured her.

Shaking, Christine picked up the message. As she, too, read tears began to flow. Her face rose to Nick's. "The money has been sent to rescue father. Without mishap, he should arrive in Williamsburg by midsummer."

"I know," Nick commented softly. "Jason is responsible for acquiring the funds to pay the bribes for Cousin Derrick's release."

Jason shrugged. "I may have sent the coin, but the real credit goes to Lord Wainwright and David Brown." Jason chuckled. "After all, it was Wainwright's money I used, and David who delivered it."

Grasping her sister's hand, Samantha closed her eyes and felt the warmth of her own tears glide down her face. Oh, Papa.

Jason lifted her hand from Christine's. Clasping it tenderly, he pulled her into his arms.

Through a watery blur she saw his gentle understanding, a comprehension that went beyond mere words. "Oh, Jason," she whispered breathlessly. "How can I ever repay you?"

His warm laughter filled the room as he drew her closer still. "Don't worry, Temptress. You'll think of something."

Dear Reader:

Since this is my first book, I'm really anxious to know how you liked it. Please take a moment to write me a note expressing your opinion of *The Scarlet Temptress*. You may send it c/o Pocket Books, or directly to me at P.O. Box 3366, Bakersfield, CA 93385.

I'll do my best to answer each and every one of your letters. Thank you so much.

Nervously awaiting your response,

Sue Rich

The Duchess

Jude Deveraux

Claire Willoughby, a beautiful young American heiress, had been trained her whole life for one thing— to be an English duchess. But when she travels to Scotland to visit her fiance, Harry Montgomery, the duke of McArran, she finds out his family is more than she'd bargained for. Fascinated by his peculiar family, Claire is most intrigued by Trevelyan Montgomery, Harry's mysterious brilliant cousin who she finds living secretly in an unused part of the estate. As she spends more and more time with the magnetic Trevelyan, Claire finds herself drawn to him against her will, yearning to know everything about him. But if Trevelyan's secret is discovered life at Bramley will never be the same.

**COMING IN HARDCOVER
FROM POCKET BOOKS
OCTOBER 1991**

POCKET
B O O K S

62-1